For my family

&

my friends

each of whom has touched this book
in their own unique way

ISBN 978-1-7366197-0-4 (Paperback 1st Edition published April 2021, reprinted September 2021)
ISBN 978-1-7366197-1-1 (eBook Edition published June 2021)

Book interior design by Shan L. Spyker/Tulip Tree Creative Studios
Additional illustrations by Thomas L. Spyker
Creative consulting and additional editing & proofing by Mia C. Spyker
Written by Shan L. Spyker, based on the original collaborative bedtime stories, *The Tales of Henry,* by Pete Lambros, 1975, with additional input from Mia C. Spyker, Thomas L. Spyker, Adrienne L.L. Blatcher, Debbie DeLuca Lambros, Kincaid F. O'Hara & Beckett F. O'Hara
Very special thanks to beta readers Sylar and Thomas
for playing a very important part in the creation of this book!

Published in the United States of America, in the state of Ohio
by Tulip Tree Creative Studios
tuliptreestudios.com

for more information visit
shanspykerauthor.com

The Way of the River

KELLANDALE WOOD
BOOK ONE

"Henry deserves an immediate induction into the literary pantheon of canine heroes....Spyker delivers a strong message of inclusiveness, love, and respect for all creatures. When the plot moves from the shelter of the forest to the darker reality of Coddlefin's circus (and animal cruelty), the kids' good intentions only grow. A safe yet magical adventure with plenty of heart." — *Kirkus Reviews*

"A high-fantasy atmosphere reminiscent of Narnia and other incredible YA realms, this story remains a uniquely plotted tale, as well as deeply symbolic. The concept of nature being a source of untold power and strength makes this novel impactful for a broad range of readers. The prose is accessible, the protagonist dynamics are touching, and the more whimsical aspects of this novel keep it balanced and compulsively readable from the first page." — *Self Publishing Review*

"A middle-school reading level and fast-paced action make this an easily accessible story for the 8+ contingent...*The Way of the River* is an adventure in the spirit of The Chronicles of Narnia, with an added emphasis on animal well-being and the interconnectedness of all living beings."— *The BookLife Prize 2021*

"So much adventure, magic, danger, and suspense. There are also several moments in the book when you see what simply being kind can accomplish. Big focus on animal rights, family, friendship, kindness, and the environment and nature as a whole. The ending was epic! Highly recommend!" — *Belle's Middle Grade Library*

"As a big lover of the fantasy genre, I loved absolutely everything about this book! I deeply fell in love with all of the characters and the friendships that emerged throughout....I am going to be waiting patiently for, hopefully, a second book." — *Iris, Goodreads Review*

"What an amazing debut...I loved reading this tale. The imagery was extremely impactful. One could picture being there right in the moment....I was inspired by the message of empathy to all living creatures." — *Stacy, Goodreads Review*

And especially for my children,

Mia & Tom

May you always trust your hearts
to enter the deep forest when you know it's right
—even when others may tell you not to.

the Way of the River

KELLANDALE WOOD
BOOK ONE

SHAN L. SPYKER

PUBLISHED BY TULIP TREE CREATIVE STUDIOS

Long ago in the country of Eldmoor . . .

Autumn

1

Elinora, Ottilie & Sir William's Tower

"Ottilie, wait for me!" Elinora's voice echoed up the dark, circular tower staircase. "I can't see a thing! Hold the flame up, will you?"

Tillie turned and raised the thick candle, illuminating a door at the top of the stairs. "Hurry up then, we're almost there. And don't call me Ottilie. It sounds like you're scolding me!" she shouted back.

"Well, I am. I told you I didn't want to come up here, *Tillie.*" As she drew closer, her brown eyes, frazzled and frustrated, became visible in the glow of the candlelight; her dress, deep burgundy-colored and practical, contrasted starkly with her pale olive complexion.

"And yet here you are anyway," Tillie grinned.

Elinora glanced at the old, splintered door that stood between them and the tower bedroom. "All right, you've seen where it is; now are you satisfied?" She set her eyes sternly on Tillie. Her hair, pulled back in a tidy chignon, further added to an illusion of authority.

Tillie disregarded her, impulsively stepping up to the landing and turning the handle before she could be stopped, but it was locked.

"Right, there's no way to get inside." Elinora drew in a deep breath, then turned and walked down a few steps, hoping her younger sister would follow. But to her dismay, Tillie didn't take the bait.

Instead, she reached into her dress pocket and pulled out a key. A look of defiance glimmered in her feisty hazel-green eyes.

"Tillie, where on earth did you get that? This part of the manor house has been off limits for ages. You know this room is meant to be left alone. I don't even know what I was thinking when I agreed to come up here."

"Oh, stop being so boring. I am sick of how dull it always is around here. Nothing exciting ever happens."

Elinora rolled her eyes. "Do you ever wonder why I call you Queen of Mischief?"

"Come on, Nor, I really want to see what's in there!" Tillie replied, her dark blonde, wavy hair swaying in time with her emphatic words.

"It's just an old bedroom and Father doesn't want it disturbed out of respect. You understand, don't you?" She folded her arms and sighed.

"An old bedroom…in a *tower*. You really are dull, aren't you." Tillie looked down at the stone landing beneath her feet, sulking, then glanced up.

Elinora was unmoved.

Tillie put her hands to her hips. "Come off it, don't be such an old lady. You're only a year older than I am but you act like you're eighty-five, not fifteen."

"I'll be sixteen very soon, thank you very much."

"Eighty-six then. It's so frustrating constantly wondering

14

what's up here. You know you've always wanted to see Sir William's room, too. What else better do we have to do on such a dreary day?"

Elinora paused a moment, then exhaled deeply. "You're relentless, you know."

In that split-second of hesitation, Tillie knew Elinora's resolve was about to buckle; she cracked a smile.

"Ugh, how daft am I to even consider listening to you?"

Her smile widened.

Elinora stood up straight and pulled her shoulders back, trying to appear as though she was still in charge. "Fine. But just for a moment."

Tillie ignored her and turned the key. The hinges creaked as she pushed the heavy door open.

"Promise you won't touch anything," Elinora whispered, as though someone could be there listening to them. "Please," she added.

"All right, I promise." Tillie took her first step into the cavernous room and looked around for a moment. "Oh, Elinora, it's marvelous!" she gushed.

Elinora peered over Tillie's shoulder, surprised by how inviting the room looked. The furniture, exotic and ornate, gave a worldly and alluring air that beckoned her inside. She followed Tillie and they both gazed up at the vaulted ceiling. Exposed wooden beams, tens of feet above their heads, infused the humid air with their smoky, earthy scent. It was the incense of old timber that had baked for centuries in the sun's rays as they streamed through the massive, arched tower windows.

Together they walked deeper into the room, toward the thick, rounded exterior wall. Originally constructed with mason stone, it had been coated with lime wash in Sir William's time. Tillie reached out and patted the wall, which made a satisfying dull thud.

The old turret in which they were standing was one of the last original architectural remains of the manor house, built more than four hundred years prior. The bedroom within it had been cared for through the many generations the Woltons had lived there, even though it had been unoccupied for most of that time. Three large windows looked out over the river, yielding an unobstructed view of the grounds. Elinora approached them, pressing her forehead to the middle window. She had never seen the landscape around their home in quite the same way before and her nervous energy was unexpectedly soothed by the stunning view. "We're up so high," she marveled.

Through the steady rainfall and haze she could see everything surrounding them—the expansive terrace and the lawn far below, the sprawling gardens that grew alongside them, and beyond that, the rushing river that ran behind the property. In the distance to the left was the old stone bridge leading to the town of Waterbridge.

Tillie came to her side, setting the candle down gently on the windowsill. She stood on her tiptoes and peered out, then teasingly nudged her sister's shoulder with her own. "See, aren't you glad you listened to me for once?"

Elinora cracked a dry smile. "Look at the garden," she pointed to the right. "And over there, I can see the entrance to the forest trail."

They stood looking out the window together, taking in their world from this new perspective.

The forest, at the height of the leaf-turning season, seemed to go on forever, the fiery autumn hues stretching on for thousands of acres. They had only ever experienced the shallow perimeter along the edge of the woods, as they were strictly prohibited from going into what their parents dramatically referred to as the malevolent forest.

"I can't believe we've never been up here. What a silly waste of a beautiful view. The forest is lovely, and I hate that we're separated from it. Maybe that's why they don't let anyone up here—they're afraid of anyone thinking it could be anything other than haunted. We're five stories up and it's as though I can see the whole world from here—I feel like I could grab it all up in my arms," Tillie said with a sigh. "And I see it's still raining. I hope we can take a walk later. I'll be utterly miserable if we don't."

"Mmhmm..." Elinora mumbled, distracted as she continued gazing out the window. She absently twirled her hair between her fingers, an unexpected twinge of curiosity consuming her thoughts.

Tillie stepped away from the window so that she could continue exploring, and headed toward an old writing desk. "Just look at all of this. It's like walking back through time. I wonder what life was like for Sir William." She let his name float through the air as she looked at his old quill, still lying in its dried-up bottle, then quietly peeked inside a drawer, hoping to find an old notebook or something that might have been written on by that very same pen.

"Sir William," Elinora echoed. "His father, Sir Edward, was our fifth great uncle. It wasn't called Kellandale Manor until over two hundred years ago when it was given to him," she said, searching her memory. "Sir Edward's brother, James, inherited it after Sir William died."

"Oh no, don't *you* start with the history lessons. All they do is tell us about Sir Edward, or Sir William this, or Sir James that, and don't go into the forest because it is treacherous, and on, and on," she grumbled, mindlessly picking up an old spyglass sitting on his desk.

"Tillie, you promised you wouldn't touch anything. And the deep forest—how do we know if it's haunted or not? No one has ever gone out there. What if it is?"

Tillie quickly put the spyglass down and walked back to the window. "I know you don't believe that, Elinora. Do you?"

"It doesn't matter, does it? Mother and Father are quite clear about how they feel."

She sighed. "I wish I knew Sir William; I bet *he* was interesting. And he probably wasn't afraid of the forest, if I had to guess. Not with a view like this." She moved to the dressing table and began looking through a carved box. "Elinora, why do you suppose it's so clean in here? I was expecting the room to be all dusty and filled with spiderwebs."

"It's been kept up and left the way it was ever since his death, from what I understand. To honor him, I suppose."

Tillie continued to browse through Sir William's things.

"Did I ever mention I once overheard Albert talking with Abigail about him? He was saying that some had believed the forest had terribly affected Sir William, and not in a good way. Can you believe that?" Elinora looked around the room guiltily for saying that, then turned to Tillie to see her reaction.

"*What?*" she stammered, giving Elinora her full attention. "Well, come on then, what more do you know?"

"I didn't hear anything after that." She paused. "Anyway, let's get back downstairs now; we've been up here far too long."

Tillie furrowed her brows. "Elinora! That wasn't very nice at all."

Elinora fell silent and regarded Tillie without another word, her eyes steadily fixed.

Tillie knew this look. "All right, all right," she relented. She walked back over to the window to pick up the candle and take one last look, lingering a little too long.

"Ottilie, come *on*," Elinora beckoned.

Tillie waved her hand to silence her. "Nor, there's a carriage stopped on the bridge."

"And?"

"And, there's a man moving about in the rain. I wonder if he's having trouble. Maybe he needs help. It's hard to tell what's going on from this far away..." she trailed off.

Elinora sighed, suspecting this was a ruse to delay leaving the tower again. But she was happy to get one more glimpse of the woods before they left, so she returned to the window. She looked off into the distance toward the bridge that crossed the Iveria.

They both watched as the man walked to the back of the carriage and opened the door. He appeared to be rummaging around inside.

Tillie quickly ran over to the desk to grab the spyglass, then returned to the window and looked through it. "He just pulled a sack out of the carriage," she reported.

The man hoisted it over his shoulder then walked over to the edge of the stone bridge. He paused and turned to look back at the carriage. He appeared to be exchanging words with the driver, his arms waving about angrily. Then, turning to look down at the rushing river below, he lowered the sack off his shoulder and held it over the water.

Tillie shoved the spyglass into Elinora's hand. She pulled it to her eyes. "What is he doing?" she asked sharply. "He'd better not..."

But he did. Not a second later he had dropped the parcel over the edge of the bridge and it floated toward them, drifting down the Iveria into Kellandale. It made its way into the forest-end of the property, then disappeared out of eyesight within the mass of trees.

Elinora furrowed her brow.

"What on earth was that about?" Tillie asked, but a loud clap of thunder interrupted her. They both jumped at the sound.

Elinora smoothed her dress nervously, then walked to the desk to set the spyglass down. "There now. I imagine Mother and

Father are waiting—they have some important news to tell us. Hopefully that was nothing," she gestured out the window, trying to shake it off.

"Hopefully."

"Now, Tillie, before anyone comes looking for us." She returned to the window, grabbed the candle off the sill, and exited the room.

"All right, you lovely, wet blanket," Tillie grumbled, hesitating as she passed by Sir William's dresser on her way out. A small monkey figurine sitting on it had caught her attention before, and she wanted a better look at it. Hand-carved from some sort of hard wood, it had eyes made of brilliant green jade and was tiny enough to fit in the palm of her hand. It was attached to a piece of weathered cording. She turned it over and ran her fingers over a small metal hinge at the top of its head. She turned it back and flipped the top up. It was hollow—a tiny wooden vessel. She debated for a second, but when Elinora called her name loudly from the stairwell again, she clasped her hand around it and put it in her dress pocket.

"Finally," Elinora said as Tillie closed the door and locked it behind her.

"I really feel like that man was up to no good, Elinora, and I know you didn't like whatever was going on, either. Shall we go outside after tea to try to find what he threw into the river?"

"Whatever that was, it's long gone already, I'm sure."

"Perhaps, but I think we should still see if we can find it anyway. We can walk along the edge of the river on the meadow trail to start. It might have gotten stuck somewhere along the way." Tillie's eyes lit up with excitement, a sly look crossing her face. "But if we have to walk deeper into the forest, well then, it will finally give me something exciting to do."

2

Announcement Over Tea

Elinora scurried down the cavernous tower stairwell, lighting the way. Tillie quickened her pace to catch up, her shoes shuffling upon the cool stone steps as she followed. They returned to the third floor where some of the household residents lived—the only floor in Kellandale Manor that was connected to the tower. Here they exited, though the stairs continued to a floor below.

Tillie peered into the darkness. "I wonder what's down there?"

"Oh no. Don't you dare think about it."

"All right, all right," she sighed.

"Hurry up," Elinora said, quickly opening the rickety old door they had passed through on their way to the tower. It led into a long, windowless corridor. The plank flooring was bare and creaky, and a mild smell of mildew lingered in the air. On the other end of the corridor was a second door. She opened it a crack to make sure the coast was clear, then they slipped past the bedrooms of Abigail, who was in charge of the day-to-day details in the manor house, her two assistants, and two manor house chefs. Abigail's door was ajar, revealing a well-appointed bedroom with a cozy woolen rug and a small fireplace, but she was not there. The other doors were closed so they tiptoed past, unsure if the rooms were occupied.

Tillie returned the tower bedroom key to a station on the wall that was filled with other keys. It was forged of heavy metal and clanked against the wall when she set it back in its place on the hook.

Elinora cringed at the noise. "How on earth did you figure out which one to take?" she whispered.

"Easy—it was the only one that looked garishly old," she replied with a snort.

Elinora blew the candle out. "Ingenious. I swear, if they find out where we've been, I'll make sure everyone knows it was *your* brilliant idea."

Tillie rolled her eyes. "Come on then, stop harassing me and let's make sure that doesn't happen," she said, pushing Elinora forward through the hall toward the side stairwell. There they hastened down to the second floor where their own bedrooms were located and traversed the hallway, at last reaching the top of the grand double staircase at the entrance of the manor house.

Elinora grabbed the balcony railing and hung her head down, catching her breath. Below was the foyer, bright and open, filled with ferns, ivy, and other potted plants. At the base of each staircase was an exquisite statue, on the left a serpent and on the right a very detailed sculpture of a monkey; vestiges from Sir William's time.

"See, wasn't that worth it?" Tillie gushed. "And no one saw where we went. Now we just need to get through tea, then we can head to the river."

Elinora glared at her, then quickly returned the candle she was still holding to the credenza in the balcony hallway.

They paused when they heard the grandfatherly voice of Albert, Kellandale's steward, greeting guests at the front entrance. Tillie peered down and could see there were four visitors, presumably there to see their father. She signaled to Elinora to halt until they were out of sight, then they proceeded down the stairs. Once at the bottom, they turned and walked through the wide hallway behind the staircase, passing the formal dining hall and the breakfast room at the back of the house before cutting through the gallery, a high-ceilinged room with a red clay tile floor.

Tillie stopped to gaze at a painting of Sir William in which he was wearing an ornately trimmed, navy velvet waistcoat with a white tunic blossoming out from underneath. His hair and eyes, exactly the color of Elinora's, were both dark brown, and his fine, tawny hands were placed elegantly upon a carved wooden staff. His smile was indicative of his kind-hearted and generous spirit. She smiled back. "Just look at him, Elinora."

She glanced quickly, then stopped to take a longer look. The gentle expression in his eyes softened her and she smiled, too. Once Tillie exited the room, she stole over to the portrait of his mother. Lady Vivienne stood confidently in an elegant green floral brocade dress with a proud grin on her face. Her straight black hair was pulled back in a low bun—it was this portrait that had informed Elinora's choice for her own hair styling. She had always held a secret affinity for Lady Vivienne, and aspired to be just how she imagined her—as a bold and fiercely independent woman.

"Elinora, you're going to be late!" Tillie heckled her from down the hall.

She pulled herself out of her daydream and rushed to catch up with Tillie, who was waiting at the entrance of the sitting room. In her haste, just as she was rounding the corner she collided with a tall woman with high, chiseled cheekbones that framed her broad smile.

"Oh, good morning, Mother," Elinora said nervously. "Right on time, aren't we?"

"Indeed, you are. Good morning, Nora." She smoothed her grey tea gown then kissed them both on the forehead.

Tillie grinned at Elinora, who pursed her lips back at her.

The rain had finally slowed, though not enough to be able to sit on the terrace as planned. Instead, they entered the sitting room, taking their seats on one of the curved, oversized sofas arranged around a low table near the fireplace at the back of the room. Shortly after they got settled, their father joined them.

"Good afternoon, my dears," he said, taking a seat across from them in the armchair next to the fire. He flashed them his big smile, his hazel eyes sparkling warmly.

"Good afternoon, Father," they replied in unison.

"Well then, I know you've been expecting big news, and I have guests arriving imminently so I will get right to it." He cleared his throat and flicked a curl out of his eye.

Tillie shuffled in her seat expectantly.

"Your mother and I have spoken with each other about this, and to your Uncle Miles and Aunt Camille as well. We have agreed that…well, how would you like it if Gray and Jamie came to stay at Kellandale for several months?"

"What?" Tillie said with an exhale of delight. She was so excited she forgot about Sir William and the man on the bridge for a brief moment.

Elinora smiled. "I would like that very much. It's been far too long since we last saw them, and exchanging letters just isn't the same."

"When will they arrive?" Tillie inquired.

"Your cousins, along with your Aunt Camille, will arrive toward the end of winter, most likely in late February," their mother answered. "They will be staying with us until your father and your uncle finish completion of the community school."

"Oh? There must be so much to do to prepare," Elinora replied. "The community project is so important, considering everything that has happened," she said to her father, growing more serious.

"Indeed, these are strange times." He shook his head. "Our plans address the current situation, but it will take some time. Your Uncle Miles and I will need to stay in the city, and your mother and I feel that an extended stay of the O'Conors would be favorable to everyone while we are gone."

Elinora continued to question him as Tillie fidgeted in her seat, repeatedly glancing out the bank of windows, hoping for a glimpse of the mysterious man and the carriage.

"How about science, history, and art education?" Elinora asked, her voice pulling Tillie back out of her thoughts.

He grinned. "My dear, I assure you, we will be offering that and more—you know how strongly I feel about all of this. And I hope that one day perhaps you'll decide to become one of our educators."

She smiled.

Tillie was also interested in her father's plans, yet she couldn't resist the opportunity to tease her sister. "Elinora likes to *read* so she's an expert on many subjects, but it won't do any good if she doesn't do anything with all she's learned," she said dramatically. "I just know I want to *do* something exciting one day. Perhaps I'll become an astronomer and discover a new planet while she hides in the library and reads about me."

"We'll see. You'll be too busy gazing up at the sky to notice when I become Head of Education and change things for the better," Elinora retorted.

"I do hope that is true," Tillie said, pulling a goofy face at her.

"Charming," Elinora said, scrunching her nose back.

"You have two very brilliant young minds on your hands, James," a booming, jovial voice broke in from behind them without warning, startling Elinora and Tillie out of their seats. They turned to see a familiar looking man standing behind them. They both broke out into wide grins. "Uncle Miles!" Tillie shouted.

"Good afternoon, family!" he said unwrapping a scarf and approaching them all with extended arms.

"Miles O'Conor, good to see you!" their father said, rising.

"James, Anna, Elinora, Tillie," he greeted everyone. He took off his top hat and bowed playfully and dramatically.

"We just heard the news about Gray and Jamie, Uncle Miles," Elinora said brightly as she and Tillie rushed over to him.

"Ah, yes, they are counting down the days until they arrive here."

"I can't wait. Please tell them to hurry up and get here!" Tillie said eagerly.

Tillie and Elinora returned to their seats as a woman swaddled in a brilliant, teal-colored waistcoat entered the room. Behind her was a man carrying several large tubes of rolled up paper in his hands which jockeyed about clumsily as he attempted to push back a length of hair that had flopped into his eyes.

From her seat, Tillie craned her neck to get another look out the window. She glanced back at Elinora, making a gesture indicating she wished everyone would hurry up so they could finish tea and get outside to explore, then she sighed loudly with impatience. Elinora flared her nostrils and put her finger to her lips to shush her.

A third man, wearing a trim grey suit entered the room a moment later. He was very tall, and bespectacled. "Thank you, Albert, good to see you," he called out into the hall before making his way to the meeting table at the front of the room where the other two men had gathered.

"Is that Everett Meade?" Anna asked James delightedly when she saw him.

"It is. Everett has agreed to come on board as our director of medical staff," Miles replied. "He's here with our architects so we can all be updated on the building progress."

"That's wonderful news—it's so good to see him. It has been far too long," Anna said, then turned to James. "I hope you don't mind us having tea by the fire. We had planned to sit outside before the rain came."

"Of course not. We just needed the table space to view the blueprints, we will be out of your hair in a moment," James said, then he and Miles made their way over to the carved wooden table at the other end of the room where everyone was waiting. "Dr. Meade! Ms. Tenfield, Mr. Rohan, good to see you all!" he said, his voice fading into the distance.

Anna rejoined Elinora and Tillie at the sofas.

Very quickly, the thought of the man on the bridge began to eat away at Tillie again. She fidgeted in her seat, searching for an excuse to get outside.

A cheerful woman, with flushed, pink cheeks, not quite old enough to be Elinora and Tillie's grandmother, entered the room as everyone got settled. In her care was a cart loaded with fruits, pastries, and a fresh pot of tea. She stopped the cart near the couches by the fire. "Cora and Jeppe have outdone themselves in the kitchen today. Help yourselves, everyone," she said.

"Thank you, Abigail. This looks wonderful. Please, join us, will you?" Anna invited.

"Of course, dear," she said. She sat down and fixed a strand of peppered grey hair that had come loose.

Anna prepared four cups of tea and handed one to Abigail, passing the other two to Elinora and Tillie.

Abigail was head of the manor house and had been welcomed into the family, just as the rest of the household staff who worked and lived there were. In addition to providing income and a comfortable place in the home, James and Anna had always made sure that everyone had access to education.

Opportunities had become very scarce as of late—an effect of the recent restriction of education to only the most influential, to those able to pay the hefty price, or to the lucky few who got in through a lottery. While Abigail and Albert had been at Kellandale for decades, the others had come to the manor house in recent times seeking alternate arrangements when their own educational opportunities had been cut off.

For the time being, Emil, Kellandale's coachperson and stable master, was being schooled by a local veterinarian. Simon and Sabine, who were Albert and Abigail's assistants, were both studying civil engineering under James' tutelage. Gemma, another of Abigail's assistants, continued her own music studies while also giving lessons to Elinora and Tillie. Now and again Cora and Jeppe, the household chefs, traveled off to faraway places where culinary schools were still open so they could continue to hone their skills. Meanwhile, Elinora and Tillie helped with the beehives, Anna cooked with Cora and Jeppe, and everyone including James, worked in the gardens and pitched in to help Emil tend the horses.

It was a chilly September afternoon—a perfect day to sit together around the fireplace. Their lanky, beloved cat, Velvet, slept soundly in front of it, her silky black fur warmed by the flames. From their seats they each had a clear view of the river through the north facing windows.

As her mother and Abigail conversed, Elinora absentmindedly clanked her spoon about in her teacup and peered out the bank of windows, attempting to catch a glimpse of the bridge off in the distance.

Anna noticed she was distracted and looked at her inquisitively.

She glanced away, embarrassed, as though her mother could read her thoughts.

"Mother, Elinora told me that Sir William was driven mad by the forest. Is this true?" Tillie blurted out with no warning, breaking the silence. Elinora froze, her eyes widening with guilt.

"Where on earth did you hear that?" her mother asked.

Her face turned red. "I...I don't remember." She glared at Tillie, then glanced sheepishly at Abigail.

"It doesn't matter, does it? Just tell us. Is it true?" Tillie pressed.

Anna hesitated as though she were tiptoeing through delicate terrain. "Sir William..." she began.

Tillie and Elinora both waited expectantly.

"His father, Sir Edward, and his family came here from Gailand. They worked hard in order to get by. Edward was smart, strong, and daring, and was eventually hired by a man who was looking for someone to represent his interests in a trading company. He sailed around the world, bringing back treasures from places in every direction—to far away to lands in the east, south, and beyond. Edward even went into regions that were closed off to trading at that time, like Miyar, Adrai, and Chanpor where he met his wife, Vivienne.

"He brought back a wealth of goods for the man who had hired him—a member of the royal family who wished to impress his subjects. In gratitude, the man bestowed titles to Edward and Vivienne and gave them this estate and large sums of money in exchange for Edward's service," she said, avoiding the question by simply repeating the same information she and James recited whenever they were asked about the history of Kellandale.

"Mother, I know that part. Just tell us, what happened to Sir William?" Tillie asked loudly, standing up in frustration.

While Elinora was mortified her sister had spoken so boldly, she was secretly pleased she had the nerve. She waited for an answer.

"Tillie, please keep your voice down," their mother shushed her without saying anything more.

But their father had overheard the exchange from across the room. Tillie sat back down when she saw him approaching.

"Tillie," he addressed her directly. "I have business to attend to as you can see. But since you insist on making a fuss, I will quickly say that nothing more than this is known; the deep woods of this estate are haunted and very dangerous. Sir William lived here alone after his parents passed on, and yes, it was said that he seemed to have suffered from some sort of delusions at the end of his life, though whether or not the forest was the cause, we cannot say. But, as a precaution…"

Tillie's eyes glazed over as he paused to take a breath.

"No one has been permitted to enter the deep woods beyond the ancient tree since Sir William's time," he continued. "This information has been passed down to us from generation to generation for our protection and it is a directive our family must honor and not question. What you are asking is, therefore, incidental. This of course is the reason why, my darling, you and Elinora are forbidden…"

Tillie sighed. "Forbidden to walk into the malicious forest. I *know*." She growled with frustration. "But Father, it's a mistake. The forest isn't dangerous, it's beautiful, and safe; I know it is. Nothing at all about it feels haunted."

He gasped. "Please tell me you respect the boundaries we have set. I fear for your safety, that is all. It's enough to bear that you go near the forest at all. Promise me once again that you will always keep to the outskirts of the woods and will never, ever stray into the deep forest."

There was a pause. "Yes, Father," Tillie relented.

"Thank you. Now I must get back," he said, returning to the meeting.

Tillie looked at Elinora out of the corner of her eye, knowing that she, too, must be thinking about everything that had happened—Sir William, the forest, and the incident on the bridge. She fidgeted again.

After a short while a streak of sunlight passed through the window, brightening the room.

Tillie overheard her father and uncle saying goodbye to their guests and she took the opportunity to make an excuse to leave. She set down her empty teacup. "Mother, I would love to get some fresh air. Would you mind if Elinora and I went for a short stroll? In the *garden?*" she clarified.

"Of course not, dear. Just don't be long. Don't forget your overcoats. And remember what you promised your father."

"Yes, of course. I'll get our coats!" she said eagerly to Elinora.

Elinora waited nervously for her to return. To be sure, she thought the forest was beautiful, but she wasn't keen about the prospect of going too far into it. They had never dared before, and she had always been content to enjoy it from afar. And yet, Tillie was right; their curiosity had been piqued, and neither of them could let it go unexplored.

3

Henry

Tillie returned wearing her long, red cloak. She handed Elinora her favorite blue woolen cape, then dashed to the bank of leaded glass doors at the back of the sitting room before anyone could delay her quest any further. She opened the middlemost door and put her hand out to feel for rain. Velvet was still sleeping by the fire and opened a wary eye to see where the cool draft disrupting her slumber might be coming from. "Would you like to come for a walk with us?" Tillie asked.

Velvet chirped then stretched and curled back up, covering her eyes with her white-tipped paw.

She laughed then turned to Elinora. "Shall we, then?"

Elinora nodded, donned her cape, and followed Tillie outside. She gently closed the door then stepped out onto the cobblestone terrace, which overlooked the sweeping grounds and extended across the full length of the manor house. The air smelled fresh from the rainfall.

Elinora glanced up at the tower looming overhead. She had never given it, or Sir William, as much thought as she had today. As she gazed upward, rainwater that had collected on the gables trickled down onto her. She wiped her face, pulled the hood of her cape over her head, and shrugged at Tillie.

Tillie cackled then turned and peered back through the glass doors. She waved at Abigail and her mother, who were still sitting on the sofas inside—guilt gnawing at her. But there was no way to deny the adventure that beckoned, so off she went.

They descended the wide steps leading onto the lawn, stopping to survey the area they had observed from the tower not a half hour before. The long stone bridge, which led to Waterbridge—the nearby town to the north—was visible in the distance to their left. It spanned across the river beyond the far west end of the property. While the foot of the bridge on their side was not a quarter mile away, there was neither road nor trail to access it directly from the property of the manor house. It was much harder to see onto the bridge from their present vantage point than it had been from high up in the tower, but they could tell the carriage was gone.

On the Kellandale side of the river, just beyond the manor house, sat the cheery cottages. These belonged to Albert, Simon, Emil, and Rufus the horticulturist who was always off tending to one of the many gardens at Kellandale. Just beyond the cottages, the rubble of the ancient menagerie rose out of a patch of overgrown rosebushes and tangled weeds. The menagerie had also been built in the fifteenth century, but unlike the tower, not much remained beyond its decrepit skeleton; no one ever went near it.

"Just as I thought. Whatever that man threw into the river must be far down river by now," Elinora said after a moment.

"I agree." Tillie gazed to the right, past the massive formal gardens over to the wondrous garden labyrinth maze on the far end of it. At the request of their father, the maze had been designed by Rufus for Elinora and Tillie when they were very young. It was a place for them to enjoy the outdoors—without going into the forest. They had loved running through it as children, playing hide and seek, and racing with Graham and Jamie to see who could reach its center first. Even as they had grown older, the labyrinth was always a destination on their walks. Beyond this was the entrance to the trail leading into the deep woods.

"So now what?" Elinora asked.

"I'm not giving up, if that's what you're going to suggest. I want to take the short path through the meadow first, but if there's nothing there, I'm going into the forest." Tillie began to walk forward, eyeing Elinora sideways, expecting she would back out and want to return to the manor house.

But Elinora followed. She at least felt brave about walking through the meadow to get a glimpse of the beautiful Iveria, and was still hopeful they might find what they were looking for before having to resort to walking too far into the woods.

They made their way to the gardens, following the damp gravel path into the stands of tall autumn flowers, grasses, and evergreen shrubs. They were tidy and still lush with cold-hearty heirloom plants, some descendants of those Lady Vivienne had planted in her time, including the large patch of delphinium. Elinora stopped for a moment to look at their spikes covered in dried seed pods. Barely a few months prior at the height of summer, they had been covered with vibrant purple flowers. She crushed some of the pods in her hand and sprinkled them into the garden. "For Lady Vivienne, and for next year's garden."

"For Lady Vivienne, and next year," Tillie echoed as she joined in scattering them. She dusted her hands off and glanced back toward the manor house. They were too far to be seen now, so they headed toward the overgrown meadow. As they made their way through the damp bramble, she teased Elinora to pass the time.

"So, you're going to be Head of Education, hmmm?" she prodded.

"Tillie, don't start again."

"You know I'm just giving you a hard time; but it is true. You spend all your time studying, and you're brilliant. You have all these grand ideas about becoming a powerful and important politician, or lawyer, or educator. Then you're accepted into a school, which is nearly impossible to do—at just fifteen, even—but then you don't want to go."

"Sixteen."

"Right. Either way, it is a very big deal. So many people would give anything to take your place. How will you accomplish all these great things when you won't even leave the manor house? You're your own worst enemy sometimes."

"Tillie!" Elinora exclaimed, clenching her teeth.

"Why are you always so afraid of everything?"

"I don't know; why are you always so hot headed and impetuous?"

"Because I am! Anyway, I just want you to be great, that's all. I want you to do big things, because you're meant to."

Tillie's words, while meant to be encouraging, stung Elinora more than Tillie realized. She defended herself. "I'm just not ready to leave home; not yet, anyway. And it's not fair—it's not right how they select who can and can't attend school now. It was sheer luck that I was even one of the few lottery winners. I can't accept in good conscience."

Tillie nodded. "I understand."

"Besides, I can't leave you here alone when I know how bored you are even when I'm right here with you," Elinora added.

"Well, that's because you stop me from doing anything exciting. Do you know why I'm always so bored? It's because you really are a wet blanket!"

"Don't blame your boredom on me! You expect the world to entertain you. And if I didn't stop you from doing half the things you think about doing, who knows what kind of trouble you'd get into."

"Exciting and wonderful kinds, I'm sure."

Elinora groaned.

"I wish Gray and Jamie would hurry up and get here already," Tillie said, deftly changing the subject. "Do you remember when Jamie was sure he could create a written language for birds?"

"How could I ever forget that?"

"Or the time he opened a school for slugs and snails to teach them to read, but then realized he was making a mistake teaching them to print instead of writing in cursive?"

They laughed, then fell in step quietly, their shoes becoming increasingly dampened by the wet ground the further they walked.

Finally, they reached the river. The Iveria flowed past to the right, coming from Waterbridge before it snaked back, curved to the west, then eventually flowed into the sea. It was at its widest within the estate at this spot, and deep enough that someone could take a rowboat into its wake if they wished.

The forest and the rushing water were a beautiful sight, but nothing offered a clue as to what could have been thrown into the river, so they continued moving along the trail which eventually led them back to the open lawn on the other side of the maze. A large bird soared overhead, scanning the land below. Tillie pointed it out. "Whatever kind of bird could that be?"

"I don't know, but it's very big. I've never seen anything like it before. It looks like it's watching us, doesn't it?"

A few hundred yards ahead, they reached the entrance of the main trail. There they entered the forest, leaving the silence of the lawn to slog through the wet mush of fallen leaves that emitted an earthy scent as they were trod upon. The trail was mossy under this shallow blanket of foliage, and much wider as it was a well-established trail, forged and worn through centuries of use by both human and animal travelers.

It was there at the forest edge that they came across the feisty little red Buckthorn squirrel they encountered almost every day. Elinora had named him Mr. Squirrel, although they simply called him "Mister." He scrambled down the towering wych elm where he made his home to greet them.

As was the routine, they both reached into their pockets to retrieve morsels of food they'd saved from teatime. Tillie bent down so she could share bits of pistachio muffin and raisins with him. He chattered in delight. "You silly little squirrel!" She laughed as he took them from her hand. "I wish I could understand what you're saying—I'm sure we'd have so much to talk about."

He scampered off, wobbling under the weight of his lopsided, overly-stuffed cheek pouches.

Tillie suppressed a giggle. "Goodbye, see you again later, Mister," she called after him as he disappeared into a hole high up in the tree.

They walked on swiftly now, trying to cover as much ground as possible before having to return home.

"Shall we keep going?" Tillie asked after a few moments.

Elinora nodded and they pressed on. After twenty minutes more, nothing out of the ordinary had caught their attention, so they paused for a break. Just then the wind picked up. Tillie put her hand out, letting the cool breeze hit her fingertips. "Do you feel that?"

"What do you mean?" Elinora looked around, unnerved by her question, already uneasy about them being so deep in the forest.

"Right, exactly. I don't feel anything different; I don't care what Father says, I am not frightened. If anything, it is the opposite—I feel safe, even protected right now. I don't think the forest is haunted at all. Do you?"

"I don't know. But you're right, it is rather peaceful out here now that you say it. We can go just a little further."

They moved deeper into the woods. The trail narrowed, the forest turning thick and dense, the trees surrounded by lush undergrowth.

Expansive stands of towering pines sprouted up in larger numbers amongst the wych elms, which were more prolific at the entrance of the forest. The ground was dry, protected by the mass of trees, and covered in soft pine needles. As the wind blew, it swept them up, scattering and weaving them into a carpet of moss and needles. Elinora breathed in deeply, taking in the scent of evergreen.

The trail turned again and ran close to the river on an embankment, giving them an unobstructed view from higher ground. The river flowed fast, the water a shimmering crystal blue and so clear they could almost see to the bottom.

"It's beautiful," Elinora gasped. Inwardly, she felt as though she could stand and silently watch it forever without a care in the world. She was surprised by this reaction.

Tillie, on the other hand, was compelled to move closer for a better look, so she ran to the edge of the embankment, tempted to plunge in and feel the river with her whole body. She only refrained because she knew how cold it would be. She looked down to a spot where the water swirled around the crest of a tall boulder sitting in the center of the river. Suddenly, she jumped back. "Elinora, come quick!"

Elinora rushed to her side, hoping she had found what they had dared to enter Kellandale Wood to come looking for.

"Over there. I saw it again!" she exclaimed, looking down into the spiraling water. "That flash in the water we've seen before from the terrace; over there, by the rock."

Elinora searched the river.

She pointed to where she had seen the flash. "Oh bother, where did it go? Same as the other times, a bright flash of colorful light, and then it just vanishes." They waited a moment to see if it would return, but there was no sign after that.

"All right, come on," Tillie said, giving up.

They moved on again and soon after found themselves at a bend in the river. They both instinctively hesitated, sensing the environment had changed even more. The forest had been quiet and still except for the occasional breeze, but now the trail was teeming with wildlife and animal sounds, as though the forest had suddenly sprung alive.

They watched a beautiful red fox trot across the path in front of them; it regarded them closely and did not shy away, then it went about its merry way. A moment later a tiny green snake slithered into the nettles off to the side of the trail. Tillie paused, sure that it seemed to be studying them, too. Then a pair of rabbits scurried past, but they were not frightened by their presence, nor was the hedgehog peering out from the underbrush. Instead, the animals were very curious, watching Elinora and Tillie with great interest.

Elinora shook her head. "There are so many animals living out here, I had no idea."

They paused, taking in the continuous chattering of forest animals, both seen and unseen. Even the insects livened up the forest with their humming and buzzing. Tillie made a trilling sound, trying to imitate them. "Hello, little critters. We come in peace!"

"This is certainly not what I pictured it to be out here," Elinora remarked.

"Now are you afraid? Do you want to go back?" Tillie asked, afraid Elinora would take the opportunity to leave the forest.

"No. Not at all. It's lovely out here. Amazing, really. If I didn't know any better I would say they are welcoming us. I think I could stay out here forever—I almost don't want to go home at all suddenly."

Tillie smiled; she loved when Elinora spoke out of character.

The embankment gradually began to slope down, and there was a clearing, giving them a view of the riverbank. Just ahead and below them they could see a rocky, freshwater beach. On it was something that was out of place, and not a part of the natural landscape.

"That must be it," Tillie gasped. She sprinted toward it.

Elinora followed, but suddenly Tillie vanished. When she called after her, there was no answer. "Tillie, where are you!" she called out, suddenly feeling very alone. She spun around, searching frantically for her sister. She tried to run, but in her panic her trembling legs caused her to trip over a slippery tree root. She tumbled down onto the trail, landing on her knees. She cried out with a sharp yelp.

"Elinora?" Tillie asked, suddenly reappearing in front of her a moment later.

"There you are!"

Tillie offered her hand. "Are you all right?"

"I am. But where did you go?" she asked, reaching for her hand. Tillie pulled her up.

"What do you mean? I was here the whole time."

"But…just before I fell, you disappeared. I thought I'd lost you out here! Oh, never mind," she said trying to brush it off. Now that she was no longer panicking, she glanced back down at her dress. "Graceful as ever," she laughed, looking up at what had created the root. She gasped. "Oh Tillie, *look!* This must be the tree Father talks about!"

"Oh, goodness, it's enormous!"

They stood aghast, staring at it. The massive twin trunks of the tree formed a V-shape, wide enough that it would take at least five sets of arms to encircle it. It towered overhead by over a hundred feet.

Tillie walked closer and reached out, gently running her hand over the bulbous knot on its left trunk. "He's all bumpy and gnarly. I'll bet he has seen a lot in his time. Thanks for the laugh, Ole Warty," she said, spontaneously naming the tree.

The wind picked up again and rustled Ole Warty's leaves. The mood shifted suddenly, becoming mysterious and elusive. Elinora and Tillie looked around cautiously. They were now in the deep woods; they both sensed it.

Tillie shook it off. "I'm still not afraid," she proclaimed. "Shall we go see what that is by the river?"

Elinora looked around. Despite the mood, nothing seemed to be threatening them. She nodded and together they walked toward it.

As they got closer, they could see that the object sitting on the little pebble beach was a burlap sack, the same shape and size as what had been thrown into the river. Something was in it. They hurriedly climbed down the sloping embankment.

Elinora approached first and quickly dropped down beside it. "Oh, no. No, no, no!" she cried out suddenly, desperately trying to open the sack.

"What is it?" Tillie asked.

"Help me, Tillie, hurry! There's an animal inside!"

"What?"

"Hurry!"

Tillie rushed to her side. "It's cinched very tight. Oh, whoever did this didn't want him to escape," she said tugging at the knot.

"Is it…is it dead?" Elinora sobbed as they struggled to open it.

"I don't know!"

Finally, Elinora found a hole in the cloth and tore at it. Together they worked quickly to rip the cloth open and pull the animal free. "Tillie, look," she said, throwing the sack to the side.

"Who on earth would do this to a puppy?" Tillie growled. She reached out and put her hand on him. "He's all right—at least he's breathing, but he feels so cold. Let's get him away from the river. Come on little fellow," she said softly, enveloping him with her body for warmth.

"Little?" Elinora half-laughed, wiping away her tears when she saw his enormous paws. Tillie struggled to pick him up, so she helped her lift him. Together they carried him back to the trail and sat down under the protection of their new friend, Ole Warty. Tillie lay him across her lap, or as much of him as she could.

He was a young pup—not a newborn, though just barely old enough to be away from his mother. He was scrawny for his size and his long, greyish-brown fur was wet and matted to his body, so they removed their overcoats and wrapped him with them.

Then, something unexpected happened.

As the puppy began to stir, Elinora and Tillie were simultaneously overcome by intense emotion. They had no control over it, and they knew it wasn't their own emotions they were feeling. They felt terrified, of what they didn't know. Vague images flitted through their minds to show them. In a flash they saw what the puppy had experienced.

Panic and fear. A struggle.
The sensation of drowning.

Elinora shivered involuntarily. A feeling of loss and a deep sadness passed over them both before more feelings washed over them.

Warmth. Security.

They saw images in their mind, like a dream, back in time to the moment the puppy had been taken away from his mother and thrown into the river. Then they felt a stillness.

"What was all that!" Tillie shouted.

"I don't know, but you saw it, too?"

"Yes, and I *felt* it. It was like watching his thoughts and feelings in my mind."

"Do you think that is what happened to him?" Elinora felt another shiver zip down her spine.

Tillie sat speechless, for once fumbling for words. "I...I think so."

Elinora leaned back onto Ole Warty. She took the puppy's front paw into her hand and looked at it. It was soft and warm now.

Tillie looked around intently. "It's the forest, isn't it?"

There was a brief pause. *Maybe Father was right,* Elinora thought. *Maybe Kellandale Wood really is bewitched after all.* She nodded.

The puppy began to squirm and stretch. He attempted to stand, so they removed their overcoats and helped him up. He shook himself off, spraying even more mud.

"Well, so much for either of our dresses," Elinora remarked.

Tillie grumbled. "From now on I'll be wearing something much more practical."

Elinora smiled lightly. "I'm so relieved he's all right. But what do we do? He needs a home; I want to bring him home, and I know you do, too. But what will Mother and Father say?"

"We can't leave him here. We don't have to tell them how far we went, just that we found him. You know how they are. Despite being anxious over just about everything, they won't be able to turn him away."

"But they will ask us how we know he doesn't belong some-where, or have a family already."

"We'll figure it out." The puppy was now beginning to walk around, so they set off back to the manor house, and he stuck very close to them. Tillie draped her cloak back over him to keep away the chill. "This is completely mad," she said, but she was grinning ear to ear.

Elinora looked over at him, sensing that he was already feeling very attached to them. She didn't care if the woods were haunted or not now, she was just grateful that this beautiful little creature had entered their lives.

"What should we call him?" Tillie asked when they reached the edge of the woods.

"Henry," Elinora replied without hesitation.

Tillie smiled. "Henry. That's a perfect name."

4

Wyches Wood

"Come on; don't be afraid," Elinora said, gently coaxing Henry through the threshold between the forest and the manor house grounds.

He hesitated. It felt less protected, out in the open with nowhere to hide, but the trauma of his recent experience was already fading in the safe hands of his new friends. He looked around, then moved forward cautiously, trusting them.

"Don't worry, this is our home. We'll get you cleaned up and get you something to eat," Tillie promised.

He understood her and wagged his tail gratefully, following Elinora as she led them across the lawn and down the moss-strewn steps to the scullery.

"Let's find Abigail," she said, opening the door. "She'll know what to do."

Inside, the entrance walls were adorned with candles. The hallway was glowing with warm light, and the aroma of savory vegetable pies baking in the kitchen drifted through. Henry perked up and sniffed the air, wagging his tail again.

"Abigail?" Elinora called down the narrow corridor that ran alongside the large kitchen and the butler's pantry.

A young man walking with a jaunty step appeared in the hall. He was carrying a sack of amaranth cultivated in one of the culinary gardens. "Good afternoon, Wolton girls," he called out brightly as he approached.

Henry sat down when he saw him coming.

"Good afternoon, Jeppe!" Tillie replied, happy to see him. Everyone could always count on Jeppe to lighten the mood.

Jeppe set the sack down, and when he stooped over to get a closer look at Henry, the red headband holding back his white-blonde hair dropped down over his eyes. Henry wagged his tail at him and tugged on it. Jeppe laughed and ruffled his fur, then pulled the headband back up and stood up. He studied Henry, then eyed Elinora and Tillie's muddy dresses, playfully furrowing his brows while breaking out into a curious grin. "My, aren't you lot a proper sight. What have you gotten yourselves into now?" he chuckled.

Tillie looked up guiltily.

"No, don't answer that. Hold on just a jiff and I'll go find Abigail for you," he said picking up the amaranth sack and trotting off.

A few moments later, Abigail came around the corner to greet Elinora and Tillie. "Why, goodness, who do we have here?" she said when she saw they weren't alone.

"Abigail, this is our friend, Henry," Tillie said scratching the top of his head, which reached above her knees.

"Henry, is it? My, he's a nice fellow." She studied their mud-caked clothing. "Well, fess up, where did he come from?" She looked at Henry intently. They locked eyes, and she paused a moment.

Elinora and Tillie glanced at one another.

"I…we, uh, we went for a walk," Elinora stammered. "We were walking near the river and found him tangled in a sack on the riverbank. He needed help. We know he doesn't have a home, and we want to keep him, but…"

"Oh, you poor fellow. You need a good scrubbing after what you've been through," Abigail said tenderly. "Follow me, all of you."

They left a trail of muddy footprints on the black and white tile floor in the corridor as she led them into the lower-level dining hall. The room was bright and open, with a long wooden table surrounded by twelve chairs. It was attached to the kitchen, divided from it by a little swinging door. In the far corner of the room was a cast iron tub. "Help me lift Henry into it, will you?" she asked.

Elinora and Tillie walked over, and Henry followed. Together they situated him into the tub.

"That's it," Abigail said gently. "Wait here. I'll have Jeppe put on some warm water and have Sabine fetch you both some dry clothes." She reached over and picked up a wool tartan blanket from one of the chairs and draped it over Henry, then disappeared through the swinging door.

After a moment she returned. "How could such a handsome fellow end up washed up on the riverbank in such a state, for Pete's sake? I can't imagine how he could have gotten there. And you say you're certain he doesn't have a home?"

Elinora decided this was her opening. "I don't know how to explain, but you won't believe it." She paused, searching for words.

"What she's trying to say is, we both had a very unnatural experience when we found him," Tillie interjected. "I mean inexplicable, really. It was as though Henry spoke to us and told us what happened, only without words. We found him tangled in a sack and felt—we *knew*—how he had gotten there; someone took

46

him from his family and tried to get rid of him by throwing him into the river."

Abigail frowned.

"I know it sounds impossible, but it really is what happened," Elinora added. She waited for Abigail's rebuff.

But she surprised them both. "You went deep into the woods, didn't you?" It was all that she said, but her words revealed that she knew even more than they realized.

Before either could answer, Jeppe returned with a cart carrying two vessels of warm water and a bowl of breakfast scraps. He picked up a crust of bread with peanut butter and offered it to Henry.

Henry took it gently and gratefully ate, filling his belly with nourishing food. He put his paw on his arm affectionately.

He smiled and scratched his head. "That's it fella, eat away."

Just then a young woman entered the room. She was dressed in woolen trousers and an embroidered linen apron, and she wore her dark reddish-brown hair in a short, cropped afro. She placed two sets of clean clothes and shoes on the table. "There you go, lovelies. Abigail said you'd need something warm," she said.

"Thank you very much, Sabine. I'll just go down the hall and change," Elinora said sheepishly, picking up her garments and exiting quietly.

"What's all this I hear about a new friend, then?" Sabine asked Tillie and Abigail. She glanced at Henry in the tub.

"Sabine, meet Henry. I have a feeling he will be coming to stay at Kellandale for good," Abigail replied.

Tillie smiled broadly when she heard this.

Sabine bent down to pat him. "He's very beautiful." Henry wagged his tail at her rigorously.

"He's very gentle, too," Tillie said to her.

Sabine smiled. "Hello there, Henry, dear. Don't worry, Cora and our friend Jeppe here will make sure you're well fed," she said, ruffling his fur as he affectionately nuzzled her.

"Of course, we will," Jeppe replied, then he and Sabine exited the room together.

Elinora returned in clean clothes a moment later. Tillie quickly resumed the conversation. "To answer your excellent question, Abigail, we didn't go terribly far into the woods."

Elinora glanced at her sister, wondering what she would share and what she would omit.

"Actually, we did. We went into the deep woods," Tillie confessed.

Abigail reached for one of the vessels and poured the warm water over Henry, then added soap and began to scrub. He wriggled in delight. "And how far did you go, Tillie?"

"We saw the tree; I named it Ole Warty," she replied guiltily.

Abigail continued scrubbing, washing away the dirt caked between Henry's toes. "Ole Warty. Now that's a nice, solid name."

"We'd been up in the tower just before tea and saw…" She put her hand to her mouth and stopped talking.

"The tower? My, you have been busy, Tillie. How on earth did you get inside?"

"I found the key. Elinora tried to stop me, as usual."

Elinora rolled her eyes.

"Right, well, I got so curious I couldn't take it anymore. Elinora did too, once we got up there and saw everything. We were looking out and saw a man on the bridge and watched him throw something into the river. We're sure now that it was Henry. But we didn't know that at the time, which is why we walked so far, to figure out what the man was doing."

"Hmmm…well it's a good thing for Henry you did," Abigail said, rinsing him off with the second vessel of water. "I had a feeling you two were up to something at tea. You're never so quiet."

"But what did we say to make you ask if we went into the deep woods, and what does Henry have to do with it?" Elinora asked.

She paused a moment. "My dears, there is a reason you have been told not to go into the woods, but it's not quite the reason you think it is. Before I go on, Tillie, perhaps you should get cleaned up, too. This might take a while."

"Oh, please don't stop now; it's torturing me to know what you're going to say." She looked down at her damp, muddy dress. She was still shivering and hadn't even noticed. "Goodness, I really do look a fright. Please, wait for me before you say anything more." She grabbed her clothing and shoes off the table and slipped out as fast as she could.

While she was gone, Elinora and Abigail fussed over Henry and dried him off in the tub. He shook his body, spattering the tub walls with his wet, but now luxuriously clean, fur. His coat was a beautiful brindle color, soft and shiny.

"Look there, he's got a sweet little patch of white fur on his neck," Abigail said, now that they could see with all the mud gone. "That's a good boy," she said softly as they lifted him out of the tub. "You've found a fine companion here, Elinora. We just need to get a little meat on his bones. Emil can look him over later, and he will be just fine."

"Henry's just beautiful, isn't he? He has such a gentle look in his eyes."

Abigail smiled and nodded. "I'll go put on a pot of tea and then I will tell you and your sister everything I know," she said, exiting the room again.

Henry could hear Tillie scurrying through the hallway. He stood up, his ears perked, and his tail wagged when she entered the room. He had never known happiness or kindness from humans in his short life and her exuberance made him very feisty.

Abigail returned with a tea pot, three cups of tea, and a fresh bowl of water for Henry. "Ah, that's much better, Tillie. Come sit down, all of you," she said.

They followed her to the table and took their seats. Henry curled up at their feet to listen with them.

"You know the legend of the haunted forest—the one in which treacherous things happen to those who travel deep into it," she began.

They both nodded.

"Now, let me tell you a tale of another kind. A tale of a good forest."

Tillie breathed in. "I knew it!"

Elinora lifted her teacup to her mouth and sipped, not taking her eyes off Abigail.

"As you know, most have lived in fear of the forest on this property. But did you know that there are those few who knew the real story? They discovered the forest possesses deep, mysterious powers—that Kellandale Wood is a safe place, and a good place. And I am quite sure Henry found his way to you because of it."

"Go on!" Tillie coaxed.

She smiled. "Well then, as you are also aware, your family members—this includes your father and your aunt Camille, and everyone else who has lived here through the ages—have been told a much more austere version of the story, one that contends that evil and treachery lurks within the deep forest. As children they, too, were forbidden to enter it and were only permitted to walk the grounds of Kellandale Manor so that no harm would come to them. Sound familiar? This is the way it has been for the Woltons all through the generations and how your family has been able to remain living here amidst such frightening tales."

She paused. "Do you know how these stories came about in the first place?" Elinora and Tillie shook their heads in unison. "The property where Kellandale sits was once an ancient hunting ground."

"Oh," Elinora gasped. Her face darkened.

"The manor house was originally built as a hunting lodge for a royal family over four hundred years ago, and it remained as such for a hundred years beyond. The old menagerie held animals they shipped in from faraway places—exotic game for the hunt. They were put on display for guests until they were released into the forest to be hunted along with the native animals. It was fashionable for the time, but here it was excessive. Countless animal lives were lost."

Tillie grimaced.

"Word of the bounty of animals quickly reached the hungry hunters and poachers in the area, and they decided they wanted a piece of the action, too. But they were prohibited from hunting on the property by the royal family."

Abigail took a sip from her teacup then continued.

"That part is all fact. Then something happened. As the legend goes, this brutal environment—the hunting, and all the death in the forest—caused the forest rise up to protect itself and all the creatures that dwelled within it. The forest began to demonstrate immense energy, dangerous and powerful. According to the tales, massive limbs from the wych elms would come alive, violently grabbing at and falling onto trespassers, killing those who dared to pass beneath. Some were rumored to have entered the forest never to return. Those who did live to tell the tale were said to have been driven mad with fear. Eventually the estate was abandoned out of fear and left to fall into ruin and decay.

"There is also a place in the forest at the far eastern boundary of the estate where the bloodthirsty poachers set fires attempting to flush out animals so they could get at them. It left the earth scorched and permanently destroyed. And it was there where all this negative energy festered, so they say. To this day it remains a desolate wasteland where no life exists—that's what began the rumors of a malevolent forest and that is the origin of the fables of

Wyches Wood. There are many who still believe it is true to this very day."

Tillie shot a glance at Elinora to see if she was just as disturbed; she certainly appeared to be.

"How did we not know any of this?" Elinora asked.

"Because your family has always wanted to protect you and spare you the fear. And yet, that is just the beginning of the story."

"Tell us," Tillie pleaded.

"Another century went by until the property was inherited by a royal duke. He believed the legend and was afraid of the forest, too. The property became nothing but a burden to him. So, to rid himself of it, he used it as payment to the young man he had hired to travel the world to find treasures for him. Eventually that man and his wife came to settle here."

"Sir Edward and Lady Vivienne," Elinora said with a smile.

"Sir Edward and Lady Vivienne. They were grateful for this gift and they renamed the estate Kellandale Wood. And just as you believe, they knew in their hearts that the forest was not a terrible place, but rather a very beautiful, magical place; they alone did not fear it.

"In his time in the trading company, Sir Edward witnessed terrible things—animals captured and exploited, people living in poor conditions. Disheartened by what he saw, he left the trading company to become a teacher. He also dedicated the rest of his life to protecting the forest and its animals, to make up for those crimes committed against fellow living beings.

"Kellandale was still known in their time for being a home to some very exotic animals, and indeed, those from the menagerie who had survived had continued to thrive. Sir Edward and Lady Vivienne vowed to keep the hunters away, protecting the land and the lives living within it as best they could until they eventually both passed. The estate was then inherited by their son, William."

Tillie grinned.

"From what I know, he wanted to protect the woods just as his parents did, and make it a sanctuary. So, using the myth of the haunted forest to his advantage, he perpetuated it, twisting it even more and leading others to believe the wicked forest had affected him adversely."

Tillie gasped. "Elinora, you didn't make that up then, did you?"

"No, but I didn't know the whole story."

"Abigail, everyone thinks the forest is haunted, and yet, what you say is nothing we have ever been told. How do you know all of this, and do you really think it's true?" Tillie asked.

She smiled. "Haven't you already discovered the answer to that yourselves?"

"Why, yes, I suppose we have," she said, looking up in surprise.

"After Sir William's passing the property was inherited by Sir Edward's youngest brother, James—your father's fourth grandfather—who was aware of the history of the forest. He, too, was fearful and refused to accept the estate. But at the end of Sir William's life, he implored his own groundskeeper—the very same groundskeeper who helped design Lady Vivienne's beautiful gardens—to convince James that Kellandale Manor and its immediate grounds would be safe to live near if the deep woods continued to be protected yet left alone. Eventually James was persuaded, which is how you have come to live here.

"Meanwhile, Sir William had shared with his groundskeeper the full truth of the goodness and magic of Kellandale Wood and asked him guard his secret and pass it down through the generations of his own family—*my* family—to keep the truth alive; he knew one day someone might need to know the true story."

Elinora's mouth dropped open.

"Oh, how *very* clever!" Tillie gushed. "So, Sir William knew the forest had powers, and that they were good powers. Yet to protect it and keep everyone out, he claimed the forest was haunted to scare them away?"

"Aye."

And it was *your* family he shared this with?"

"Yes, indeed. 'The forest will only reveal its true nature to those who care and understand,' is what I was told as a child. No one in your family since Sir William's time has dared go near the woods out of fear, and my family stayed away from it to respect his wishes. But I feel it is my duty to tell you the truth now because something unusual has happened—you have dared to enter the forest and have shown no fear; you pose no threat to it and have demonstrated only love and respect. I suspect perhaps the forest can sense this," Abigail said, nodding toward Henry.

Tillie was shaking with delight; Elinora's eyes were wide.

"Oh, your parents would not be happy if they knew what I have just told you."

"They're such big worriers," Tillie moaned. "If they had it their way, we would forever be stuck inside and would never have found Henry. Who knows what would have become of him."

"I don't want to think about that," Elinora said, brushing away the thought quickly.

"But you did find him. And I truly believe, as you do, that the woods are not dangerous. There is a reason you found Henry and are able to communicate with him; the forest allowed you to experience some of its powers, and that was no accident."

"Can you hear him, Abigail?" Tillie asked. "I mean, can you hear Henry's thoughts and feelings as we do?"

Abigail looked fondly at him. Henry lifted his head and looked at her with full awareness. Brief, fleeting images of him being comforted by Elinora and Tillie at the river's edge entered her mind. "I believe I can," she said. "I also sense he can communicate with whomever he wishes—and that he chooses to do so only with those he trusts." She smiled.

"What are we to do then, if we're not supposed to know what you told us?" Elinora asked. "And what do we do about Henry? We can't tell Mother and Father what happened, that we can speak to him through our minds because of the magical woods, or where we found him."

"I know your parents, and I know they won't give you a hard time about keeping Henry," Abigail replied. "But you're absolutely right—you should keep the rest to yourselves. It's an extremely delicate subject, and one that your parents have always been very nervous about."

Tillie snorted.

"Tillie, dear, your parents can't be told the truth about the forest, because in order to understand it, they must experience and discover it for themselves, just as you have. And that has always been up to them. Thus far they have been too afraid." Henry looked into her eyes again and she winked back. "As for Henry, he knows not to let anyone else know of his abilities, at least not now. I don't think your parents would accept this so readily as you have, and Jeppe, Sabine, and the others shouldn't be under the pressure of knowing such matters as this, either."

Henry wagged his tail in response, promising the secret of his empathic abilities would remain safe with the four of them.

"For now, he has found his way to you. You are the ones meant to hear him and help him. Just promise you will be careful."

"Promise," Elinora reassured her.

"I believe what we have here is a beautiful Morlish Wolfhound," she added, coaxing Henry into the hall. "He will get much bigger and he will be a wonderful, faithful companion. Wolfhounds are among the most intelligent and loyal as they come. Now, we need to get you all upstairs. Give me a few minutes, then we will introduce Henry to your parents. I will let them know about the delivery man who came today—you know, the kind gentleman who brought me this poor puppy in need of a home."

"Oh, Abigail, I knew you would know what to do!" Elinora exclaimed. "Come with us Henry, you need to rest," she said.

He followed her and Tillie to her bedroom. Once there, Tillie closed the door and breathed in deeply.

Henry looked around the room and was surprised to see a lanky black cat sleeping on Elinora's bed.

"Henry, this is Velvet," Tillie introduced them. "She was once a stray, too. She stays inside now because she doesn't like to wander far. And because she thinks it's far cozier in here."

Velvet let out a little welcoming chirp.

He nuzzled her with a wet nose then curled up on the lounge chair next to Elinora's dressing table. He drifted into a deep, restful sleep.

Velvet stretched and moved next to him. She felt what he was feeling. They all did.

Love. Hope. Belonging.

"I can't believe the day we've had. Or the day he's had. *What the heck in the world?*" Tillie said, looking over at Henry.

"Rather dull, wasn't it?" Elinora said, cracking a smile as she sat down at her dressing table.

"The worst." Tillie grinned, then flopped onto Elinora's bed. The sound woke Henry and he bounded over to her playfully.

Then came a knock. "It's just me," Abigail whispered through the closed door. "Hurry now, let's introduce Henry to your parents, shall we?"

And so, the tales of Henry began.

Winter

5

The Heart of the Forest

"Dress warm, it's snowing Tillie!" Elinora called down the hall before making her way from her own bedroom to the grand staircase. Once downstairs, she took a seat on the foyer settee and set the small woolen blanket that she had been carrying, onto her lap.

Henry heard her voice and came rushing out of Tillie's room to wait with her.

"She probably isn't paying attention; she'll come out wearing summer clothing if she hasn't bothered to look out the window," she said when he approached.

He wagged his tail and dutifully turned and trotted back up the steps to convey this message to Tillie.

Elinora smiled when she heard him pawing at her bedroom door, reminding herself the way in which they could communicate with Henry was actually highly unusual.

It was the thick of winter now, but not even cold weather kept Elinora and Tillie from their daily walks with Henry. Kellandale

Wood was filled with such mystery and wonder, and they craved their journeys into it. The animals loved Henry, and they loved Elinora and Tillie, too; they had made them feel as though they were a part of the forest as much as any other woodland creature—they just happened to be woodland creatures of the human sort.

In the few months following his rescue, Henry had likewise become part of the Wolton household, a canine member of his human pack. He was adored by everyone at the manor house, and as a social creature by nature, he loved them back just as deeply.

A daily routine had quickly fallen into place after Henry's arrival. During the early morning hours as Elinora and Tillie were dressing, Henry made his rounds, visiting everyone in the manor house before setting off to join Velvet in front of the fire in the library. Besides those moments, he was never more than a few footsteps away from either of them.

Their father conceded and allowed Elinora and Tillie to take Henry on walks, a necessity of course, though he had very firmly and constantly harped on them, reminding them where they were, and more importantly, were not allowed to travel. This meant Elinora and Tillie had to keep secret their forays into the deep woods, which had become a daily occurrence.

Meanwhile, Abigail had been correct in her prediction; once a runt, and a frail, abandoned, muddy puppy, Henry had blossomed into an elegant, intelligent, and exceptionally large six-month-old wolfhound, the same one who was descending the stairs again, this time with Tillie by his side.

Elinora stood up and ruffled Henry's fur, the top of his head almost reaching her elbows. "Here, you'll probably want this, too, not that you could fit anything else on your body if you tried," she said handing Tillie a knitted hat.

She took it and placed it on top of the one she was already wearing. She curtsied and grinned at Elinora. "Two hats, father's winter boots, double overcoats, and my woolen stockings—check. Satchel with provisions—check."

"All right, are we ready then? Lead the way, Henry," Elinora said and they followed him out the door and onto the trail. During the milder autumn afternoons, they had spent time sitting beneath their favorite tree at the river's edge, sometimes stopping for a picnic, always hopeful to catch sight of the flash in the water they had last seen on the day they had found Henry.

Out on the trail now, the sun was shining from behind dotted clouds, but the early January air was bone-chilling. Thankfully, the thick cover of the towering evergreens gave them protection from the wind. Tillie breathed in the familiar scent of pine as they traversed delicate sheets of ice, everything cold and quiet except for the occasional crackling sound as the ice buckled under their feet. Though the river was still flowing, a thick slush had begun to accumulate along its edges.

"Hello, old friend," Tillie said to Ole Warty when they reached him. She gazed down at the river.

"No bright flashes in the water?" Elinora asked, reading her thoughts.

She shook her head. "We haven't seen Mister yet, either. Can we walk just a little longer until we find him?"

Elinora nodded and they continued on.

The clouds began to knit together, eventually forming a murky grey blanket overhead as the snowfall began to intensify. Elinora was concerned Henry's paws were getting too cold so she suggested they move away from the river and seek out a fallen tree to sit upon. Once she found a satisfactory spot, she began to unroll the blanket she had been carrying.

But Tillie quickly began pulling things out of her satchel. "Banana, anyone?" she said holding the slightly bruised fruit up.

"No thanks?" Elinora asked, as though this might be the

wrong answer, her voice rising into a giggle.

Tillie unpeeled the banana and tossed it aside for any lucky creature who might happen upon it. "I brought extra socks and galoshes, too, in case we were out here awhile."

Elinora watched with amusement as she struggled to put them on Henry.

He shook his front paws, curious about the odd sensation, then tried to walk, but his paws flopped out of them.

"Worth a try," Elinora laughed. She scooped them up and handed them back to Tillie, then looked around intently. In her hunt for a place to sit, without realizing, she had led them to an area they had never been before. She was surprised to find fresh footprints in the snow. She pointed them out to Tillie.

"Who on earth would be all the way out here besides us?" Tillie asked.

"Maybe a bear?" she replied, thinking of the mysterious white bear they had often seen in the distance within the forest.

"No, I don't think so."

They looked around suspiciously, then cautiously followed them. Elinora grimaced. "Those are definitely human footprints. But who made them?"

They continued to follow them and eventually the tracks stopped near a mass of tangled bushes, then backtracked. Tillie pondered this a moment, then glanced ahead beyond the felled tree. Something there caught her eye. "Elinora, what is *that?*" she asked.

Elinora turned to look. Her eyes widened when she noticed the bright light coming from deep within the forest.

"Stay here, I'll be right back," Tillie whispered.

"No, Tillie, you're not going in there alone."

"Then you're going to have to follow me," she replied.

Elinora put her head down and sighed, then she and Henry cautiously followed.

As they traveled, the snow began to recede, eventually revealing a narrow, overgrown trail. Once on it, the jumble of foliage that had been concealing the trail faded as they walked, revealing the path one step at a time, like an earthen sign pointing the way. A cathedral of trees bursting with flowers leaned in from both sides, forming a natural archway overhead. Tiny purple petals rained on them as they made their way, luring them deeper. Tillie put her hand out to catch them.

"Flowers in the winter?" Elinora marveled.

At the end of the archway a moat of tangled buckthorns guarded the area beyond. They pushed through them to the edge, surprised to discover their angry thorns did not scratch them as they passed through. From where they stood they could see into a clearing; it was circular, wide open, and as though someone had been keeping a tidy campsite, except, there was no evidence of a fire ring or tent, nor was there any sign of a human presence.

Beyond the buckthorn, they could see dense stands of ferns and ancient pines surrounded a clearing. Within this clearing was a tiered slope that formed what appeared to be a rustic amphitheater. The air smelled earthy, of damp moss and rich soil. They moved forward, lingering on the edge of the open area. On the other side of it they could see the forest continued, and from deep within the trees came a rising mist and the sound of a powerful, rushing waterfall.

"Where *are* we?" Elinora asked.

Tillie removed her satchel from her shoulder and began peeling off the multiple layers of overcoats, setting them on the ground next to her, then she took off both her hats. "I haven't the faintest idea, but I am so uncomfortably warm all of a sudden."

Elinora shielded her eyes. There was not a cloud in sight now, and the sun was shining again. Flowers were in full bloom in dazzling colors, the foliage lush and green. They could no longer see their breath in the lightly breezy, warm, humid air, and the frigid January snow was replaced by what seemed to be a proper summer's morning in an exotic tropical oasis.

Without warning, Tillie suddenly advanced toward the center of the ring.

"Where are you going now?" Elinora asked nervously.

"I'm going to see if someone's here," she said as though that was the natural thing to want to do.

"Tillie, please don't," Elinora protested.

Tillie put her fingers to her lips to silence her then crept forward into the amphitheater. But the moment she stepped out into the open, an ominous growl came from somewhere beyond, shaking the ground beneath her feet. She froze. She could hear Elinora stifling a scream.

Then came more noises—at first, an indistinguishable chattering from the trees, but it grew in intensity, louder and louder, as though the sounds were coming from every direction. The sounds melded into a singular moan, then erupted into a piercing screech. Branches, acorns, and bits of tree bark began to drop violently from the trees around her. Tales of the malevolent Wyches Wood screamed out in her mind.

"Come back!" Elinora croaked weakly. Henry crouched down, ready to pounce.

There came a stirring from the underbrush, and the sound of an unknown something charging at Tillie. There was more chatter, this time so deafeningly high-pitched she flinched and covered her ears. When the branches parted, she screamed and turned away, racing back to the safety of Elinora and Henry. But she stopped running when she heard laughing. It was Elinora's laugh. And she could see Henry's tail was wagging.

"Are you both crazy!" she exclaimed, her heart pounding.

Elinora laughed even harder and pointed behind Tillie.

She pivoted abruptly just in time to see a tiny creature sailing through the air and landing on the ground in front of her. Its tail ballooned into a mass of fuzz as it shrieked back. Tillie let out a high-pitched yelp. "Mister?" she asked incredulously as she stooped forward for a better look. She heaved a deep sigh. "Oh, Mister, you *really* startled me! But what are you doing all the way out here? I thought you lived on the other side of the forest."

He chattered about very deliberately, running circles around her feet. Four additional sets of eyes peered out from the underbrush, watching her. Elinora and Henry emerged from the cover of buckthorn as Mister continued to chatter and chirp.

Tillie turned to Elinora and they locked eyes. They looked back at Mister.

"We can understand you!" Tillie exclaimed.

In a flash they knew everything he was trying to tell them, in the very same manner they could with Henry.

"I'm so sorry we frightened you so badly," Elinora replied gently to him after he explained why they had been making such an awful racket.

He was relieved though, delighted even, to find it was only them, and not the hunters that had been in the forest earlier. Then he expressed amazement they had been able to find the trail to the amphitheater in the first place.

"Hunters, out here?" Tillie asked crossly. She glanced around. "And where exactly are we?"

We are in the heart of the forest.

Mister explained that the area in which they were standing, the amphitheater, was where the animals gathered, especially in times of danger. The amphitheater was part of a much larger area, known as the heart of the forest, which included the deep woods that Elinora and Tillie were so fond of, and was guarded by the Lady of the Forest.

Recently hunters had been coming much too close to the path to the amphitheater. Though it was hidden from them, the woodland creatures were uncomfortable and threatened by their presence and they were attempting to drive them away. Elinora, Tillie, and Henry had been mistaken for these hunters, which was why they had been attacked so rudely. Mister quickly reassured them that he knew they could be trusted, not only because they were his friends, but especially because the forest had just invited them into the amphitheater.

"The forest *invited* us?" Elinora asked.

Yes, only those it trusts
are able to see and enter the amphitheater.

"And who, might I ask, is the Lady of the Forest?" Tillie inquired.

Mister's thoughts continued.

The Lady of the Forest is our protector.
She watches over the forest and all
the creatures within it. She is elusive and
remains shielded from the world.
To most she is only a myth.
But there is one who rightly believes she exists,
and he is filled with greed.
The tales are not enough to frighten his men
away, and they return again
and again, seeking her.
Just as she, along with Monkey, the Messenger,
and the protective energy of the forest watch
over us, we, the council of beings, protect her.

"Monkey? And who is the Messenger?" Tillie pressed for more answers.

"And the council of beings?" Elinora added.

We, the creatures that dwell within the forest,
all belong to the council.

"It was the council that made the noises when we arrived, then," she replied.

Yes.

"Well, you do a very good job of protecting the forest," Tillie said with delight. "My heart was ready to jump out of my chest. I've never heard a sound like that in all my life,"

Another Buckthorn squirrel came forward. She confessed to Tillie that she and the other squirrels had made the sounds—that is, all except the deepest growl, which only one of the creatures in the forest was capable of making.

"It's all right, it was exciting! But who made *that* sound, then? And how is it that we can understand all of you?" Tillie asked.

Here, within the amphitheater,
all creatures can communicate and understand
one another. Come see!

He scampered ahead without elaborating any further, leading them into it.

Elinora and Tillie glanced at each other then they, along with Henry, followed Mister.

Mister motioned to the moss-covered ground on the sloped edge of the amphitheater and invited them to sit while the council met. Then he stood up on his hind legs and chattered loudly, calling the council forth. The four other Buckthorn squirrels scurried to his side as animals of all sizes and sorts began emerging from the fringes of the forest. Some of the animals they had seen by the river appeared: a pair of marled rabbits, raccoons, green snakes, porcupines, cottage mice, turtles, deer, and an opossum Elinora had named Ronda.

The bear was there, too. They had never seen him so close before and had only ever caught glimpses of him running through the forest. His fur was dusty white, like smoke. Tillie named him Pipe on the spot. Henry ran forward to greet him and they leapt about, playing and tussling with one another, immediately becoming fast friends.

Tillie clutched Elinora's arm. "Erm, look over there."

She gasped.

Two Bekanan tigers and an indigo water buffalo entered the amphitheater, followed by a handful of spotted warthogs from Kinsori, and a Grouse's blue pangolin, which Tillie was able to identify from all her reading about animals. There was also a very strange, large rodent-like creature that they didn't recognize, not to mention many other exotic animals—all descendants of the ancient menagerie. They were unafraid of Elinora and Tillie, and just as the encounters with other animals in the forest had been, they were non-threatening.

Elinora and Tillie had a hard time keeping their mouths from hanging open. But they politely listened as the council conferred about the urgent matter of the hunters. The discussion was silent, passing through their minds just like their communication with Henry.

Mister took charge, reporting the sighting of the two hunters. They had appeared in the forest not long before Elinora, Tillie, and Henry had arrived. This explained the extra footprints.

Pipe reported they had been chased off, but everyone knew it was only a matter of time before they would be back. The council resolved to remain on high alert for further human activity. There was a brief pause, then Mister conveyed to Elinora and Tillie that they were an exception to and were always welcome in the forest.

Thank you," Elinora said, addressing the animals. She paused and sighed. "This has been utterly remarkable, so much so we've lost track of time. But we've been gone far too long and I'm afraid we must leave now."

"Elinora is right," Tillie said to the council. "As much as I don't want to leave, we really must, and straight away. Our parents are just not so, well, to be polite about it, they're not quite so keen that we travel so far away from our home. But we will find a way to return soon, I promise."

Mister scampered forward, offering to lead them back to the trail. Henry stood up and he and Elinora followed as Tillie gathered her hats and pile of clothing.

When they reached the edge of the buckthorn moat, Tillie turned and called out to the council, still gathered together in the amphitheater. "Tell me now, who was it that shook the ground with a roar when we entered the Heart of the Forest?"

"Monkey!" was the reply.

6

Graham & Jamie

"Dearest Graham and Jamie," Elinora began her letter. *There, that part is done at least,* she silently congratulated herself. She stopped writing and tapped her ink pen on the blotter, struggling to find the words to explain to her cousins what she and Tillie had discovered over the course of the past several months. She had been putting the task off for weeks, but the O'Conors were due to arrive soon and she couldn't delay any longer.

Tillie had written to them shortly after they had found Henry, but Graham—not quite half a year older than Elinora—was wise beyond his years, and a relentless skeptic. He had replied that while he thoroughly enjoyed her creative writing, he knew he and his younger brother, Jamie, were on the receiving end of an elaborate scheme with one Ottilie Wolton's fingerprints all over it. "A talking dog? You're an award-winning fiction writer! Next you'll be telling me that Velvet is singing opera. It sounds like Tillie is even more bored than I thought! But don't worry, we will be there soon enough to entertain you," he had written back.

Elinora knew he was teasing, but she wanted to follow up to make sure he understood Tillie wasn't just dreaming up a fanciful story. She tapped again a few more times, then exhaled. The flame of the candle sitting on the desk flickered as she began to write.

I hope this letter finds you both well. Tillie and I cannot wait until you arrive! It really does send me into a giggle fit thinking what your faces must have looked like as you read Tillie's last letter. I know it sounds ridiculous and like something she would invent, but you must trust me, this is not the case. We have so much to share and to show you.

You remember the stories about Kellandale Wood? Well, we have found there is some truth to them, but overall, what we have been told is a very misleading version of the truth. I do wish you would just believe us, but I know the only way is for you to see for yourselves. I at least wanted to prepare you so it wouldn't be such a shock when you arrive. Things really have been quite abnormal lately—the strangest you could ever imagine, but in a good way.

Nobody knows about any of this except for Tillie, me, you, and Jamie, and also Abigail, with whom we have shared everything. And would you believe, she knew more about the forest than we ever realized?

I am writing again now as other curious things have occurred since Tillie's last letter. But you must <u>promise</u> to keep to yourselves what I am about to share with you.

She paused to underline the word *"promise"* a second time, then recounted their discovery of the amphitheater and the council of animals, their ability to communicate with them, and even what little they knew of the Lady of the Forest.

Elinora groaned when she read what she had written. That they were empathically connected with the dog they had found by the side of the river was far-fetched enough. But she also expected them to believe in a forest full of animals they could talk to, an unseen growling monkey, mythical creatures, and tropical weather in the middle of winter. Why would they believe it? It was the stuff of dreams and fairy tales.

But her letter would have to do. She folded it neatly and sealed it in an envelope, then set out to find someone to deliver it—someone she could entrust it to. She closed her bedroom door and headed down the staircase, passing by Albert at the bottom. "Good evening," she said looking up at him with a smile. Albert, a very tall, older man with greying hair, was energetic beyond his years. A resident at Kellandale for three generations, he had become steward when James and Camille were children. Elinora and Tillie looked to him like a grandfather and she knew she could go to him in confidence with such an important matter.

"Good evening, Elinora, dear," he replied warmly, glancing at the envelope in her hand. He could always tell when she was on a mission.

"Albert...is there any way this can be sent to my cousins right away? It's urgent they receive it before they arrive here."

He smiled. "I'll have Emil and Simon deliver it when they take your father to the Waterbridge train station first thing tomorrow morning," he said reaching out his hand and taking the letter from Elinora. His skin was tinged with a few age spots, and slightly wrinkly—the only visible signs hinting at his age.

"Thank you." She sighed. "My father will be gone for a long while, won't he?"

"It would seem so, but don't worry. From what I understand Graham and young James will be coming to stay, something to look forward to, I'm sure."

"Yes, you're right. You always know how to help me feel better, thank you," she said.

"Of course, Elinora, dear," he replied, heading down the hall toward the back of the house.

Just then Henry approached her, anticipating where she was headed.

She patted his head. "You're always one step ahead of me. What would I ever do without you?"

He nudged her and wagged his tail, then led her to Tillie.

"Ottilie! It's done!" she called triumphantly as she and Henry entered the spacious library. It smelled of old books and the smoke of the crackling fire. She plopped down on the soft plum-colored sofa across from her sister, who was surrounded by heaps of books strewn about on the couch, the carpet at her feet, and the large table in between them.

Henry walked to the back of the room. Velvet was already there, napping by the fire. He playfully nudged her with his nose before curling up beside her in his favorite spot. She lifted her head and greeted him with a chirp.

"I finished the letter. Albert is sending it off tomorrow," Elinora continued, then waited for a reply, but she was met with more silence. "You're welcome."

Tillie's face was buried in a large book she had plucked from one of the many towering shelves lining the walls of the library. "I can't wait to see their expressions when they realize this isn't a practical joke," she finally responded, peering over the top of the book. "I had to climb the ladder to the very top to find this one. I wish I could have sat up there while I read, but it's so big and heavy I probably would have fallen over trying to hold it up. It's a book about nature and wildlife in this part of the country, and there's another about animals from around the world. I'm reading about the species of fish and birds and animals that are native to our area.

"Indigo water buffalo and Bekanan tigers definitely do not belong here, but we know that already. And that one animal we weren't sure about? It was a giant sienna capybara. They're from the rainforests in *Pedora,* can you believe it? A lot of the animals we've seen in the forest are from countries in completely different continents from ours, like the Debarian okapi, and the Myarian grey serval. And our bear friend Pipe? He's a ghost bear from all the way in Northern Auria," she reported. "No mention of monkeys supposed to be living here in our part of the world. Or Ladies of the Forest, for that matter."

She and Elinora had been intrigued by this bit of information Mister had shared, but he was an enigmatic little squirrel, as mysterious as the forest itself, and he had said nothing more about the Lady of the Forest after that first mention.

Elinora scanned the pile of books in front of Tillie. "A sienna capybara?" she asked with interest.

Tillie flipped through the book then turned it toward her sister to show her an illustration.

"That is certainly what we saw. Jamie and Gray really are going to be absolutely stunned, aren't they?"

Tillie grinned with delight. "Better than that. They're going to completely faint!"

The big arrival came a few weeks later when a small fleet of carriages—one full of people, the other stuffed with their belongings for the long visit—approached Kellandale Manor. As they turned onto the long gravel drive, they left tire tracks and hoof prints in the fresh dusting of snow.

Tillie and her mother were already waiting for their arrival at the entrance of the manor house.

Emil was also there, ready to assist the O'Conors, stepping forward to help with the horses when the carriage stopped.

"Jamie!" Tillie shouted when she saw a shock of red-blonde, wavy hair appear in the carriage window.

"Tillie!" he yelled, stepping out with a large case.

She ran to greet him. "Your viola! Will you finally be playing for us?" she asked when she saw it.

"We'll see," he said, which was his typical reaction to that particular question. He grinned at her, his dimples showing on his fair-skinned, freckled, round cheeks. A budding, talented musician, he was not shy except for when it came to his musical talents. Somehow self-doubt reared its ugly head, making him uncharacteristically self-conscious when he was asked to play.

"Oh, please, I hope you do. I won't stop asking until you finally do."

He scrunched his nose, brushing off the request with a roll of his blue-grey eyes. "Come on, let's go say hello to the horses," he suggested when he saw she was holding a bunch of carrots. He waved hello to his aunt, set down the case, then followed Tillie to the front of the carriage. Emil was already helping the driver to unhitch four beautiful horses.

"Thanks for the ride, Peachy," Jamie said to the chestnut mare as he gently rubbed the white blaze that ran down her velvety nose. She nickered contentedly and nibbled on the white embroidery on the lapel of his blue tweed coat.

Emil grinned, peering over Peachy from the other side. They ran a hand over her beautiful ginger mane that was almost the same color as their own hair. "It's good to see you again, Jamie. The horses sure worked hard the last two days to get you here," they said. Emil removed the bit from her mouth and put on her halter, readying her to be taken into the stable to rest with the other horses when they noticed the carrots Jamie and Tillie were holding. "Go ahead," they nodded. "I'm sure Peachy will appreciate that very much."

Jamie nodded back at Emil, held out a flattened hand and set a carrot onto it, and offered it. Peachy took it gratefully. Then Jamie and Tillie did the same for the other horses.

Graham and his mother, meanwhile, had stepped out of the carriage. Anna approached, greeting them warmly. "You must be so tired, but we're all so happy to see all of you. James left for the city yesterday morning and I'm sure he and Miles have met up by now."

"Yes, indeed! Hello, Anna, love," Camille said, stepping out in a lemon-hued linen traveling dress. Her hair was dark blonde like Tillie's, but cut short, and she possessed Tillie's demeanor as well—fiery and energetic.

Graham stretched his legs, pulled off his cap, then brushed his floppy, dark brown bangs out of his face. "Hello Aunt Anna," he said with much charm, breaking out in his signature broad, infectious grin, his pale cheeks flushing from the cold air.

As they continued to talk, Elinora emerged from the manor house with Henry by her side. "Gray! Aunt Camille!" she called out and bolted down the steps toward them.

Henry stepped out from behind her to get a glimpse of the new members of his pack. His tail wagged fiercely.

Graham lifted Elinora off her feet when he saw her.

"I'm so glad you're here!" she laughed. She always felt like nothing could go wrong when her cousins were around.

Tillie and Jamie rushed back to join them when they saw everyone gathered.

"So, *you're* Henry," Jamie gasped when he saw him. He rushed over to meet him.

Henry didn't let any of his thoughts and feelings come through though—not yet—but he knew without a doubt he could trust

76

Jamie. He wagged his tail again and brushed against his legs playfully. Then he jumped up and rested a paw on his shoulder. His weight was so great that Jamie's knees buckled, pushing him down into the snow-covered cobblestones.

"He's *huge*! I love him already," Jamie laughed. He continued to fuss over Henry before pulling himself back up and dusting the snow off his trousers.

"Gray, you're here!" Tillie said as he grabbed her and gave her a bear hug, his hazel eyes sparkling along with his wide grin.

Elinora stood quietly observing for a moment, full of great anticipation and excitement over the extended stay. None of them realized it yet, but this was one of those subtle moments—an instant in time which would eventually come to be remembered as the start of a fantastical adventure.

"Hello, Henry," Graham said warmly. He paused and looked intently at him, and Elinora wondered if he was waiting for Henry to talk. Tillie wondered, too, and smiled amusedly.

"Wolfhound then, eh?" he asked, though that detail hadn't been mentioned in their letters.

"Yes," Elinora said, smiling.

"Morlish Wolfhound to be exact. I've read all about them and they're really smart."

"Exactly right! He's incredibly smart, and very gentle, despite his size. But he needs lots of exercise; Elinora and I take him on walks every day to make sure he's content. We'll take a walk after you're all settled in, if you'd like," Tillie offered.

"I would love that," he replied with a wink.

Elinora felt her hear skip a beat, but still Graham said nothing about the letter she had written.

Everyone began picking up the heaps of luggage to bring their belongings inside. "Are you planning to stay here a while or something?" Tillie teased, picking up two bags.

Graham and Jamie did likewise.

Jamie grinned. "A long time. You're going to be very sick of me soon!"

"Come on, follow me," Tillie said laughing, leading them inside.

"I'll join you in a moment, I'm going to help Aunt Camille get settled first," Elinora called after them.

"All right; let's take Graham and Jamie for a stroll with Henry when we're done!" Tillie shouted back, then she turned to her cousins. "They usually put the luggage on the service lift to carry it up, but my way is much faster. You get to bunk together," she said as they hauled the heavy bags up the grand staircase. She led them to their room—a spacious bedroom with two beds and a view out a front window. They followed and set their haul down.

A young man entered with the rest of their luggage and placed the bags on the floor. "Here's the rest. You're doing my job better than I am again, aren't you Tillie," he laughed.

"Never!" She replied to the dark haired, tan-skinned young man who looked to be slightly older than Graham by only a few years. "Simon," she said, "you've heard of Graham and Jamie, my cousins," she introduced them. Simon nodded hello.

"Graham, Jamie, this is Simon. Simon has been here with us for almost a year now. He helps Albert, and is studying with my father while he's staying here. And he knows how to play Knaves... *tiered* Knaves!" she said to Graham excitedly. She turned back to Simon. "Graham *loves* to play. Obsessed, really."

"Regular Knaves...but, really? You know how to play the tiered version? Where did you learn?" Graham asked with eagerness.

"I do! My parents are from Idi. My grandfather was a tiered Knaves—tiered Helijot, that is—champion back in the day."

"Whoa!" Jamie exclaimed.

"I would do anything to learn how to play Helijot. I've only heard about it; it sounds really intriguing—and very hard!"

"It's definitely a challenge; I'd be happy to teach you," Simon offered. He reached out a hand and he and Graham shook.

"Really?" Graham replied excitedly.

"Anytime; come find me when you're ready. I'll leave you all here to get settled for now," Simon said with a smile before leaving the room.

"I'll be right back," Tillie said to Graham and Jamie, stepping out into the hall. "I'm going to Aunt Camille's room to give her a proper hello."

Elinora was already in the bedroom next door with her mother, helping Camille unpack.

"This lovely old view—it brings back so many memories. So many things from my childhood are still here," Camille said, looking out the window overlooking the drive as Tillie entered.

Anna and Elinora smiled.

"Oh, Aunt Camille, I am so glad you could come stay, we're so happy you're here," Tillie said approaching her and giving her a kiss on the cheek. Just then she heard hoofbeats outside. She moved to the window to look out in time to see another carriage pulling up. "Who is that now? Are we expecting someone else, Mother?"

"Oh, yes, I meant to mention it. Everett Meade is helping your father and your Uncle Miles in the city," she replied. "We had invited him to send Penelope and Madelina to come stay with us while he is away, too, and they decided to take us up on the offer. The Meades live so far away now, it will bring Penelope and Lina much closer to Everett so they can visit easier now and again. It will be wonderful for us all to be together, don't you think?"

Elinora's eyes darted to over to Tillie.

"Oh, Mother, why?" Tillie moaned. She smothered her face with her hands.

"What? Oh, don't tell me the two of you never settled whatever happened between you the last time."

"No, we didn't and nothing happened. Lina just decided she didn't need me as a friend, and I have no idea what made her feel that way suddenly!" she said, twisting her face. "It's probably because I'm not living in as modern or fancy of a house as the rest of her friends or something dull like that."

"Maybe not, though. It could be a misunderstanding. I certainly hope you can work things out now that she's here. It's been a long time since you last saw her. I'm sure things will have changed. You used to be so close."

Tillie shook her head. "She would never; she's too stubborn."

Elinora turned to Tillie with raised eyebrows. She stifled a snort.

"Well, I would like all of us to go downstairs together to greet them," Anna replied.

Tillie took a moment to reply. "I can't, not right now."

"Tillie," Elinora scolded. "Be reasonable. Whatever it was that happened, don't forget you were just as disagreeable as she— possibly even more so, if you ask me."

Tillie glared at her. "Well, that's what you think. And like I said, nothing happened. She doesn't like me and I can't do anything about it. Anyway, we promised Graham and Jamie we would take them on a walk in the garden with Henry right now, remember?"

"Yes, I suppose," Elinora replied.

"Come along then, we should find Henry," she said, grabbing Elinora by the arm. "See you at supper," she called to her mother from the hall, rushing away as fast as she could.

"Tillie!" Anna called back, but they were already gone.

"Oh dear," Camille said.

Anna exhaled deeply. "Tillie and Lina were so close—just as close as you and Penelope have always been. It's very upsetting to learn they're still in a quarrel. Has Penelope ever said anything about what might have gotten into the two of them?"

Camille shook her head. "No, she's been just as perplexed as we are."

Anna sighed. "And these long walks...Tillie and Elinora of course have been told to stay close to the manor house and away from the deep woods, but sometimes I wonder if they're listening. I do feel a bit silly because I don't want to stop them from enjoying the grounds, but they are out there even more than ever now that we have Henry. And James and I get so worried that, well..." she drifted off.

Camille nodded. She, too, had grown up at Kellandale with the legend of the forest hanging over her head. As children, she and her brother, James, were frightened by the stories and made a pact they would not go anywhere near the woods. They had never broken this promise. "Trust me, I know," she said. "Graham and Jamie of course know as well. We can only hope they listen. James and I never wanted to find out if the tales were true or not. I hope for their sake they are sensible and do not try to find out, either."

7

The Skeptic & the Storytellers

"Magical forest, is it, then? Do tell me more," Graham said, eager to initiate the unavoidable conversation as they exited through the prep room door on the first floor. He pushed back his bangs and tucked them under the brim of his cap, revealing a devious grin. Despite his desire to heckle, however, his instinct to be protective of Elinora and Tillie was always first and foremost, so it was only after slipping outside and making their way to the garden maze that he mentioned their letters. But now, out of earshot of anyone else, he felt free to relentlessly tease. "Oh yes, and the talking animals, how could I ever forget." He arched his eyebrow playfully.

Tillie put her hands on her hips and furrowed her brows.

He glanced at Henry, who was trotting down the stone steps beside him. "How do you do? Splendid. I am doing quite well, too, thank you," he said to him. He looked at Elinora and smiled.

"Oh, stop now. He can understand you whether you believe it or not," she said, flapping him in the stomach with the gloves she was carrying before slipping them on.

He winced, pretending to be hurt. "Right. Have you ever actually seen this so-called monkey, or are you just letting your imagination get the best of you?" He rubbed his hands together briskly and breathed on them for warmth.

Before she or Tillie could respond, he fired off more questions. "Could it have been your grumbling stomach you heard, and not Henry's thoughts? Oh, wait, please, tell me more about that Lady of the Forest; I think that was the most creative bit of all. How did you come up with that? Oh right—a talking squirrel told you!" He looked at Tillie and feigned doubling over with laughter.

"I can't wait to see you eat your hat, Gray, because you will," she replied. "You are going to fall over onto the ground and faint when you find out it's all true. And when you do, I will shake you awake to make sure you finish every last bite!"

"Oh, come on, you can't really communicate with animals, just admit it. You're just a bunch of story tellers; rather inventive story tellers at that, to be honest."

"Graham O'Conor," Tillie said rolling her eyes.

"Will you two please stop!" Elinora tried to sound like she was scolding, but even she was laughing.

"If you say so." Graham pulled his cap down over his face protectively to shield himself from his cousins.

He continued to pester them, and as he did Abigail's words floated through Elinora's mind. *The energy of the forest will only reveal itself to those who truly care.* Graham had always teased them relentlessly about many things, but it was always in good fun. She knew deep down he was actually sensitive and kind and would come around sooner or later. She just wondered how long it might take.

"All right, Gray," Jamie said. "We'll find out soon enough."

They walked ahead, and for old time's sake Jamie made his way to the center of the snow-covered garden maze, stalking the others and jumping out every now and again from behind the towering hornbeam shrubberies. "I'm going to get you!" he threatened.

"Come, this way," Tillie said laughing and catching her breath after being chased by him through the hedges. She led them out of the maze to the entrance of the forest trail.

"Ah yes, the infamous Kellandale Wood," Graham said ominously as they approached.

"Puckish, aren't we," Tillie teased.

"Puckish, eh? Did you find that word in the mythology book that helped you make up your stories? And you do know that my mother would not condone this illicit activity; what kind of trouble are you trying to get me into?"

"Oh Gray, she'll never know as long as you keep quiet," Jamie said, pushing forward.

"Yes, just shush and come on," Tillie needled Graham.

Just then came a familiar rustling. "Hello, Mister," Elinora said when he jumped out of a pile of ice-encrusted leaves. She ruffled the fur on the top of his head, then bent down to give him a few peanuts.

Mister put his paw in her hand and gently took them. He turned and regarded Graham and Jamie, then scampered down the trail.

"Gray, Jamie, that was Mr. Squirrel, but you can call him Mister," Tillie explained. "He's usually here waiting for us when we take our walks."

"He's adorable I'll admit, but it still proves nothing," Graham said, giving a sideways glance at his brother.

Jamie, meanwhile, was thrilled by the interaction with the friendly squirrel. "I believe what they've told us could very well be true. I mean I really, really hope it's true, because how amazing is that?"

"It *is* true!" Tillie protested.

Elinora walked ahead. Graham smirked, but he continued to follow; Henry was still at his side.

Jamie walked a little slower, exploring and inspecting the trail closely. "Why would they make up such an elaborate story and not let it go by now if it weren't true?" he said quietly to his brother.

"That's the question of the hour, isn't it?" he replied.

"Hold up a minute, I want to try something," Jamie said, stopping on the trail. He put his head down and remained silent. Henry sensed his intention and came to his side. Jamie's eyes widened and he smiled. Then he reached out and placed his hands on each side of Henry's face and closed his eyes dramatically. Graham watched closely and stifled a laugh when Jamie lowered his head and touched it to Henry's forehead.

But he didn't need to make a production of it; all Henry needed was absolute trust, and he had already felt he had Jamie's when they'd met. Now he was letting him in completely.

Jamie's eyes popped open and he stumbled back, a rush of strong feeling coursing through him. "Gray, it's not a joke, it's for real!" he shouted. "I know what Henry is thinking and feeling right now, right this very minute. He's happy we're here!"

Elinora and Tillie heard shouts and turned back on the trail.

Graham raised his eyebrows. "I certainly didn't hear anything."

"No, it's not like that at all, it wasn't words, or even sounds I heard. I just felt a whole lot of things; I just know what he's thinking and feeling."

Graham folded his arms.

"He thinks you'll come around, too, by the way," he snickered.

"Is that so."

"It *is* so."

Graham strolled over and knelt so that his face was at the same level as Henry's, then he looked directly into his soft brown eyes. Henry's tail wagged and thumped on the ground playfully. Graham flicked his wrists, then mimicking Jamie, put both hands on either side of Henry's temples like a fortune-teller would to a crystal ball and...he waited.

Henry sloppily licked his face. He wagged his tail again and panted, which gave him the look of someone laughing.

Graham pulled away, laughing, too. "Nothing. I heard absolutely nothing," he said, releasing his hands and rubbing his cheek with his sleeve. He turned to Jamie. "So, you're in on this too, now? All right, three against one—no worries, I can handle it. This is going to be a long visit, fella," he chuckled.

"For crying out loud, Gray," Jamie groused.

Graham looked into Henry's eyes again and couldn't help but feel lighthearted. "He really is beautiful, and I can tell he's really smart, talking or not. And the woods are magnificent. I don't need magic to enjoy any of this, you know." He stood back up and spun around to take it all in.

Tillie watched him closely.

He turned to her abruptly. "Now I get it. You know you don't have to cook up a fantastic adventure so I won't miss the city."

"Oof, you're absolutely exhausting," she groaned.

Henry wagged his tail again, aware, and very much enjoying the game. He liked Graham a lot, and his resistance was making him feel very playful. Even he knew Graham would come around; he just wanted to make him work a little first.

Elinora, Tillie, and Jamie sensed this. Jamie snickered when he realized Henry could understand Graham and was playing with him.

"Just give it time, Gray," Elinora said gently.

"Can you take us to the place in the woods with the animals? Maybe he will believe us when he sees it," Jamie asked.

"It's where we are headed now—the amphitheater."

86

"It's another world there, you'll be amazed. It won't be so cold either," Tillie said, then exhaled and looked cross-eyed at her breath.

"Righto. By all means, lead the way," said Graham, shivering and laughing.

Henry wagged his tail again. He continued to walk next to him and even gave him a little nudge.

Graham ruffled Henry's fur once more and noticed he did seem exceptionally aware. It made him pause, even if only for a moment.

The snow began to fall lightly again as they moved through the stand of pines on the trail.

"Has Graham told you that he's applied for school again?" Jamie asked Elinora and Tillie.

"Gray, that's wonderful," Elinora said. "I'm sorry you've been having such a hard time getting in. It's not right."

"Don't worry, I'll just keep at it. And hopefully things will change. A lot of people are angry about all of it."

"Gray wants to study international law," Jamie added proudly. "It's proper good, but I thought he'd become an inventor." He looked at Graham, who smiled.

"I think that's what *you're* going to be, James. You certainly have the mind for it."

Jamie looked down and smiled, glancing over at Henry again. He still couldn't believe he could understand Henry. But in some way, it just felt natural. He smiled again.

Henry wagged his tail. He didn't need to see Jamie's face to feel his joy.

"And how about you, Nor?" Graham asked. "You actually got in, but I heard you declined your acceptance. I was really surprised to hear that. Why did you do that?" He looked at her intently.

"She's afraid of leaving home," Tillie said bluntly. "I think she's making a huge mistake."

"I am *not* afraid," she said defensively. "Maybe I am a little… but that's not the only reason. I told Tillie I don't feel right about it—I only got in through lottery and that feels so unfair. We are getting by here, so for the time being, I would rather figure out what I could possibly do to help change things in the long run. At least the community school is being built. It's a start. As long as they aren't shut down like some of the other schools have been. I don't know, there's got to be something that can be done about it. Now can we talk about something else right now?"

Jamie shrugged. "It's all right, Elinora, you'll figure it out."

"What are we going to do about Lina?" Tillie asked. "She is certainly going to tattle if she sees us going into the woods every day, I just know it. She has always wanted to get me into trouble."

Jamie shrugged. "Don't be so angry with her, Tillie. I quite like her. And we haven't seen her in a long time. Maybe it will be different this time."

Tillie snorted. "Unlikely."

"What happened between you two?"

"I don't want to talk about it."

Jamie sighed. "All right. I like your outfit," he said, quickly changing the topic.

"Oh yes, thank you for loaning me the trousers," she said looking at the baggy brown pants and heavy stockings peeking out from under her long overcoat.

"You can keep them if you'd like. They'll keep you warm when we walk," he offered. "I hope we can walk out here every day."

"Brilliant. Dresses are unbearably impractical. I feel much more comfortable, and I want to be able to run and climb and wade in the river and not have to deal with a stuffy, ridiculous dress," she said.

Jamie nodded approvingly. "Tell us more about Kellandale Wood," he prodded.

"You mean *Wyches Wood*," Graham interjected, holding up his hands and wiggling his fingers.

"Yes, those who are *afraid* of it call it that," Elinora teased, then recounted the history of the estate as she and Tillie had been recently told by Abigail.

"People used to hunt tigers here?" Jamie asked.

"Yes, animals of all kinds, from all over the world," Tillie replied.

"That's horrible," Graham remarked.

"Apparently when the manor house was built, the hunting parties were excessive; loads of animals were hunted. Abigail said they brought in game from other places; not just tigers, but rhinos, giraffe, bear, water buffalo—anything big and exotic. The menagerie we used to wonder about was used to display them for guests, like a zoo, until they were released for the hunt."

Jamie wrinkled his nose.

"Awful, isn't it?" Tillie agreed.

"That's why the animals of the forest formed a council, to protect themselves." Elinora looked over at Graham, expecting his reproach, but she continued. "Kellandale Wood is so vast that hunters sometimes still enter the forest without us even knowing. The forest council works together to chase them away when they do."

Graham had been listening attentively to the history and was engrossed, but the part about the forest council made him shake his head. Yet his mind wandered, and he couldn't help but wonder—if it were all true, why was he alone the one that was unable to sense Henry's thoughts. *Bah, what am I even thinking? It is impossible*, he thought. He glanced over at Henry, who had been watching him closely. They locked eyes. Graham sensed his deep intelligence and awareness and he flinched. Elinora, meanwhile, had continued with her story, so he turned his attention back to her.

"...and the reason Kellandale Wood was thought to be haunted in the first place was because the forest really *does* possess some sort of magic," she said. "The ability to experience it depends on whether you are here out of love, and want to help and be part of it, or if you're here out of greed, and trying to take from it or destroy it. That's what we believe, anyway."

"Wonderful," Graham teased.

They walked on for a bit then Tillie stopped. "Right here. This is where we found Henry," she said, pointing to the riverbank and the little rocky beach. She lowered her head. "It was so awful, Graham."

Henry gazed over toward the riverbank and sat down.

"We thought he was dead," Elinora said, her voice low and solemn.

As they shared more of the story, Graham suddenly breathed in deep and began to feel a tightening in his chest. He looked at Henry, imagining the trauma, and what his cousins must have felt. All of the emotions he had tried to hold back, the hiding behind disbelief, suddenly came crashing down on him. "How could someone do that to Henry? To any living being?" His voice cracked as he said this. The rising emotion was so strong it overwhelmed him. Then he realized it was not just his own emotions he was feeling. Henry had let him in, and now Graham felt everything. He saw fleeting images in his mind—all that had happened to Henry on that day, just as they had said. Then, in another flash, he knew what Henry was feeling right at that very moment.

A sense of belonging. A teasing nudge.

Love.

"That was...oh, Henry, did that really happen?" Graham blurted. He moved over to him and stroked his fur. He looked around, dazed.

90

Tillie pushed him playfully "I told you!" she needled.

"But how?"

"It's the forest, Graham…we're sure of it," Elinora replied softly.

Suddenly, another rush of feeling slipped out of Henry; something he had been holding back even from Elinora and Tillie. Only Graham perceived it.

Sadness. Horrible, aching sadness. Fear.

"What is it, boy?" Graham gasped.

Henry's ears dropped, but he went silent.

Elinora quickly looked over. She, too, felt something pass through Henry's mind. She shivered.

"Gray?" Tillie asked.

He shook his head. "I don't know. But it felt like something is really bothering Henry."

Henry quickly stood up and wagged his tail, shaking off whatever had caught Graham's attention. The feeling lifted.

"You sure you're all right?" Graham asked him. Henry wagged his tail again.

Tillie raised an eyebrow at them both. "All right then, let's get moving to the amphitheater," she beckoned. Graham, Jamie, and Henry followed.

Elinora, meanwhile, fell behind a few steps, keeping her eye on Henry. She, too, had sensed something within Henry that unsettled her, but she did not know what to make of it. She felt another shiver pass through, but composed herself, running to catch up.

8

The Energy of the Forest

"That's the tree, isn't it? The one we aren't supposed to walk out to," Jamie said as Ole Warty came into sight ahead on the trail. He quickened his pace, eager to see it up close.

Tillie ran ahead with him. "It's him all right—this big guy marks where we turn off the trail to enter the amphitheater. His name is Ole Warty." She patted him.

"Ole Warty." He looked around. "Why is it that we aren't supposed to come out here, again?" He snorted a laugh.

"Evil. Haunted. Remember?" Graham joked when he and Elinora caught up to Jamie and Tillie. "Anyway, that's a sycamore tree."

Elinora nodded. "Isn't he extraordinary?"

"Yes, he really is a giant—he's got to be hundreds of years old, at least."

Tillie smiled and patted Ole Warty again. "We'll come back later to visit him. Come on, there's a waterfall somewhere in the amphitheater. Elinora and I keep hearing it off in the distance, but so far we haven't been able to find it," she said, grabbing Jamie's hand.

As they approached the unmarked trail, they caught sight of Mister again, waiting to lead his new guests into the hidden sanctuary of the forest council. They followed him through buckthorn and ferns, then out into the grassy opening. Tillie stretched out her arms, presenting it to Graham and Jamie. "Here we are. This is the amphitheater, and we're in what the forest animals call the heart of the forest. As you can see, it's all very real."

"Unbelievable," Jamie gasped. Without wasting a moment, he took off to explore the area. Henry chased after him, play-nibbling at his ankles as they ran. Along the way he made sure to say hello to each of the animals he encountered—rabbits, deer, turtles, even a hedgehog, all of them roaming freely. It was warm and dry in the amphitheater so he removed his boots and stockings, pulling them off and tossing them away so he could feel the soft moss between his toes. He waved at Graham from a distance.

Graham covered his face with his hand, then shook his head. He turned to Tillie, looking utterly befuddled. "I really don't understand how any of this is possible."

"Don't try, just enjoy it. By the way, you're lucky I'm not going to make you eat your hat, you know."

He took it off and pretended to take a bite. Elinora snickered.

"Brilliant. Now, come sit down a moment when you're done with that," Tillie said, walking toward the center of the amphitheater. Graham and Elinora followed. Together they sat watching Jamie and Henry play with Pipe, the squirrels, and a little fox that came out to meet everyone.

A tiny green snake slithered up to Graham, crossing over his outstretched legs. He put out his hand and let it wind through his fingers and back down to the mossy ground. He looked up and grinned.

Tillie was busy studying a tiny ant marching past. She lowered herself down onto her stomach and watched as it attempted to haul a piece of leaf five times its size. It struggled for a moment then dropped the leaf, so she picked it up gently between her fingers and held it up for the ant to grab. "Here you go," she said as the ant took it from her. "You're welcome." She smiled.

Jamie came running over and plopped down onto the ground to catch his breath. Henry followed. "The animals were just as interested in me as I am in them. Do they know what we're thinking, too?"

"I'm certain they do," Elinora replied. She looked back at Graham, whose smile was wider than she had ever seen before.

A loud call pierced the air, commanding attention.

"What was that?" Graham looked into the sky.

"I'll wager a guess it's the bird we've seen, but we don't know what kind it is. It's certainly not in any of the books I've been reading," Tillie replied.

Mister skittered forward eagerly.

> *The Messenger is the eyes and ears of the forest,*
> *the bearer of news. He watches over, soaring*
> *high, protecting the forest from above.*

"Mister! We really can understand you, too!" Jamie exclaimed.

At this, Graham clutched his hat again and looked at Tillie. She smiled wryly.

"The Messenger?" Jamie asked Mister.

> *Yes—he is intelligent and strong, and very, very*
> *old. The energy of the forest has allowed him to*
> *live a long time, just as it has for all of us.*

"The Messenger! What kind of bird is he, then?" Tillie asked.

He is the Messenger.

Tillie shook her head. "If you say so." She turned to Graham and Jamie. "You need to see something else. Mister taught us this. You're able to see the heart of the forest and the amphitheater only because it is allowing you to—which means you have been invited here."

"I like being invited here," Jamie said, eagerly following her.

"And being invited here means you should probably be able to hear it, too. Just lie down and be quiet a moment. You're going to feel things, but don't be afraid."

Graham obediently did as he was instructed. He lay down in the center of the amphitheater, then laced his fingers together and rested his head in his hands. The others did the same. "Righto, let's have it then," he said, closing his eyes.

As if in reply, the wind picked up. Softly and slowly, the heart of the forest began to speak to them.

Just as Henry did, it communicated in feelings and images that lilted through their minds. It spoke of the sky, the water, and the earth—the plants, animals, trees, birds, and insects within the forest that it protected. It told them that they were a part of, and connected to, all of it. Then the wind slowed to a gentle breeze.

Graham sat up. The forest council had gathered and surrounded them, watching intently.

"The heart of the forest was telling you about its energy, the magical stuff that protects the creatures who live out here," Tillie explained. "The energy comes from the power of the earth, the sky, and the river; we are only barely beginning to understand it all, but I think we've come to realize *how* powerful it is."

"I heard it," Graham said.

"Me, too," Jamie whispered.

95

Graham nodded solemnly. He looked around carefully at the amphitheater again, taking it all in once more.

Tillie smiled, then turned to Elinora. "You're so quiet," she said, studying her face.

Elinora gazed over at Henry, who was curled up next to her. A much-welcomed sense of ease had passed over her while the heart of the forest was speaking, but there was still another feeling nagging away at her that not even the forest could calm. A wave of nausea gripped her and she shivered once again despite the warmth in the amphitheater. A seed of unease had been planted when she had felt something was upsetting Henry, and it lingered. She looked at him more closely with concern, but he wagged his tail happily. She sighed. "I'm all right," she finally replied. She paused. "Tillie..."

Tillie groaned. "I know what you're going to say." She turned to the council. "It's maddening how frightened our parents are of this place, but Elinora's right—it's time we head back home for now. But we will return again soon. Thank you for allowing us to come here today."

"What! Already?" Jamie protested.

"Sorry, we really must go, Jamie," Elinora said gently to him, rising from her seat. "Keeping our visits short is only way we can keep coming out here without anyone knowing."

"Come on James, we'll come back again tomorrow," Graham added.

"If you say so," he said, getting up, following the others. "Oh, wait, my shoes!" he suddenly exclaimed. He hurried off to find them as the others made a start for the trail.

Once at the far edge of the amphitheater, he could hear the powerful rushing of water in the distance. He turned and dashed back to Tillie. "I heard it! I heard the waterfall. Can't we stay just a moment longer to look for it?"

"Tomorrow, I promise," she said, nudging him on.

His shoulders slumped in resignation. "All right. Goodbye for now," he called to the animals, as they disappeared into the buckthorn. They chattered back happily.

When they reached the edge of the woods, Tillie glanced across the lawn to the manor house. She pointed and grumbled.

Elinora, Jamie, and Graham turned to see Lina off in the distance, standing out on the terrace. She had seen them when they exited the forest, and when she saw them looking her way, she quickly slipped back inside through the sitting room door.

"She's going to tattle on me for sure," Tillie announced.

"Don't jump to conclusions," Elinora replied.

But Tillie ignored her. "I'm going inside this way," she said, changing course and heading toward the scullery.

Jamie looked at Graham and shrugged, but they followed.

Inside, Tillie stopped to visit Abigail and Gemma, biding her time before going upstairs to get ready for supper.

9

Supper at Kellandale

Later in the evening, Tillie reluctantly made her way to the dining room, following Elinora, Graham, and Jamie. Anna, Camille, Penelope Meade, and her daughter, Madelina—Lina as everyone called her—were already seated around the long dining table, the room lively with their conversation.

"Well just look at all of you!" Penelope said when they entered. Penelope, Camille's best friend since childhood, had spent much of her youth at Kellandale, and the Woltons, O'Conors, and Meades all considered each other family.

"Aunt Penelope!" Jamie called out to her when he saw her.

"Hello, my love! It's been far too long," she replied, familiarity and warmth ringing in her voice as she spoke. Her long black hair was in twists and adorned with Adraian rivulons, tiny glass beads which made an enchanting tinkling sound when she turned to greet them. She reached out a hand to take Tillie's into hers.

"Hello, Auntie Pen, we've missed you," Tillie said brightly, clasping her hand and giving her a kiss on the cheek. "I hear Uncle Everett is with father at the new community school."

"Yes, he is. And hello to you," she said warmly to Elinora and Graham as they moved closer to embrace her. "Come, join us," Penelope said, offering Tillie the open seat on the other side of Lina.

Tillie did as she asked, and the others also took their seats— Elinora next to Tillie on her other side, and Graham and Jamie across the table. Anna, Penelope, and Camille returned to their conversation as everyone got settled.

Lina was seated next to her mother. She was her spitting image, sharing her round features and delicate frame. She wore a lavender evening dress, beautiful against the dark brown tone of her skin, and the intricate beadwork sewed into the dress's neckline glimmered elegantly in the candlelight.

When she'd heard Tillie enter the room, she had glanced up briefly at her with searching eyes, hoping they would be able to get past the argument they'd had the previous visit. But Tillie was busy talking and hadn't noticed this at all; in turn, Lina had misread this lack of reciprocation as avoidance. Annoyed, and sure that Tillie had purposely ignored her, Lina decided right in the moment that perhaps mending their friendship wouldn't be worth it after all; she had plenty enough to stay busy and knew she would be content keeping to herself while staying at Kellandale.

As Tillie took her seat, Lina turned her back toward her.

"Good evening, Lina," Tillie said once she was seated.

Lina turned around suddenly. "Hello, Ottilie," she said guardedly.

To Tillie, the coolness in Lina's voice was proof enough of her firm belief that Lina really did hate her and that there was no way they would be able to resolve their quarrel. She furrowed her brow.

Elinora closed her eyes and shook her head, wishing to be

anywhere else but near the two of them—a duo of equally stubborn friends unwilling to admit perhaps they both might be suffering from erroneous assumptions.

"Hello, Lina, how have you been? It really has been a while, it's nice to see you again," Graham said. He grinned warmly, hoping the tension between her and Tillie would pass quickly.

"Hello, Gray. It's been so long since I've seen you," Lina said, brightening a little, allowing her broad, friendly smile to shine through.

"Good evening, Lina," Jamie said, smiling and waving.

"Hello, Jamie," she replied, then leaned forward to talk to Elinora. "I've been wanting to show you this, Nora. How do you like my necklace?" she asked unexpectedly. She held it in her hand with admiration and care.

Elinora glanced over at the large translucent blue, sparkling gem. "It's really beautiful, Lina, and it's lovely with your dress. What kind of stone is that?" she asked.

She smiled. "It's a cobalt oumolira stone from Adrai and is very old. My grandmother gave it to me. I'm told it's worth—well, I'm not really supposed to say."

"Is that so. Well, I'm not really a fan of expensive jewelry," Tillie countered tartly. "Sparkly things don't do much—they're not worth anything really, are they? They're just that—things. I'd much rather put on a pair of trousers and boots and enjoy the outdoors than staying inside and ogling over trinkets."

Elinora looked at Tillie and glared.

Lina blinked and hesitated for a moment, but then she composed herself. "Speaking of trousers and boots, I noticed you were wearing some earlier today when you went out into the forest. You should have trousers on for an adventure like that, though I've been told the forest is off limits; perhaps I heard wrong," she said loud enough that their mothers overheard this.

Tillie, Elinora, Graham, and Jamie froze.

Anna stopped talking to Camille and Penelope and quickly turned to Tillie. "Is this true?" she asked in a strained, angry voice, looking across the table back and forth at her and Elinora.

"That I was wearing trousers? Yes, it is," Tillie replied cheekily.

Anna furrowed her brows. "The trousers don't bother me, Ottilie Wolton; what upsets me is that I am hearing that you went into the forest. I don't like hearing this."

Camille quickly intervened. "Graham, James...Penelope has already reminded Lina about staying out of the woods. Your Uncle James and I also forbid you from walking into the deep forest. You may *only* walk in the gardens and along the edge of the lawn where Elinora and Tillie are permitted to walk Henry—which is where we assumed you were."

Anna eyed her daughters sternly.

Tillie braced herself to be scolded further, but Lina continued. "I tried to stop them, but I think Tillie might have been avoiding me." She shrugged.

"Well, thank you for letting me know, Lina," Anna replied. She turned back to her daughters. "You shouldn't be surprised that I am rather upset about this. Your father would be beside himself if he knew. You are never to do that again, are we clear? Otherwise, someone else will be taking Henry for his walks."

Tillie groaned.

Lina glanced sideways at Tillie. She had meant for only Tillie to hear her comment and was surprised, even sorry, just how strong of a reaction her comment elicited from Tillie's mother. She tried changing the subject. "I met Henry in the library just a bit ago, I like him very much, and I think he likes me," she said with a genuine smile.

At this Tillie set her glass of water down loudly.

Lina turned her head away from her, revealing a ring of

glimmering beaded hairpins that fastened her dark, tight curls into a high bun.

Everyone sat in the awkward silence that followed, but thankfully, Albert and Simon entered the dining room, breaking it. They each carried a large, covered silver tray loaded with supper. Albert set his tray in the center of the table and Simon followed suit before they removed the lids simultaneously.

"Look at that. Cora and Jeppe must be two of the finest chefs in the world," Penelope remarked.

"Indeed. To the chefs, and also to you," Camille said, raising her glass to Albert and Simon, grateful for the diversion. The others did the same.

Dinner began and Lina and Tillie settled into a silent truce. Then came dessert.

Anna sensed the mood had calmed somewhat, and grasping at straws, tried to try to make peace. "I'm hoping the two of you can sort things out," she said to Tillie and Lina. "Why don't you all head to the music room? Perhaps you can entertain on the piano, Elinora? It will give everyone a chance to talk."

Elinora winced.

Tillie stared at her mother in disbelief.

"I think that is a wonderful idea," Penelope encouraged.

"Sounds lovely, but I must return to my room," Lina replied. "I have to write a letter to my friend Belladonna. Bella lives in a stunning manor house. They even have electricity now. And I hear they will soon have an *automobile*."

"Is that so," Tillie replied.

"Her parents are having a grand party, and I need to figure out if any one of my gowns will be appropriate or if I should have a new one made. I know that sort of thing is a bit grown up for you, Tillie. Maybe you'll be interested when you're more mature. Oh wait, you're my age."

Tillie stood up abruptly. "Why don't you just go write your letter to your new best friend Belladonna then, and you can discuss your fancy dresses and her *grand party* without bothering me!"

"Tillie," Anna said.

"Madelina," Penelope said at the same time.

Elinora rose from her seat and put her hand on Tillie's shoulder. "Enjoy the rest of your evening, Lina, it's nice to see you again," she said diplomatically. She stretched and yawned, pretending to be tired. "I think it's time to head to my room. I'm a bit tired from all the activity today. You must be too, Tillie. May we be excused, Mother?"

"You may," Anna replied with notable disappointment.

Tillie growled as they exited.

"I think I'll head to my room for the night as well. Good evening then," Jamie said, rising from his seat, also excusing himself. "Good night, Lina. I'm happy you're here." She looked up with surprise but smiled back when he said this.

"Good night, Gray," Lina said to him when he stood up.

"Good night, Lina; it's nice to see you and your mother again," he replied before exiting the room.

Elinora and Tillie were already in the foyer, ready to head upstairs, when Graham and Jamie caught up with them.

"How do you like my necklace, Nora?" Tillie mocked.

"Tillie, come on," Elinora said, stopping her.

"That was very uncomfortable," Graham muttered.

"She's insufferable," Tillie replied.

"Do you have any idea how *you* sounded?" Elinora countered.

"All that bickering was exhausting," Jamie added. "I'm going to go practice my viola now—but Tillie, I saw how Lina looked at you when we walked into the room. She didn't look angry, but actually the opposite, like she wanted to talk to you. She's staying here a while, too, and now that you are both arguing, she'll be all by herself. Maybe you should just try to find out what's wrong."

"Are you serious? She doesn't want to have anything to do with me, you saw for yourselves," Tillie said defensively. "And what did I tell you—she did tell on me. And all of you, too."

"True," Graham replied.

Elinora nodded somberly. "I am a bit worried what might happen if she sees us going into the forest again."

"I don't know; I still think you should talk to her," Jamie said again.

"We'll see," Tillie replied.

"How about if I talk to her?" he offered.

"What? No! I'll figure it out. For now, I'm going to head to my room for the night. I'll see you in the morning."

"All right Tillie," he replied as she made her way upstairs.

"Why is she so angry with Lina?" Jamie asked Elinora quietly once Tillie was gone.

"I don't know for sure. It's been over a year since they've seen each other. Last time Lina was here, she had recently moved and made new friends. You know how Tillie and Lina have been best friends since forever...well, she would never admit this, but I think Tillie maybe felt like she had been left behind. I really don't think that was Lina's intention, but then they both got very defensive and they've been in this horrible argument ever since. And there's no talking to either of them."

"Well, I hope they can sort things out quickly," Graham said.

"Me, too," Jamie agreed.

"All right, I'm going to see if there's a book about tiered Knaves in the library, I need to study before I play against Simon. See you in the morning," Graham said, then retreated.

"Good night," Elinora called to her cousins as she climbed the grand staircase and headed to her room.

A moment later Tillie entered. She closed the door behind her, pressing her back against it. "You do see what I mean, don't you?"

Elinora waited for her to continue.

"No matter, though. I'm not going to let Lina stop me from going into the forest. I'll just have to watch out better next time."

Elinora pondered this. "You're right. But Tillie, I also don't think Jamie is wrong. You were as argumentative with her as she was with you. Don't be so stubborn. Just ask her what's the matter, why don't you?" Elinora suggested.

Tillie paused, then growled. "As if—whatever have I done? And anyway, how about Mother? Won't she and Father *ever* stop harping on about the forest? Why can't they just go see how beautiful it really it is, once and for all?" she moaned.

"That will never happen—they're too afraid of the forest, you know that," Elinora replied.

Tillie snorted. "Ah, well, maybe *you* could learn something from that, then," she said as she opened the door to head to her own room across the hall.

Elinora sighed. "Good night, Tillie. And please try to calm down a little."

"Good night, Nora," she sighed, closing the door. She glanced down the hall again, just in time to see Henry entering Lina's room. She pursed her lips.

She knew Henry was kind and gentle and was above all the angry nonsense between herself and Lina. But still, she was aggravated thinking that he would want to spend any time with someone so unreasonable. She decided the next time she was with him she would let him know how unfair she thought Lina was being to her, which would certainly put an end to that.

Spring

10

The Song of the Earth

The weeks passed quickly, and soon tiny blades of grass nudged through the lingering patches of frost. Glimpses of wild violets peppered the ground, and the days grew longer and warmer with each passing sunrise. Within the Heart of the Forest however, it never ceased to be anything other than a tropical paradise, the air within always warm, humid, and teeming with life. Birds and woodland frogs filled the air with their peeps and chirps and the thick mass of plant life engulfing the amphitheater flourished.

It was a welcome respite from the weather, and for Tillie, a way to avoid further confrontation with Lina. A stalemate had befallen them, and the two had given each other space ever since the encounter at dinner the day Lina and her mother had arrived. Their mothers' well-meaning encouragement to repair their friendship had thus far remained futile.

As an antidote to the situation, Lina spent time in her bedroom, content to read, paint, and draw, taking music lessons from Gemma, and also in the kitchen, learning to cook from Cora and Jeppe. On occasion she left Kellandale to visit her friends.

Jamie, Graham, and Elinora couldn't help but feel unsettled by the silence between the two of them, and Jamie took it upon himself to check in on Lina, often stopping to chat with her to make sure she was all right. Lina continually assured him she had enough to keep busy and was just fine. But he sensed a sadness in her, and he knew Henry felt it, too. He also knew how stubborn Tillie could be, so he was forever trying to find a way to talk to her about it without her becoming too frustrated with him. For the time being, he knew Henry spent time with Lina, and knew he would be a good friend to her.

Meanwhile, Elinora, Tillie, Graham, and Jamie continued to seek the adventure of the forest. The woodland animals quickly bonded with Graham and Jamie, just as they had Elinora and Tillie, and it wasn't long before they were all asked to be human representatives within the council of beings—an honor that came with great responsibility. It didn't need to be said, but they knew they were walking in Sir William's footsteps, and they took it upon themselves to properly learn the ways of the forest to help protect it as he had.

Mister, along with the other squirrels, spent time schooling Elinora, Tillie, Graham, and Jamie in their cunning tactics to make Kellandale Wood seem treacherous and fearsome. Tillie devoted herself to learning how to recreate the deafening racket the squirrels made, and was also rather fond of making the bizarre, throaty sound she referred to as the Warble. Elinora and Graham focused their time on learning the art of illusion, which often involved throwing stones and acorns, and shaking tree branches, while Jamie spent time with Mister learning to mimic the sound made by Monkey—that terrifying low growl that rippled through the forest and caused the earth to rumble.

At the end of the lessons, they would take time to lie in the center of the amphitheater, the sun's rays warming them, and the breeze cooling them, until they were lulled into a quiet sleep. In these moments, they were rewarded by the heart of the forest with more of its secrets.

Intense and overwhelming thoughts and images drifted into their minds. Moments in time, both past and present, were shared with them. It was like gazing through a mysterious kaleidoscope while serenaded by the songs of universe, filling them with feelings, visions, and sounds. After this rush of feeling came a stillness, then lightness and clarity, and an unspoken understanding of the mysterious connection to of all life, and to nature. In this way, the forest spoke to them, using its own language. It was the very same language that allowed them to communicate with Henry, and it enabled them to understand the forest animals when they were near him, just as they could while they were visiting the heart of the forest.

In time, the forest also divulged to them more of the terrible histories of the animal lives lost hundreds of years before. During this dark time, the forest had been clouded in fear, and the animals were tormented by the humans plaguing the forest with their weapons, fire, and thirst for blood. The children felt the anguish and pain the hunters had inflicted upon the forest creatures, and devastating images of animals being hunted drifted through their minds.

Later came visions of the uprising, when the torrential powers of the earth, river, and forest combined with that of the animals of the forest and manifested into a singular protective force. It shielded the forest's inhabitants—some who had lived there from the beginning, many who had been brought into it from faraway lands, and others who had come seeking shelter and safety—all of whom had been invited to live there by the forest. This energy also had a side effect, dulling and warping the passage of time, which allowed the creatures of the forest to live for a very, very long time.

The Lady of the Forest, Monkey, and the Messenger had eventually come to dwell there, and they joined forces with the energy of the forest. This alliance created a force unique to Kellandale Wood. It allowed the energy to grow even stronger— strong enough to drive out the hunters who desired dominance over the natural world. Finally, peace had returned to Kellandale Wood and had remained ever since.

11

The Gift

In the following weeks at Kellandale, Jamie had begun music studies with Gemma, herself an accomplished musician. He was in the music room, writing passages of a sonata. The smooth sounds of his viola resonated throughout the wing as he played. His newest assignment required him to create a viola accompaniment he could eventually play with Tillie on the piano; he was presently working through a particularly difficult measure and was practicing slowly.

A baby grand piano stood in the center of the room, surrounded by other exquisite instruments. Sitting in the corner was a hand-stretched drum from Debari. On a stand next to the piano rested an ebony, long-necked string instrument from Chanpor, and sitting on a table near the picture window where he stood was a zither from Tukora—Jamie was eager to get his hands on all of them once he perfected the sonata.

Henry was lounging on one of the settees with Velvet at his side on the other, as usual. It appeared that they were napping, but

Henry's perked ears and intermittently wagging tail gave it away that he was awake and enjoying the concert.

Just outside the door, Tillie crouched in the hallway, listening in awe of her cousin's concealed talent.

He worked his way to the end of the stanza a third time, and just as he reached a crescendo, he missed a note. He stopped playing abruptly when the bow scraped over the string, creating a harsh, screeching sound. "Mustard!" he grumbled.

He lifted the bow again and placed it back on the viola between the fingerboard and the bridge, setting up to play again, but paused when he heard scratching at the window. He lowered his bow again and pulled the sheer, cream-colored drapes aside. There he found Mister, perched on the exterior windowsill looking in, his two tiny front paws on the glass.

Mister had been drawn to the music room the first day Jamie had begun his practices, intrigued by the mysterious sounds coming from within. Since that moment, he made sure to be there for every practice. The instrument was intriguing enough on its own, but the way Jamie could make it sound, Mister believed was pure magic.

Jamie grinned and pried open a window. "Would you like to come inside to listen? Come on, you can hear much better from in here."

Mister had never been inside a house before. He hesitated, his tail twitching. Jamie leaned over to let him climb onto his shoulder so he could carry him to the piano. Mister scurried up, clinging to his shirt collar for the ride, then hopped off onto the shiny black piano, slipping a little as he jumped down. He lifted his front paws repeatedly, feeling the foreign surface. Jamie smiled, watching him investigate. Eventually, Mister found his footing and settled down on the top of the piano. He looked around the room at all the strange objects. Then he caught sight of Velvet. He stood back up, his fur bristling uncontrollably. He had never encountered a house cat, and instincts that he had never felt before took hold. For the first time in his life, another animal frightened him.

Henry jumped off the armchair and walked over to Jamie and Mister, his proximity allowing them to understand one another. He welcomed Mister with a wagging tail, quickly letting him know that Velvet was friendly. She confirmed this with an affectionate chirp.

"Don't worry, Henry's right; she won't hurt you, I promise," Jamie reassured.

Mister relaxed considerably. He looked up and chattered.

"Oh! You want me to bring my viola to the amphitheater? Well, let me think about that. I've never performed in front of anyone apart from my teacher, or the three of you, and never before an audience. It scares me." He pondered a moment more, picturing the council circled around him, watching and listening.

Mister chattered again, encouraging him.

He sighed. "Well...I hope I am good enough, but I would be honored. And it would be good practice for me..." He smiled, wincing bashfully.

Outside the door, Tillie was growing impatient. She could hear the music had stopped, and now Jamie was talking to someone. She flung the door open and barged into the room.

Jamie jumped at the sudden noise.

"A ha! And who are you talking to about playing your viola?"

He looked to the piano and back to Tillie, then grinned.

"Mister!" she exclaimed. The squirrel greeted her warmly.

"He wants me to play for the other animals in the forest."

"Brilliant! Does this mean I finally will be able to hear you, too?"

"I suppose," he said nervously.

"Oh, Jamie, it will be wonderful. Hurry, let's find the others."

She darted out of the room before he could take it all back.

Mister scampered to the window and Jamie opened it again. He jumped down the ledge and onto the lawn, then dashed off, eager to gather the animals.

Less than an hour later, Jamie met Graham, Elinora, Tillie, and Henry out on the terrace. He gripped his viola case tightly by its handle. Anna, Camille, and Penelope were outside playing a game of croquet on the lawn. They descended the steps quietly, hoping to make it to the forest trail without them noticing, but Camille spotted them and waved.

"We'll have to make this a much shorter visit now," Tillie sighed.

Jamie muttered something under his breath, then waved back to his mother with a feigned smile. "We're just letting Henry stretch his legs a moment," he shouted.

"Don't be long!" she called back.

"All right!" He checked his pocket watch to note the time.

A sharp crack from a croquet mallet sounded as it connected with the wooden ball, then it went sailing through the air, off course, and Penelope went after it in the underbrush beneath a stand of trees. They continued walking toward the forest as she searched for it.

They moved on quickly, and in their haste, they hadn't noticed Lina had been watching from the sitting room.

She had just returned by carriage after a visit to her friend Belladonna's grand estate. Belladonna's family coachman had driven her back to Kellandale, and Belladonna, along with their friend Sosanya, had accompanied them. It was a long ride, so Lina invited them inside, eager to introduce them to Henry while the coachman and his horses rested.

But Lina's face fell when she saw that Henry was outside with the others, walking across the lawn, undoubtedly on their way to the forest.

"Well, there you have it. Now's your chance, Lina," Belladonna said, her eyebrows arching antagonistically. She primped her hair, exquisitely coiffed and pulled back with a pearl comb.

"What?" she replied. But she knew exactly what Belladonna meant.

"Tillie is so boorish; imagine *wanting* to go into the forest. And I recall you saying they weren't allowed. Now you have the perfect opportunity to see what they're up to. I'm sure their parents would want to know all about it." She pulled the matching pearl-beaded clutch she was carrying to her chest and laughed.

Sosanya cast a quick glance at Lina. "That's really not very nice, Bella," she replied quietly. She twisted her hair between her fingers nervously, waiting for Belladonna's rebuke.

"Oh hush," Belladonna snapped. "You're younger than Lina and I—you wouldn't know about these kinds of things." She turned to Lina. "Why is it that they get to spend time all their time with Henry, and not *you?*"

Lina paused. "All right, but you're coming with me," she said, opening the sitting room door.

Belladonna followed eagerly. "Come on, Sosanya," she beckoned and they descended the terrace steps into the nearby garden. When Lina saw her mother fishing her croquet ball out of the shrubs in the distance, they ducked down behind the fountain grass and crept over to the lawn. Belladonna had to pull up the hem of her cream-colored gown to keep it from dragging on the ground on their way to the forest trail.

But once Lina found herself standing at the edge of the woods, she hesitated. Just as her own mother, James, and Camille were, she was genuinely afraid, and truth be told, she wanted nothing to do with Wyches Wood.

"Tell me you're not going to back out *now?*" Belladonna taunted.

"You don't have to," Sosanya said to her.

But Lina shook her head, quickly swallowing back her fear.

Sosanya paused. "I think I'm just going to wait here," she said.

Belladonna rolled her eyes. "But you're dressed perfectly for the occasion," she said, eyeing Sosanya's light-blue traveling attire, far less showy than her own.

"It's all right, stay here, we'll be right back," Lina said to Sosanya, then entered the forest. She made sure to trail the others from behind at a safe distance.

Along the way she began to take in her surroundings. To her surprise the soft spring breeze and the warmth of the sunlight seemed to soothe her, and the trees and the river were more beautiful than she had ever expected. Very quickly she lost herself in the beauty of Kellandale Wood, and a sense of inner peace overpowered the angst and sadness she carried with her. For a long moment, she forgot why she was there. She recalled that Tillie had said she preferred to be outside in the forest rather than fussing over jewelry, dresses, and other trivial matters. In that moment, she thought perhaps she understood her.

"Oh, this place is *awful!* Look at how filthy my shoes are!" Belladonna said suddenly, pulling Lina out of her thoughts.

As she caught sight of Henry walking beside Tillie, Lina's jealousy was rekindled. She had bonded very deeply with Henry ever since coming to Kellandale and he had become her friend; he understood and loved her. It hurt her deeply to see the five of them happily walking the trail together—without her. She felt a lump rise in her throat. Her emotions began rocking in conflicting waves, from anger and jealousy to a sense of peace and calm, then back again.

Then, just as she came upon the ancient tree that she had hoped to catch them walking beyond, they all seemed to vanish from the trail. She blinked to see if her eyes were playing tricks on her. But they did not reappear.

Frightened, she pulled Belladonna over to a pine tree at the edge of the river so she could catch her breath and collect her thoughts. She looked down at the river, and as she did, the sense of peace involuntarily returned. She was again soothed by the sound of the flowing water, mesmerized by its motion, and by the sunlight reflecting on its surface. She tried to shake it off, but this time it took hold.

A sudden violent splash in the water made her lurch backward. Belladonna looked at her in confusion, having not heard the sound. Then came a bright flash of light just beneath the surface. Lina squinted up at the sky to see if perhaps it was only the sunlight, then looked down into the water again—just in time to see another flash of color and the long, cascading fins of an unknown something swimming past.

The water bubbled suspiciously as a creature rose to the surface and skimmed the water with its huge mouth. Then, peering out of the water, it turned with deliberate movement to face her.

Lina felt its eyes—big, intelligent, and aware, gazing at her. She felt as though it was looking directly into her soul, studying her. It blinked thoughtfully at her, inviting her into the heart of the forest, right at the same moment Tillie and the others reappeared on the trail in the distance.

Lina crouched down, backing away, panicked thoughts of a haunted forest terrifying her. With haste, she turned and bolted back toward the manor house, leaving Belladonna to follow her in confusion. She hadn't seen or heard anything that Lina had.

The creature, startled by these quick movements, plunged back into the river and disappeared into the depths of the Iveria.

Henry was looking back toward the riverbank where Lina had been hiding and wagged his tail. He sensed she had been there.

Tillie, Elinora, Graham, and Jamie, however, still unaware that she had been following them, had noticed the flash in the water from a distance. They had seen the creature emerge, and heard the splash, and were now frantically searching the river.

"Elinora! Did you see it, too?" Tillie shouted.

"I did! I can't believe it!"

"What the heck in the world was it?" She paced back and forth along the trail.

"Whatever it was, it was *huge!* It must be a giant fish of some sort," Jamie suggested.

"It had to have been at least ten feet long. There is no way it could have been a fish. It looked more like a water dragon or a serpent," Graham replied.

"A water dragon, Gray? Are you serious?"

"Oh, I hope so!" Tillie exclaimed.

A familiar voice entered their minds suddenly, interrupting the conversation. Mister scurried over to share the exciting news.

The Lady of the Forest has allowed you
to see her!

"*That* was the Lady of the Forest?" Tillie choked out the words. Mister confirmed this. He raced around in a circle in excitement.

You have been given rare gift!
The gift of her trust.

"Are you telling us that all along that flash of light in the water we have been seeing was the Lady of the Forest?" Elinora asked.

But Mister turned away without a reply, darting away toward the amphitheater in anticipation of Jamie's performance.

12

The Viola & the Vortex

"Hurry!" Jamie called to the others. He grabbed his viola and off they sprinted, chasing after Mister.

Tillie fired away questions as they ran. "Is she a fish, or is she a river serpent? A water dragon? Mister! What is she?"

She is the Lady of the Forest!

"Agh!" she yelled back.

"I'm telling you, it was a water dragon," Graham shouted.

Mister raced ahead, disappearing into the buckthorn.

Jamie, Tillie, Graham, and Elinora quickly traversed the hidden trail, cutting through the thorny patch in a daze, still astonished by what they had just seen. Then Mister came into view again, already waiting for them in the amphitheater. He stood on his hind legs and chattered eagerly at Jamie, inviting him to come over and take his place next to him. He spoke nothing more of the Lady of the Forest, and everyone knew asking about it wouldn't make a difference if he wasn't ready to explain.

Jamie stepped forward and set his viola case down in the center of the clearing then looked around. Creatures of all shapes and sizes had all already gathered—water buffalo, Bekanan tigers, the sienna capybara who Tillie had named Popo, rabbits, turtles, lemurs, foxes, deer, even the tiniest of creatures, the bats, butterflies, salamanders, bees, and a tiny chipmunk that Jamie loved to feed, who he had named Mitch. Mister was beside him, as were the other Buckthorn squirrels, attentively watching his every move.

Jamie opened the case and took out his viola. He smiled at Mister then stroked the bow across the strings to warm up. The sound caught the attention of the other forest animals that had been roaming about the amphitheater. They watched with intensity as the vibrations filled the air, ears twitching and hooves pawing the ground.

Tillie, Elinora, and Graham followed Henry and sat down on the second tier of the amphitheater to watch the performance. Pipe ambled over and joined them, as did a tiny fawn with spindly little legs that had recently come to the forest seeking shelter. Elinora had named her Vita when they had first seen her. Vita came over and curled up in Elinora's lap for the performance.

Once everyone was settled, there was a moment of quiet anticipation.

Jamie nodded and raised his bow in the air, placed it on the strings, then let the music flow freely out through his heart, into his viola, and back out into the forest, not thinking about anything but the music. This helped him forget he had an audience. Gorgeous, mystical sounds, foreign to the animals, flooded the amphitheater. Some of the more elusive creatures, those who lived deep within the forest, had been listening from the fringes and were drawn closer by the music. A kudu and a clouded leopard peeked out and watched from the edges. Others came out in the open, too. Jamie was able to remain composed when a beautiful panther trotted out of the woods and sat beside him; he even continued playing when a shy okapi emerged from the undergrowth, but he almost dropped his viola when a pair of white rhinoceroses entered the amphitheater to listen.

Despite the surprises, Jamie finished the first movement of the sonata without making a single mistake, then bowed, his cheeks flushed. Elinora and Graham clapped and cheered as Tillie jumped up and shouted in delight, finally getting to hear her cousin play. The animals flitted about in a buzz celebrating the performance. Jamie bowed again, then looked around, secretly hoping the Lady of the Forest had been able to hear, too. He set his instrument down in its open case and invited the animals to come look at it, then he plopped down onto the grass to relax. "It's all right, Boing, go ahead and have a look," he coaxed the tiny rabbit, picking him up and setting him on the viola so he could explore.

Vita watched this with great interest and jumped up from Elinora's lap to get a better look. Mitch followed eagerly. Elinora watched the little deer, the chipmunk, and the rabbit as they studied the instrument with wide eyes.

Jamie reached over and plucked a string of the viola. Boing popped into the air playfully when he felt the vibration beneath his feet, then he, and Mitch, and Vita scampered off together.

Jamie chuckled, then sat quietly for a moment watching all the animals, very much enjoying their excitement. He felt the time slipping away, but was certainly not ready to return to the manor house, especially since now that he could hear the rush of the waterfall again. Graham, Tillie, and Elinora were a short distance away, engrossed in conversation, so he took the opportunity to slip away and investigate.

"Where did Jamie go?" Elinora asked after a short spell when she noticed he was no longer lying next to them.

"Jamie?" Graham called out, but there was no reply.

Tillie pointed into the distance. "I know where he's headed." Sure enough, they could see him off in the distance, heading to the far side of the amphitheater, into the forest.

"Now?" Elinora sighed. We've got to get back home."

"Jamie!" Graham shouted again.

Jamie turned back and waved, but kept going, determined to find the waterfall. Very quickly he found himself scrambling down the rim of a deep gorge; the red rock terrain was slippery from the moss and spraying mist, so he climbed carefully, working his way toward the sound of the waterfall. Louder and louder it thundered the closer he got.

Graham, Elinora, and Tillie reluctantly followed him.

Then came the sound of cracking branches. Then a yelp.

"Jamie!" Elinora yelled as they ran to the edge of the gorge.

"Oof!" his voice echoed from below. "I'm fine! But I banged my leg up. Oh dear, I think it's going to be a bit tricky to get back out," he shouted over the din of the raging water. "There it is! There's another level of ground below me, between me and the base off the waterfall, but I can see it! I wish you could all come down here. It's...well, it's not normal."

"We can't see anything. And it's so loud we can barely hear you," Tillie yelled through the rising mist.

"There are *three* waterfalls," he shouted back even louder. "They form a circle around a pool at the bottom! I'm on a ridge above everything, looking down at them. Water is coming in from everywhere! One of the waterfalls is rocky and stepped, another flows much more gently, then a third one on the other side of the gorge plunges straight down. It's incredible, the pool below is spinning like mad! But, there's no more river after that. It's like the water disappears into a hole!"

"Oh Jamie, please come back," Elinora pleaded.

"Do you think you can make it out by yourself?" Tillie shouted.

"I don't know...wait a moment, I just saw a flash in the pool beneath the waterfall, I think the Lady of the Forest might be down there!"

The others looked over the edge and could just make out faint flashes of light through the haze.

"Hello?" he called out. His voice echoed in the gorge. "I wish we could stay out here longer. Oh fiddlesticks, she's disappeared again!"

"James, for crying out loud, just climb up. You can tell us about it later!" Graham coaxed.

"Just give me a moment." He picked his way through the rocks, being careful where he stepped, then grabbed at the rocky wall. "I can't get a grip to climb up!"

"Try grabbing onto some tree roots. If you can get high enough, we can reach down and grab you," Graham yelled.

"Maybe we can tie our clothes together into a rope," Tillie suggested.

Henry, meanwhile, had been tussling and playing with Pipe in the amphitheater, but he sensed something was amiss. Quickly, he ran to the gorge to see what was happening, and Pipe followed. They reached the edge and looked down. Henry turned to Elinora with a distressed whine, then paced back and forth, surveying the terrain. He conveyed to Pipe to wait for him, then he climbed down. Rocks plunged into the chasm around him as he struggled to keep his footing.

"Henry!" Elinora exclaimed. But he was swift and nimble, righting himself and quickly making his way to Jamie. He grabbed him by his trousers with his teeth, then hauled him up the side of the gorge.

As Henry came back into view carrying Jamie by the seat of his pants, he made his way back to Pipe, who reached down and grabbed Jamie in his large, soft paws. Graham was there and together he and Pipe pulled him over the cliff edge, up to safety. Henry bounded out of the gorge and rushed over to them.

"Well then," Jamie said, collapsing to the ground when he reached the top. "Hoisted by my own petard! Well, not really. Hoisted by my own *pet*, more like." he chuckled.

Tillie groaned at his quip, but Pipe grunted when he saw his pant leg, dirty and torn, with a tinge of blood soaking through.

Jamie sat back up and reached over to ruffle his scruff. "I'll be all right. Thank you both for helping me." Then he put his head to Henry's.

"Oh Jamie," Elinora lamented.

"Really, it doesn't hurt that bad. And I'm sure that was the Lady of the Forest down there. The water was glowing before she vanished. I have a feeling that's her home." He shifted his body as he sat on the ground. "Ouch, all right, I guess this does sting a bit. I feel a tad woozy now," he said, looking closely at his leg. He pulled up the cuff of his torn pants, revealing a deep gash on his shin. It was bleeding more than he had realized.

Tillie gasped.

"We need to get you out of here right away," said Elinora.

By this time, word of the accident had reached the forest council. Mister approached and implored Jamie to go to the river. He chattered, asking him to follow.

Tillie grabbed Jamie's viola. Pipe leaned down so Jamie could climb onto his back. With help, Jamie heaved himself up, lying flat on his belly and holding on to Pipe's soft fur as everyone followed Mister out of the amphitheater to the rocky beach beneath Ole Warty. Pipe set Jamie down at the river's edge when they reached it, then Mister instructed him further.

Step into the water. It will soothe you.

"If you say so; I trust you," he replied. He pulled off his boots then pulled up his pant cuffs again. He waded out ankle-deep into the water then cupped his hands, dipping them into the river and splashing the water onto his legs and arms. The ice-cold water felt good. Mister spoke to him again.

Take the earth, mix it with the water. Hold it in the air, then rub the soothing clay onto your wound.

Jamie mindfully did as he was told, rubbing the mixture over his leg. "Ah, it feels so much better, and it's stopped bleeding," he reported to the others.

The waters of the Iveria, the earth, and the sky together are healing.

"But of course they would be, wouldn't they? Thank you, Mister," he said, stepping out of the water and returning to shore. He looked again. The wound began to fade—not wholly, but the healing process was quickly setting in.

Tillie climbed down the slope to join him. She looked at his leg. "Oh, what a relief! Whatever is in that water?" She looked to the river, then quickly pulled a necklace from around her neck—the little monkey figurine she had taken from the tower. She scooped up some of the crystal-clear river water and silt, combining them as Jamie had, then flipped open the figurine's tiny lid and filled the vessel with the mixture. She saw Mister watching and quickly stood up, fearing she had done something wrong.

But Mister encouraged her.

It is yours to take. Keep it close for times of need.

"Thank you." She smiled then put the necklace back around her neck.

Jamie looked up the embankment to Elinora and Graham who were standing on the trail. "I'm sorry I've taken so much time. I'm sure they'll all be wondering where we are by now—we'd better hurry back." But Mister intervened.

You have been to the vortex and have set the
energy of the forest to work.

No one will know you were gone, they will not
have had the time to notice.

Then he scampered away, leaving them standing there looking at one another blankly.

"Now, what does *that* mean?" Jamie scratched his head.

"That tricky little squirrel!" said Tillie.

Jamie pondered Mister's words on the way back, the phrase turning over in his mind. *"No one will know you were gone, they will not have had the time to notice."*

As they passed by Ole Warty, Jamie checked his pocket watch. He lifted it closer then put it to his ear. "Rubbish. It must have stopped working while we were gone. Who knows what time it is now," he said winding it, but it wouldn't budge.

"Come on," Elinora beckoned.

They rushed back onto the grounds, pausing at the edge of the gardens before heading down the steps.

Tillie peered out from behind the towering fountain grasses and pulled a puzzled face. "They're on the lawn in the very same spot they were in when we left. Aunt Penelope is over there looking for her ball still."

"My watch is working again," Jamie said, furrowing his brow. It was ticking, but only a few minutes had passed. He tapped it, then looked up into the sky. The sun was in the same position as it had been when they had left for the forest. "They will not have had the time to notice," he said out loud.

Tillie shot him a sideways glance.

"I'm going to go have a chat with them."

"Jamie, please," Elinora said. "Let's just go in through the scullery and hope they don't see us."

"But you heard Mister. I think I know what he was trying to say now." Before anyone could stop him, he walked toward his mother with Henry at his side, taking care to hide his torn, bloodied pants behind some shrubbery.

Elinora, Tillie, and Graham hovered in the background.

"Hi, Mum!" he called.

She turned to him in surprise.

"We're off to let Henry stretch his legs for a bit."

"Yes, dear, you just said that not a moment ago."

"Oh, right, silly me. Don't worry, we will stay in the gardens and will be back in time for supper."

"Very well then, see you inside."

He looked over to the others and shrugged. "They didn't have the time to notice we were gone," he said, with a wild grin. Just as Mister had said, the energy of the forest had been at work. Jamie had encountered the vortex, and to his delight, he had discovered that time had been disrupted by the powers of Kellandale Wood.

13

The Phantom Carousel

It was a sunny, fresh, mid-March morning, one that began like most days for Elinora, Tillie, Graham, and Jamie. They joined everyone in the breakfast room, and as always, they ate quickly, eager to set off on their daily adventure into the magical realm of the forest.

Anna, Camille, and Penelope were there, as was Lina, who sat at the far end of the table with their mothers. Though their unresolved argument still hung in the air, she and Tillie had continued to keep their distance, sparing themselves and everyone else from their quarrels.

After poached eggs, fresh fruit, and toast with elderberry marmalade were served, Elinora and Tillie's mother announced she would be going into the nearby town of Waterbridge for the day. "Your Aunt Camille, Penelope, and Lina will be joining me. We need to send some things to your fathers. We'll be back in time for supper."

Tillie glanced at Lina briefly, realizing she wouldn't have to worry about being caught going into the forest today.

But Lina had been terrified the day she had trailed them into the woods—so startled by the creature in the water that she no longer had the desire to know if they went into the forest or not anymore.

"Will you be visiting Lovii's while you are there?" Elinora asked.

"Absolutely," she said with a smile. "I'd never miss a chance to visit her shop. And yes, I'll bring back some macarons."

After finishing breakfast, Elinora, Tillie, Graham, and Jamie excused themselves, anxious to make their way downstairs to find Henry. Jamie's recent discovery of the vortex's time-disrupting powers had gained them a particularly useful advantage. Now, their visits into the deep forest could be as lengthy as they wanted without anyone noticing, so long as one of them visited the vortex before returning home. Jamie eagerly took on this duty.

Jamie poked his head into the busy, cavernous kitchen.

Cora was hovering over the large copper roasting pan, already preparing supper. She reached over and dropped a bowl full of fresh chopped vegetables into it, her long, black hair tied up in a knot to keep it from getting in the way.

"Is Henry in here? Mmm, something smells delicious!" Jamie said.

She looked up. Cora was in her twenties and had a youthful, round face, and light brown skin. She broke into a smile when she saw Jamie. "Henry's right here, dear." She set the empty bowl down on the long, wooden work table, then pointed to her feet where Henry was strategically camped while she cooked. "I'm making something my grandmother in Bekana makes for me whenever I visit her."

"Oh? What is it?"

"I'm making gojini—roasted cauliflower and root vegetables

131

seasoned with cumin, paprika, and turmeric. What my grand-mother adds to it is her secret." She flashed a playful eye at him. "But I'm sure she would want me to share it with you. She makes a lovely, savory sauce from roasted almond and sesame seed pastes, spiced honey, lemon and cipra juices, garlic, and sea salt. When the vegetables are done, she drizzles the sauce over them, then tops it with fresh pomegranate seeds, straight from the tree. You'll be able to taste some later tonight."

"Mmm, I can't wait," he replied.

"Come on, Henry, let's go for a walk!" Tillie called from the corridor. "Thank you for breakfast, Cora, it was so delicious."

"You're welcome!" she replied, putting the roasting pan into the oven.

Henry stood up, but not before finishing the warm, crusty bread she had tossed him. He swallowed it in a single gulp and wagged his tail, then took off to catch up.

Once gathered outside, off they went. As they entered the woods and set upon the trail, Jamie demonstrated his newly perfected impersonation of Monkey's growl. Tillie laughed and plugged her ears. "So loud, Jamie! I have to admit, you do sound quite wicked. You've really done it; I wouldn't last long in the forest if something made that sound."

He grinned.

"I always knew you had it in you," Graham chuckled.

As they approached Ole Warty, Jamie stopped to investigate a large slug inching its way across the trail. He knelt beside it and he and Henry watched curiously as it maneuvered past. Graham waited for them. Meanwhile, Elinora and Tillie continued ahead, and not unpredictably, Elinora stumbled over one of Ole Warty's sprawling roots. Tillie tried to catch her, but it only threw her off balance more. Elinora slipped out of Tillie's grasp and landed on her knees with a thud. "Agh!" she grunted.

"Elinora Wolton, you *must* learn to watch your step," Tillie said trying to stifle a laugh.

Graham and Jamie had seen her fall, too. "You're not hurt, are you?" Jamie called out.

She looked up and shook her head, groaning with embarrassment. "No, I'm fine. I don't know how I always manage to do that."

"Because despite you being so utterly proper all the time, Nor, you're completely clumsy. At least you've learned to fall with panache," Tillie teased.

Elinora began to pull herself up, but she immediately flattened to the ground. Tillie looked at her with confusion, but Elinora put her hand out, motioning for Graham and Jamie to stop walking toward them. "Tillie, get down. *Now!*" she ordered, grabbing her hand and pulling her down.

Tillie quickly dropped down next to her, turning her head to see what Elinora was looking at. That's when she noticed three men prowling through the forest not ten feet away.

As feared, the hunters had returned. They crept through the forest, guns slung over their shoulders, nets on long wooden poles gripped firmly in their hands.

Graham pressed his fingers to his lips when Jamie gave him a nervous glance.

The hunters moved forward with purpose through the thick cover of the trees, nearing the overlook of the little rocky beach.

They were so close now, Elinora and Tillie could hear them talking. Henry came bounding down the trail, his back arched, fur bristling, and stood between them and the hunters.

This concerned Elinora, but the hunters did not seem to hear or see any of his movements; they continued to skulk about, oblivious to the eyes fixed on them.

In a fit of anger, Tillie grabbed a rock and cocked her arm back.

This alarmed Elinora even more. She put her hand out to try to stop her.

"Trust me," Tillie whispered.

"Tillie, no!"

But she hurled the rock at the hunters anyway; it flew past them and tumbled down the slope into the river, making a loud splash when it hit the water.

The tallest hunter, a solidly built man with a rough demeanor, pivoted toward the direction the rock had come from and instantaneously discharged his shotgun. Bullets sprayed the air.

Elinora screamed and braced herself, but the bullets seemed to pass right by without hitting anyone. She looked over at Tillie in horror and confusion.

Tillie's eyes widened. "I..."

"What'd you do that for?" a second hunter, smaller and more slender, suddenly blurted out, rattled by the sound of the gun. It appeared that Elinora's scream had gone unnoticed.

"Quiet!" the rough looking hunter hissed. He held his gun up again and listened for movement. A violent splash drew their attention back to the river. "There it is again. I'll bet it's the creature. Come out, come out!" he clucked, creeping closer to the water's edge.

Tillie and Elinora remained on the ground, while Henry continued to stand guard.

"You don't really believe it's true, do you? There's no monster out here, it's just a tall tale. Isn't it?" a second hunter asked, following cautiously.

"Hush, and keep your eyes peeled, Oliver," a third hunter, also tall, but wiry, snapped at him.

"Course I believe it. The boss knows all about it," the rough one replied tartly.

"And what would you even know about that, Ghant? It was me that was with him when he saw it all those years ago. You weren't

134

even a twitch in your mother's eye then, so don't you go running your mouth about things you don't understand!"

"Why can't we just go after one of the other animals? Something we can handle, something that *exists,* like a bear. I think I saw a nice white one out here last time," Oliver pleaded.

"We've already got our hands full with bears. We're going to do what the Boss told us to do, and we're going to find it once and for all. Oliver, go check it out while Mudd and I stand guard," Ghant commanded.

"Ease off, I'm the one in charge here," Mudd growled back at him.

Tillie turned to Elinora. "Are they talking about..."

"Hush!" she scolded.

"But Elinora..." she said even louder. "Don't you realize? They don't see or hear us—watch!" She stood up and moved toward the hunters to prove it.

Elinora shrank back and covered her head with her hands.

But Tillie was standing in plain sight now, and still they did not notice her. "We're being protected—we're in the heart of the forest; it's shielding us. We're invisible to them, and their bullets can't hurt us," she said loud enough for Jamie and Graham to hear.

Henry crept toward the hunters, trailing them to the river's edge.

Graham looked at Jamie. "We need to get them out of here."

Jamie nodded, and recalling everything Mister had taught him, closed his eyes, threw his head back, and breathed in deeply. He held his breath for a long moment, then let a roar explode from his lungs; it was louder than any growl he had ever been able to produce. This, the forest allowed the hunters to hear. His growl echoed throughout the forest. Then came a deep rumbling, a low infrasonic growl in response to his call, shaking the earth beneath their feet. Jamie grinned.

"What the..." Ghant snapped.

Oliver staggered back, fanning himself.

Before the hunters could flee, the forest animals joined in and descended upon them. It was a united, disorienting strike—Mister, Pipe, Popo, Vita, Mitch, the other Buckthorn squirrels, birds, mammals, and reptiles of all sizes and sorts coming at them from every direction. The butterflies, bees, and dragonflies came out in swarms, adding to the confusion. Graham, Jamie, Elinora, and Tillie threw stones, yelled, and shook the tree branches. The forest came alive with terrifying sound.

Monkey growled again. This time it came from much closer, raging like a fierce wind, and the vibrations caused the earth to shudder again.

Oliver shrieked as he ran. "I don't care what the boss sent us looking for, Mudd, Théodore is mad! And it doesn't matter if it's a river monster, a whale, or a unicorn he's after. No creature is worth risking coming out here for. This place is the home of demons and monsters!"

Mudd and Ghant followed without dispute and the three men bolted out of the forest.

The Messenger, the leopard, and one of the rhinoceros trailed them to make sure they were completely out of the boundaries of Kellandale Wood. Boing followed.

"Go away, and never come back!" Tillie yelled at the hunters.

Elinora was still on the ground, trembling.

Graham and Jamie rushed over, and Jamie helped her stand up, but she was still too shaken to speak.

"I heard every word they said," Tillie growled.

"They deserved what they got," Jamie shouted.

Tillie dusted off her trousers, then looked around. "Henry?" she called after him when she noticed he was gone. But he didn't respond.

"There he is!" Jamie said, pointing in the distance.

She turned to the river.

Henry stood silently at the edge of the embankment, staring intently at the rocky beach below him where he had been found.

Elinora, Tillie, Graham, and Jamie rushed to his side. Tillie threw her arms around him and he let out a sorrowful whimper. She could feel him shivering.

In a flash, they knew. They could see the man's face in their minds. It was the man they had heard called Mudd.

"*He* was the one who took you from your family?" Tillie asked.

Henry's head sagged.

Jamie gasped. "One of the men on the bridge who threw you into the river?"

Elinora, Graham, and Jamie also reached out to comfort him as the traumatic memories pulsed in stormy waves.

"Why on earth is he here?" Tillie asked, furrowing her brow.

More of Henry's thoughts continued to flood their minds. They were vivid, and not just of Mudd, but of the place he had come from. They saw Henry's family, there were five of them— his mother and four siblings, still puppies—all beautiful just like him. Then they saw Henry, the smallest of them all, weak, the runt of the litter. They were huddled together in a cage. They could see piles of straw, cages, other animals, and people walking around everywhere. A shadowy figure approached and arms reached out, grabbing at Henry. They felt his panic and fear as he was pulled away from his family. Then, there was nothing but darkness.

Henry was so distraught by this memory that everything he was conveying to them suddenly faded into a scrambled blur. But they knew they had just been given a glimpse into his early life.

Tillie pressed her head against Henry's.

"That man, Mudd. He was on the bridge last fall," Graham repeated.

Tillie nodded.

"And he came in a carriage, with another man—perhaps one of the others that was with him today, even. They had Henry, and they threw him into the river."

"They left him to die. But why have they come back?" Tillie snarled.

"They're hunters, that's why. But the real question is why would hunters dump a puppy into the river?" Jamie wondered.

"Well, it seems like they come here looking for other animals. They've seen Pipe, too. Maybe they know about the rest of the animals in Kellandale. And as Mister has said, someone suspects the Lady of the Forest exists," Graham replied.

"How would they know about her? The animals have kept her hidden, and it doesn't seem like anyone else has ever seen her besides us. What would they want her for, anyway?" asked Elinora, who had finally recovered from her fright.

"For a trophy, or something," Jamie replied.

Elinora gasped; Tillie's face darkened.

"Come on, I am sure the council is on alert and is gathering. Maybe we can find out more," Graham urged.

Elinora put her hand on Henry's head and stroked him gently.

"It will be all right, we promise," Tillie said to him softly.

As they drew near the amphitheater, they could hear a sound, strangely out of place, even for Kellandale Wood.

Jamie cupped his hands around his ears. "Is that...music?"

They followed the sound, muffled and distorted and growing louder as they approached the buckthorn.

They pushed through it and walked into the clearing.

There at the edge of the amphitheater, a massive structure had appeared. It was spinning slowly as it played a faint, eerie, and garbled melody.

"A *carousel?*" Jamie blinked his eyes incredulously.

Henry stood still as another flood of memories washed over him with intensity. The thoughts and feelings came rapidly. Fleeting images passed through all of their minds again—a tent, an arena, animals everywhere. They saw the very same carousel that was in front of them there in the forest. Henry was trembling again.

Graham turned his head quickly and looked over at him. The same swell of dread that Graham had perceived from Henry the first day he had met him, returned. This time Henry could not stop it. "Guys," he said to Tillie, Elinora, and Jamie.

But they had already felt it, too.

Henry could no longer hold back his sadness. He conveyed to them more about his past, and about the man who had taken him from his family. The place he had come from was harsh and cruel. And Henry's family—his mother, his sister, and his brothers—were still there living under those conditions.

"Why didn't you tell us this before?" Tillie asked, throwing her arms around him. "How can we help him?" she begged the others, tears spilling from her eyes.

Graham shook his head solemnly, then turned his head, as though in deep thought. "Well, it's a good thing the hunters came here," he finally said.

"You have to be joking!" Jamie replied, turning to look at Graham, brows furrowed, eyes filled with dismay.

"I know it sounds terrible, but think about it. Now we know one of the men is called Mudd. I also heard him say the name Théodore. We have real information—information that could help us and Henry find out where his family is."

Silently, they all gazed at the carousel, dumbfounded and puzzling together what it meant that Mudd was one of the hunters. They were paralyzed by the sadness they knew Henry had been suffering in silence.

Jamie suddenly stood up and moved closer to investigate the phantom machine—a misty apparition of a carousel, but there nonetheless. He could see well enough to make out the large, carved wooden animals on its platform. Henry recognized some of them—figures of a large, black horse, a handful of dogs, a lion, two tigers, and several more horses.

The carousel continued to spin, and as it did, its form became more and more substantial until finally it was as real as any other carousel. It made another revolution, and this time five wolfhound figures came into view.

Henry lowered his head and cried out.

Tillie gasped.

"It's them," Elinora said quietly.

"Oh my, of course," Jamie said. "That's it then, isn't it?"

"What is?" Tillie asked.

"Where he came from. He came from a circus. Those men must be coming here looking for animals for the circus."

A stunned silence followed. Graham turned to Elinora and Tillie. "He's right, isn't he?"

Elinora and Tillie looked at one another. Elinora nodded.

"A circus," Tillie finally said. "Henry's family is at the circus."

14

Sir Edward's Treasure

It was very late into the night on the day Mudd had returned to the forest and the carousel had manifested. Thought to be a projection borne from Henry's traumatic memories, it had given Tillie, Elinora, Graham, and Jamie insight into his origins, and even more importantly, clues that might lead them to his family. They had sought the privacy of the tower to discuss how they might go about figuring out which circus he had come from. This time, Abigail had given them the tower key and made sure no one knew where they were headed.

"Here we are then," Tillie said as she opened the door at the top of the stairs.

Jamie stared in awe from the entrance. "This is where Sir William slept?"

They all entered and Graham walked straight to the windows. "Come over here, James," he called.

Jamie joined him to look out. The night sky was clear, treating them to an infinite field of stars above, and a brilliant full moon that cast long shadows across the garden landscape below. A gentle fog hovered over the river. "What a view," he said, resting his chin on his hand as he looked out.

Tillie had brought blankets, which she spread out carefully on the floor. She watched Graham for a moment as he gazed out into the night sky, then she glanced over at Jamie, who was now off exploring Sir William's belongings. She smiled, amused that he was inspecting every little item he came across, just as she had. She was also pleasantly surprised that Elinora was no longer henpecking anyone about it.

Graham came over and sat down next to her beneath the arched windows. Elinora followed.

Jamie finally joined them, settling in on the blanket. He pulled out a cloth napkin from his pocket and unfolded it, revealing a handful of tiny macarons and a biscuit that his mother had brought back from Lovii's earlier that evening. He offered them to everyone, saving the biscuit for Henry.

He came over and gently took it, crunching on it happily, then he curled up next to Jamie, resting his head upon his lap and settling in for a nap.

More candles were lit. The shifting moonlight shimmered through the arched windows, which helped to further brighten the room. Tillie realized it was the same moon and the same view Sir William would have had when he called Kellandale home. Thoughts of him moving about, looking out the tower windows, or perhaps sitting at the desk writing a letter, passed through Tillie's mind once again.

Henry lifted his head and looked upon his friends before wearily lying back down. It had been an emotional, exhausting day and he was tired, but he still listened intently.

"Well, how do you think we should go about this?" Jamie

142

asked, wiping a crumb from his mouth.

Elinora closed her eyes, fear gripping her. Henry's family was out there, somewhere unsafe, and to help him meant…what, she did not know. She wanted nothing more than to be able to help him, but her fear of change was strong. Life seemed so perfect now and she was afraid to lose it. She tried to stifle these confusing thoughts and hide them from Henry. She sighed loudly.

"Well, for starters, brooding certainly isn't the way," Tillie replied to Jamie, shooting Elinora an angry look.

"There's really nothing we can do." Elinora replied, her voice strained. "You saw those men—they could have killed us. They *would* have killed us if it weren't for the forest protecting us. I don't even want to think about what they would do to us if they caught us stealing from them. And besides, how can we go to a circus if we don't know where it is, let alone which one it is? Even if we do figure it out, do you think we're going to just walk away with five large dogs without anyone noticing?"

"I don't know, but I'll do whatever it takes; we can't just leave them there. You saw how frightened Henry was just thinking about that place." Tillie squeezed her hands into fists. "I'll go there by myself if I have to. And we wouldn't be stealing Henry's family; they don't belong to those men, they are being forced to live there."

"She's right," Jamie said, looking down and picking at the blanket fibers. "We have to help them—somehow."

Elinora rolled her eyes up to the ceiling and sighed. She felt the same in her heart, but the nagging fear inside her mind would not cease, and it was beginning to consume her thoughts. She hated it—fear, her cursed fear, always getting in the way of doing anything bold, anything daring to make a difference.

Graham got up and paced around the room, his shadow flickering upon the wall as he moved about. He folded his arms. "All right, let's take a step back. We know that Henry's family is living at a circus. We know it is likely that the circus is located nearby, or at least close enough for them to travel here now and again, in any event. And the hunters we saw, we know they are the ones who threw Henry into the river. That's how Henry got here in the first place."

Henry lifted his head when he heard his name.

"It sure seems like it," Jamie replied. He patted Henry. "It's all right boy."

"Go on, Gray," Tillie said.

"Well, the first order of business is easy enough; we need to investigate which circuses come through here in the summer. You can handle that, can't you, Elinora?"

"Perfect!" Tillie replied eagerly. "Waterbridge is an easy place to start. That's where the circuses will travel closest to us," she added, encouraged that a plan was finally taking shape.

"And if we discover which circus it is, then what?" Elinora asked pointedly. "You're still suggesting we steal from them in the end."

Tillie stood up. "Precisely. I will go there, and I will walk in and grab them, then take them home with me. It's very simple."

"Otillie, you're a fool. You think you're invincible, but you're not. None of us are. We could never overpower those men and walk away with Henry's family. It's impossible."

"Elinora," Tillie growled.

Henry shifted uncomfortably.

"We could sneak in when everyone is sleeping," Graham suggested.

"We could even dress up like we are part of the circus," Jamie added.

"Those are terrible ideas," Elinora said flatly.

"What, then? Ignore the fact that Henry is devastated that his family is trapped in an awful place and leave them there? Don't you even care about him or his family?" Tillie scolded.

Elinora recoiled in horror. "How could you even say that? Of course I care!"

The room fell silent.

Jamie leaned over and hugged Henry when he felt him trembling. "Don't worry, we'll figure something out."

"I'm sorry," Elinora whispered. Tears flooded her eyes; she was terribly sad and frustrated that she alone was such an impediment. She stood up and moved to the window and looked out. "The animals are probably out there discussing what to do." They came over to look out with her. "Maybe the council can do something! Perhaps they can send scouts to find Henry's family. We can wait for the circuses to come around and try to help them then," she suggested, her face lighting up.

"Elinora, you can't be serious. We can't leave Henry's family at the circus until summer, or ask the woodland animals to put themselves in danger by leaving the protected forest. It isn't right," Tillie said, trying to keep herself calm. "We're humans, and we can move around more safely outside the forest. I would never want any of them to get hurt, and I'm sure you wouldn't either."

Elinora's face fell. She growled in frustration, trying to suppress the urge to cry.

"Don't worry, we'll find a way that doesn't seem so scary," Jamie said softly.

"Something will come to us," Graham agreed.

She nodded, wiping away the tears and trying to put on a brave face. She looked over at Henry and sighed again. "I want to help you, Henry, I really do. Your family could come live here, and it would be so wonderful for all of us."

Henry stood up from his spot on the floor, then walked over and brushed against her.

"There's not much we can do tonight, anyway. We should go back downstairs and sleep on it," Graham suggested.

Jamie stretched and yawned. "Yes, let's. And perhaps we can go to the forest council tomorrow morning," he replied sleepily. "We have the forest, a magic forest that gave Henry the ability to communicate with us. A carousel showed us where Henry came from—*a carousel*. Who knows how else the powers of the forest might be able to help."

"Yes, I like that idea very much," Elinora said quietly.

"It's a deal then."

They gathered up the blankets, collected the candles, and filed back down the circular staircase. When they reached the third floor, Graham held his candle up so the others could see. In doing so, he revealed the door tucked in the corner of the stairwell on the floor below.

"Elinora wouldn't let me see what's down there the last time," Tillie said pointing it out.

"We were in a hurry," Elinora replied.

But Graham's curiosity was piqued. He continued down the narrow stone stairwell to the next level. "Let's have a look now then, shall we?"

Tillie followed, holding up the key to the tower room. Graham nodded and Tillie slid it into the rusty iron lock, which was a perfect fit. It clicked as she turned it. She raised an eyebrow at him, then opened the door slowly.

Graham held the candle out again to light up the room. Just like the tower bedroom, it had been kept tidied—another room Abigail perhaps knew a thing or two about, he thought.

Jamie and Elinora came down the stairwell and peered inside. Henry remained at Jamie's side.

The room was windowless and dark as night except for the candlelight. In the dim glow, they could see the silhouettes of hundreds of items—clothing, furniture, masks, hats, swords, pieces of furniture, and more. "Look at that," Tillie whispered.

146

"There are heaps of things everywhere."

"More of Sir Edward's things," Jamie said.

"I could spend hours in here." Tillie surveyed the room and found a case nearby. She walked over and opened it. It was filled with hats and headpieces. A black velvet bonnet, piled almost a foot high with olive green fabric bows and embellished with silk flowers sprouting from every direction, caught her attention. It was old and tattered, still elegant, yet slightly absurd. She reached for it and placed it on her head then smiled and curtsied at Henry. He wagged his tail back at her.

Jamie jumped out at Graham wearing a large mask with angry eyes and exaggerated features. "A soul mask from Chanpor, just like I read about, Gray. They chase away evil spirits!"

"Graham took it from him to look closely at it. "It's beautiful."

"Bwah! You look like a bird," Jamie said to Tillie when he saw her hat.

"It suits you," Graham said to her with a grin. "What time is it? Abigail has been waiting up for us and it's really late—there's no vortex here to help with that," he reminded everyone.

Tillie nodded. She returned the hat to its case and they began filing back out of the room.

Elinora had also been quietly exploring the room, and a book had caught her eye. She picked it up and opened it. "It's a journal," she said with excitement. She ran back to the door, holding it out for the others to see. "Look, it's Sir William's journal!"

"I don't think anyone would notice if you borrowed it; come on, take it with you," Graham said with grin.

Elinora smiled. "I can't wait to read it."

Tillie smiled back, happy to see her sister's mood lift. She turned and locked the door, then they met Abigail at the key station. She handed her the key and asked about the room.

"Most of Sir Edward, Lady Vivienne, and Sir William's

belongings are kept there," Abigail confirmed.

"I found a journal," Elinora said, holding it out.

"Ah! Sir William kept a journal his whole life from what I understand. I'm sure the rest of them are somewhere in the room."

"I should love to find them all," Elinora replied.

"We would like to come back, if that is all right," Graham asked.

"I will be happy to give you the key again when you need it. But let's keep that to ourselves, shall we?"

"Of course. Thank you, Abigail," Tillie replied, then they all said good night, retiring to their rooms in the hopes of finding enough peace to get some sleep.

It would be difficult with their minds still racing, but they were so exhausted it wasn't long before they all drifted off into deep slumber.

Still deeper into the night as the moon dropped lower in the sky, Henry stirred. He had been plagued with fitful sleep, having felt Elinora's distress while they were in the tower room. It pained him, and he knew that the children—even Elinora—would eventually find the resolve to help him, and that would likely mean putting themselves in harm's way. He couldn't bear the thought and knew there was only one thing to do. He needed to find his family, and he needed to protect the children, and that meant leaving Kellandale, alone.

He quietly rose, making sure he didn't brush against Tillie's bed, and gently nudged the door open with his nose. Then he made his way to the prep room where he knew the door would be kept unlatched for him as it always was on milder nights.

He remorsefully made his way outside and down the stone steps, a ritual which usually marked the start of a happy journey into the woods with his beloved family members. He glanced back at the manor house, taking comfort in knowing the children were tucked away safely inside.

He lowered his head and let out a big sigh. He was desperate to help his mother and siblings now that he had some memories that might lead him to them, but he was also filled with great sorrow, distraught that he was leaving the new family he loved so much. But he used that emotion to strengthen his resolve to quickly find his family and return to Kellandale. He would be back again soon; he was sure of that.

Henry crept quietly down the shadowy path, the low hanging moon lighting the way to the forest council. He knew the raccoons, mice, and perhaps the fox would still be active at this hour, so he set off to find them and confide in them about his plan. As he approached the amphitheater, he could see the carousel was still spinning. He paused, trying to reach the depths of his memories for clues as to where he should go.

Mister had heard Henry enter the forest and had left his tree at the start of the trail to follow him. He approached Henry, knowing he had news to bear.

Henry quickly conveyed his plans. Mister asked if anything else could be done so that he wouldn't have to leave, but Henry knew there was no other way. He asked Mister to discourage the children from following him to ensure their safety.

Mister obliged and wished him well. He vowed the council would do whatever they could to help, and that they would watch over the children in the meantime.

With that, Henry bade him farewell. He slowly walked off, then broke into a sprint, quickly making his way to the northeast, to the outer edge of the protected boundaries of Kellandale Wood.

There he caught up with the Iveria again, but after a spell he sensed a drastic shift in the environment. He stopped and sniffed the air and pricked up his ears. His fur tingled. The air suddenly soured, turning putrid and hazy. The river here was murky and filled with debris, and the few trees left standing were mangled and burned. The rest had fallen and covered the ground. He felt something sinister in the air.

Destruction. Greed.
Maleficence.

It was nothing like the forest he knew. This was the part of the forest he had heard Abigail speak of to Elinora and Tillie. He recalled what she had said about the swath of festering energy left behind from the ancient fires and knew he had found that place— the malevolent forest. He turned away, breaking into a full gallop, putting a great distance between himself and the fallen forest.

Back in the heart of the forest, word of Henry's departure had spread like wildfire, and the animals gathered quickly. They sat together in silence in the amphitheater. Pipe put his head down and let out a sorrowful grunt when he was told the news. He knew Henry was strong and brave and was sure he would find his way back with his family. But in the meantime, until his return, Henry's absence would be mourned by all.

15

Missing

Tillie opened her eyes abruptly, roused from deep slumber by a terrible feeling in her gut. It was her turn to have Henry in her room that night, but even without getting up to look, she sensed his absence. "Henry?" she called softly.

There was no response; no sounds of him stretching his long legs, no sign of stirring.

She jumped out of bed and searched her room, her heart racing. When she was certain he wasn't there, she pulled on her robe and slippers and flung her door open. She crossed the darkened hallway to Elinora's room and barged in. "Nora," she whispered. "Wake up. Please!"

Elinora rolled over onto her back and opened her eyes, forcing them to focus. She reached over and stroked Velvet, who was curled up next to her, then she looked at Tillie. "Hmm?" she mumbled groggily.

"It's Henry. He's not in my room, or yours. He's gone."

Velvet perked her head up. She also sensed Henry was missing, and without him there, she didn't understand the words Tillie was saying. But her cat instincts enabled her to sense Tillie's panic. She stood up and brushed against her, trying to comfort her. Tillie rubbed her soft fur.

Elinora yawned and stretched her hands above her head, trying to wake up. "It was very late when we left the tower. Maybe we just overslept and he's downstairs charming Cora and Jeppe, waiting for some food."

Tillie quickly grabbed a robe and handed it to her, then opened the curtain a crack. It was still dark outside. "We haven't overslept. The sun has barely just come up. He's usually here at this time waiting for us to wake for breakfast, you know that."

Elinora looked out the window and sat up abruptly, then looked about nervously, realizing the gravity of the situation. She thought of the conversation they'd had in the tower.

"I hope he is in Graham and Jamie's room." She tossed Elinora's slippers at her.

Elinora got out of bed and pulled them on, then donned her robe in haste. "Stay here, Velvet, we'll find him," she said, patting her. Velvet chirped with worry as Elinora and Tillie exited the room and closed the door.

They tiptoed across the hall to the other side of the stairwell.

"Gray, Jamie," Tillie whispered, tapping lightly on their door. When there was no answer, she knocked louder.

A moment later Jamie opened it and peered out. His hair was wildly mussed, his eyes barely open. "Do you know what time it is?" he whispered back, teasing Tillie, then falling silent as he felt her sense of urgency.

"Henry's gone!" said Elinora, her face now dark and serious.

"What's that?" Graham asked, rubbing his eyes as he joined Jamie at the door.

"We can't find Henry," Tillie repeated. "Is he here with you?"

"No, he isn't." He frowned.

Elinora closed her eyes. "Something's not right." She pressed her back to the wall and sat down, covering her face with her hands. "I have a horrible feeling it's my fault."

"What do you mean?" Jamie asked.

"He has been so sad and worried about his family, and I think yesterday was more than he could bear."

"This isn't your fault," said Graham. "He has to be around here somewhere. Come on, let's find him." He helped her to her feet, then he and Jamie returned to their room for their slippers.

They hurried down the side stairwell to the prep room, and when they arrived, the exterior door was ajar. The room was cool and crisp from the early morning breeze, but otherwise empty. They rushed to the door and looked out.

"I see paw prints. I think he's gone outside from the look of it," Tillie said.

Jamie sighed. "Maybe he went to the forest council for help?"

"Let's go find out," Graham said leading the way onto the lawn.

They dashed off, the morning dew dampening their slippers as they ran. When they arrived at the amphitheater, the carousel was slowly spinning and Mister was quietly sitting beside it, watching for them. It was apparent he had been anticipating their arrival.

"Mister, where is Henry?" Tillie called to him.

In a flash, the news was delivered.

> *He will miss you greatly but in time he will*
> *return with his family. Please do not worry*
> *yourselves while he is gone.*

"I knew it! How could I be such a coward?" Elinora exclaimed. "I drove him away—I made him feel like he had to do this alone.

How will we ever know if he made it to his family? And how can he find his family when he has no idea where he came from to begin with? What if he gets lost along the way or hurt—or worse!" A string of terrible thoughts paraded through her mind; so many tears fell from her eyes that she couldn't see.

"Elinora, why did you have to scare Henry away like that!" Jamie yelled abruptly.

She looked up, startled by his shout, panic and shame reflecting on her face.

His eyes opened wide. It was the first time he had ever shouted at her about anything. He, too, began to cry; he cried for Henry, and he cried at his own insensitivity.

But Tillie was very angry, too. "You've ruined *everything*, Elinora, you've chased him away!" she accused.

Elinora turned away, her sobs so violent she lost her breath.

Pipe had been watching and listening from the edge of the forest. He quietly came over to Elinora's side, engulfing her in his big bear arms. She grabbed onto him. For the first time, he tried to communicate directly with them.

> *Do not lose heart. You did not chase him away.*
> *Henry needed to find his family,*
> *and he needed to do it alone to protect you,*
> *just as you have been doing for him.*
> *Trust that he will return,*
> *and do not be angry with one another.*

Graham felt his throat tighten. He moved over next to Elinora and Pipe and put his head down. "He's right. We can't start fighting each other. You didn't make him leave, Nora. Henry is strong and independent, and he's very smart. He must have felt it was the only way. We need to believe in him."

Before they could recover from the shock, even more

discouraging news was shared by the council. As the hunters fled the forest the day before, the Messenger had chased after them. In the chase he had traveled far beyond the boundaries of the protected area, becoming visible and vulnerable. The hunters had eventually regained their wits and seizing the opportunity, they had captured him. Boing had seen from a distance, and the tiny rabbit watched helplessly as he was netted and locked in a cage. The hunters then disappeared, and the Messenger had not been seen since.

Elinora sat upon the ground, shaking.

"What are they going to do with the Messenger? Force him into the circus?" Tillie growled. "I can't stand this anymore. I'm going after them! Those awful men will lead us right where we want to be—right to Henry."

Mister chattered desperately, imploring her to respect to Henry's wishes. He promised her that Monkey had already gone to look for the Messenger and then to search for Henry and aid him in his travels. He pleaded with her to remain at Kellandale until Monkey returned with news.

There was a pause. The carousel continued to spin, its eerie music echoing in the forest. "I wish you would just be quiet!" Tillie yelled at it. But somehow she was drawn to it; she walked over and climbed aboard, looking closely at the carousel animals. She found the figure of a beautiful horse and climbed on its back, hoping the carousel would perhaps transport her right to where Henry was. She waited a moment, and though nothing happened, the slow, quiet hum of the carousel calmed her, distracting her from her tangled thoughts. She climbed back down. "What if Monkey doesn't find the Messenger, or Henry?" she asked.

Monkey has his ways.
He will find them, and he will return with news.
This is the truth.

She hesitated. "I believe you." She sighed. "I promise I will not go looking for him—for now. But please, I want to hear you say again that he will come back soon."

He will return. He will be successful in finding
his family and he will return to you soon.

"Just know, if I somehow discover he needs help, I will go looking for him, and I will bring him back here at all costs." She glanced at Elinora and recognized how distraught she was and softened a little. "Don't worry. We just need to be prepared to do something if the time comes for that."

Elinora nodded.

"I'm sorry, Elinora" Jamie said. He walked over to her and reached his hand out to help her up. "We all know how scared you are. I am, too. And I know that you want Henry back just as much as the rest of us. None of this is your fault."

She took his hand. "I'm sorry, too, though I do still feel it is my fault; maybe he would still be here if he thought we were going to help." She looked around and noticed that they were suddenly surrounded by the animals of the forest. "Thank you for being here for us," she said.

They said their goodbyes, then turned back toward the manor house, without Henry by their side.

Back home, they quickly found Abigail and confided in her first. When the news was delivered, a cloud of sadness fell over everyone, except for Lina, who was still in her bedroom and had not yet been told.

"Don't worry, he couldn't have strayed far," Emil reassured everyone. Though tall and lanky, and naturally standing with excellent posture from all the horseback riding they did, Emil was now crumpled over from the grief of learning about Henry's absence, their head down, and shoulders sagging. "I'll take the horses and we'll go out looking. We will make sure everyone in the area is watching for him, too," they said quietly. "He'll be back here in no time."

"Thank you, Emil," Tillie replied. She sucked in her breath. "I'm sure you're right." But there was a faraway look in her eyes. She turned to her mother. "I won't be coming to breakfast today," she said quietly, then made her way up the grand staircase to her room.

Abigail cast a solemn but consoling glance at Elinora, Graham, and Jamie.

Anna put her arms around Elinora. "He will return soon, my dear."

Elinora wiped her eyes and nodded. "Thank you, Mother."

As Tillie reached the top of the staircase, a muffled voice came from the direction of Lina's bedroom. She made her way down the hall, then stood silently outside her closed door. Lina was crying. "Henry, where did you go?" Tillie heard her shout. Tillie's eyes widened; in that moment she understood the bond between Henry and Lina was very real—strong enough that she knew he was gone without even being told.

Moved by Lina's deep emotion, she placed her hand on the doorknob—perhaps she would try to comfort her, she thought. But the sound of something smashing to the floor stopped her. Lina shouted out in anger, and Tillie's already cautious desire to help her wilted. She turned away so she that could seek solace from the quiet of her own room. She knew she was going to have to quickly pull herself back together and draw strength from within in order to endure Henry's absence.

16

Through the Forest

Alone and a long way from Kellandale, Henry journeyed on in search of his mother, sisters, and brothers. He fixed them firmly in his mind's eye. The sorrow of their loss, and the worry from knowing they were at the circus drove him forward. The pain of separation from Elinora, Tillie, and the others gave him the will to complete his mission as fast as he could. He had been running for hours, only stopping when necessary for water or to catch his breath.

The sun was now high overhead, so he veered off the road and headed into the forest to seek cover while continuing to travel in a northeasterly direction. He had quickly realized that most of the people he encountered along the road were frightened by him, which resulted in some chasing him away with their guns; others were so awestruck by his size they had very much wanted to capture him as a prize.

He tried not to feel defeated so early on in his quest, but eventually his body gave in and he collapsed on the ground on the bank of the Iveria. Though it was the very same river that flowed past the manor house and ran through the forest there, the sense of security and protection within its boundaries was absent once he had left behind the sanctuary of Kellandale Wood. He let out a sorrowful groan. The cool water lapped over his body and soaked his fur as he leaned his head over to take a drink. As he lay there panting, and for the first time feeling hopeless, a large fish crow flew down into the tree above.

The bird startled when he saw Henry lying on the ground beneath him. He flapped his wings defensively, flying higher into the tree. He had never seen a dog before; the only canines he knew were the wild wolves that dwelled in this part of the forest and he was mistrustful.

Henry remained still, passively lying down, not wishing to frighten him any more than he had.

The fish crow studied him closely, cocking his head from side to side with curiosity. When he no longer felt as though he was being looked upon as a meal, he hopped back down onto a lower branch.

Henry stood up and shook himself off, then greeted the fish crow, who cackled with delight when he realized he could under-stand Henry's thoughts.

Henry told him his story and shared how it had come to pass that he was there by the river.

The fish crow listened intently, squawking passionately and struggling to find his own voice. He was eager share information he believed could help set Henry on the path he was desperately seeking. Once he figured out how to communicate back, the fish crow began to convey what he had seen.

During his daily flit around the forest the day before, he had happened upon some men stuck on the side of the road—three noisy louts yelling at one another and disturbing the peace as they attempted to fix a wheel on their carriage. Curious and welcoming the entertainment, he flew to a nearby bush to watch. But from his perch he caught a glimpse inside the vehicle; there he noticed a large and colorful bird confined in a cage. It was in distress and needed help.

Henry's ears perked up.

The fish crow told Henry how he had flapped and fluttered at the men to chase them away, but they quickly drove him back into the treetops with their guns. Once they were on their way he had followed the men a long distance to a village. "Garibaldi!" he squawked, repeating a word he had overheard one of the hunters say just before they had disappeared into a building.

He expressed great sorrow that he had not been able to find a way help a fellow bird. But those very same men had appeared in his thoughts when Henry had conveyed his tale to him, leading him to believe the men with the bird and the hunters Henry had encountered back home were one and the same.

Henry was shocked when he realized it the Messenger had been captured, and agreed it was Mudd and his men the fish crow had encountered. He told the bird this and thanked him for his help, for without him, he would have been lost. If he could find the hunters, he knew they would certainly lead him straight to his family at the circus. To show his deep gratitude, Henry told his new friend how to find Kellandale Wood and invited him to make his home there.

The fish crow bobbed his head, showing interest in the offer, then he pointed his beak in the direction of the carriage path that led to the village.

Henry thanked him again, promising he would free the bird, then dashed away to find him. An excellent runner true to his breed, his stamina allowed him to travel at a swift pace. The days he had spent in the woods while he grew, playing with the animals, running free, and wrestling with Pipe, had conditioned him physically. He may have started life out as a runt, but his time at Kellandale had allowed him to grow to his full potential; the heart of the forest had helped him grow even beyond it. But still, he was gentle, loyal, and affectionate, and his only instinct toward other animals was to play hard; he knew no fear of them.

Now things felt different as he began to encounter wild animals unaccustomed to the ways of Kellandale Wood. Many were aloof, skittish, and on guard. He could see some of them hovering at the edge of the forest, watching, and even sensed a tinge of aggression creeping in from some of them. For this reason, he purposefully steered clear of any interaction.

After a time, the sun lowered in the sky. A few stray clouds moved in and rain droplets began to sprinkle on the carriage path that Henry was following, so he moved deeper into the forest. Hunger and despair began to consume him. He paused and sniffed the air. Something was tracking him, and it wasn't human. He shivered involuntarily when he felt several sets of eyes fixed upon him.

A pack of wolves crept out from of the shadows, revealing their leader—lean and riddled with scars. He had Henry in his sights and he advanced quickly.

The rest of the pack was close behind.

Henry tried to scan the leader's thoughts, but he couldn't connect with him as easily as he could with others. These were wild animals driven by the necessity to survive, operating on instinct, defensive and aggressive. They were oblivious to Henry's thoughts, but still, they could sense something different about him.

Henry hesitated. He considered running as there was a chance he could get away. Then he contemplated standing his ground, though every instinct made him feel uncomfortable about fighting with a fellow being. He didn't want to risk injury, nor did he want to hurt anyone. But the pack was creeping low to the ground now, and it was clear they were preparing to attack. Henry needed to think fast. If there had been one lone wolf, he knew it wouldn't have dared to approach him. But there were many, and together they were bold.

In an instant the pack was on top of him; one of the wolves struck from the rear as the leader lunged at him from the side. The others waited for an opening.

But Henry was quick and agile, dodging between the two, then turning on the pack leader who had grabbed his flank with his teeth. Henry quickly flipped him on his back, closing his mouth around his neck, pinning him to the ground. The wolf lay motionless. Henry sensed his fear, and he did not bite down.

Without injuring the leader, Henry attempted to communicate again as he cautiously began to release him. The rest of the pack paused to listen.

Though Henry's demeanor had subdued the wolf, it confused and him and he defensively jumped back up, baring his teeth and growling.

Henry continued speaking using the language of the forest.

The profound sense of empathy the wolf felt was overwhelming; he tipped his head, pricking his ears, then signaled to the rest of the pack to stand down.

Henry conveyed to them that he was not a threat.

The wolf understood him clearly now. He conveyed back to Henry, and told him about the plight of their pack, that they were hunting aggressively out of desperation and near-starvation. As the last surviving pack in the area, they had been able to evade hunters and remain hidden from humans; they viewed anyone as a threat, even other animals. The wolf leader apologized for their misguided attack.

Henry told them about Kellandale Wood, where they would be protected and nourished by the energy of the forest, and where they would no longer have need to hunt for food—a place where they wouldn't have to fear other animals or humans and could make a new home and live in peace. He offered its shelter to them. Then he told them of the kindness of Elinora, Tillie, and the others. The wolves listened intently as he shared his story and what he had learned from the fish crow.

A lanky wolf with shaggy fur and a striking splash of white fur across her chest stepped forward. She thanked Henry for refusing to fight and for his kindness. She knew of the human called Garibaldi—a man known to lure wolves into his traps with food—and warned Henry to be wary. Then the wolves formed a protective circle around Henry and led him to Craggybog.

When they reached the village, the sun had just begun to set. Shouts and laughter were coming from the people ambling along the dirt road running through town, so they hid at the edge of the woods. The wolf leader showed Henry the building that belonged to Garibaldi, which was where he hoped to find the hunters and the bird he was searching for.

Henry again invited the wolf pack to Kellandale Wood and wished them safe passage if they chose to make the journey.

The wolves thanked him, promising they would meet again one day back in his forest. Then they wished him luck on his quest, and retreated into the darkness.

Henry hunkered down and waited. He thought deeply about his encounter with the wolves; it had ended well, but it was the first time he had ever been pitted against another being. Truth be told, he was surprised by his own strength and that defending himself had come so easy. But this knowledge also grounded him, increasing his resolve. He now knew he had the physical ability, the means to communicate, and the fortitude to carry on.

17

Grotelby's Inn & Tavern

The village of Craggybog wasn't so much a village as it was a small cluster of homes in the middle of nowhere. The downtown was comprised of a single crossroad, twelve ramshackle shops, and twelve streetlamps—one for each storefront. These had been tended to and lit by the lamplighter for the night and were flickering in the gentle breeze as people moved about beneath their eerie, pale glow. Henry continued to hide in the shadows, his ears twitching back and forth as he kept a sharp eye, waiting for the town to settle.

Although Craggybog's population was small, it was a popular stopover for travelers on their way to better places, not to mention a notorious haunt for some unsavory types, and it was usually humming with activity. No matter their reasons for being in town, all visitors made sure to visit Craggybog's biggest draw—Grotelby's Inn and Tavern. Famous for its gruff owners and an abundance of gourmet food, drink, and gambling, the tavern's adjoining inn served as the only place in town for guests to lay their weary heads at night's end.

At last, only a handful of people lingered on the streets, the rest now tucked away in their homes or crammed inside Grotelby's. Once an upscale establishment, the inn had deteriorated over time, though it still retained a certain quaintness. A weathered wooden sign hung out front of the four-story building, and each of its rooms had its own balcony overlooking the dirt road.

Henry was so hungry it was becoming unbearable, and despite the warning from the wolves, the smell of food at once lured him from his hiding spot. He stood up and sniffed the air, hoping to find scraps while avoiding Garibaldi's traps as he desperately needed to eat.

He slipped out of the woods and trotted quietly along the edge of the little alley that stretched beside the inn, following his nose to the tavern kitchen at the back of the building. A thin rope had been strung lengthwise down the lane, and animal skins of all sorts had been draped over it. Some looked fresh; many of them were wolf hides. Nightfall was the only thing holding back the buzzing flies. Henry's stomach pitched.

He advanced cautiously, hunkering down when he heard the back door creak open, then slam shut. A young man stepped outside with a barrel of trash in his arms. Henry could see him better when he passed under the light of an alley lantern—he was just a bit older than Graham and Elinora, and he had wavy, dark brown hair and warm brown skin. He was not very tall, but he was excessively strong and agile, carrying the heavy barrel with ease.

The young man started down the alley toward the nearby trash heap, but froze when he noticed Henry's looming silhouette ahead.

Henry instinctively sensed the boy was inquisitive and friendly. He stood back up and approached slowly with his head down, then sat so he would not appear to be a threat. For a good long moment, they eyed each other. Henry finally wagged his tail. He looked deep into the young man's eyes, dark brown and soft, though they had a certain confident steadiness to them. Henry locked into his mind to calm him.

In a flash he knew Henry's past. He stumbled back.

"Uhm, what was that?" he asked, setting the barrel down and glancing around. He dusted off his trousers and fixed his dark blue button-down shirt.

Henry continued to convey his story.

"Ehalēa Henry...that's "hello" in Cortinian." He furrowed his brow, confused by everything. He looked around to see who might have been talking, but there was no one nearby. "How do I know your name? And why do I feel like I know everything about you?"

Henry explained how he could communicate as he did.

He looked intently at Henry. "Well, that certainly doesn't happen every day. I can speak three languages—Cortinian, Morlish, and Gai....and now "Canine," it seems," he grinned. "All right, then."

Henry liked him very much already. He came closer.

"I'm sorry to hear you had a rough beginning, but I'm glad you're here, Henry. You're safe with me. I'm Alister. It's nice to meet someone friendly for a change."

Just then they were interrupted by a large, unkempt man who barged outside through the kitchen door. "Alister Grotelby!" he boomed, his already pink cheeks flushing red. His mangy, greying beard was peppered with bits of food. A sharp stench drifted from his pores, and his clothes were spattered with food from cooking.

"Quick, don't let him see you," Alister warned, and Henry shrank back into the alley.

"Alister!" he shouted again.

"Ah, yes, it's your same-smelling self," he muttered.

"What did you say?" the man roared, his body shaking violently as he spoke, but he ignored the comment. "What's keeping you?

Hurry up with the trash, customers need to be waited on." Then he noticed Henry backing away in the shadows. "Yeow! Get inside before that beast tears us apart, lad! Rodene! Get my gun, woman!" he yelled to someone inside.

An arm, ensnared in a mangled shawl, reached out from the other side of the door. Henry couldn't see a face, but whoever the arm belonged to, it was holding a rifle.

The man grabbed it and swiftly took aim.

Alister jumped between them and lunged after the gun, pulling the barrel downward just before it fired. There was a loud blast and a large clump of mud thudded up into the sky before raining back down on them. They both wiped dirt off their faces.

Henry disappeared back into the forest before the man could reload.

"What'd you do that for! That beast could have taken our heads off in one bite!"

"He won't hurt us," Alister spit back.

"What? You must have a thick skull, kid—that was a vicious beast if I ever saw one. Well, he's gone in any event. You're lucky I saved your hide! Boy would I sure like to have *his* hide, though. Maybe I'll find him in one of my traps later." He scratched the grey scruff on his chin, looking around for Henry.

"Garibaldi Grotelby! Get that boy back in here. The customers are getting antsy," Rodene yelled. She opened the door again and stepped out with a smelly mop in her pale, almost grey, withered hand. She came after Alister, swatting the air. Her rat's nest of a hairdo, yellow-grey and piled high, somehow remained sturdy even as she moved about violently. "Get in there! Your father needs your help! It's a wild lot this evening!"

"He's not my father," Alister reminded her coolly, brushing away her attack.

"What did you just say?" Rodene pounded on his back with

the mop, bits of fiber and debris scattering in the air. "Ungrateful boy! Garibaldi, shut him up!"

Alister glared at her.

"Don't you look at your mother like that, you're making her angry. Rodene, mop him up again!" Garibaldi yelled.

Henry's fur bristled when he saw what was happening. He also heard the name and knew for better or for worse that this was the place he needed to be. He hovered behind the bushes until the Grotelbys disappeared back inside.

"I'm sorry you had to listen to that. You're really a nice fellow, Henry," Alister said patting him when he came out of hiding. He picked up the barrel again and dumped its contents onto the trash pile, then set it down and returned to Henry.

Again, they communicated silently with one another, and Henry shared more about his mission to find his family.

"I'm going with you," Alister replied firmly. "I will help you find and rescue them, and I'll figure out where to go after that. All I know is I need to get out of here. I'm dying living here." He nodded towards the inn. "They pretend they're my parents, but they're really not. They think they did me a big favor, bringing me here to live with them when I was very young, but I would have been better off if they had just left me alone after my parents disappeared. I wish they would have. I'm sure I would have been just fine."

Henry's ears drooped.

Alister sighed. "It's all right...no one ever told me what happened to my parents, and I've accepted the fact I probably won't ever see them again. As for Rodene and Garibaldi—I can handle them. For now, I have to get back inside—that way they won't suspect anything. We can leave in the middle of the night when they're sleeping."

Henry wagged his tail, grateful for a new friend.

"Say, there's a depot not far from here. We can hop a train and figure out the rest along the way. I've been itching for a reason to leave, but I needed somewhere to go first; now I've found it. We can look out for each other."

Henry understood this. He wagged his tail, then shared more about his journey from Kellandale and asked if Alister had come across a bird.

"I've heard all about Kellandale Wood. Lots of stories about it float around the tavern. And to answer your question, yes, in fact, there's a very unusual bird here, it sort of makes sense now." He told Henry about three men, regulars at the inn who worked for a circus. "They're still here. Rodene is nosy and asked about it. She wants the bird for herself—to entertain the patrons—but they refused. Garibaldi wasn't happy about that." He looked at Henry. "I don't know why I didn't think of this before, but I'll bet my life on it that your family is at the circus those men are from. It's a big operation and known for its animals..."

Henry listened intently.

"The animals are transported by train. Once a week, after they bring in the big animals by ship from overseas, they load them onto a train, which passes through the Craggybog depot. A train will come early tomorrow morning, in fact, which is why those men are here tonight; they're scouts looking for animals in our neck of the woods. They stop here overnight while they wait to catch a ride back to the circus. I'll bet that train will take us right to the place you're looking for."

"Alister!" Rodene shrieked from inside the kitchen.

He cringed. "All right, wait here and hide. I'll come get you as soon as I can. When I get a second, I'll bring you some food— you look really hungry. There's some water over there for now," he whispered, then disappeared through the door.

Henry crept under a patch of scraggly shrubs and found the

little water bowl Alister left out for stray animals. He lapped up the water thirstily.

Alister entered the kitchen, tiptoeing so the slanted wooden floorboards wouldn't creak. He stirred the soup simmering in the iron kettle, then peered into the tavern through the swinging doors. Rodene and Garibaldi were busily socializing with the patrons, so he grabbed a fresh loaf of bread, dunked it into the soup, then placed it in a bowl. He ran back outside to Henry. "Here's something to hold you over for now," he told him. "I promise I won't leave you out here all night."

He dashed back through the kitchen and into the tavern. It was bustling at both the bar and the dining tables, with fifty hungry and thirsty customers waiting to be served. As usual, not a seat was empty. Card players, business folk—respectable and not so respectable alike—shysters, locals, and wealthy travelers all sat elbow to elbow. A saloon pianist had come to stay at the inn and was plunking away on the upright piano. His tip jar held a few meager coins, and those were the ones he had placed in it himself. The conflicting aromas of fine cooking and the stench of the musty, smoke-filled saloon combined and filled the air.

Alister dutifully choked back his disgust. Another night of insults from the ungrateful customers, another day being worked to the bone. But he served everyone efficiently, filling their mugs and tankards, trying his hardest to block them from his thoughts. He had plans now and it wouldn't be much longer until he was free; he set his sights on that.

And yet, he couldn't resist taking an interest in a peculiar gentleman at the back-corner table—at least he appeared to be a gentleman at first glance. He stood out from the rest in part due to his unusual attire. It wasn't a modern military uniform, but more antiquated and of some foreign origin, which gave him an air of sophistication. But his primitive, almost ape-like body movements and ragged clothing quickly dispelled that illusion.

Upon closer look, Alister noticed his arms were exceptionally long and hairy, and that he moved about in an awkward manner. He smoked a cigar and with difficulty lifted his tankard, which was overflowing with frothy humberth, a special, tart, and potent drink that Grotelby had invented himself, the ingredients secret, and changing slightly every day with whatever was on hand. Today's version involved lyleberry, sour currant, beet, and lemon juices, and honey mead. The gentleman was completely silent, merely nodding or tipping his hat if someone happened to look his way. A very small monkey was clinging to his back, looking around intently, which drew even more attention.

Alister watched amusedly trying to figure them out, but his attention was diverted when two men barged into the tavern, loudly arguing.

"Aww, it'll be too much trouble to catch 'em, he looks pretty wily! *And*, his fur is scruffy and dirty. It's not worth the time, Mudd," argued the first man, who was shorter and more petite of the two, with short, dark hair, and olive skin. He smiled a wide, bright smile, hoping to appeal to Mudd's sensible side.

They sat down at a nearby table. "Not worth the time? What are you talking about, Oliver?" Mudd finally replied loudly. He aggressively fiddled with his oddly coiffed red-brown hair which was parted on the side, brushed sideways and stopped just short of becoming a pompadour.

Oliver shrank back in his seat.

"He'll clean up and we both know the Boss would certainly be interested in a dog of that stature. You saw him, he's enormous." He rubbed his ruddy hands together in delight.

Alister listened intently. He knew who the two men were. But a third man that he didn't recognize, with sharp features, an antagonistic gate, and much more solidly built than the other two, came in and joined them.

"Look what the cat dragged in," Mudd snorted as Ghant sat down with them.

"Evening, Ghant," Oliver said with a nod.

Mudd turned back to Oliver. "Look, who's the scout here? Whose job is it to recognize the exceptional? Mine. That's what I'm here for. You're here to do what I tell you. And why are you even here?" he asked, directing the last question at Ghant.

Ghant curled his lips and stared at Mudd with piercing eyes so blue Alister could see the color and rage in them from far away.

"Théodore would be thrilled if we brought in a dog like that," Mudd continued. "He looks like Azalea and her lot, except he's much, much bigger."

"But we already got a bird, a pretty neat looking bird at that," Oliver moaned. "Isn't that good enough for now?" He raised his thick, dark eyebrows. "All I want to do is eat, drink, then go to sleep. I don't want to spend any more time working for the boss than I have to."

Alister saw the man in the military uniform had taken an interest in their discussion.

"You don't want to end up like Bernard, now, do you, Oliver," Ghant said in a way that was more like a threat than a question.

Mudd clucked. "No one wants to end up like Bernard."

"The boss is a beast, a flippin' horrible man. What am I doing working for him anyway? This is no life," Oliver whined into his drink.

"Where do you think you're gonna go? There's nowhere else. You don't know a thing about living life outside the circus. I'm *sure* the Boss would be pleased to let you go if he thought you were that unhappy," Mudd replied with sarcasm.

Oliver cringed.

"He'd off you in a heartbeat if he thought your loyalty was wavering," Ghant said with a gleeful laugh. Mudd laughed with him, which made Ghant angry. "What's so funny, eh? You got nothing to worry about, you smug boss's-right-hand man."

"Pfft," Mudd said, brushing off the hostility, which only further inflamed Ghant. "It's settled then. We're gonna get that hound and take him with us tomorrow. Train comes by at six o'clock in the morning sharp, so you'd both better be in tip top shape by then and be ready with the bird *and* the dog." Mudd picked up his tankard and took a drink, not taking his eyes off Ghant.

Ghant narrowed his eyes and turned away. That's when the silent man caught his attention, and he realized he had been watching them and listening.

Alister had heard every word, too. He was certain they were discussing the circus Henry was looking for, and now he knew they needed to get to the station for the six o'clock train...without them capturing Henry first.

Garibaldi returned to the tavern from the kitchen wearing his signature red apron as he made the rounds, greeting customers as they entered.

"Hey, Garibaldi, how much for your mutt?" Mudd yelled over the din of the crowd.

"Eh? My dog?" He walked over to the table.

"The beast. The mangy wolfhound out front." Mudd paused. "I see. So, he's not yours then, eh? That makes things easy." He looked over at Oliver and Ghant.

"Ah, my dog," Garibaldi said, remembering the animal in the alley. He wrinkled his nose. "Settle yourself down, Mudd. He's my prize, and he will cost a pretty penny if you want him. Ninety smacks."

Rodene was nearby, listening in, and scurried over. "One hundred...and the bird, too," she demanded.

Mudd laughed. "I already told you, we're not letting that bird go for any price, sweetums, so you can just forget it."

"Don't you talk to Rodene like that," Garibaldi said, getting in his face. "I know that bird's in your room and it would be easy as pie for us to just take 'em if we wanted."

"No deal. I'm not even going to bother *paying* for the dog, now. If you don't hand them both over, I'll make sure that Théodore sees to it this place gets shut down."

Garibaldi laughed. "Théodore, eh. Well, if I tell him *you're* coming here and causing trouble, you'll be the one getting shut down!"

Oliver was happy that something more exciting than catching a dog was happening, so he joined in. "Back off, *Mister Sweetums!*" he shouted at Garibaldi.

"What are you staring at, you big buffoon?" Ghant shouted at the silent man before Garibaldi could respond to Oliver. He got out of his seat and walked over, pulling his shoulders back, ready to fight.

But the silent, hairy-armed man simply pulled the cigar out of his large mouth, leaned in casually toward Ghant and breathed out, belching directly into his nostrils.

"Aw, that's awful! Sewer breath!" he shouted, waving his hands and fanning the smoke and odor away. He composed himself. "Listening in on our private conversation, eh? Do you have a problem or something, you big ugly…thing?"

Without warning, the silent man stood up abruptly. He was considerably larger than any of them expected—even Ghant backed away slightly—and he effortlessly flipped the heavy wooden table he had been sitting at, onto its side. A lantern had been on the table and it toppled off, along with three heavy brandy glasses and his tankard full of humberth. Everything crashed to the ground, smashing and splashing, and causing everyone to jump in their seats.

Ghant remained still, unsure what he'd gotten himself into. On a normal day he would have countered with a walloping punch, but his knees were quivering. He tried to hide it.

174

Mudd, who was tired of arguing with Garibaldi, came over to see what the commotion was. He saw the mess on the ground then attempted to swing at the silent man, not because he cared to defend Ghant, but because it seemed like something entertaining to do.

The silent man dodged the blow and swiftly grabbed Mudd by the hand. He squeezed it and bent it behind his back.

Mudd tried to retract his hand, but he was quickly flipped over, and he slammed onto the ground. He cried out in pain. "You know martial arts, eh? Looking for somewhere to perform by chance?" he wheezed as he lay there, stunned and waiting for his breath to return fully. Stillness fell over the tavern patrons as everyone gawked at the scene. Then everyone went wild.

They cheered, celebrating the brawl and joining in the skirmish, smashing their glasses against the walls, throwing wild punches, and wrestling each other to the ground. A body soared through the air after one overzealous customer grabbed the pianist and tossed him across the room. He landed hard, but he jumped up and threw his arms in the air like he was a champion. Everyone cheered louder.

But the fight escalated, and quickly turned fierce. Everyone—that is except for a few of the more respectable patrons who ran out the front door of the tavern, and also Oliver who had fled to his room to hide—began to fight ruthlessly. Bottles and fists flew. Rodene was running about swatting anything that came near with her mop. The din was so loud no one could hear Garibaldi's angry shouts.

Meanwhile, amidst the chaos, the lantern that had fallen to the ground was still lit and had ignited the leg of a nearby chair. The flame grew, spreading along the floor. Yet for the moment it went unnoticed.

No one saw that a giant Morlish wolfhound had entered the tavern, either. Even Mudd and Ghant were so busy brawling they had forgotten completely about him.

Henry had come to help Alister, swiftly making his way over to the back of the bar where he was hiding. The unexpected chaos had created the perfect opportunity to escape and the two of them quickly communicated a plan, then headed toward the door. But just before they exited, Henry saw the silent man with the monkey on his shoulder, standing aside and observing the pandemonium they had started. He dashed over to them.

Alister could see tell Henry was communicating with them. Then, amidst the shouts, the tinkling of breaking glass, and the crashes of airborne furniture, the silent man and his monkey slipped out of the tavern and up the darkened stairs to the adjoining inn.

Henry returned to Alister's side and Alister led the way to the door intending to make a break for the train depot.

"Hey, where're you going!" Rodene shrieked when she saw him.

He turned back to see Garibaldi lumbering after him, his towel still draped over his shoulder. But there was a surge of screams and a stampede erupted when the tavern patrons discovered the growing fire and rushed toward the door. They quickly fled into the street as smoke billowed out of the inn and engulfed Alister and Henry in the confusion.

"Alister Grotelby, get back here!" Garibaldi shouted, but it was too late.

Once far away from the tavern, Alister turned to take one final look at the burning building in the distance. He shook his head. "Come on, Henry, let's go," he sighed.

They quickly turned off the road and slipped into the woods under the cover of darkness. As they ran, the Messenger trailed them to the station from the sky.

18

Wildflower

Alister awoke, tense and unsure where he was. He clenched his right hand into a fist, ready to clobber anyone who might happen to come near, then looked around in confusion. He was beneath the rusty iron leg of a train trestle perched at the top of a deep ravine, with a very large dog sleeping next to him. Below, a branch of the Iveria flowed past. Then the memories came rushing back—meeting Henry, the fight at the tavern, the escape, the bird called the Messenger, and the mysterious apelike being with the monkey on his shoulder. More snippets from the night before returned. He remembered everything. After fleeing the tavern, he and Henry had made a run for the train station during the fire.

The fire.

They had fled the scene while it was still burning, so he was unsure how it had ended for the Grotelby's, or if the inn was even still standing. But he cared little to know; he was finally free, and his only hope was to never see Garibaldi or Rodene again.

When they had reached the station, it was boarded up for the night, but the bird and the silent man with the monkey were there waiting. Monkey was no longer wearing his archaic military uniform. Their reappearance had surprised him, though Henry seemed to know they would be there. This time, Alister had been able to understand everything conveyed between them. He learned that the bird, as well as the strange duo—Monkey, as Henry referred to them collectively—were from Kellandale Wood. Deep into the night, the pouring rain and the cold air had driven them to seek shelter. Down the tracks and around a bend Alister had found the bridge, and he and Henry had climbed down, wedging their bodies into the rocks so they would not fall into the ravine as they slept.

Alister sat up and rubbed his eyes. The chill of the dawn air hit his damp clothing. He shivered, pulling his arms around himself, then looked over at Henry, who was still fast asleep. "I hope I did right by you," he said quietly. He looked around for the Messenger and Monkey, but they were not there. He stood up, brushing the dirt from his trousers and coat and moving his body around. He turned to Henry. "Hey, fella," he said, waking him.

Henry roused himself. He stretched his long legs, flexing his toes, and wagged his tail softly.

"I think we slept pretty hard, though I'm not sure how, considering our accommodations. I hope we didn't miss that train. We'd have to wait another week, because I don't know how to find the circus without it."

Henry stood up and together they climbed the embankment, intending to walk along the tracks back to the depot. Just then, there was a deep rumble and the trestle above shuddered as it grew louder. A train whistle sounded in the distance.

"Son of a mop bucket, we missed it," Alister muttered. He watched as the nose of the train appeared from around the bend, then he ducked back down beneath the trestle with Henry. "It's not going very fast yet. We can jump on as it passes by."

Henry understood him and got ready to leap.

Alister wasn't sure his plan was the best idea, but he didn't want to let Henry down. He closed his eyes to concentrate, but opened them again as a loud crack cut through the air, followed by a dull thud as something heavy dropped onto the tracks just above them.

The train whistle blew again, this time long and loud, then the train came to a full stop with a piercing squeal of grinding metal.

Alister covered his ears, then nodded toward the embankment. Together they crept back up to see what had happened. The train was a mere twenty feet away and had stopped just short of hitting a mammoth-sized, uprooted, dead tree now splayed across the tracks. Alister could see through the underside of the train as a pair of enormous, ape-like feet flitted by, disappearing into the woods on the other side. A bird called out from the treetops.

Alister looked up, then back to the tree trunk and smiled to himself. Quickly, he scrambled behind a large boulder. Henry followed. Alister crouched down and looked up at the train, just barely able to make out the words *"Amazing Feats"* painted on one of the cars. The rest of the letters were chipped off, but the fanciful images of animals were a giveaway. "This is our ride, all right," he said to Henry. "Looks like Monkey and the Messenger made it possible for us to get on after all."

The conductor disembarked and three men emerged from the car behind the engine room to join him. They all walked to the front of the train.

Alister groaned when he saw it was Mudd, Ghant, and Oliver. They had obviously made it to the train depot from the tavern despite their eventful night, though without the prized bird or dog. To Alister's relief, they hadn't spotted him or Henry.

"What happened!" Mudd snapped as he surveyed the damage.

"The wind?" the conductor suggested weakly.

"The wind? There isn't even enough of a gentle breeze to bend a daisy!"

The argument that followed, along with the droning of the idling train engine, gave Henry and Alister the perfect opportunity to slip on board without anyone noticing. "Over here, Henry," Alister said as he reached up and grabbed the latch of the nearest train car and opened it slowly. Henry quickly jumped in.

They could hear Mudd barking more orders off in the distance just as two more men, neither of whom had been at the tavern, emerged. "Hey, boss!" one of them called out.

"What is it, Byron?" Mudd shouted back at the man.

"Looks like we got a hop-on. Saw some legs scrambling into car three."

Mudd looked back at the train with annoyance. "Freeloader, eh? Come here and help get that consarned tree out of the way; I'll take care of it."

Byron walked to the front of the train as Mudd stormed over to the car and slid the door open abruptly.

Alister froze. His mind raced trying to figure a way out, but Henry's thoughts washed over, steadying his nerves. He also connected the dots, recognizing that Mudd had played a crucial part in Henry's past.

While Mudd didn't recognize Henry as such, he did recognize him as the prize he had wanted to capture the night before, and he knew Alister from the tavern. "Well, look who we've got here. Not only did I not have to pay a dime, but I didn't even need to lift a finger to catch that giant. You made it easy for me, lad. I thank you for that. I'll just keep the dog, and you can hop right back off this train and get yourself back to town. The tavern was looking pretty rough when we left, but the inn is still standing. Right, get out son, I'll handle the dog from here," he chuckled.

Henry continued to silently communicate with Alister, giving him an idea.

He followed Henry's lead. "I don't think so," Alister said to Mudd. "This dog is wild and unruly. You're not going to be able to handle him without my help. I'm the only one he will listen to."

Henry snarled to show Mudd exactly how unruly he was.

"It's all right, boy," Alister said, pretending to subdue him.

Henry immediately sat down at his command.

Alister turned to Mudd. "We have a bond. He listens to me, and only me. So that means wherever I go, he goes with me. Take me with you, and I promise I'll look after him and I will teach him amazing tricks. Anyway, you can't make me go back to Craggybog. It's miserable, and I've got nowhere else to go."

Mudd looked at Alister suspiciously. He reached out to grab Henry, who growled fiercely and snapped at his hand. He backed away.

Alister watched Mudd without breaking his gaze.

"I'm not so sure about this, kid. You're just another mouth to feed and I'm not sure the boss will go for that." He paused for a moment, then hollered to the front of the train. "Ghant Louis, get over here!"

He stormed over.

"Seems like you might have a purpose after all."

Ghant's eyes blazed.

"What can you do with this beast? Make him listen to you."

"Here boy," Ghant said gruffly to Henry, attempting to coax him out of the train. Henry didn't budge so he stepped up into the car and approached him. "I know who you are, you mangy mutt. We were gonna snatch you up at the tavern. Come on then, don't make me get rough."

181

Henry's fur bristled as he stood up to reveal his full size. He showed his teeth.

Ghant lurched backward. "He's a wily one. Forget it, he'll be too much work, and we've already got wolfhounds that look just like him," he said, stepping out of the car.

"Here boy," Alister said to Henry. Henry turned and wagged his tail at Alister again. "Up!" Alister commanded. Right on cue Henry reared up on his back legs.

Alister looked back at Mudd and Ghant with a grin.

"Ready!" a voice from the front of the train shouted.

Mudd stepped forward to get a look. "All right, everyone back on! That means you, too, Ghant," he ordered.

Ghant sniffed and walked off.

Mudd turned back to Alister. "You might think it's miserable back at the tavern, but you have no idea what you're getting yourself into, son."

Alister didn't flinch.

"All right, you pesky kid. We need to get moving. You got lucky; you can hitch a ride with your dog. But remember, he belongs to us now—you're just here to handle him. And you'd better be prepared to pull your own weight." He slammed the door shut.

A few moments later the train began to creep forward. As it picked up speed, Alister searched for a spot to sit down, unsure how long of a ride they were in for. In the dappled light weakly shining through the spaces between slats of the car, he and Henry could just make out the shape of a small animal riding with them. It was facing the wall and its feet were shackled with chains to a bolt on the floor. Shriveled, dusty hay was spread around for food, but the animal's head was hanging low and it showed no interest in its surroundings.

There was a jolt as the train lurched forward. The animal tried to maintain its balance, but the movement caused it to knock its head into the wall. Its rear legs buckled from the impact, and it fell to the ground.

Alister quickly rushed over to help and it turned to look up at him, quivering. It was very small—a tiny Rahsican grey elephant, just a baby.

She was breathing hard. She coiled her tiny trunk in the air repeatedly, trying to soothe herself.

Alister could understand her and realized that because Henry was beside him, he could communicate with her in the same way they could. "Don't be frightened," he said.

The tiny elephant was confused and instinctively shrank back, but when Henry looked into her eyes she relaxed. He told her his story, and Alister's. Then images of her capture raced through their minds.

Her family, while searching for water, had become entangled in hunters' traps. Then they were attacked, and many of them were killed. Then more men, different men than the hunters, had appeared and captured her. Other elephants who had heard her cries had come to help, but they, too, were attacked as she was taken away. She was put on a ship, then loaded onto the train by some of the very same men who were there now. She was far from her homeland and mourning her family, alone and frightened, with no hope of returning.

Henry moved over to her and lay by her side. Alister did the same, leaning his head next to hers. "All three of us are without family, now," he said. "But we can be family to each other, if you want." She wound her tiny trunk around his arm and he patted her gently.

Henry conveyed to her about his family at the circus. He promised she could trust them, and that they would take her to Kellandale to a new, loving family one day.

"You need a name," Alister said gently.

She rumbled softly, her long eyelashes reflecting in the light. There was a tiny dandelion lying in the hay next to her and she picked it up in her trunk, offering it to him.

"How about we call you Wildflower," he said with a smile.

For the first time since she had been captured, Wildflower had a moment of feeling safe, protected, and even loved. It helped ease her fear and deep sadness, even if just a little bit.

The train picked up speed, taking them to a place they did not wish to be taken. For the time being there was no other choice, but they had each other now. There was power in numbers, and now there was hope. The newfound comfort that came with a sense of unity allowed them all to drift into a quiet slumber as they raced onward to their new home together.

19

Arrival at the Circus

"Move it you ghastly beast," a stocky man wielding a bull hook screeched at Henry. He jabbed at him with the hook in manner that seemed more out of pleasure than necessity, prodding him forward into a long line of slow-moving animals.

Henry recognized him from the train and knew he wasn't friendly, but he refrained from taking his hand into his mouth to stop him as he knew it would not end well. Instead, he glanced back, searching desperately for Alister and Wildflower. It was early afternoon, and he hadn't seen them since their arrival at the circus training grounds after they had disembarked from the train and been forcefully separated.

"I said go on, get!" The man said, furrowing his thick, unruly, auburn brows at him; this time he used his foot against Henry's ribs to move him.

Henry yelped, then snarled viciously. To be sure, the kick hurt, but he channeled the pain into a disproportionately formidable growl to show he was the uncontrollable beast Alister had claimed him to be. Inside, however, he felt very vulnerable.

The handler pulled his foot away quickly and raised his bull hook above his head in retaliation.

"Byron! I told you to keep that dog with the boy. Idiot, hold up!" Mudd's voice came from behind and the line stopped moving at his command. He pushed Alister and Wildflower forward toward Henry.

Byron froze and stroked his meager chin scruff, his pale cheeks suddenly flushing in embarrassment.

"Leave him alone!" Alister shouted, rushing at him. He had been leading Wildflower by a short rope, and she trotted to keep up. When they caught up to Henry, Alister grabbed Byron's arm and held it firmly in the air, knocking the hook out of his hand.

Byron tried to wrestle his arm free, but Alister was too strong. He bared his teeth and growled.

Ghant was close by and had seen the scuffle. He sauntered over and roughly pushed Alister's arm away, stepping between them.

Byron shook his arm free dramatically and spit at Alister, then picked up his bull hook.

"Who do you think you are, ordering Byron around like that? I told him to get that dog through the inspection line, and that's what he's gonna do," Ghant snapped, giving Alister a shove.

"Ghant!" Mudd shouted, suddenly stepping out from behind. They locked eyes. "The boy, the dog, and the elephant stay together. The boy is going to train them, and they're under *my* watch. You have a problem with that, you'll have to get past me."

Henry moved to Alister's side defensively.

"Train them? *Him?*" Ghant scoffed.

"I can handle them," Alister replied coolly.

"Boss has already been apprised of the situation," Mudd said to Ghant.

His lip curled into a snarl and he feigned another a swipe at Alister. "Is that a fact. *Sir*," he hissed at Mudd.

Mudd remained still.

In frustration, Ghant turned to face Alister again. "You'd better hope those animals can learn some snazzy tricks really fast or else..." he trailed off and motioned his finger across his neck, then laughed wickedly.

"Get outta here!" Mudd boomed.

"I've got my eye on you, boy," Ghant called over his shoulder as he stormed off. Byron scuttled away at his heels.

Alister made note of the interaction between Mudd and Ghant.

Mudd shook his head. "Ghant Louis is a proper menace, always trying to climb the ranks and make trouble. But he's not wrong; when the boss is mad, it's bad for everyone. He can be a bit...unpredictable. No one wants to press their luck with him.

"Meanwhile, don't forget what I said—you're here to handle and train the dog and the elephant and nothing more. Get in line here so they can process the lot of you, then keep your head down, do your job, and things might not be so rocky for you. Now get moving!" he ended his speech with a shout to keep Alister on his toes. He sauntered off, leaving Alister with Henry and Wildflower to navigate on their own.

Alister stepped forward in line, which led them into a poorly ventilated arena on the outskirts of the circus training grounds. This was where the newest human and animal acquisitions were judged for their potential value. The people, most of whom were intended for the side show acts, were divided up and moved into the sprawling tent encampments. Those who weren't of use this way, or as performers, became hard laborers to keep the training ground operating.

Meanwhile, the stronger animals and the more unique specimens were fast tracked into cages and assigned to a trainer. The other unfortunate animals, those too ill or weak to perform, or without some sort of potential show value, were made use of in other ways—and those ways were some of the secrets the circus liked to keep from the general public.

Wildflower walked slowly, cowering behind Alister. She had been handled roughly when she had been loaded off the train, before Mudd had placed her under Alister's care. Her legs trembled, watching how the handlers were treating the animals. Their calls of distress filled the air. Some of the people were visibly distraught, and others were openly crying, but most just looked lost. Now and again a man with a dirtied apron would appear and haul away a wagon loaded with the animals that had been rejected. Those were taken to another barn at the back of the building.

It's all right, Henry and I are here with you. I promise I won't let anything happen to you, Alister conveyed to Wildflower. He felt her lean into him. Henry moved closely to her side and together he and Alister huddled around her as they walked.

"Hey, boy! Where'd you get that dog, anyway?" Byron barked as he passed by on his way to fetch another animal.

"He was lost and was wandering through town, so I took him in," Alister replied.

"Is that a fact. Mudd said you're the lout who hopped the train. I caught a glimpse of those weak legs of yours flailing around when you tried to get in the car. I was the one who ratted you out." He grinned a wide, smarmy grin.

"Mighty appreciative of that," Alister replied smoothly.

Byron moved closer. "Ghant and I could train that dog easily on our own, just so you know. If you don't watch out, you might find yourself not so useful around here. And what do you want coming to this place, anyway? No one comes here by choice. You a spy or something?"

"No. Mudd wants me here because Henry can do just about anything I ask. Same with Wildflower." He ignored the other questions.

"Henry and Wildflower, is it?" He lurched antagonistically at them but then had to catch himself from tripping over his own feet when the fur on Henry's back bristled.

Henry let out a long, low growl. Alister smiled.

"What's so funny," Byron snarled, but he noticed Mudd was watching. He signaled to another man to indicate that Alister and his companions had already been looked over and accepted, then he pushed them forward. "Have fun, Mr. Big Britches," he snorted.

Alister, Henry, and Wildflower were shuffled to a corner to await placement. Henry and Wildflower were destined to be kept in cages, and in Alister's case, some sort of living arrangement would be made for him in the tent city.

They stood together in silence, observing. The animal handlers were cruel, the environment raw and unforgiving. Wagons moved in and out, picking up animals. Others walked by on foot in a long procession, flanked by trainers. The horses pulling the wagons were skin and bones and whipped hard to make them move. Some of the more unmanageable or dangerous animals were transported in thick iron cages that were loaded onto the wagons.

Lions, tigers, ostriches, bears and bear cubs, alligators, poisonous snakes, and every other sort of animal one could think of, were shuffled around. There were plenty of very young animals in the mix, and they were treated just as roughly as those that were full-grown.

"This place is unbearable," Alister muttered.

Just then man dressed in tan trousers and a heavy button-down jacket approached. He looked to be in his thirties and was tall and muscular, with dark brown skin. He was walking slowly but purposefully toward Alister, Henry, and Wildflower. "You're certainly right about this place," he said to Alister. "I'm supposed to show you around and get you settled. "I'm Nigel," the man said, reaching out his hand.

Alister took it and they shook. Nigel's handshake was firm and strong, just like Alister's. They both nodded to each other.

"Follow me. Bring your dog and elephant with you, and keep your head low, got it?" he said as he led them away, leaving the processing arena behind.

"Usually, the animals are kept with their own kind." He nodded toward Henry and Wildflower. "Mudd wants you to stay with the dog and the elephant for some reason. But the dog and elephant can't live with the people, which I guess means you'll be staying with the animals, too." He laughed apologetically and stroked his goatee.

"Fine by me," Alister replied.

"Fine by me," Nigel echoed contemplatively. He pursed his lips and nodded, surprised by how amenable Alister was to the unusual living arrangements. "All right then," he added.

They walked silently through the tent city where the circus workers lived when the circus was camped during the off season. The air was ripe with the scent of rotten fruit and musty hay. The people looked exhausted, and empty bottles and trash littered the ground around them. A few of them gazed up at Alister and his companions. They showed no sign of emotion, or that they had even noticed anyone was walking past.

A wave of despair hit Alister and he drew in a deep breath, wondering what he had gotten Henry and Wildflower into.

"Yeah. I know what you mean," Nigel said, noticing the look on his face. "They don't have anywhere else to go now, so at least they have a place here. The Boss keeps them content enough, I guess. That's what I'm supposed to say, anyway." They continued moving through the camp. "Everyone does get a bit of a buzz when the circus is touring, at least…"

Alister frowned.

"I know, I know. This would've been your place." Nigel pointed to an unoccupied tent slightly larger than the rest. "Would have been a nice spot. Fast Man Dan lived there until the other week, but he's not—he's not with us anymore. He did some impressive stunts in his time, but he was getting a little weak in the britches, not pulling his weight, so, well, he's not with us anymore." He sniffed and tightened his jaw. "Not worth feeding and housing, I suppose is what they figured." He wrinkled his nose and sniffed again, running his hand over his short, spiky afro.

"I'm really sorry," Alister replied quietly, sensing his sadness.

This response really surprised Nigel. He looked hard at Alister, his eyes intensely trying to read him, but the sternness of his gaze was quickly eroded by a gentle smile that formed on his lips. He sighed. "Thanks, kid," he said, then he continued leading them along on a smaller path.

In the distance through a patch of trees, Alister could see another group of much larger tents—separate living quarters that were notably more luxurious than the others he had seen so far.

"That's where the Boss and his men and the star performers live. Don't ever get caught going over there," Nigel warned. Alister nodded to show he understood.

As they walked out in the open Alister noticed a large shadow seeming to be following them. He looked up to see the Messenger flying above them.

Finally, they walked past a large, red barn. "That's where you'll start your training," Nigel pointed. "Front of the barn is the arena where you'll go. Back of the barn and the other buildings behind them are all strictly off limits. You don't want see what goes on there, anyway."

Alister turned back to give it a good look. He shook his head, unable to fathom Henry had been born into this place.

They strolled for another hundred yards then Nigel led them to a large stable. "The bigger animals and the ones that need more warmth are kept inside here. You'll have some neighbors—horses, a zebra, and maybe you'll see the giraffe or musk ox now and again." He waved Alister, Henry, and Wildflower inside; the sound of a horse's hoof kicking violently against a stall door startled them.

"That's Alexander. He's always angry," Nigel said, walking over to a dark corner where there was a larger stall that could temporarily house Wildflower while she was young. This was next to two smaller stalls; one was meant for Henry, and the other for Alister. "I would've put your dog with his own kind—we've got others that look exactly like him, except they're a bit smaller—but Mudd has all kinds of crazy ideas. He doesn't want your dog mixing with the others. He thinks they'll ruin his potential."

Henry's ears pricked up at his words. Alister took note, too.

Nigel pointed for them to enter. "He wants you to stay near the dog and the elephant and keep them in your sights at all times while they're training. He said the dog's too wily for anyone else to handle."

"If you don't mind, Henry and I will stay together with Wildflower in her stall," Alister replied.

"Henry and Wildflower, is it? Suit yourself. Settle in then, they'll call you for supper and show you the ropes later. Do your best—Mudd expects them to impress the Boss in a few days."

"I'm not worried about that."

"You don't seem as worried as you should be. Just keep an eye out; folks around here aren't too kind to one another."

"Why don't you all just leave if it's as awful as you say, and it certainly looks as though it is. Anywhere else would be better than this. Except for Craggybog, maybe, but I think I would almost pick that over this place."

"Huh," Nigel replied. There was a faraway look in his eye. "I only know a few who have tried to leave, and it didn't end well for them. Everyone's either so afraid that they don't make a move, or else they have some big ideas about trying to please the Boss to move up in the ranks to try to cope. Funny, you just don't seem to be callous and calculating like most everyone else here."

"Well, I'm not like the rest of them. It doesn't seem like you are, either."

Nigel smiled faintly, but warmly. "Oh yea, well…" he mumbled. "Glad to hear that."

"You said there are others that look like him," Alister said, motioning to Henry. "Where are they?"

"Be careful asking too many questions," Nigel warned, then he paused. "I guess there's no harm in telling you. You'll probably run into them sooner or later, anyway. They're off in the other stable where the dogs and smaller animals are kept. Why, do you think you can train them, too?"

"Perhaps," Alister said, lying down in a pile of hay. He put his hands behind his head and stretched his legs. "You don't happen to have a blanket or two, do you?"

Nigel laughed. "A blanket, huh? Now, don't get cocky—you're lucky you have a space here at all. The Boss would tear you apart if he suspected you had too many needs." He walked off, but called back much more gently. "If I find one, I'll bring it to you, yeah?"

"Thank you," Alister called after him. "Well, here we are, home sweet home, my friends." He sighed.

Henry and Wildflower lay down next to him and they quickly began to drift off to sleep. Moments later they were awakened to the sound of the Messenger landing on the stall windowsill. Monkey was behind him, hiding in the woods next to the stable.

Both Monkey and the Messenger were beginning to weaken from being away from the forest for so long, and they were preparing to leave. The Messenger offered to bring news to everyone back home, but Henry asked that he refrain from divulging his location and details of the conditions in which he would be living, fearing the children would come looking for him. The Messenger flapped his wings and bade them farewell, then he and Monkey set off on their long journey back to Kellandale Wood.

"We'll get out of here soon," Alister reassured Henry and Wildflower.

As they lay there, Henry began to share more about his human family. Memories of them poured out and washed over Alister and Wildflower. Henry sighed, thinking of the happy times walking through the forest or lying next to the fire with Velvet by his side.

Wildflower trumpeted softly as she listened.

Alister caught a glimpse of Elinora, Tillie, and everyone else at Kellandale in his mind, and it made him smile. "I wish I knew them, too. I can already tell they are good people," he said wistfully. "I promise I won't let any of you down. We will get you and your family where you belong, and I won't stop until we do it."

20

Lovii's Sweet Shop

It had been only two days since Henry had been gone, but back at Kellandale he was missed so terribly that a haze of sadness clouded every waking moment. To help, Abigail had arranged a carriage ride to Waterbridge, which was a welcomed distraction from the sorrow plaguing Elinora, Tillie, Graham, and Jamie.

The trip had a two-fold purpose—Abigail had asked Emil to drive them into town that evening for dessert at Lovii's, but she had also encouraged them to inquire about the circuses that come to town. "Lovii and Lucerne know everyone and everything that goes on in Waterbridge. I'm sure they will be able to help you in some way," she had said.

The ride was a beautiful jaunt through the forest to the northwest, about forty minutes by horse and carriage. En route they crossed the bridge from which Elinora and Tillie had seen Henry dropped into the river.

To keep their spirits up while they traveled, Jamie played a game he called Worst Dessert—a thinly veiled excuse to disgust Tillie for entertainment's sake wherein he named stomach-turning sundae combinations, then dared her to eat them. Her favorite thus far was his Triple Beast, an anchovy-flavored ice cream topped with earthworms, marmalade, and capers.

"I'll be ordering one of those as soon as we get to Lovii's," she threatened.

"Ottilie the Unflappable," he replied.

After driving a bit longer, they reached town. Emil hitched the horses to a post on the tree-lined side street, and the four of them emerged from the carriage.

"Thank you, Emil, we'll be back soon," Elinora said. "Would you like anything from the shop?"

"Take your time," they replied with a smile, holding up a book they planned to read while waiting. "And the usual, for me!"

Elinora nodded and smiled back.

Jamie made a quick stop to feed the horses a few carrots before they headed to the shop.

"Lovii's is just down this way," Tillie said, walking briskly. She turned the corner onto Main Street, already tasting the sodas and meringues in her mind.

"I remember being here when I was little," Jamie said when he spotted the cheery sign with two giant, candy stripe lollipops where the "i's" in *Lovii's* would be.

"You mean little-*er*," Graham said.

Jamie slugged him. "I was five. I was little then—I'm not now. And anyway, what's wrong with being little."

Tillie cackled. "All right, close your eyes, James," she said when they reached the storefront. She reached for his hand and led him up the step. The silver bell at the top of the door jingled as she opened it. "You can open them now but try not to go bananas;

196

pretty much every sweet you could ever ask for is here," she said as they entered the bright and colorful shop.

The aroma of homemade fudge, hot buttered caramel, and sugar-dusted delicacies, along with the sight of candy-jar lined walls and display cases filled with rainbow-colored desserts, overwhelmed their senses. Jamie gasped then hurried to a case overflowing with freshly made macarons and other delicate confections.

"Tillie! Elinora! How wonderful to see you!" called out a voice from the back of the shop. A moment later a short, curvy woman with long, black coils pulled back in a bright pink kerchief appeared. Her face was round, the tone of her skin dark brown, and her long, full eyelashes framed her kind eyes.

"Hello, Lovii!" Tillie exclaimed. She and Elinora raced over to give her a hug. Lovii embraced them tightly.

"Is Lucerne here today?" Elinora asked.

"Yes, I am!" came a voice from the back. Lucerne, taller than Lovii by about six inches, had long black, flowing hair, arched, black eyebrows and tawny skin. She waltzed into the room and embraced Elinora and Tillie warmly. "How are you, my darlings?" she asked.

"Happy to be here!" Tillie replied. "You remember our cousins, don't you? It's been a while since they've been here. Graham, Jamie, you remember Lovii, right? This is her partner, Lucerne. They run the shop together now." Graham and Jamie both smiled and greeted them both.

Lovii grinned, her hidden dimples revealed as she unleashed her infectious smile. "Graham O'Conor, is that really you?"

"Aye," he replied, taking off the hat and bowing.

"And that must be Jamie, but you're all grown up now. Last time I saw you, you were just a tiny sprout!"

"Hello, Lovii, hello Lucerne!" Jamie replied with a wave, looking up from the macarons. "I remember being here, even though I was so little, *before*." He grinned at Graham.

"Come, come, have a seat, all of you," Lovii offered, smoothing her candy-striped apron.

The four of them gathered around the long counter and climbed up into the tall, high-backed purple and white striped seats as Lucerne headed toward the shop door. "I'm off to the market to get the rest of the ingredients for the cakes we're making tomorrow, dear," she said, passing by Lovii and giving her a kiss on the forehead. She turned to the others. "I'm happy you caught me before I left so I had a chance to say hello!"

"Goodbye, Lucerne! See you later!" they called back and waved. The bell jingled as she exited the shop and closed the door.

"Now, what can I get you?" Lovii asked as they rocked back and forth in the swiveling chairs.

"One of everything, please," Tillie ordered very sincerely.

"Ah, yes, your famous, standing order, 'one of everything,' which would be a starter course of a meringue, with vanilla and caramel ice cream, I believe?"

"Correct!" Tillie laughed.

"Chocolate syrup and almond slivers on top?"

"Yes, please!" Tillie answered, wiggling in her seat.

The others gave their orders and Lovii began scooping ice cream, mixing shakes, and adding dollops of sauces and whipped cream on top of everything.

"Emil would like some custard, too," Elinora added.

"Of course!" Lovii replied.

While Lovii was preparing their treats, Graham asked her about the town's activities. "Summertime is probably exciting around here," he led in casually. "We will be staying with Elinora and Tillie until at least until the end of summer. I'll bet there'll be all kinds of things to do here in town—festivals and such, I imagine?" he asked, getting right to business.

"Oh indeed! I'm sure Elinora and Tillie have told you all about the parades and the traveling showmen and circuses that come through here. This shop never sees so much business as it does when they come to town in the summer. If I recall, your family was never one for attending the circuses though, am I right? I have to say, I am in agreement on that. Others seem to love it, but I feel for those poor animals when they're paraded out in the heat and made to do tricks. But I'm getting myself into another conversation altogether."

"So, which are the best circuses?" Jamie asked, trying to keep the conversation going.

"Oh, just give me a moment," she said, then bustled into to the back of the shop. Her muffled voice carried into the shop from the storeroom as she yelled, "I've got some things to show you that might help answer that!"

Jamie dug into his sundae as they waited. "This is nothing like the Triple Beast," he mumbled, stuffing a heaping spoonful of homemade vanilla ice cream topped with hot fudge, broken bits of toffee, and fresh whipped cream into his mouth.

Elinora sipped on her malt as Graham ate his homemade lemon roseberry ice cream cone. "This is amazing," he said when Lovii reappeared with a stack of large, colorful papers in her arms.

She smiled. "I thought you'd like that. My newest creation. I hope they'll be a hit this summer. Now, all of you, have a look at this. I've been collecting these over the years." She turned the stack over to reveal vibrant, colorful posters.

Circus posters.

Graham leaned in for a better look.

"All the traveling acts that come through here bring me these to post in my shop windows." She turned them around and pushed them forward toward Graham. "I don't like to advertise, but I keep them anyway—after all, they are rather nice looking. These are from last year."

"Thank you! This is great," he replied, reaching for the stack.

"You're welcome, dear." She began cleaning up when a few customers came in. She set down her bright, white-and-purple towel then took their orders while Graham leafed through the posters once he had finished his cone.

Elinora, Tillie, and Jamie climbed off their chairs to get a closer look. The posters were well designed and colorful. Each one declared *"The Biggest!"* or *"The Best!"* or *"The Most Bizarre in All the Land!"* Some of the posters announced acrobat troupes but had no animals. They put those aside. Some announced rare and daring human acts, and the more unusual they appeared to be, the more boastful they were about it. Some were classic circuses, with big top tents and the usual animals. They focused on those that seemed to look more like what they had seen in Henry's vision.

As they combed through the stack, Tillie noticed a circus solely for trick dogs. She picked it up and looked closely. There were dogs of all sorts, big ones, little ones, and a few other circus animals thrown in for good measure. In the foreground, the image of a large face was peering out at the reader. His garish smile summoned the viewer of the poster to *Come See! Harold Piston's Incredible Canine Stunts!* "Look at this one," she said pointing it out.

"Do you think it's where Henry is?" Elinora asked. She looked again. In the background were a few dogs almost as big as Henry, and they looked somewhat like him.

"It's possible," Jamie whispered.

Lovii came back over and tapped the poster. "I've never heard so much yapping going on as when these folks come through," she laughed. "At least Harold Piston seems to really love his dogs, though. Not many care for their animals like he does."

"When do they come around?" Graham asked.

"Early summer usually, but not always. They travel all over the country. Funny people, too. Mr. Piston himself has been in this shop many times."

"Do you know if they will be here this year?" Tillie asked.

"They like it to be a surprise to the town folk so they don't announce too much ahead of time, but they'll be here—maybe mid-August if I had to guess. That's when Stan Dillon and some of the others usually travel through here, too."

"We have a dog—he looks just like some of the dogs in this poster," Elinora said, showing it to Lovii. She sighed and caught herself almost starting to cry.

"We've lost him," Tillie said quietly. "He went outside the other morning on his own, and he hasn't come back yet."

Lovii looked at her with concern, "Ohh..." she started to say.

"He went looking for the rest of his family," Jamie blurted out, then covered his mouth.

But Elinora nodded. "It's all right, we should tell her," she said, and he explained.

"Why, that's the most horrible thing I've ever heard!" Lovii replied after Jamie, Tillie, Elinora, and Graham told her the whole story. "It is absolutely incredible what you say about the forest! And as for Henry, you're right in trying to help him—you've got to get him back, that's for sure." She stroked her chin. "If you say he looks like the dogs in Harold Piston's poster, perhaps that's where they are. I'm not sure where he is off season, but ask around town before you head home—maybe someone will know. I can do the same, and I'll send word to you if I find anything out."

"Thank you, Lovii," Elinora said, wiping away a tear.

She nodded. "I know you'll find them. If there's anything else we can do to help Henry, just ask. You know Lucerne and I will always be here for you." She looked at the four empty bowls on the counter. "Finished?" she asked.

"Yes—that was better than anything I've ever had, thank you," Jamie replied.

201

"Any time. Now good luck finding Harold's place, and I hope he's gracious and hands them over to you, where they belong."

They got up from their seats to leave. When Elinora reached over to pick up the poster, another one lying underneath was revealed, catching her attention.

Graham noticed her studying it. "Coddlefin's Amazing Feats and Extraordinary Traveling Menagerie," he read out loud.

"Oh, now *that*'s a production," Lovii said. The best of the best of them all, according to just about everyone. It's Théodore Coddlefin's circus."

All four of them looked up.

"Théodore," Graham said. He glanced over at the others. "That's the name we heard in the forest, Lovii."

"Is that so?" She shook her head.

"What more do you know?" Tillie asked.

"Well, his show is best in all the world. At least *he* says so," she said pointing to the poster. "Maybe it's true, and his audience sure believes it. He certainly knows how to dazzle. He's got so many people and so many animals in his show, all spectacular performers. They have it together, all right. Lions, tigers, elephants, and other animals. They've got trick horses and loads of acrobats, and the Sabre Sisters."

"Who are they?" Tillie asked.

"Two acrobats, and also highly skilled swordspersons. Coddlefin adopted them as children and they've grown up in the circus. They do crazy aerial stunts with knives and swords. And he certainly has dogs, more than Stan Dillon or Harold Piston combined, and so many different breeds."

"When do they come here?" Jamie asked.

"Every summer. But they keep their schedule even more secret than the rest. They create quite a stir when they come into town, usually just after dawn is all people can predict. But Coddlefin is a crafty man. His training ground is up north quite a way, and for a price he allows visitors to come in to watch them train in the off-season. Helps create excitement when they finally come around. He's outdone Stan Dillon's Magical Menagerie, which he's been aiming to do since the start—they're in big competition with one another.

"Dillon's big on all the exotic animals, but Coddlefin's got that, and even more. And his animals mind him, but I question how he gets them to perform so well." She shook her head. "If that's where Henry and his family are, Coddlefin might not be as amiable about surrendering them as Harold Piston would be."

"That's got to be where Henry is. How do we get there, Lovii?" Graham asked.

"I'm not exactly sure. The man isn't very social, and he and his people don't mix with the locals when they come to town, so I've never asked. But take that poster with you and show it to the stationmaster; he'll know where to send you."

"Thank you, this is exactly what we needed," he said, rolling it up. "How much do we owe you?"

"Today? Nothing," she said. "Hang on, I'll go grab Emil's custard and berries," she said, returning to the back of the shop.

While she was gone, Graham reached into his pocket and placed a stack of coins into a jar on the counter.

"Thank you kindly, Mr. O'Conor," Lovii said warmly, noticing this when she returned. She handed a small package sealed with one of her signature lollipop stickers to Graham then she folded her arms. "Now go find that pup of yours, will you?" she said. "Be sure to give everyone else a warm hello from me, too, and come back soon," she said as they walked to the door.

"We certainly will," Elinora replied.

Goodbye, Lovii!" Tillie exclaimed.

"See you next time!" Jamie shouted as the door was closing.

On the return home there was fervent discussion. They were certain they knew where Henry had come from, and now Tillie was determined to go to the training grounds to find him.

"How do you know if Henry has even made it there yet?" Elinora asked quickly. The same surge of fear she had felt the last time Tillie suggested going to the circus returned with a vengeance. "Monkey hasn't even returned with the Messenger yet. I think we need to wait to see what news comes first before we go anywhere."

"I can't wait any longer for news that may or may not ever come. We *know* where Henry is now, or at least where he is headed. The sooner we find him, the better," Tillie said firmly.

"Tillie's right," Graham said. "I'm going to have to side with her on this one, especially since they welcome visitors. I don't see any harm in trying to get there to have a look."

"I want to help Henry, too," Jamie said. "But what if something bad has happened to him and he's lost or hurt, and he isn't even there, like Elinora said. What if news does come and we're not there to get it?"

"Two versus two," Graham said, looking at Tillie.

She huffed. "If the Messenger or Monkey aren't back when we get home, I will be going to Coddlefin's circus immediately, even if I have to go alone."

There was silence as the carriage turned down the drive at Kellandale Manor. "Can we give it until tomorrow?" Graham finally asked. "If no news arrives by then, Wednesday we will pay him a visit." He looked at Elinora and Jamie. Everyone agreed that this was the plan, even Elinora.

When the horses reached Kellandale, they came to a halt. Graham opened the carriage door, stepped out, then held it open for the others. "So, it's settled then, right? Anyway, what harm could it be if Coddlefin is welcoming visitors to his training ground?"

21

Madelina

The very next morning, everyone was seated around the breakfast table, and as always, the aromas of Cora and Jeppe's freshly baked breads, savory curry, fresh brewed coffee, and tea filled the air.

Anna Wolton reached for the coffee carafe sitting in the center of the table to refill her cup. Rays of the sun, shining through the bank of leaded glass windows in the breakfast room, caught the steam rising from the pot as she poured. "We received a message from your father yesterday evening," she said, setting it back down.

"Oh, what did he say?" Elinora asked.

"They are making good progress, but there's so much that needs to be done yet. Your aunt Camille, Penelope, and I will be traveling to the city to join your fathers for a spell; they are very busy and need all the help they can get."

"That's very good news," Tillie said with delight. Getting to the circus training grounds was going to be much easier than she thought.

Lina was sitting at the far end of the table. She looked up quickly, trying to keep from crying, then she turned away.

Jamie frowned, saddened to see her so upset. "How long will you be gone?" he asked his mother quietly.

"A week or two at the most," she replied.

Abigail was also at the table. "Albert and I, and all the others will be here to take care of things, don't you worry," she reassured everyone.

"When do you leave?" Graham inquired.

"Emil and Simon will take us by carriage to Waterbridge Station early tomorrow morning," his mother replied.

Lina's face darkened. "Why do you have to go?" she suddenly snapped at her mother. "And why do you have to get so involved?" Everyone turned to look at her. She furrowed her brows and turned away again.

"Madelina," Penelope said with a sigh. "I promise we won't be gone for long."

"Two weeks? Why are you leaving me here alone with them. You and father are just so helpful to everyone, aren't you? But what about me?" Tears streamed down her cheeks as she spoke.

"I didn't think you'd mind so much. You'll be in good hands here with Abigail and the others, and perhaps you can visit Belladonna again."

Tillie looked at Lina. For the first time in a long while, they made eye contact; Tillie felt a surge of emotion and found herself wanting to protect Lina. But before she could say anything, Lina stood up, turned, and fled out of the breakfast room to her bedroom without another word.

Elinora sighed and looked down, unsure what to say. Tillie had a worried look in her eyes.

"Don't worry, dear," Abigail said to Penelope. "We will take good care of her. Simon made sure he picked up extra supplies for her last time he was in Waterbridge so she can continue painting while you are away, and I am sure Emil would be happy to take her to visit her friend if she wishes."

"Thank you," she replied quietly. "I'd better go check on her," she said excusing herself.

The others rose from the table and began to exit the room, but Anna, who remained seated, called Tillie over to her. She walked over without protest. "Tillie, this has gone on far too long—you must make peace with Lina."

"But she doesn't want my help, she doesn't like me," Tillie objected. But only half-heartedly.

"Why on earth do you keep saying that?" she asked, taking her hand. "I know for a fact she considered you her best friend—and she was yours. And I think it's still the case. You're both just too stubborn to be the first one to start the conversation, aren't you?"

Tillie sighed and nodded.

Anna gave her a sideways glance. "Talk to her, Tillie," she said.

She nodded again. "I will," she replied quietly.

"Good." Anna squeezed her hand, then let go.

Tillie left the room to catch up with the others, who were already outside on the terrace waiting to tell Mister and the council about their plans to visit the training grounds. She opened the sitting room door, but then hesitated. "Go on ahead, I'll catch up with you. I want to change my shoes," she said unconvincingly.

"All right," Elinora replied, looking at her feet quizzically.

"What's wrong with those shoes?" Jamie asked.

"Oh, never mind. I'll be there in a bit," she said then quickly disappeared.

Once upstairs, instead of going to her room, she turned the other way and headed down the hall to the guest wing. She had been so deeply affected by Lina's emotional reaction to the news of the trip that it surprised her. But she realized that her mother,

Jamie, and Henry had all been right. Although Lina's behavior toward her still confused her, Tillie was beginning to realize that maybe she had been so blinded by her own assumptions that she had never bothered to find out what the actual problem was, let alone admit to her own behavior toward Lina. But today she felt different. Resolved that she would not let Lina push her away this time, no matter how mad she might be, she walked to her room and knocked firmly on her door.

"I told you, I don't want to talk about it anymore, Mother," Lina's voice came from inside.

Tillie opened the door and peered in.

Lina was sitting on her bed and turned around when she heard the door open. Her dark brown eyes widened when she saw that it was Tillie standing there. "What do *you* want?" she asked.

"Why do you always have to do that?"

"Do *what?* Why are you in here! Why aren't you outside with the others? I know you'd much rather be with them." She turned her back, trying to retain an aggressive attitude, but it failed, and she began to cry.

"Lina," Tillie said softly, entering the room. It was filled with books and art supplies. Paintbrushes and used tubes of paint were scattered on a cloth on a little side table. Three easels were propped up in various places around the spacious room. Two held paintings of the gardens at Kellandale, and the third, a portrait of a wolfhound. Tillie smiled when she saw it.

"It looks just like Henry. I can tell you must practice every day; your paintings are incredible." She sighed. "Please talk to me, Lina. I know you're very sad about Henry being gone. I am, too. But I know there's more to your sadness. And I want to know why we are like this," Tillie said, motioning back and forth to herself and Lina.

Lina turned to look at her, her eyes still puffy. She bit her lip. "What does it matter? My mother is leaving me here with all of you, and I know you hate me. Please, just leave me alone."

"But I *don't* hate you. In fact, it's just the opposite—you hate me!" Tillie said, her voice strained.

"What?" Lina gasped. But she let Tillie continue.

"You have a new best friend and could care less about me anymore. You used to my best friend...and Elinora's, too. But once your family moved away and you made new friends, everything changed. You seemed to be much more interested in all the sparkly things, and you didn't want anything to do with me at all."

Lina frowned. "First of all, do you have any idea what my new friends are like? They're more interested in sparkly things and being impressive, just as you've said. But I'm not like that, and it's been very hard trying to keep up with all of that nonsense. I've had to spend a lot of time with Bella because she lives nearby, though sometimes I wonder if she is truly a friend. It was very difficult to move away. You've never had to deal with that, and it's all made me feel like I don't belong anywhere anymore."

Tillie's mouth fell open. She was surprised by how protective of Lina she suddenly felt. Her voice softened considerably. "You belong *here*. You always have...you know that."

Lina shook her head. "That's not what it feels like," she said, her lower lip quivering. "You have and Elinora, and you both have Graham and Jamie, and Henry—you all have someone you can trust. I don't. I did have that feeling with Henry for a time at least, but now he's gone."

Tillie came and sat down next to her. "So that's the reason you've been angry with me."

Lina huffed. "Tillie, I'm *not* angry. Don't you understand?" Lina's tears came faster and harder. "I did push you away—but not because I hated you. Not at all. I was anxious and felt alone. It made me sad and jealous knowing you and Elinora have each other no matter what, and when I got upset, it seemed like you didn't care at all. I know I didn't handle it well, but then you seemed so eager to believe I thought all those terrible things about you that you quickly accepted being my enemy." She looked up, then continued.

"Maybe I was silly to feel so hurt, but when you didn't even seem to notice why, I guess it did make me angry, and everything got jumbled up. I'm really sorry that's how things went."

Tillie's shoulders slumped. "I had no idea. I think I was hurt, too. But I've really missed you, just so you know. Terribly, to be honest. I also know you love Henry, and that he loves you back. I'm sorry, too, Lina." She wiped away a tear falling down her cheek. "I don't know why I couldn't bring myself to ask you what was wrong."

"Well, none of that matters now. We've figured it out," Lina said with a smile.

"We have, haven't we," Tillie replied.

Lina smiled and wiped her eyes.

"Silly how long it took. So, are we friends?"

"We're *best* friends," Lina replied, her smile widening. She nudged Tillie with her elbow, and at last they put their quarrel to rest.

Tillie reached out and they hugged tightly. Then she paused a moment. "Speaking of Henry, I need to ask. Were you able to talk to him? I mean, not talk, but…"

Lina nodded. "Yes. I could understand him. I know he was happy here. And I know he didn't want us fight. He encouraged me to talk to you, but silly me, I never listened. I also knew he was very sad for some reason, though I wasn't sure why. I didn't know if anyone else could communicate with him like I could—he seemed to keep it a secret."

"We can understand him, too," Tillie replied. "And he tried to tell me the same thing."

Lina's eyes widened as Tillie shared with her everything they had discovered. "I didn't realize how sad Henry was. He hid that well. So, the forest really is haunted," she said, thinking back on her experience.

"Haunted isn't the word I would use to describe it. It's more… magical. More than we even knew. Graham didn't believe us at all at first; he was the last to discover Henry could communicate the way he does."

"Why am I not surprised," Lina snickered.

Tillie laughed with her. "But I have to tell you. We know where Henry is now, or at least where he is headed."

Lina looked up. "What? How?"

"It's a bit complicated, but let's just say we made a discovery recently. We know he left to find his way back—to a circus where he came from, to find his family. When we visited Lovii's yesterday in Waterbridge, she helped confirm everything we suspected—now we even know exactly which circus it is."

"Tillie, what on earth are you waiting for? Why haven't you gone after him already!"

Tillie snorted. "I forgot how much alike we really are. I've been wanting to go after him since the day he left, it just took a while to convince everyone else. But now we will go as soon as possible. And I want you to come with us."

Lina looked up, her face brightening.

"I'm heading to the forest to meet the others right now to make plans, in fact. You want to help Henry, too, right? Come with me…he needs our help," Tillie pleaded. Lina hesitated briefly. "Lina, it's *not* haunted; I promise. Not in the slightest—I wish you'd trust me."

Lina reached for her hand and squeezed it, sighing deeply. "I do trust you, Tillie."

22

Visions

Tillie and Lina sat by the river's edge, stopping a moment to take in the view before continuing into the heart of the forest. Tillie was in her trousers, seated on the ground, resting her back against Ole Warty. Lina sat at the top of the embankment, dangling her legs over the edge, eyes transfixed on the clear rushing water below. "I saw something when I followed you out here," she suddenly confessed.

"When?" Tillie asked, then brushed it off with a laugh. "I suspected you might do something like that. What did you see?"

Lina scrunched her nose up. "Sorry," she said guiltily. "A monster or something; it looked like a fish or a serpent, but it was enormous. It peered out of the water and looked right at me."

"You saw The Lady of the Forest," Tillie gasped.

"Who?"

"I'll explain as we walk, but tell me, what did she look like?"

"I saw her eyes. They were very dark, and she had long and

colorful fins—greens and blues. But she startled me so badly I ran away, and she swam off."

"You must have been here that day we finally saw her. Graham is convinced she's a water dragon or a river serpent." She shared more of what they knew and told her about the day they found Henry.

Lina's eyes were glassy. "I'm so sorry, I can't imagine seeing Henry like that. I'm glad you were there to find him."

It was a peculiar moment for both, in one another's presence no longer as enemies, but as friends, and a united front at that. And although the absence of Henry cast a long shadow, because of him, they were now together sharing in one another's sadness, and that made everything just a little more bearable. "Funny how things can change so fast," Tillie sighed.

"I think our mothers did everything they could not to scream with joy when we told them we're friends again. My mother can leave now and feel at ease—and so can I." Lina wiped her eyes and looked up. "What will Elinora, Graham, and Jamie think?"

Her voice sounded so vulnerable Tillie was taken aback. She let the question linger in her mind a moment before responding. Elinora would never have predicted that Tillie would invite Lina into the heart of the forest, let alone share their secrets with her. She knew she would be taken off guard at first, especially since Tillie had convinced everyone that Lina would try to ruin their chances of going into the forest. But at the same time, Jamie, Elinora, and Graham had all been encouraging her to make amends with Lina.

"Elinora might be a little difficult at first—but only because she's so nervous and scared about our plans to rescue Henry. But she and Jamie and Graham have been wanting us to work things out since you arrived. Let me handle them when we get to the heart of the forest. Don't worry, everything will be fine."

"Thank you, Tillie."

"That's what friends are for!" She stood up then motioned

toward the unmarked trail. "Shall we then?"

Lina nodded.

As they walked, Tillie watched Lina's face. It reminded her of how she and Elinora had looked when they had first dared to enter the forest—overwhelmed by the magnificence of their surroundings, yet enveloped in a sense of peace and calm.

"No wonder you want to be out here all the time. And to think, I almost ruined it for you," Lina said after a moment.

"It's all right, you kept things interesting." She grinned. "You'll make a formidable adversary for Coddlefin. And I know together we'll figure out how to get Henry and his family back."

Lina smiled. "Tillie, just so you know, I like your trousers. They're practical and smart—and they suit you."

"Thanks," she said. She looked down, grabbing her trousers by the pockets. "You won't catch me in a dress ever again," she replied with a cheeky curtsy. "And so *you* know, I actually think your pendant from your grandmother is very beautiful."

Lina smiled. "I should tell you. When I said I wasn't supposed to say what it's worth, I didn't mean how much. It's not worth anything, except it's a lucky stone from Adrai, where her family came from. She says it keeps me safe. I never take it off." She put her hand to her neck, feeling it. "It connects me to her, too. She said I inherited her intuition."

"Lina, that's incredible...and I'm sorry I made such a ridiculous comment. Here we are now, I should mention that Ole Warty marks the spot where we become invisible to others that shouldn't be out here." She patted him as they walked past.

Lina looked up suddenly. "You disappeared when I followed you out here," she confessed. "Right here at this very spot."

Tillie reached out and took her by the hand. "Well, you see me now, and that's what matters. It's a sign the forest is welcoming you! Come on," she said pulling her forward. "Over here, this is

214

the way to the most magical part of all."

Mister suddenly scurried down a nearby tree. He had been sitting above, listening, and now came down to meet Lina and to lead them to the amphitheater.

"Hello, Mister," Tillie said. "This is Lina—she's a friend and is here to help. She misses Henry, too. I want to show her the amphitheater, if you don't mind. You can trust her."

Mister studied her for a moment, then brushed against her leg affectionately. He chattered at them both. Lina stooped down to pat his head.

"Mister knows everything that goes on out here. Just wait, once we're in the amphitheater, you'll be able to sense his thoughts and feelings, just like you can with Henry. And so you're prepared, some of the animals aren't what you'll expect to see. You should also know about the carousel before…"

But it had come into view as they pushed through the buckthorn, and Lina rushed over to get a closer look before Tillie could finish her sentence. Lina was so awestruck she didn't notice that Elinora, Graham, and Jamie were sitting in the grass on the other side.

"Tillie?" Elinora called when she heard footsteps.

Lina stopped running and turned to face her.

"Hello!" Tillie called back from where she stood amongst the buckthorn. She waved and grinned tentatively.

Elinora glanced back to the carousel and Lina, then stood up suddenly.

Tillie rushed over. "Don't worry, Lina's with me."

"Tillie, what's going on?" she asked with visible agitation.

"I know, I know, Elinora. But…"

"But what? Aren't you the one who repeatedly told me we would never be allowed near the forest if she found us out here?"

Lina turned away in embarrassment, and she caught sight of

Graham and Jamie still sitting on the other side of the carousel. She shrank back, wishing to flee the forest.

But Tillie spoke up. "Lina and I talked," she said to everyone. "Really talked. We worked things out, just like you all hoped we would. It's just that things went badly and got confusing between us, and we both just made it worse. We fixed that. I told her everything and she wants to help Henry."

Elinora paused, her anxiety heightening.

Jamie stepped forward. He walked over to Lina and without a word he wrapped his arms around her and gave her a hug. "It's all fine by me. If you and Tillie say things are all right, then I know they are. I'm really glad you're here. I knew neither of you should have been fighting, and I'm usually right about everything."

Lina stepped back and took both his hands in hers. "Thank you, Jamie." She squeezed his hands and smiled. He smiled back.

"Lina can communicate with Henry, just like us," Tillie added.

"You can?" Elinora asked with surprise.

Lina glanced at her and their eyes met. "Yes. Henry made me feel accepted and loved, and it was the first time I've felt that from a true friend in a long time. When I realized he was gone, and then when I found out my mother was leaving me here alone I..." She looked at Elinora, then to Jamie and Graham, fumbling her words.

Elinora smiled warmly. "It's all right, Lina. If you and Tillie have made peace, that's all that matters. I'm sorry the way things have been between all of us, and I'm glad you're here with us finally."

"Thank you, Elinora," she replied, reaching for her hand.

Graham got up, took off his hat and walked over with a dramatic sigh. "Well thank goodness! It's been frightfully tedious listening to the two of you." He grinned. "I'm teasing. I'm really happy you're here, too, Lina. I know with all of us working together, we'll be able to help Henry and his family." Lina smiled.

"She knew Henry left Kellandale before she was ever told

216

about it," Tillie added.

"You did? How?" Elinora asked.

"I don't know. I suddenly couldn't feel his thoughts or his feelings anymore. That sort of thing happens to me sometimes, I just... sort of feel things, and I just trust my gut." She got back up and walked over to the carousel. "But this, I can't even believe," she said climbing up the wooden plank onto its platform. "Has it always been here?" she asked.

"Not until recently," Elinora replied.

Jamie boarded and followed her. As they explored, he related the story of the day the hunters appeared in the forest. "Henry had a flood of memories when he saw them, and he recognized one of them. We learned what had happened to him before he came to us. Has Tillie told you we think he is trying to find the circus belonging to a man named Théodore Coddlefin?"

Tillie came up from behind and joined them. "I've told Lina all we know; I just hadn't gotten to the part about the carousel yet."

On cue, the carousel lurched forward and made a deep grinding sound, then started to spin slowly. Eerie, distorted music began to play.

"I know it might seem a stretch," Graham called out to Lina from the ground below, "but this seems to be a projection from Henry's mind, like a memory. I suspect the forest helped with that, so we could help him."

"I don't think it's a stretch at all," Lina yelled back. "It seems just about anything is possible anymore." She walked ahead, looking closely at the carvings, inspecting every animal, and running her hands across the lifelike wooden figures. Jamie and Tillie followed.

"Is that...Henry?" Lina asked suddenly.

Elinora and Graham rushed onto the carousel when they heard this.

"That wasn't here before," Jamie said, looking at the figure.

"There are others that weren't here before, too," Tillie said, pointing. "There, next to Henry."

Elinora's gaze fell upon the figure of a young man standing confidently by Henry's side. She studied his face for a moment. There was also a little elephant with them. "Look at them," she sighed.

They continued to circle around the carousel, examining the new figures. As Lina walked, the wide center pole, elaborately carved and embellished with gold leaf, sparkled brightly and drew her in closer. This, in turn, caused her to notice a tiny door within it. She gasped, then pointed it out to Jamie.

"I've never noticed that," he said, intrigued.

They walked up to it. The little door sat next to the music box, which was still quietly playing music. The door had a small wrought iron latch. Lina reached out and unlocked it. Behind it was a mirror, which she peered into. At first, she could barely make out her own reflection, but then that faded. She wiped the mirror and looked again. "Jamie, look at this."

He leaned in and peered through. "Lina, you're brilliant!"

"What is it?" Tillie asked.

"I'm not sure," he replied.

"I have a feeling we might be seeing into the circus grounds where Henry is..." Lina whispered.

Everyone rushed over. Tillie approached the little door and peered in. The silvering of the mirror was tarnished, and the view hazy, but she, too, could see what they were seeing. "Oh Lina, you're right—there's a tent, look! A circus tent!" she exclaimed.

Elinora and Graham took turns looking through the mirror. As they did, the woodland animals began to gather in the amphitheater.

"Look," Tillie whispered to Lina, nodding her head toward them. "It's the forest council."

Lina sucked in her breath when she saw the Bekanan tiger, followed by a rhinoceros, and an okapi who was peacefully trailing the rabbits, squirrels, and the rest of the animals. Pipe, Mitch, Popo, and Vita were there among them.

There was a brief stirring among the council, then Mister reappeared from the back of the pack, hurrying to the center of the amphitheater.

All five of them stepped off the carousel and followed him.

First, Mister introduced Lina to the council, and they warmly welcomed her. Then he shared the news just received from the scouts. Monkey had been spotted just outside Kellandale Wood and he was with the Messenger. They were on their way and were expected to arrive momentarily.

"Oh goodness gracious, yes!" Tillie yelled. Everyone stirred with excitement.

A large shadow fell onto the ground a few moments later, then the Messenger landed in a nearby tree. The sunlight illuminated his feathers, smoky grey and tinged with vibrant turquoise, green, and red markings on his body and wings.

"Whoa," Jamie exclaimed. He turned to Lina. "That's him! He keeps watch over the forest. We've only ever seen him from afar. I didn't realize just how enormous he is."

The Messenger noticed the children and acknowledged them with a flap of his wings, then rested silently for a moment before recounting what had transpired after his capture. He spoke of the young man from the inn who was now with Henry and a young elephant, who were both under the young man's protection. It was Henry's plan to eventually bring them both to Kellandale Wood with him, along with his family.

There was a flurry of conversation, and the Messenger waited for it to quiet. He repeated Henry's wish for the children to not come looking for him, keeping his promise to Henry that he would deliver that message. But he had seen the suffering of the animals and people of the circus. Though Henry was brave and determined, the Messenger knew Coddlefin's circus was far worse than anyone had imagined and that Henry was up against more than he had expected. Reluctantly, against Henry's wishes, the Messenger broke the grave news of the harsh and inhospitable environment of the circus, confirming that Henry and his companions would most certainly need help if they wished to ever be able to make it home to Kellandale safely.

There were gasps from the humans and rumbles from the animals.

Tillie stood up. "We have news, too! We know where Henry is—and the Messenger has just confirmed it—and we have the means to get there. Now that we know the situation, we can't leave him to do this alone any longer."

The reaction was deafening. The animals of the council unanimously pledged to help Henry in any way they could. Mister stepped forward to introduce the new inhabitants in the forest—the fish crow and the wolves who had helped Henry find his way. The female wolf bowed to the animals, then conveyed to the council how they had met Henry. She was grateful to be there, and they, too, pledged their help.

"Thank you," Tillie said. "There's got to be a way we can help them without putting all of you in danger. For now, I intend to go to him. I know Henry would do the same for me."

Lina stood up. "I will go there with you, Tillie."

"So will I," Graham replied.

"I will, too," Jamie echoed.

Elinora hesitated. She had no doubts that Lina would help, but now she felt a shift at the root of her worry. Together Tillie and Lina had always been a dervish of activity. They were both fearless. She suspected they would make hasty, heroic, and quite possibly risky decisions, and this was causing her panic to swell. But she held her tongue. She had already agreed to visit the training grounds and knew her anxiety was getting the best of her. *I can handle a trip to a circus,* she reminded herself. She stepped forward. "I will go, too," she said as boldly as she could.

Tillie smiled. "Mister?" she asked, turning to him.

He responded with approval.

> *Go to him.*
> *We will be here to help in any way we can.*

Tillie exhaled with great relief.

"Let's head back and get some rest. I think we're going to need it. Then we can talk about how we will get there," Graham said. He stood up and the others followed.

"I'll be right there," Jamie said, then walked off deeper into the woods on the other side of the amphitheater.

Tillie saw the puzzled look on Lina's face. "He's visiting the vortex," she said, as though that was a normal phrase used every day.

"He *what?*"

"Just wait, he'll be thrilled to tell you all about it," she teased.

When he returned, Jamie explained what he was doing as they walked back. "The vortex has the power to slow time outside the forest while we are here. Or speed it up in here. Or slow it down all over. I really can't figure out which way it is. I just know that when we get back, you'll see—our mothers won't even have begun to pack their bags yet, and they'll be almost exactly where they were before we came out here."

Lina walked on without a word, but her eyes were wide.

"That face happens a lot around here," he teased.

"Our mothers will be leaving early in the morning," Tillie reminded everyone. "Just think, if all goes well, we could be home with Henry and his family by tomorrow evening!"

23

Reunited

Three days had passed since Henry's arrival at Coddlefin's circus. On the fourth morning, the sun rose, sending warm light through the uncovered stall window and into Alister's eyes, waking him. He sat up and rubbed them groggily then noticed that a blanket had been placed over him sometime during the night. "There's only one person who would have done that for us." He cracked a smile at Henry and Wildflower. "All right, guys, it's breakfast time. I'll be right back," he said, then headed off to find food for everyone.

He left the stable to get in line at the mess hall two buildings over, where he was given three pieces of bread and a bowl of lukewarm slop. He had asked for a dried gourd, boiled milk, and sugar, hopeful that he could at least forage some leaves and herbs from the field outside the barn to cobble together a version of qitza, a traditional drink he used to watch his mother brew when he was a small child. But he had simply been laughed at for asking for anything other than bread or gruel. On his way back to the stall, he stopped at a nearby spigot to fill a container with cold water, then grabbed a handful of limp hay. "Doesn't look any more appetizing today than it's been so far," he said returning to the stable and offering the rations.

Henry nudged a piece of stale bread over to Wildflower and took one for himself. Alister dunked his crust into the gruel and took a bite. "Bleh. This is awful." He pushed the bowl away and ate the bread. "I never thought I'd say this, but they could learn a thing or two about food from Garibaldi. Anyway, we'd better get moving, I don't want to get off to a bad start. I hear Mudd is coming to observe today."

Henry and Wildflower understood; all three of them knew an exceptional performance was key to their survival. They exited the stall together and walked down the trail to the Red Barn, ready for whatever was to come.

"Well, if it isn't the train hopper," Ghant jeered when they entered the building. "I haven't seen you in a few days, what have you been doing, hiding?"

Byron walked over and yanked on Wildflower's lead, trying to move her.

Alister stepped forward. "She stays with me," he said pointedly, taking the lead back.

Byron's face turned red.

"Never mind him, it's not worth getting your britches bunched up over again," Ghant said, then he turned to Alister. "All right, wise guy, bring your animals and follow me. What's your name anyway, you never did tell us before."

"I'm Alis, er, Gar...i...geoff-oree..." he mumbled, trying to invent a new name quickly.

"Whatever you say, boy."

"We're headed to the big top today. Hurry it up, you don't want

223

to keep Mudd waiting, you hear me, *Alisar Jeffries?*" Byron added.

"How about we just call him Alice," Ghant barked. He led them through the compound to a massive, ruby-red tent at the front of the grounds. They entered and passed through the center of the ring.

Strong and powerful horses thundered around them, some with acrobats on their backs. Across the arena, a bear cub was being led into the ring. There were other animals there as well—two tigers, a lion, and a handful of small monkeys—practicing their routines, jumping through large hoops, balancing on tiny cones, and doing flips in the air. Henry scanned for signs of his family.

Ghant walked on, taking them to a back corner where two trainers were working with another group of canines. They trotted by in synchronized formation, taking turns leaping over one another or walking on their hind legs.

"That's right, very good," cooed Hector, one of the small dog trainers. He was a slender but muscular man with pimply skin and a goofy smile. "Over here, Snicker, Guinness, Ginger, Sir Billings, come this way. Clover, Magnolia, Cherry, Princess!" He patted each member of the canine gaggle within his care as they each returned to his side.

Another trainer named Ellis who was much taller, skinnier, and somehow even more pale skinned than Hector, left the tent then returned with five more large dogs who followed him obediently. "Sit! Now, stay?" he meekly requested. When they were all still, he exited the tent again.

Even from a distance Henry recognized his family. His tail thumped the ground frantically, but he quickly stifled his excitement, fearful of drawing attention. Alister and Wildflower felt the surge of emotion coming from him and looked over.

Henry's mother had felt it, too, and she turned and locked eyes with Henry. She never knew what had happened to her littlest pup after he had been taken away, and since that moment she had been filled with deep sorrow. She stood up, pricked her ears, and wagged her tail vigorously.

Ghant noticed she was moving around. "Stupid animal!" he growled. "He said stay until he comes back!" He walked over and swiftly came down on her, striking her on the backside. Hector turned his head away when she yelped.

Henry growled and his fur bristled. But his mother gave him a pleading look, warning him not to interfere.

Ellis rushed back into the barn when he heard the commotion. "Azalea, at attention!" he warbled in a panic, cracking his whip on the ground.

"She didn't do anything wrong!" Alister shouted, creating a diversion when he noticed Henry was baring his teeth. He turned to him and conveyed silently. *Don't get yourself into trouble, fella. We will go to her later to make sure she is all right. For now, I'll get us closer so you can speak to them.*

Henry calmed down and silently followed Alister over to Azalea and the rest of his siblings—Aster, Basil, Sage, and Yarrow. Again, he stifled his joy. But he had at last found his family.

"Well now, Alice Big Britches," Ghant heckled. "I'm surely looking forward to seeing what kind of magic you supposedly possess. If you're as talented as you say—show us."

Byron snickered.

"All right then, I'm taking requests, but don't give Henry and me any tricks that are too easy." He winked at Henry, then continued to taunt Byron and Ghant to buy time for Henry and his family.

Henry quickly explained how it had come to pass that he had returned to the circus, and why. He told them about Elinora, Tillie, and the others, and the plan he had with Alister to free them and get them to the safety of Kellandale.

225

Hector, meanwhile, was busy trying to quiet his canine troupe, who had begun to bark excitedly. They, too, were able to understand Henry and were letting the other animals know that he, Alister, and Wildflower were friendly and there to help.

All the while, Ghant had continued to bicker with Alister. "You don't think getting that dog to jump through a hoop is hard enough? Well let's see you get him to walk on his hind legs then, you cheeky little twerp!"

"Not a problem," Alister replied. He looked at Henry and winked. *Let's show these idiots what we can do. We'll make it fast, so it isn't too painful for you.*

On command, Henry reared up and stood on his hind legs, his head well above Alister's—almost six feet in the air. He took several steps forward; it was difficult, but he endured the pain and humiliation, aware their livelihood depended on it.

Alister felt his discomfort. "Good boy, you can stand down now," he said quickly.

But Henry continued to walk toward Byron. Then he stopped and rested his front paws on his shoulders.

The weight of his body caused Byron's legs to buckle. "Right then," he grimaced, forcing a laugh as he struggled to stand up. "All right, all right, enough! Call him off, Alice!"

"Well done. Come, Henry," Alister called.

Henry abruptly pulled away and Byron fell to the ground.

"That might get you a few claps. Some of the other dogs can do that anyway, I'll bet," Ghant said with a shrug as he watched Byron awkwardly pull himself up.

"What do you have in mind?" Alister asked coolly.

He looked off in the distance when he saw someone approaching. "Perfect timing," he said, grinning when he saw it was Mudd. "How about you show us something that is actually impressive now…" he said but fell silent when he noticed Mudd was leading another man into the arena. The man was tall and menacing, with flushing red cheeks that changed color like a mood ring. Everyone became noticeably ill at ease by his appearance.

Mudd saw Alister standing with Henry. "Ah yes! We have been watching you from outside the tent," he called out.

Sage let out a warning bark to Henry. Ellis frantically tried to quiet him.

"Good morning," Alister said steadily.

But the man with Mudd had heard the bark and was irritated by the sound. He walked over directly to Ellis. "What have you been told?" he asked him pointedly.

"To keep them minding," he replied sheepishly.

"As I have said countless times, to do this you must keep order by showing your power. Use whatever means necessary to make them listen. No, no! Don't frown like that, it's all for the greater good, and it's what makes our show the best in the world." He grabbed the whip from his side and unfurled it, then snapped Ellis with it.

Ellis grimaced, stifling a full-fledged yelp.

"That is how you keep your animals in line. Now, let me see you do the same, so I know you understand."

He took the whip back and struck Sage weakly.

"Not good enough."

He struck again, harder, enough to make him cry out.

"Now, get your dogs out of here, I don't want them mixing with the new talent," the man ordered, brushing him away with his hands.

Alister could feel Henry's body shuddering with anger and he put his hand on him to calm him.

Ellis collected himself, then quickly led Henry's family away.

Sage glanced back at Henry, who whimpered when he watched helplessly as his family was pulled out of sight.

227

"Now then, back to business. Can anyone ride that stubborn mule of a horse yet?" the man with Mudd demanded.

Ghant grabbed a bamboo pole from off the ground. A clown hat was tied to it with a rope. "Alice, let's see you get on that horse. Better yet, how about you get your dog to ride him so the Boss can see just how fabulous you are." He snickered, pointing at Alister with the pole.

"Just give me a moment," Alister replied, then bowed his head congenially at the man with Mudd.

He put his hand to his chin, waiting, and said nothing in return.

"Leopold!" Ghant shouted to another trainer in the stables behind the ring. "Get Alexander over here!"

A moment later the beautiful, shiny black Inbeke, captured in Myar, was led to the center of the ring. Alexander stomped and snorted as a burly man, with dark, curly hair appeared from the wings tried to keep hold of his halter.

The horse's hatred for the trainers ran deep and he always put up his best fight, sometimes becoming violent toward them, even to his own detriment. The Boss particularly loved him, though. He was fierce, regal, and independent-minded—a specimen to parade around the ring with pride. Now and again a performer was ordered to try to ride him, something that was dreaded as everyone knew there would only be one outcome.

But Alexander had heard Henry communicating with his mother and sensed that he, Alister, and Wildflower were allies; he could also tell Alister had a big heart. He let them know he understood what he needed to do to help, and that he was willing. Very quickly, Henry and Alister communicated the plan with him.

A small audience had assembled as other trainers and workers in the arena stopped to watch the show.

"I've been bragging about you, so don't you go and make a liar of me!" Mudd nervously yelled at Alister.

He grinned, turned to Alexander, and commanded him to lower himself down, then nodded at Henry.

Alexander obliged, bending his back legs and letting Henry jump up without bucking him off. Then he stood up with the wolfhound balanced on his back.

"There it is! That a boy! What did I tell you! Unbelievable!" Mudd exclaimed. "Who else here can do that? Come, come, let me introduce you," he said grabbing Alister's arm and pulling him closer to the man. "This is the boy I was telling you about. This is..." he said, hesitating.

"Alice Jeffries," Ghant said flatly.

"Yes, yes, right, Alice Jeffries. He's the one that's been training the dog and the little elephant. Alice, this is Coddlefin, the man behind everything you see here...the man you will need to continue to impress."

The sound of Alexander's hooves beating the ground when he suddenly bolted, galloping high-speed around the ring diverted everyone's attention. Henry was still on his back and he held on steadily and gracefully as they made the circuit together, then rounded the bend, making their return.

Ghant walked over to the edge of the ring and raised the pole he was still holding, giving the impression he was going to set the hat on Henry's head as they rode past. But at the last minute he took a swipe, attempting to knock him off Alexander's back.

Henry had anticipated this, and grabbed the pole in his mouth, yanking Ghant off his feet.

Ghant shrieked and tumbled to the ground as Alexander and Henry made another lap around the arena.

Coddlefin and Mudd roared with laughter.

On their next pass, Alister sprinted off toward them, leapt onto Alexander's back behind Henry, and together the three made one last circuit.

"Bravo, Mr. Jeffries! Never has anyone been able to stay on that horse," Coddlefin shouted. He turned to Mudd. "All right then, we'll call the dog Snapdragon. But keep him away from the rest of the dogs. This one needs special attention. Make sure he and the boy are both fed well enough; upgrade them to the grade-B fare at least every day or two. His elephant can have some, too. They will continue training to ride Alexander. Have the boy come up with a trick for his elephant and have them ready for the show by spring. They'll need costumes, too. Good work!" he boomed, then abruptly exited the tent.

Ghant cracked his whip, not taking his eyes of Alister.

Mudd flicked a hard stare back. "You heard the Boss. Don't mess with Jeffries or his animals, or you'll have to answer to me—and him. You hear that, kid?" he asked slapping Alister on the back. "You're in for good, whether you like it or not. Welcome to Théodore Coddlefin's Amazing Feats and Traveling Menagerie!"

24

Waterbridge Station

It was just past eight in the morning the very next day. Elinora, Tillie, Graham, Jamie, and Lina had been waiting their turn in the long line at Waterbridge Station for some time, their eyelids heavy after an early morning carriage ride. It was a busy station, and it served as a hub that connected several lines across the country. Emil had driven them at Abigail's request shortly after having delivered Anna, Penelope, and Camille to the very same station, allowing enough time to pass so that crossing paths with their mothers at the station would be avoided.

Elinora looked up when she saw that the last remaining person between them and the ticket window had been helped.

"Finally," Tillie said impatiently when they reached the front of the line.

"You get the tickets," Elinora whispered sleepily.

She nodded and stepped up to the window, her hands tucked in her trouser pockets. "Excuse me sir," she said to the ticket salesman, standing on her tiptoes to get a better view.

"Yes…" came the monotone reply from a visibly haggard man sitting behind the counter. His tenor reflected the tell-tale signs of someone worn out by a repetitive job dealing with the impatient public. It took him a moment to bother to look up. When he did, his brows furrowed as he set his eyes upon her.

Tillie wrinkled her nose back at him.

"Yes, how can I help you, child? Are you lost or something?" he asked flatly.

"Lost? Oh! Goodness no, I know exactly where I am." She looked back and shrugged at the others, who were listening to the exchange.

She tried again. "I was wondering, what train would we need to take to get to the circus training ground of Coddlefin's Amazing Feats and Extraordinary Traveling Menagerie?"

The man scrutinized her more closely. "Train 273. That's train two-seven-three, to Brookeamble, with a transfer to train one-zero-zero to Cavenwell," he recited from memory. He looked past her, his intrusive gaze falling onto the rest of the group. Like Tillie, Elinora and Lina were also wearing trousers, which, while not uncommon in Eldmoor, was something he was used to only seeing on adults. He shook his head absently.

Tillie raised her eyebrows back at him. "Five tickets to Cavenwell then," she said firmly.

"Where are your parents?" he asked abruptly.

"Excuse me?"

"Do they know where you're going?" he interrogated. "It's a very long trip."

"Why, yes they do," she fibbed. She gritted her teeth.

"Hmmm. Five tickets you say. I'm not so sure about that. There are no seats left going to Cavenwell today, not for the next several days, even weeks perhaps, if at all."

"What? Oh please. Are you absolutely sure? We *must* get there today."

She sounded so genuinely distraught that she managed to elicit a spark of kindness in him, the first in a very long time. "All right, let me have a look. But don't get your hopes up," he said, leaving the window abruptly.

She could see him rummaging around at the back of the ticket booth. He pulled out a register and looked it over then walked back over to her. She watched him expectantly.

"Most folks purchased their tickets to the grounds long ago, and even more couldn't get their hands on them at all. *Everyone* wants to go to Coddlefin's, and today happens to be opening day. Right pain if you ask me, this place has been so busy with his rabid fans. But it just so happens there's an empty train car in the back that's available. It's a storage car, not the most luxurious, but it'll do—it's got seats at least. There's no porter or car attendant, so you'll be on your own. The tickets to Cavenwell will get you into the training grounds, too—so don't lose them."

"Oh, that's wonderful, thank you so much. It was very kind of you to take the time to find a way for us." She turned back to the others nodding triumphantly.

"All right, all right. Eight each," he said, softening slightly.

"Eight? Blimey, are we going to the royal ball or something?"

"Might as well be. And these are half price. But from what I understand there's quite a show at the other end of the line, and all you can eat is included in the ticket, too. But between you and me, you're really just paying dearly to be able to say you got the first glimpse of the season ahead of the rest of the crowd. What a racket."

She reached into her pocket and counted out silver coins. She looked up at the ticketmaster. "I only have five..."

"Whatever, that'll do, considering your accommodations." He stamped five tickets and handed them to Tillie. "Don't forget to transfer trains or you'll end up on the other side of Eldmoor. Platform three, and you have less than four minutes before it arrives. Now step aside. And…have fun." He waved her away and pointed them all to the side with his stubby, ink-stained finger.

"Thank you again," she said to him, grinning. He grunted but she could see he was trying to suppress a smile. She walked back to the others.

Lina was laughing. "Charmer," she teased.

"Indeed. You handled that rather well," Graham snickered.

"Honestly, it took all I had not to leap over the counter and find the tickets myself!" She glanced up at the oversized clock. "We'd better hurry. If we miss this train, we won't have another chance to get there for some time." She pushed the tickets into Graham's hand and clutched the little jade-eyed monkey figurine she was wearing around her neck, then dashed off to the platform in a run. Elinora, Lina, Graham, and Jamie followed on her heels.

Once the prior passengers disembarked, they were motioned to come aboard. Graham handed the tickets over to the inspector who madly clicked away with his ticket punch. "One, two, three, four, five!" he counted out loud. "You'll switch trains about fifty minutes from here at Brookeamble for the One Hundred, north-bound to Cavenwell, another hour and a half away. Thank you, enjoy your trip." He pointed them toward their compartment at the back of the train.

They made their way up the steps and down the narrow corridor to their cabin. Graham slid open the door and held it for the rest of them. The car was sparse yet clean, and the seats, while not luxurious like the recliners in the other cars, were benches upholstered with emerald green cloth, and quite cozy. "This isn't as bad as he made it out to be," Tillie remarked.

Jamie stretched out and placed his feet on the edge of the seat across from him, then leaned back. "Not at all, this is splendid."

The others each took a spot and settled into the seats around him as the train pulled out of the station and made its way down the tracks amongst the wildflowers and rushes that filled the countryside landscape. The sound of the train quickly lulled them all into a moment of quiet. Tillie chose a window seat and pressed her head against the window while she looked out, as if that would somehow make the train go faster.

Two hours and one train later, Graham nudged his brother awake as they neared Cavenwell station.

Jamie stirred. It was warm and even more comfortable in the number One Hundred train and he had fallen asleep soon after they had transferred. He stretched and yawned, trying to regain his bearings, momentarily forgetting where they were. "Are we there yet?" he asked when he remembered.

Graham shook his head.

"Where is everyone?"

"They went searching for sodas. You missed quite a show earlier, but you looked so relaxed I didn't want to wake you." He filled him in about the exchange between Tillie and Lina in which they discussed the various scenarios they imagined for rescuing Henry.

Graham of course had felt it was his duty to interject common sense. Elinora, meanwhile, had been horrified by all of their ideas, and although she knew most of what they said was purely for entertainment's sake, she had swiftly rebuked them. She'd reminded them that they needed to find Henry as quickly as possible and sneak him and his family away without attracting attention. "I even had to make Tillie and Lina promise they wouldn't set anything on fire as a diversion to get Henry out of there," he joked.

"Sounds like a normal conversation, then," Jamie chuckled.

"You missed the best part—Lina and Tillie's brilliant suggestion involving Coddlefin and some tranquilizer darts."

"They'd do it in a heartbeat if they had the means," Jamie chuckled. "Did anyone come up with actual, sensible ideas, then?"

"Nothing beyond 'let's see what we find once we're there,'" Graham replied.

Jamie sniffed a laugh then stretched again, peering out the window at the horizon. The undulating hills he was accustomed to seeing near home were slowly beginning to give way to flat grasslands densely dotted with sheep the further north they traveled. He looked up at the sky. "Is he still following?"

Graham got up and moved to the seat across from him to look out. "I would count on it. Look, there he is," he said pointing in the air to the elegant wings soaring overhead.

"He's got to be exhausted. How long has he been flying, then?"

"It was an hour from Waterbridge to Brookeamble, and almost another hour has gone by since. Don't worry though, I think he's mostly been riding on the top of the train, but now and again I've seen him stretch his wings like that. It's incredible."

The cabin door opened. "Who's incredible, me?" Tillie asked upon entering. Lina and Elinora followed her.

"*Him,* silly," Jamie replied, pointing out the window. "The Messenger."

"Oh, let me have a look," Elinora said, nudging Jamie over so she could see. Just the sight of him made her feel more at ease, like they weren't quite so alone with him watching over.

Twenty minutes later the whistle blew, and the train pulled into the station just ahead of schedule. They gathered their belongings and climbed out of the car, one step closer to Henry.

25

Coddlefin's Amazing Feats & Extraordinary Traveling Menagerie

Tillie stepped out of the train and was overwhelmed by an oversized sign posted on the cavernous station walls. *Welcome to Cavenwell, Home of Théodore Coddlefin's Amazing Feats and Extraordinary Traveling Menagerie!* it proclaimed in bright, cherry-colored letters.

"Hurry up! Henry is out there somewhere!" she beckoned the others and weaved through the marble tiled station amongst an elbow-to-elbow crowd.

Cavenwell Station, modernized and gorgeously detailed, was even larger than the station at Waterbridge; it had been built to accommodate the mass of visitors to the circus training ground, the sole destination for the stop, as no one other than Coddlefin and his entourage lived in the remote area of the country. The passengers had traveled long and far, paying a large sum to be there for this very special day, and everyone rushed through the terminal, eager to grab a good spot in the stands of the big top for the show.

"Where is Coddlefin? I've been waiting all day!" a child stomped his foot and shouted at his mother.

"He's just so talented and handsome!" a woman overdressed in a fine, violet-colored crepe evening gown bragged to a group of ladies. They clucked back in delight.

"You've never seen one of his previews before? Oh, amazing doesn't even express half of it," another fan gushed. "Coddlefin is marvelous, everyone *adores* him."

"Oh, do they now?" Tillie muttered under her breath as they walked past.

Lina snorted a laugh.

They continued to dodge between the passengers, busking musicians, and wandering circus performers donned in bright colored silks, all milling about in the crowded station. Music blared from trumpets, drums, maracas, cellos, and flutes.

Tillie, Elinora, Lina, Graham, and Jamie followed the masses down a manicured trail, making the pilgrimage from the station to the training grounds. While the terrain outside Coddlefin's universe was barren, the plush oasis they had entered stood out in startling contrast. Lush trees, fountains, meticulously manicured gardens, and flickering torches and lanterns surrounded them on all sides. The main circus tent, crimson-red and looming like a castle on the horizon, came into view long before they reached the front gates. It was the largest tent any of them had ever seen. Jamie let out an involuntary gasp when he saw it.

Circus performers were everywhere, hundreds of them now. Performing animals, including lions, tigers, and giraffes, walked obediently with their trainers. Vendors were busily selling food and souvenirs from their little carts that lined the inner perimeter of a long, spiked, white fence. The public area abruptly ended at the back of the big top, the fence concealing the private areas where Coddlefin and his staff lived.

"I've never seen anything quite like this," Graham remarked, walking ahead with Lina.

"Nor have I, it is rather impressive." She looked at him guiltily. "I wonder where Henry is?"

He sighed. "Indeed, we need to stay focused. Let's see if he's part of the show to start, shall we?"

They walked on, but as they neared the big top, Lina hesitated.

"What is it?" he asked. Her eyes were fixed onto something in the distance and he turned, curious to see what she was looking at. "It's just like the carousel in the forest," he said with surprise.

Tillie, Elinora, and Jamie had heard what Graham said and rushed to catch up, but a man with shiny black hair stepped out of the tent holding a megaphone. "This way folks! This way to the show!" he called loudly.

"We'll go look at the carousel later. I think we need to be in there," Graham said, motioning for them to follow to the big top.

Elinora walked slowly, trailing behind, her stomach pitching nervously. She was unsure how things would play out considering their plans were not very well thought out.

"Look, the tent is made entirely out of velvet!" Jamie marveled when they arrived at the entrance.

Tillie reached out to touch it, and the tent flap opened slightly; Elinora peered through, hoping to catch a glimpse of Henry inside.

But a man inside pushed the flap fully open and stepped in front of her, blocking her view. He stood over seven feet tall, with long, silk trouser-clad legs and skin as white as his ruffled blouse. "Welcome. Please take a seat anywhere and make yourselves comfortable. The show will begin soon," he said with polite melancholy, directing them into the stands.

"Thank you," she replied, surprised by his demeanor as she had envisioned everyone in Coddlefin's circus to be aggressive and frightening.

Jamie took the lead, heading to a remote corner in the tent. He made sure to choose five seats near the front of the ring but at the end of the row, close to an exit. Soon after they sat down and got settled, the lights went down and the tent flaps closed again, shrouding them in darkness.

A collective gasp was followed by excited whispers. Seconds later, the crowd was startled back into silence as a single, focused spotlight switched on with a loud pop. It was very bright, and it illuminated the man standing in the center of the ring.

"A velvet tent, *and* they have electricity all the way out here? Who are these people?" Jamie whispered to Tillie.

The ringmaster, a young man with black hair, the same man who had called everyone to the tent, was holding a baton, which he lifted in the air to command attention. He then pulled the megaphone dramatically to his mouth with the other hand. "Welcome Guests! Welcome Children! Your attention please!" his amplified voice echoed in the tent. His glittering, red-sequined pants sparkled under the spotlight as the band began a cascading drum roll.

"You have made it this far, and we applaud you—for what a long journey you must have made to be with us." He paused for a trombone slide, his round face breaking into a grin. "We welcome you on this special opening night of the season. I know who you came to see; you know who you came to see! So, without further ado, it is my pleasure to introduce the man that you adore, here, in the flesh, before your very own eyes, the dazzling, the extraordinary and most amazing, the one and only Théodore Coddlefin!"

The crowd screamed madly as he swaggered into the ring accompanied by the feverish music of the circus band. He cut a striking form in his eccentric outfit—the sleeves and chest of his black suit were emblazoned with crimson-red sequins that matched the velvet big top and the ring master's own sparkling, sequined pants. Beneath his jacket was a button-down black shirt, and on his feet he wore shiny leather boots.

He was handsome—much more handsome, and certainly more beguiling than Tillie, Elinora, or any of the others had expected. He was an older man, and though time had roughened his face a bit, he moved about with flair and energy, smiling broadly. The spotlight hit his gold-plated front tooth and it glinted brightly, giving him a wild, toothy grin.

He bowed deeply then threw his arms dramatically in the air. "Good evening folks!" he shouted, then took the megaphone from the ringmaster. "Children, my dear children. Thank you all for coming! It means so much that you would travel far and wide to pay me a visit. It will be worth it, I promise you. What you are about to see, what you are about to experience, is unsurpassed, and more amazing than your wildest dreams.

"Our animal trainers are not *among* the best in the world, they *are* the best in the world. Our performers are the most skilled of any performers you'll ever see, and they accomplish *Amazing Feats!* Our animals, well, do I need to say it? We've got the most extraordinary, exotic animals ever amassed in a single collection, and they will perform for you just as spectacularly as our human performers." More applause and shouts followed. Single yelps swelled into a fervent wave of cheers, hoots, and hollers.

Coddlefin lowered his arms, dramatically lulling everyone back into silence. "Hold on to your hats and behold an exclusive advanced viewing of our Amazing Feats and our wild and wonderful Traveling Menagerie! Our show this season will be the best ever, and you are the select, lucky few to see it for the very first time. We are just beginning to put the final touches on the show, and I know you will love it." He handed the megaphone back.

The band played again and another roar of cheers erupted as three beautiful mares raced into the ring—one black, one white, and one grey appaloosa. They galloped side by side in perfect step making two circuits around the arena.

"My dear audience, let me introduce our trusty stuntman, the Great Quackenbush!" the ringmaster interjected when an incredibly muscular man with curly brown hair, and wide and woolly sideburns tumbled into the ring doing back flips, then proceeded to gracefully pounce onto the back of the appaloosa. He continued on, performing handstands in the saddle and somersaults in the air as he jumped from one horse to the next. "Ho!" he finally yelled, and the horses stopped at his command. They reared up and snorted as he jumped off the black stallion.

"I introduce to you...Thunder!" the ringmaster introduced the horse to the audience. Then he turned to the appaloosa and the white stallion. "Earthquake, and Typhoon! And the Great Quackenbush!" he exclaimed.

The crowd cheered frantically. Tillie jumped up to give a standing ovation but quickly caught herself. She looked at the others guiltily, but they, too, were on their feet applauding.

The music continued, flowing into the next act. Violins swelled serenely as two women dressed in vibrant purple silk costumes dropped down from the ceiling of the tent, their legs entwined in ropes. They plunged downward, headfirst into the arena, twirling upside down, faster with each rotation, hair spinning freely. Then one of the acrobats pulled out a long, slender sword, pointing it at the other. The second performer responded by unsheathing her own and a fierce sword fight began.

"My dear audience, now I introduce to you Kano and Rikona, known far and wide as the Sabre Sisters!" the ringmaster roared as the ropes pulled them up and out of sight. Next came a parade of animals. One by one, tigers, lions, an ostrich, a giraffe, and a man with a bright yellow python wrapped around his neck entered the ring. They were followed by a humongous rhinoceros who obediently followed his master. Coddlefin smiled proudly and applauded each act, encouraging the audience to cheer louder with him.

"And now, for a very special treat," the ringmaster continued. Fresh off the train, straight from the wilds of Rahsica, a young elephant able to perform after only four days in our care—a testament to both our animals and our trainers. I introduce to you for the very first time in the ring, the youngest elephant in captivity anywhere in the world—Wildflower, the baby Elephant!"

The audience cheered wildly.

But Wildflower did not appear.

The announcer shifted in place for a minute and tried again. "I introduce to you...Wildflower, the baby Elephant!" The band played jubilantly, but she still did not enter. To fill the awkward silence, he improvised.

As he rambled, Elinora's attention drifted into the sidelines. There she caught sight of Wildflower, cowering with fright by the loud noises coming from the ring and from the audience. A man hulked over, prodding and poking at her. Despite the attack, the tiny elephant remained still.

The man raised his bull hook then jabbed her hard in her flank with it.

Elinora gasped. "Look what he's doing!"

Tillie turned to look. "No!" she exclaimed as they watched helplessly as he stabbed at her with it again.

At the last minute, the trainer took out a thin wire loop and caught it around Wildflower's tiny trunk, then he twisted it roughly. She trumpeted in distress and lurched forward. The trainer quickly removed the wire, then pushed her into the ring, confident no one had seen what he had done.

"Daddy!" A young child in the audience stood up and exclaimed when she noticed the bloody gash on Wildflower's trunk.

"Why is the poor little elephant bleeding?" her father yelled.

A collective gasp arose from the crowd in response. Everyone stood up to gawk.

Jamie booed, and the rest of the audience chimed in, heckling and shouting at the trainer.

Tillie stomped her foot. "Hideous man!" She turned to Elinora. "I don't care how much people love Coddlefin and his circus, they're horrible monsters!"

Elinora nodded, not taking her eyes off the young elephant.

The ringmaster paused awkwardly, then stuttered. "Ah yes," he said, turning to Coddlefin, whose face twisted as he tried to suppress his anger. The ringmaster turned back to the audience. "No, no, don't do that, you don't understand. Ahem. You are very observant, my child," he addressed the little girl directly. "This little elephant is lucky to be alive! Thanks to the endeavors of our beloved Théodore Coddlefin, some of his men happened to be in the right place at the right time. While overseas just this past week, they chanced upon poor little Wildflower.

"Her family had just been attacked. She was left on her own but remained loyally by her family's side until our scouts found her and took her into their care, bringing her back to us. Here at Coddlefin's Amazing Feats and Extraordinary Traveling Menagerie, the welfare of our animals and performers is our greatest concern. Rest assured, Wildflower is in a much better place and will live a far better life than she would have ever lived in the wilds."

Coddlefin picked up the story from there. "Wildflower suffered these wounds during the attack. Do not concern yourselves, as we are working hard to heal her. It's just a little blood, nothing to be concerned about. She is very well and in good spirits, as you can clearly see!"

The trainer followed behind Wildflower, bowing to the audience, a wide grin forming to disguise his relief. He turned and smiled at Coddlefin.

Coddlefin turned on him abruptly, locking cold, steely eyes on the trainer.

Elinora watched closely and sensed something rise within Théodore Coddlefin, something unsettling. The others felt the shift in his demeanor, too.

His body was now stiff, clenched, his face darkened, and his mannerisms nothing like what they had been when he had first greeted the audience. He leaned in to say something privately to the trainer, who cowered in response. Then the trainer quickly coaxed Wildflower onto four pedestals.

She stood with one foot on each, quivering uncontrollably. Then, at his command she lifted her front leg in the air as he removed the pedestal, leaving her balancing on three legs. The trainer pointed his bull hook at her, and she raised the opposite back leg, after which he removed that pedestal. To the audience it seemed as though she was being gently persuaded into a difficult trick; they stood up and applauded with pleasure.

But Elinora knew better. Her face was contorted with disgust and sheer horror. The others were no longer fooled, either.

A sharp crack of a whip came from another trainer as he entered the ring with his act. Five dogs—wolfhounds, huge and elegant—trotted in as Wildflower was led away. The crowd rose to their feet once again.

"Look!" Jamie whispered.

Elinora drew in a deep breath.

"Is he there?" Lina asked.

"No, I don't see him, but that's surely his family; he's got to be around here somewhere, too," Graham whispered back.

"I can't watch this any longer. We need to get out of here and find him," Tillie growled. She stood up, and before the crowd had a chance to settle down and take their seats, she led them out of the stands and into the grounds outside the tent.

"That poor elephant," Elinora snarled.

"We've got to do something to help," Jamie said pulling out his pocket watch. "It's half past twelve. How much time do we have?"

"The first train back leaves at two o'clock," Tillie replied. "We need to hurry and be on that one if we want to get home before the crowd disperses and everyone notices what we're doing."

Lina paused and eyed the carousel again.

"Should we go look at it?" Jamie asked.

"Let's find Henry first, while Coddlefin and the others are busy in the ring," she answered.

"What about Henry's family? And the elephant. They're still in the tent, too," Elinora said.

"We can't get to them. We need to find Henry now while we have a chance," Graham replied, looking down, realizing the gravity of the situation.

"You remember what the Messenger said about this place," Jamie replied with a heavy sigh. "We need to do what we can, while we can. If there's anyone else we can help along the way, we will, but right now Henry is our priority. He's not going to like it if it means leaving his family behind again, but we can come back for them."

"Right then," Tillie said quickly. "We should split up. Lina and Jamie, how about we go that way," she said pointing behind the white fence. "Elinora, you and Graham go the other way. If one of us finds Henry, encourage him to come home and we will meet at the train."

"Watch for the Messenger—he's already scouting for Henry. Hopefully he has found him by now," Graham said to the others as they parted ways.

Elinora could feel her heart racing. She was shaking. "Don't do anything stupid, Tillie," she warned. "Be careful, all of you."

"You, too," Tillie replied. She looked intently at Elinora, then slipped behind the white fence, squeezing her monkey figurine tight.

As Elinora and Graham made their way through the grounds, hiding in the shadows of the trees, the Messenger spotted them and flew down to get their attention. Then he turned his back, coaxing them to follow. The alternating voices of the ringmaster and Coddlefin shouting in the arena, the roars of laughter from the audience, and the music of the band faded into the distance as they moved deeper.

Meanwhile, Tillie, Lina, and Jamie were already working their way toward the living quarters on the far edge of the encampment. A few circus performers wandered by, but nobody approached or tried to stop them. "Watch yourselves—you're asking for it if they catch you out here," one of them finally said.

Tillie ignored the warning. "Come on, it sounds like we're headed in the right direction," she said, leading Jamie and Lina further.

Upon rounding a bend, they came to an area separated from the rest by another fence. They ducked under the fence and continued walking. The landscape was manicured just like at the entrance of the grounds, the tents increasing in size the further they went; the first few were very clean, but still somewhat modest in size. The next several were a little larger. Finally, they saw a tent, the largest of them, made from the same crimson velvet as the big top.

Cautiously, Tillie crept forward. She looked at Lina, who nodded back and coaxed her forward.

"Jamie, will you stand guard while Tillie and I have a look around?" Lina whispered.

He grimaced, but they advanced anyway. "Be careful!" he demanded.

Tillie peered into the tent, opening the flap quickly when she saw no one was inside. Then she and Lina entered Coddlefin's lair.

26

The Red Barn

On the opposite side of the encampment, Graham and Elinora continued following the Messenger, who was drawing them deeper into an area that was tucked away and hidden from the public eye. The glamour of the big top and entrance to the grounds was absent here in the residence areas of the circus laborers, where the path was sloppy with dried mud, and hay was strewn about in a meager attempt to keep it tolerable. The air was stagnant, and tattered tents were crammed closely together, giving their inhabitants little protection or privacy.

A quiet young girl with pink, dirt-flecked cheeks gazed up at Elinora with wide eyes as she and Graham passed by. Elinora and Graham both felt discourteous wandering through in clean, tailored attire, sensing they stood out amongst the circus workers who were dressed modestly in their well-worn uniforms. There were adults and children alike living there, some of whom Coddlefin had plucked from their homes in Eldmoor or from distant lands, having been lured by hollow promises of a grand life—of fame and wealth. Others had been blackmailed or were indebted to him for various reasons—business loans and gambling debts mostly—and were forced into labor to work it off.

Elinora took off her blue, woolen cape and quietly gave it to the girl.

She remained silent, but she nodded, thanking Elinora.

Elinora slogged forward, tears filling her eyes as she tried to process what they were seeing—the harsh reality and foul living conditions borne from a cold, calculating heart. In that moment, she felt her fear of Coddlefin and his men begin to transform into something much deeper and more complex, and a defiance she had never known she possessed was sparked. She was certainly frightened, but her rising rage toward the cruelty he inflicted on others revealed a profound sense of strength and determination within her.

Graham shook his head. "This is awful. I hope we find Henry quickly. How could we ever leave him—or anyone—behind in this mess?"

She nodded and drew in a deep breath, then moved forward purposefully.

Together they continued following the Messenger, cautiously moving through the patch of woods that surrounded the area.

He soared overhead, then landed on the roof of a very large, red building in the clearing ahead and shook his wings.

"The red barn," Graham whispered.

"What?" Elinora whispered back, creeping forward.

He pointed to the top of the massive barn. "The sign—up there. It says *The Red Barn, Keep Out. Training in Progress.*"

She glanced up. "Do you think he's in there?"

He raised his eyebrows. "The Messenger certainly seemed to know where he was going." He put his fingers to his lips and looked back at the barn again.

She nodded. There was no one around so they moved out into the open together, approaching cautiously.

But the violent crack of a whip came from inside seconds later, stopping them. It was followed by the chilling trumpet of a horse in distress. "You stupid beast!" they heard a man yell as another snap cut through the air.

Elinora bristled. She looked over at Graham.

He furrowed his brows and looked around again. Then, spotting a door on the side of the building, he motioned for her to follow him. There was a large stack of barrels piled at the entrance and he crouched and tucked himself amongst them, making room for Elinora to squeeze in next to him.

The door was opened a crack, just enough for them to look through.

"I can see everything going on in there," Graham said, peering through. "They're definitely training animals here. I can see the horse we heard—boy he's beautiful—and two tigers, and... Elinora, look." He moved aside.

Elinora leaned over and peered through the crack. Inside she could see two trainers, one off in the distance at the back corner of the ring working with the tigers, the other in the foreground, red-faced with anger, fighting with the horse. She gritted her teeth—if only she could rush in right then and there and stop him; she knew Tillie would have. Then she looked to the far right and reflexively drew in a deep breath. Not twenty feet from her was a large, beautiful wolfhound. "Henry!" she gasped.

Graham looked up and signaled to the Messenger.

He flapped his wings silently, then bounded into the sky to find and alert Tillie, Jamie, and Lina.

Elinora quickly realized Henry was not being treated like the other animals; he looked well, almost relaxed—not at all in the condition she expected to find him in. He stood beside a young man, who was treating him respectfully and with compassion, unlike what was going on elsewhere in the arena. He carried no whip nor anything with which to prod or discipline; instead, he was using hand signals and verbal commands, and was smiling. Even from a distance, she sensed the boy's confidence, and his kindness. Her face lit up when she saw who it was. "Gray, look!" she said.

He peered back in. "That's who we saw on the carousel, isn't it?"

She nodded, smiling.

"There are too many people inside; we can't get to him yet. What do you think we should do?"

"Let's wait a minute and watch, all right?"

Graham nodded. They remained in their hiding spot and kept their eyes on Henry and the young man with him, who of course, was Alister. He and Henry seemed to be very in tune with one another. They watched breathlessly as Henry broke into a run, his powerful legs pounding the ground at top speed. Then, leaping high into the air, he touched his nose to a ball that had been suspended seven feet off the ground. He landed gracefully and shook his body, invigorated by the jump, then returned to Alister's side.

Elinora smiled again when she saw Alister ruffle his fur lovingly. Henry wagged his tail back.

Meanwhile, some of the other less fortunate animals were receiving a much harsher workout. They could see the horse they had heard in distress earlier. He was a proud and beautiful, but the scars on his back hinted at the treatment he'd suffered at the hands of his trainers. Now and again, when he wasn't being hit with the switch or cracked with a leather whip, he would let out an angry snort.

"That horse was on the carousel, too," Elinora whispered.

The horse stomped his foot, which made a dull thud when his hoof hit the earthen floor of the arena. Sawdust clouded the air.

"Alexander! Canter!" the trainer shrieked, whipping him again.

Alexander didn't budge, refusing to make the circuit around the ring. He trumpeted again, then gave a single sharp kick at the trainer.

"Bloody horse!" the trainer cried out and crumpled to the ground when his hooves connected with his knees.

"Serves him right!" Elinora whispered to Graham.

Another man with a sparse beard barged into the arena gripping a flaming torch in his right hand. He was coaxing a bear cub forward with an iron poker he held in his other hand. "Leopold, you're a sorry excuse for a trainer. Someone other than fancy britches over there should be able to ride that horse by now," he said, casting a dark look at Alister. "Alexander is lucky the Boss hasn't already turned him into horse meat, and you with him. Watch this," he snapped, picking up a ball.

"Shut up, Byron," Leopold barked back.

Byron nudged the cub with the poker to make him catch the ball.

But the cub was startled by this and fell backwards onto the ground. He rocked back and forth anxiously, not understanding what was wanted of him.

Byron swiped at him with the torch, causing him to scramble back up onto his hind legs, then he pressed the flame into the bear's tender front paws.

The cub cried in agony. He remained on his hind legs, crying and growling.

Byron tossed the ball into his outstretched paws. "That's it, you big, ugly beast," he chuckled. He turned back to Leopold, laughing. "How about that." A second later he was on the ground, flat on his stomach. He looked up in confusion.

"Don't ever let me see you treat any animal like that ever again," Alister growled as he stood back up, having tackled him.

At that moment Ghant entered with Wildflower. Just as he

had done in the wings during the performance, he was using a bull hook to move her. He poked the sharp end of the hook into the tender flesh of her armpit and nudged her forward into the center of the arena. "Get in there!" he yelled.

She made a feeble trunk call of distress to Alister when she saw him.

He jumped up, releasing Byron, and he rushed to her side. "What is wrong with you!" he shouted.

Byron got up and brushed himself off.

"Why is she here, Ghant?" Alister said between clenched teeth. "She should be in her stable where I left her to rest."

Ghant flashed a gnarly smile and raised the bull hook over her head.

She fell to the ground onto her knees, shrinking in fear, struggling to curl her tiny trunk around herself for protection. But the wound on her trunk was deep and painful, making it difficult to move.

Ghant leered, then smiled. "What will you do to stop me, Alice?"

"Don't you dare touch her," Alister said, stepping between them. "You know Mudd's orders."

Ghant scoffed, but Henry approached him with his back arched and stood at Alister's side. Ghant winced, though he still didn't back down. "No biggie, I just had her in the ring for the show."

"What did you just say?"

He cocked his head and smiled, raising his voice. "You heard me, *I took her into the ring for the show.*"

Alister suppressed his urge to fight with Ghant and instead turned his back and knelt beside Wildflower. Henry watched over them. He placed his hand gently on her back then ran it down her side and discovered the cut on her trunk. He touched it, then pulled away when he saw streaks of fresh blood on his hands. His face twisted with rage, a tear forming in his eye when he sensed Wildflower's pain, but he refused to allow Ghant and the others to see he was upset. "What have you done to her?" he asked steadily.

"I wanted to see what she could do. But she was a flop in the ring—you should have seen it. That worthless little runt still needs a lot of work. You might want to do something about that." He laughed wickedly.

Elinora and Graham could see that Wildflower was trembling. Graham clenched his jaw. Elinora stood up abruptly, but he put his hand on her shoulder and she lowered back down. "Hang on, I think he's handling them," he whispered.

"She isn't ready for the ring, and you know it," Alister said tersely to Ghant. "You stay away from her."

"You need to stop trying to make us look bad," he hissed, but he stepped back when Henry curled his lips and bared his teeth.

Leopold, however, had witnessed Coddlefin's reaction to Ghant's performance in the ring and pulled him aside.

Ghant sneered at Alister, but he backed off and walked away, stepping right in front of Elinora and Graham.

Elinora stifled a gasp when she realized he was one of the hunters who had been in Kellandale Wood. Her eyes narrowed.

"Just let her be," Alister said coolly. He grabbed the cloth that was draped over his shoulder, and tearing it into thin strips, he fashioned a tourniquet to tie around Wildflower's wound.

"Oh sure, of course, anything you say, Alice, dear," Ghant taunted again from a distance.

Alister rose to face him. "Let them all be. They trust me. Let me do it my way. You can take all the credit if you want, I don't care. I just want them to be left alone. They shouldn't be treated like this. You see Hector over there; he's not tormenting his tigers to teach them. You don't need to, either."

Hector froze when he heard his name.

"Oh yeah? Hector is weak then," Byron sputtered, but he quickly closed his mouth and glanced back at Ghant.

Ghant waved his hand in the air to silence him as he pondered Alister's offer. Even though he didn't want to agree with anything he said, he knew he was right; clearly, Alister could handle his animals and get them to do what he wanted. He especially liked the idea that Coddlefin would think that he was doing a great job without having to do a thing. He thought perhaps it would get him out of hot water after his failed performance. "Byron, come on, let him at it. We've got to go help Hector and Ellis get the dogs from the big top and put them away for the night, anyway," he finally said.

Byron shuffled his feet in the sawdust.

Ghant walked back over to Alister, pressing his face close. "It's a deal. But you'd better have these animals doing some top tricks, real fast. And you better be sure to let Mudd and Coddlefin know about the great job I've been doing." He paused. "There's something fishy about you that I haven't figured out quite yet. Sooner or later it'll catch up with you, and mark my words, I'll be there to make sure your life is miserable when I find out what it is."

"You heard him. Sooner or later it's all gonna catch up with you, Alice Jeffries," Byron echoed.

"You're filled with original thoughts, aren't you?" Alister snapped.

"What's that mean?" Byron asked. He turned to Ghant. "What's he mean by that?"

They both ignored him.

"Leopold, Nigel, get your animals and head back to the stables," Ghant barked.

"Right, mate," Leopold replied.

Alister locked eyes with Ghant. "I'll take Alexander and the others back to their stables myself."

"Suit yourself," he said, spitting on the ground, then he abruptly turned and exited the barn out the front door, along with Byron and Leopold.

Nigel followed with his head down, jaw clenched, glancing back at Alister with a mix of smoldering frustration and sadness on his face.

Alister nodded to him as he passed by, acknowledging this. Then Alister sighed loudly. "Come over here, guys," he said standing up. The bear cub, the tigers, and Alexander came to his side.

Elinora and Graham watched silently as Alister patted each of them and checked them for injuries, then walked over to the side of the barn and out through a back exit. They could hear a spigot being pumped, and then he returned with a bucket and two new rags.

He approached the bear cub and reached for his paw. "That's it, easy there, Caelus," he said dipping the cloths into the bucket and putting the cool rag on it. He turned to Wildflower and placed the other cloth on her back. "I should have never left you alone. I thought it would be all right to let you get some sleep for a moment, but I won't leave your side ever again. I'm going to keep even closer watch on all of you now; I won't let them hurt you anymore. Meanwhile, we're all going to find a way out of here sooner or later, aren't we Henry?"

Elinora listened to the sound of Alister's voice, gentle and reassuring. She closed her eyes and tears ran down her cheeks. "Oh, Henry," she said quietly.

Henry was standing beside Wildflower when he suddenly turned and looked to the side door. He pricked up his ears.

"Who's there? Show yourself!" Alister demanded, turning to face the door. But he felt Henry's demeanor shift—he was suddenly relaxed and not afraid, and even seemed happy. Curious, Alister waited for a reply from whoever might be outside.

Elinora, trusting him instinctively, took a risk and pushed the door open. She slipped through, revealing herself and Graham.

Henry recognized them immediately. He bounded over to greet them, his tail wagging frantically.

"Elinora!" Alister called out, grinning when he saw her. He stood up.

She looked over to him, surprised by his familiarity. "How do you know who I am?" she asked, then looked at Henry. "But of course. Henry, I've missed you so much!" She threw her arms around his neck and burrowed her head into his shoulder. He turned and licked her cheek.

Graham stepped forward. "Hello," he said to Alister.

"Hello, Graham. Henry has told me all about you," he replied, coming over to greet him. He shook his hand. "He's told me about all of you," he said looking back at Elinora with a warm smile.

Elinora felt a bit of a jolt when their eyes met and an unexpected wave of familiarity washed over both of them. She composed herself and smiled back. "I see you can understand Henry, too?"

Graham cracked a smile. "I'm not surprised. Henry trusts you, and I can see why. Thank you. He's really lucky to have you." He gave Henry a ruffle on the head.

"Yes, thank you—Alice, is it?" Elinora asked.

Alister laughed. "It's Alister, actually. Alister Jeff…Alister. It's Alister Pedronyn," he said firmly, shedding the surname he had inherited from Garibaldi and Rodene and reclaiming his parent's last name. He stepped closer and put his hand out for her to shake. She took his hand and he felt his cheeks flush slightly.

Henry communicated to Elinora and Graham the tale of how he and Alister had come to meet. Alister's story also passed to Elinora and Graham in a flash.

"Thank you for helping Henry," Elinora said to him. "And I'm sorry, it sounds like you were living with some not so nice people."

He nodded. "Yes. It's all right now, and Henry and I have been a good team."

"You have probably guessed that we've come to bring him back home," Elinora replied. "Henry, we want to take your family back with us, too, if we can get to them in time." She looked at Alister. "We saw them in the ring. Do you think it's possible?" She had hoped Henry would be relieved to hear this, but she felt panic rushing through him.

Alister paused a moment and sighed. "Henry is beautiful and magnificent, not to mention he's extremely intelligent. Mudd, the man who brought us here, recognized this and now he's Coddlefin's prize, which unfortunately complicates things greatly. They keep close watch on him; Coddlefin would know if he went missing in a heartbeat."

Elinora and Graham looked at each other when they heard the name Mudd.

"Coddlefin only sees money and fame—he thrives on adoration. Henry, he believes, is a way to all of that. He wants him trained to be the star of the show. If you try to take him back with you, Coddlefin will go to great lengths and do terrible things to stop you."

Elinora looked down.

"I'm sorry, Elinora," Alister said quietly.

Henry's thoughts washed over them again. He was overjoyed to see Elinora and Graham and wanted nothing more than to go home with them. But he couldn't leave—not now, not without his family, not without Wildflower or the other animals, and not without Alister.

"This is not a kind place. But I'm here, and with Henry at my side I can communicate with all the animals. They're able to learn tricks quickly, which will help keep Coddlefin satisfied, and them safe for the time being. Eventually we can work out how to get away, when the time is right," Alister reassured her.

"I do think we could figure out a way to get him out of here quickly, right now," Graham replied.

"Please, Alister," Elinora pleaded. "You can come to Kellandale with us, too. You would have a safe place to stay." But she looked at Wildflower, Alexander, Caelus, and the two tigers, Jazz and Tango; she thought of the people she had seen, and she understood Henry's dilemma.

"First of all, it will take more than just the three of us to pull anything off," he answered.

"There are six of us; Tillie, Jamie, and Lina are also here," Graham said hopefully. "They went looking for Henry on the other side of the grounds, behind the fence. We have the Messenger with us, too."

"Oh no, they're headed into Coddlefin's compound? They'll be discovered immediately. He has people watching—always. He's not anyone you'd ever want to be caught double crossing."

They were interrupted by the sound of footsteps. "Alice Jeffries!" Ghant's voice echoed from outside the arena.

"Quick, hide," Alister said to Graham and Elinora. They slipped out the door and crouched behind the barrels again.

"Hey, boy! All hands on deck!" Ghant yelled again as he entered. "Three runts were just seen nosing around Coddlefin's tent. I'm gonna go take care of them myself. Leopold is searching for Coddlefin to tell him. You might want to help him out, Alice." He rubbed his hands in excitement.

"I'm right behind you. I'll take Henry and the others to their stalls first," Alister said, feigning concern.

This seemed to satisfy Ghant, who rushed off to the tent.

Elinora and Graham stepped back into the arena.

"You need to go help them," Alister said quickly. "If you take the shortcut, there's a good chance you will get to them before Ghant does. If you do, get them out of here as fast as you can, and

259

don't worry about us; Henry and I will figure out how to get out of here later." He reached for Alexander's halter. "But if they get caught before you arrive, don't panic. Stay put, and stay out of sight. I will be right behind you, and I can diffuse Coddlefin. First, I have to take these guys to the stable. I'll have Henry and Alexander watch over Wildflower while I'm gone. She needs to rest and heal."

Elinora and Graham nodded.

"I'll see you there. Cut back through the woods. Look for the big red tent—it's hard to miss. And be careful, all right?" he said quickly rushing to the door.

Henry followed but turned back to look at Elinora and Graham, his eyes filled with grief.

"Henry, we love you. We will come back for you," Elinora called out.

His ears drooped and he wagged his tail, then he turned and followed Alister out of the Red Barn.

Graham put his hand on Elinora's shoulder. "Alister's right. We've got to help them. We'll come back for Henry and the others soon; at least we know they're in good hands for the moment."

"Oh, Gray, what will they do to them?"

He took her hand. "Come on, we just need to get to them first before they can do anything at all," he said as they ran.

Moments later, Coddlefin's velvet tent came into view. They made a mad dash toward it, but Ghant appeared from around the corner and approached the tent from the other side. They quickly ducked down to hide behind a stand of tall grasses outside the tent.

Elinora kept her eyes fixed, listening and waiting. She looked at Graham anxiously.

"We've got to trust Alister," he said. "But we've also got to be ready to do something fast to help them if he doesn't get here very soon."

27

Into the Fire

Ghant quickly spotted Jamie standing outside the entrance of Coddlefin's tent and he crept over quietly. Jamie hadn't seen him coming. He ambushed him from behind, quickly locking him in a strangle hold and covering his mouth so he couldn't alert anyone.

Tillie and Lina, meanwhile, had been snooping around inside and had plucked two journals from Coddlefin's desk. They had frantically searched through them for information that might help them find Henry and were shocked by things they had read. Equally shocking was the sound of the activated tripwire as Tillie unwittingly stepped onto the booby trap set for Coddlefin's enemies—spies from other circuses, people he had swindled, or authorities who might have finally caught onto one of his many illicit enterprises.

Ghant pulled Jamie into the tent, which served as Coddlefin's sleeping quarters as well as a workspace, with a tidy desk, a collection of books, and drafting materials. There he found Tillie and Lina hanging from the ceiling, strung up by their ankles from rigged trapeze cables. He laughed as they struggled and thrashed, thrilled at his own competence in catching them in the act. He continued to squeeze Jamie.

"Ow!" he gasped. "You really don't need to do that, I'm not going to run. Could you please just let me go and help them down? We didn't mean to hurt anything, we just got lost."

Ghant laughed. "That's what they all say."

Byron entered the tent suddenly. He snickered when he saw Jamie in a headlock.

Ghant turned abruptly. "Big help you are. Why don't you just head back to the big top to help Ellis. I can handle these three myself. No need for two heroes here."

"Aw, Ghant, I thought I could..."

"Go on," Ghant growled and Byron skittered off quickly.

Tillie was starting to feel lightheaded, and also very annoyed to be hanging upside down. "He's telling the truth, we just got lost!" she shouted.

Ghant stormed over, dragging Jamie with him. He pressed his face to hers, which was eye level with his own, but upside down. "I told you. I don't care what you say, you're not supposed to be in here. The Boss will decide what happens to you."

"Please," Lina pleaded. She winced from the pain of the rope lashed tightly around her. Thankfully, the thick woolen socks she and Tillie were wearing with their trousers offered at least some protection to the skin of her ankles.

Tillie squirmed. Ghant saw this so he gave her a little nudge, causing her to swing back and forth. "Rock-a-bye, little spy," he laughed.

"You'll be sorry if you don't let us down!" she threatened.

Ghant looked at her with narrowed eyes.

Rikona and Kano entered the tent abruptly and Coddlefin

stormed in from behind. He looked down at Jamie, around his tent, and then over to Tillie and Lina.

"I caught these three snooping around; I thought I could help," Ghant offered.

"Yes, yes, we can take it from here," Coddlefin replied, waving him away. Ghant opened his mouth, but he stopped him. "You're not needed any further, you've done enough already today." He waved him away again much more curtly.

Ghant let go of Jamie, pushing him to the ground, then he turned and hurried off.

Coddlefin moved closer to Tillie and Lina, his face flushed. He nodded to Rikona and Kano to restrain Jamie. They walked over and grabbed him by the arms.

"Honestly, we didn't mean to cause any trouble," he pleaded, pulling himself back onto his feet as they lifted him.

The color left Coddlefin's face suddenly. He decided another approach. "I see. Let's try this again more civilly, shall we? Now then, what brings you here into my home, my dear children?" he said, with eerie congeniality.

"Nothing, sir. We were looking for cotton candy and got lost. We tried to find our parents, but we got distracted by this beautiful tent," Lina answered. He was standing close enough she could smell cigars and a light tinge of garlic on his breath.

"Wonderful," he laughed. "And tell me, did you choose your clothing purposely?" he said, eyeing her grey velvet trousers that were identical to Tillie's, except for the color, which were a dusty, dark blue.

"What do you mean?" Lina asked.

"Yes," Tillie said, furrowing her brows, what does that have to do with anything?"

Lina groaned. She was feeling quite fuzzy now, the blood rushing to her head. "I know we shouldn't have come in here, we just started exploring."

"Well, isn't that something. And here I thought maybe you were some of the little vagrants, *spies,* sent by Dickerson's Circus. Your costumes are very much what they wear when they try to blend in here," he said, glaring at Tillie and Lina's clothing, gauging their response.

"What?" Jamie gasped.

"No? Then it must be Stan Dillon and his men you're working with. Yes, that makes more sense—that slippery man is always trying to get his hands on my ideas and inventions. Well, he won't get away with it this time." Spittle flew from his mouth as he spoke.

"Oh no, no, we're here to see your show," Tillie protested. He turned sharply then studied her closely with no expression. For a fleeting moment she thought he believed her.

But he turned away and looked at the ground, catching a glimpse of one of his journals lying beneath her. It was open. He bent over and snatched it up. The veins in his neck pulsated. He moved closer, his steely gaze burning a hole through her. "Peeking at my diaries? Who else are you with!"

"I didn't, we didn't . . ." she said, panicking.

His face contorted, turning an even deeper crimson than his tent. He nodded at Rikona and Kano, then Kano unsheathed her sword and approached.

But Rikona put her arm out to stop her.

Coddlefin cocked his head, grabbing her sword from her hand. "Don't you dare challenge me. I've never seen this side of you before, Rikona. Think carefully."

Kano didn't move. She remained ready to strike on his word.

"Kano, he's asking too much this time—they're *children,*" Rikona protested. She looked at Coddlefin pleadingly.

He ignored her and nodded to Kano again.

Kano moved toward Tillie, raising her sword above her head.

"Wait! What? What are you doing?" Tillie asked, frantically struggling to free herself from the cables.

"Please!" Jamie shouted.

"Don't hurt her!" Lina yelled. Within seconds Coddlefin was at her side and he punched her in the stomach; the sound was dull and sickening. Lina recoiled in pain, struggling to breathe.

"Lina!" Tillie yelped and struggled again, but Coddlefin stepped toward her. "Somebody help!" she screamed again.

"Tillie!" Elinora called out reflexively from outside the tent when she heard her sister's cries.

This distracted Coddlefin for moment—long enough to spare Tillie from the blow he had intended for her. But it also gave Elinora's presence away. He turned to look out the tent, scanning for intruders. "Kano, find whoever that is!" he ordered.

She exited and bounded over to where she suspected the voice had come from, stealthily moving amongst the grasses. Her sabre glistened in the sun, her body poised to spring into action. "Show yourself!" she demanded.

Elinora was so frightened she felt lightheaded. But she took a deep breath. "Stay down," she quickly whispered to Graham. "I'll go with her. When I'm gone, go find Alister. I'll be all right, I promise."

Graham looked shocked.

"Please, just do it."

He nodded and hunkered down deeper into the grass.

She stood and gave herself up. "It's just me. I am looking for my sister and cousins. We got separated. I think they got lost," she said trying to keep her voice from trembling.

Kano grabbed her by the arm and pulled her toward the tent. "Very well. Come with me. Someone wants a word with you."

Elinora did not struggle. She breathed deeply, letting fear pass through as she was shoved forward into the tent in front of

Coddlefin. He was sweating profusely, glaring at her. She stepped back to get away, but Kano pushed her forward. Behind him she could see Tillie and Lina suspended in the air, their faces flushed. Lina was still reeling from the pain. Rikona held Jamie tightly.

Tillie looked up in horror when she saw Elinora. "Nora, no!" she cried.

"I'm sorry, Tillie. I should have never let you wander off."

Coddlefin eyed Tillie when he heard her name. He moved over to her and dug the tip of Rikona's sword into her collarbone, stopping just short of breaking the skin.

She whimpered but held her tongue.

"Tillie, is it? Well, I'm sorry to say, clever Tillie, you and your cohorts have been caught red handed in a place you'll wish you'd never found."

Jamie looked up at Elinora, tears falling down his dirt-stained cheeks.

"Do you know what I do to those who take from me?" Coddlefin asked in an unnervingly pleasant tone. "I take something back—sometimes an arm or a leg. Sometimes just a hand." He studied Tillie, calculating the space between them, then without warning, he swiftly brought down the sword upon her. But it was with planned precision, and he only just nicked the tip of her littlest finger on her left hand with the razor-sharp blade. Not so much of her finger that it would cause her to lose too much blood, but enough to make her suffer in pain.

She shrieked when she saw the blood dribbling from her hand onto the ground. She clutched her hand protectively.

"Leave her alone!" Lina raged.

He grinned. "Did you forget that I'm quite a marksman myself?" he said to Rikona. He raised the sword again, this time aiming at Lina.

"Stop!" Tillie screamed at him.

Before he could strike at Lina, Alister appeared in the tent, distracting everyone.

Elinora looked pleadingly at him, terror in her eyes. He winked at her, then smiled calmly.

Jamie and Lina immediately recognized him from the carousel, but kept quiet.

Alister returned Jamie's glance with a subtle nod then looked around the tent assessing what had happened. He saw that Tillie was bleeding so he quickly moved over to her, pulling another handkerchief from his pocket to tend to her. He kneeled down and wrapped it around her hand. "Looks like you might need some help," he said.

She looked up at him with recognition but he pursed his lips, hoping to silence her. Then he looked up at Coddlefin. "Well, hello, Boss. I just put the animals away and was going to see if anyone needed help at the big top, but I heard the commotion in here."

Coddlefin didn't reply.

Alister stood up and looked around the tent again. "So, what happened?" he asked.

"Just a little business I need to attend to," he said evenly. "Don't worry yourself about it. These fools got caught looking through my things. Stan Dillon has crossed me one too many times; I've decided it's time we showed him we mean business." He shrugged Alister off. "Get rid of them, Kano," he said casually, as though he was asking someone to close a window.

"What?!" Elinora screamed.

"Wait. Are you sure you should do that?" Alister asked, stepping protectively in front of her.

"Quite sure," Coddlefin replied curtly. He raised his right eyebrow, his face beginning to pulsate again. But he decided to let Alister speak.

Rikona and Kano remained motionless, waiting for orders.

"Well, *I* am quite sure I saw them in the crowd with their parents earlier today," Alister said without missing a beat. "I suspect it might be very bad for business if they went home without the rest of their family."

Coddlefin cocked his head.

"They aren't spies, I promise. Why not just let them go."

"They've read my diary."

Alister didn't know what that meant, but he could tell it was something he certainly didn't want anyone to do.

Coddlefin looked at Tillie wild-eyed, like his mind was off in another world as the rage coursed through his body. "*What*, pray, did you read in my journal?" he interrogated.

"I…I only read about the new baby elephant. The one we saw in the show. She's beautiful, everyone loved her. You're so kind to have helped her."

"But *why* were you looking through it in the first place?"

"The cover just looked intriguing, so I picked it up out of curiosity. I'm silly like that, but that's really all that I read, I swear," she lied again. But she noticed Coddlefin's skin tone change back to a light pink again. His eyes stopped bulging.

"Really, sir, we love your circus, it's amazing. We didn't mean to cause you any trouble," Jamie said.

Coddlefin lifted his head proudly.

"We saw the show, it's the best I've ever seen. We were very impressed," Lina added, joining in on the flattery.

"Is that so." Coddlefin straightened his posture.

"Oh yes, *extraordinary*," Tillie said.

"It's going to be quite a show this year. We have other surprises in store. But I need to be assured you won't share the little tidbit about the elephant. It's one of our newest attractions and meant to be a surprise." He paused. "Jeffries, make sure you escort these fine young children out of here. And take them to get their cotton candy before they return to their parents. On the house."

"Will do," Alister said, wiping a bead of sweat off his brow. He turned to Elinora and locked eyes with her. She exhaled with relief.

"And be sure to walk them off the grounds," Coddlefin said abruptly. "Their parents can find them outside the gates. I am trusting you, Jeffries." Then he turned to Tillie to address her directly. "I'll let you go—this time. But to be safe, I don't ever want to see your darling little face again, not here on the grounds, and not ever at our shows. And if I find that you have read anything else in my diary and share it with *anyone*, I have the means to find you, and your parents will never, ever know what became of you. Do you *understand!?*"

She gulped.

Elinora glared at him.

Coddlefin smiled congenially. "Thank you for coming. I hope you enjoyed the show, have a wonderful trip home," he said, then exited the tent.

Kano shoved Jamie forward toward Alister. "Leave. Now," she warned, then she and Rikona followed on his heels.

Elinora doubled over, trying to catch her breath. Alister moved to her side and put a hand on her shoulder. "Don't worry, they're gone," he said. She nodded and breathed deep. "Are you all right, Jamie?" she asked. He nodded and she moved over to his side to check him for injury.

A moment later, Graham slipped into the tent.

Alister quickly found a small knife on the desk and Jamie, Graham, and Elinora untangled Tillie and Lina as he cut the lines that were holding them.

They dropped to the ground and Lina scrambled over to Tillie, throwing her arms around her.

Tillie grabbed her back. "I can't believe he punched you! Are you hurt?"

"I'm not, somehow…thankfully, but that's nothing compared to what he did to you! Look what he did to your hand!"

Tillie cringed. "I'll be all right. Thank *you* for trying to protect me."

"And thank you, Alister," Graham added. "I don't know what would have happened to them if you hadn't come in here when you did."

"Glad to help. I know it was hard for you to stay hidden, but you're the only one Coddlefin won't recognize now. Let's keep it that way."

Jamie put his hand out to help Lina and Tillie to their feet, then Tillie unwrapped the handkerchief. "Ouch," she said looking down at her hand. "Who needs a fingertip, anyway?"

Elinora rushed to her side. "What on earth were you thinking, Tillie? Why did you come in here, of all places? Were you trying to get yourself killed? You're lucky this is all he did to you!" She grabbed her sister's bloody hand. Tears fell down her cheeks. Then she saw her necklace. Quickly she pulled it from her neck and opened the monkey figurine. "Here," she said, soaking the handkerchief with the water inside the vessel, then holding it firmly to her wound. Tillie took it and continued to squeeze her finger to stop the blood.

Alister came to her side, watching intently.

"You have to stop doing such stupid things without thinking! This is by far the worst decision you have ever made in your life," Elinora scolded, but she grabbed Tillie and was hugging her as she yelled.

"I read his journal. Hopefully what I read is worth losing a fingertip for," she replied, then paused. "I'm really sorry, Elinora. I wasn't thinking. I'm sorry I put all of us in danger—I'm just desperate to find Henry."

Elinora sighed. "It's all I want, too. We all do."

Tillie looked up in surprise. "So, you're not angry with me?"

"How could I ever be? I just don't want anything to happen to you. But I finally realize what we are up against and the risks we're going to have to take—that I'll have to take, too—in order to help him. Henry can't stay here. None of them can." She paused. "We found him. He was with Alister," she said, reaching out and touching his arm. She pulled it away quickly, catching herself for being so familiar. But he smiled at her. "Alister is taking good care of Henry; he will be safe with him until we can figure out better plans."

Tillie looked up; her eyes were wide. "You have him? Where?"

Alister nodded. "He's back at the stable, watching over Wildflower."

Elinora removed the handkerchief; just as the water had healed Jamie, Tillie's finger had already stopped bleeding. The tip was still missing, but it was visibly healing all the same. She covered it again. "I think we need to get out of here, I don't want to get caught again. I'll explain that on our way out of here," she said to Alister, gesturing at the figurine.

He nodded. "I'm assuming you don't really want cotton candy?" he asked with a slight grin, glancing at Elinora. He felt his face flush again and turned his head quickly to hide it. But when he glanced at her again, she was grinning right back at him. "Come on, we need to get you out of here," he said to the group, his grin now a full smile.

They followed him out of the tent, through the encampment, and back under the white fence. As they made their way to the exit, they passed by the carousel.

"Can you give me a moment?" Lina asked. "I really feel like we should have a look before we go..." She ran to it, stepping up onto the platform and quickly moving to the center pole. She circled it, inspecting carefully. "I knew it! Come here!" she called to the others.

Jamie joined her. "Oh, you genius!" he said opening the little door. "It's just like..." He turned to the others. "I'm looking right into the forest!"

The others rushed onto the carousel.

"Our forest?" Tillie asked.

"Yes! What if we were able to communicate through it!" Lina exclaimed. She turned to Alister. "Can you come back here later? You, here on the carousel, and us, there at the carousel in the forest."

"I can come tomorrow night, just after sundown," he replied. "That's when Coddlefin and his men disappear for the night, and there's lots of diversion while the animals are being fed. I could get away for a moment without anyone noticing." He looked off in the distance. Rikona and Kano were headed in their direction, flanked by several circus performers. "Coddlefin's people are making sure you aren't sticking around. We should hurry," he said. "Graham, stay out of sight, away from us."

"Will do. See you tomorrow, Alister," he said then quickly made his way to the trail back to the train station ahead of everyone.

The others filed off the carousel. Before parting ways with Alister, Elinora said something quietly to Tillie, who nodded.

"Here, Alister, take this," Tillie said taking off her necklace and pressing the monkey figurine into his hands. "This will heal Wildflower. You can use it on the other animals, or yourself even, if you ever need to. Shake it, then hold it in the air before you apply it. And don't worry, it doesn't seem to run out. Thank you for saving us, and for watching over Henry."

Alister pulled the strap around his neck and held the figurine in his hand. "Glad to help. Thank you for this. I will keep it safe and I will return it when I see you again. I hope that I won't need to use it, but it's good to have." He glanced back to Rikona and Kano.

Elinora saw them coming, too. She turned to Alister. "I meant it when I said you can come with us."

"Thank you, Elinora," he said to her, reaching out for her hand. "I would like that. I'll be there one day, and it will be as soon as I can. For now, I promise I will protect Henry and the others. I will be at the carousel tomorrow and I will see you again then. Now hurry, before they notice that you're still here...and be safe!" he said as he led her to the exit.

"All right, you be careful, too, Alister," Elinora said, letting go of his hand, then she, Tillie, Lina, and Jamie fled the grounds of Théodore Coddlefin.

28

Contact

Alister held the stable door open for Henry and Wildflower. They quietly filed in and Henry curled up by Wildflower's side on one of the blankets Nigel had smuggled in for them. The sounds of other animals shuffling into their own stalls droned in the background as they got settled. He sighed deeply. "You both did well today. You should rest for a while—that was hard work." He closed the door then sat down and nestled in between them.

Once the activity quieted down and the trainers had returned to their tents for the evening, he checked Wildflower's trunk again. It had already healed considerably since he had applied the tincture Tillie had given him. He pulled the monkey figurine out and turned it over in his hand. "Whatever is in this little vessel, it's magic."

Wildflower rumbled contentedly and curled her trunk around his arm.

It was still an hour before sundown, so Alister had time to ponder how best to get to the carousel with Henry and Wildflower without being noticed. He knew everyone at Kellendale would be waiting for him. He thought of Elinora, and a wave of anticipation hit him. He realized how much he was looking forward to seeing her again. He sighed and leaned his head against the stall wall. "If we can talk to them through the carousel, that will be something, all right; it will change everything. We can make plans and band together. Maybe we'll get out of this place sooner than later."

Henry's mind wandered as he thought about Elinora and Tillie, Graham, Jamie, Lina, the forest, and all his friends he missed so terribly. He shared more memories of them with Alister and Wildflower as they rested for comfort.

It had been a surprisingly decent day, relatively speaking, compared to the confrontation with Coddlefin the day before. Not only had they been spared from interacting with Ghant and Byron thanks to the deal Alister had struck with them, but Henry had seen his family again. And this time he had taken the opportunity to convey more about the rising plan to escape.

The sound of the main door of the barn opening and closing echoed in the stable, pulling Alister out of his thoughts. "Who could that be, this late?" he grumbled.

But it was only Nigel, making his last rounds to check on Jazz and Tango and a few of the other animals in his care. "In you go," he said gently as he shut the stable door behind Jazz.

Alister stood up, an idea crossing his mind. "Hey there," he called out casually. "Want to join us for a bit, Nigel? No one will miss you this late."

Nigel acknowledged him with a tired hello but came over. He entered the stable, then sat down in the hay with them. It was slightly cramped, but no one minded. A spot of solitude, no matter the conditions, was rare and welcomed. "There's not many places where I feel I can let my guard down here," he finally replied. "Thanks, Alice, you're a good guy."

"You are, too. And actually you should know, my real name is Alister," he said with a grin. "But it's all right if you call me Alice. I just don't want Ghant and the others knowing. But I'm glad to share it with you."

"Alister. That's a good name."

"My real mother named me after my grandfather, so I've been told. Anyway, I've been wondering. How did you end up here? You don't seem to like it very much—more than most of the people I've met so far."

Nigel studied him for a moment, then looked up at the stall ceiling and watched as a black and yellow moth drifted in through the bars of one stall window and out the other. He scratched his head and thought for a moment. "No one's ever asked me that before, not in the ten years I've been here." He sighed.

Alister waited for him to continue.

"I'm here because of the debt my father had with the Boss. When he died, his debt didn't die with him. So Coddlefin came after my mother for it. Since she wasn't able to settle it, I stepped in—to protect her. But I didn't have enough to settle it either and in the end I couldn't protect her. I was overpowered by his men and didn't stand a chance against them. Then, I was given a choice. I could work off what my father had owed on the loan, a loan he had unwittingly taken out with such a crooked man to start his business, or Coddlefin threatened to take everything we had—even the house. Then he hinted to me in private that something bad might happen to my mother if I didn't take the first option. Can you guess what I chose?"

Alister nodded.

"He said I was smart, that I would be working for the best circus in the world, and I'd be rich in the end. He even sweet-talked my mother and convinced her to be proud of me for joining his circus." He looked down with a scowl. "I haven't seen her since that day."

"I'm sorry about that."

"Thanks, Alice. Alister. So, now here I am. Turns out he wanted me to do animal training—the rough kind. That's what he claims gives results. But I can't lay a hand on any animal. Ghant and the others, they seem to like the power it makes them feel, beating and harassing those poor animals. But no matter what, I'm stuck, because I know too much about how things work here. There's more to Coddlefin than just his circus, and there's a lot going on in those back barns. Really ugly stuff—some illegal stuff; stuff you don't want to know about, because you probably couldn't stomach it, and also because if you knew about it, you wouldn't ever be able to leave, either. Really, you can't leave now as it is anyway, because once you're in, you're in. That's how it is for all of us." He looked hard at Alister.

Alister fell silent as he pondered everything he had just been told. "Thanks for confiding in me. I came from a pretty bad place. My parents—well, I refuse to call them my parents, but the folks that looked after me after my parents went missing—they were awful. Yet I'm beginning to realize things can be much worse still. I've already seen and heard Coddlefin do some pretty terrible things. I don't like it here either, Nigel. It really is miserable."

"Boss has his sights on bigger things all the time. I swear that man is deranged. He's hungry for attention and doesn't care who he steps on or destroys to get it. Now and then he loses it and gets a look in his eye; it's terrifying, like a banshee staring down at you."

Alister nodded. "I've seen that look. I'm sure glad I got to meet you. You're the only sane person I've met so far, apart from the animals, Hector, and Ellis, and some of the other circus folk. Maybe we can help each other." As he said this, he could feel Henry's feelings wash over him. He felt Wildflower's, too. They all trusted Nigel, and knew he was kind at heart. Henry silently encouraged Alister to continue sharing their plans with him.

"So, Nigel, I might as well tell you. Henry, Wildflower, and I plan to break out of here. They want to take as many others as we can with us, animals or people—anyone who wants out. I do, too. I know everyone is too afraid to leave, but we have friends outside and a place to go. They were here yesterday, in fact, and we are working on a plan. We would be thankful to have you on our side."

"Well, that's not what I expected to hear." He thought a moment, then he broke into a wide smile and laughed. "Henry and Wildflower told you that?"

Alister let the question hang a moment. "You'll see eventually."

"Well, I guess there's nothing to lose. But I don't know if you'll be able to pull it off. It's risky, especially since Coddlefin's got Rikona and Kano, and all his men watching."

"Oh, I can handle them," Alister replied confidently. "Ghant and Byron are worthless."

"No, not just them. His army. You know about Coddlefin's army?"

Alister turned his head to the side. "A little..."

"Do you know how many he has guarding him?"

"Quite a few?" Alister replied.

"Try hundreds. It's a full-scale operation. He's in command of a lot of people, some you see, some you don't see, most you don't even notice. They do what he asks without question. Some are like me, trapped here against their will. The others he takes care of much better, and they stick around because they have aspirations themselves." He eyed Alister, who looked surprised for the first time. "You sure you know what you're getting yourself into?"

"Not entirely. But I do know we have a lot in our favor. In fact, I need to get to the carousel at sundown tonight, and I need to take Henry and Wildflower with me. I can't explain why yet, but I need someone to stand guard, someone I can trust."

Nigel's eyes narrowed as he pondered doing anything against Coddlefin. "Wait a minute. I think maybe I'll get Stinky to help. Stinky is the one who shovels all the bad stuff around here. You know who I'm talking about I'm sure, because he just smells pretty bad. It's not his fault, it's his job; he thinks the smell might be permanent. But he's a good kid. His real name is Flynn, but he prefers to be called Stinky—he came up with the name himself. He says it keeps Coddlefin's men a good distance away from him," he chuckled. "And he would like nothing more than to get out of here, too. He's a tough one; he'll help for sure."

"Stinky, I like that. And the more help, the better. Tell him he can come talk to me if he wants. Maybe you can find others we can trust, too. For now, when the sun starts to set, meet us out front. We'll sneak over when the trainers are busy feeding the animals and Coddlefin and his men are two sheets to the wind in their tents for the night. One of you can stay in our stable to make an excuse if someone comes looking for me, and one of you can stand guard at the carousel."

"Sundown," Nigel said, getting up. "We'll be there."

"Thanks, my friend. So, now that you know we don't plan to stick around here for long, you might as well tell me what we're really up against. I've seen Coddlefin angry. But you said things are going on in the back. What kinds of things? Tell me."

Nigel sighed. "You really want to know? Some of it is just crazy inventions, things like that, nothing harmful. But some of the other stuff is plain wrong. And some of it is pretty awful how they use anyone and anything that doesn't serve a purpose to the Boss; I hope you don't get upset easily."

Alister was thrilled when he heard the stable door open at sundown. True to his word, Nigel had returned with Stinky, and Stinky had brought yet another helper—a dark-haired young girl his age named Lark, which meant they now had three new allies.

As planned, Nigel remained at the stable sweeping and cleaning up in the event someone came in looking for Alister, while Stinky and Lark followed Alister, Henry, and Wildflower to the carousel. Stinky was no more than thirteen years old. But he was talkative and full of energy, with wild, dark brown curls, and light tan skin that had been covered with a layer of dirt from all the hard barn work. And he was loaded with questions. He hated Coddlefin just as much as Nigel did and was eager to help fight their way out from under him.

Lark, who was as short as Stinky, with big blue eyes, smiled a lot, but she was very shy and chose not speak much at all. She resorted to shrugs, nods, and eyebrow expression to communicate, and relied on Stinky to do all the talking for the both of them. They were inseparable.

Stinky was very protective of her and he told Alister that Lark was even stronger than he was, and ten times as brave, even though she was ten times quieter. True to form, Stinky had to be shushed when he and Lark experienced Henry's ability to communicate firsthand, though Alister certainly didn't want to quash his exuberance—he quite liked both of them and knew they would be reliable. He also tried to remain upwind from Stinky as they walked and Alister told them all about how he and Henry first met.

They were both completely engrossed in the story. "I remember when your brothers and sisters were puppies," Stinky said to Henry. "I didn't know they got rid of you, and I'm sorry you're stuck here again," he said, baring his teeth. "I can't wait to get us out of here."

Henry raced over to Lark when he saw her blue woolen cape.

He knew that cape, and he wagged his tail frantically. Lark clutched it tightly when she realized who had given it to her. Alister noticed this and smiled. They walked on quietly the rest of the way, Lark hugging Henry often as they went. She could sense there was something different about him and he made her feel safe.

"All right, stay hidden and keep a look out. If you see anyone coming near, throw a rock to let me know," Alister instructed once they reached the carousel.

Lark nodded.

"Will do, Alice," Stinky replied dutifully, getting into position.

"You can call me Alister. And thanks, we make a good team."

Stinky saluted him, then Alister made his way onto the carousel with his companions. It was large enough even for Wildflower to step onto it. They worked their way to the little door in the center pole that he had seen Lina open. It was quiet and dark, and they made sure to stay in the shadows. From a distance, Wildflower and Henry looked as though they were part of the carousel.

Alister opened the portal and peered inside. He could see a clearing within a forest on the other side. It was sundown there as well, but he could still see clearly. "Hello," he whispered. There was no response, but the carousel began to hum quietly a moment later. He glanced over to Stinky, who gave the signal that everything was all right, and he relaxed a little again. Then came the sound of a muffled voice, distant and somewhat choppy, but certainly coming from the other end of the portal.

"Hel-? Is an-one th-re?" the voice called out.

"He-o!" Alister replied. "Who's ther-? I can he-r yo-."

"It's me, Jam-e," the voice said. "I ca- hear -ou, a lit-le. And I *see* yo-!"

Henry came bounding over to Alister's side, jumping up with his paws onto the pole so he could see Jamie.

"Henry! I'm so happy to see you, too, boy," Jamie said, now conveying his thoughts to Henry without speaking.

"Jamie, we can hear you loud and clear," Alister replied to him in his mind.

"It's working! Hang on, someone else really wants to see you." He stepped away from the portal.

"Henry!" Elinora exclaimed. She was smiling ear to ear. Tillie moved in next to her and peeked in with her.

Elinora looked back through the portal again and saw Alister. "Oh, I'm so happy to see you!" she blurted out. "I've been worried about you and Henry," she said.

"It's really nice to see you, Elinora," he smiled back, then paused and took a deep breath. "We're doing just fine for the moment."

Tillie looked at her sister, then to Alister and back to her sister again with a grin. Then she stood on her tiptoes and called out, "Hello, hello!" excitedly through the portal. Henry's tail pounded the ground.

Graham and Lina leaned in so they could see Henry. His tail wagged even faster.

"How are you doing, sweet little Wildflower?" Lina asked when she saw her. She raised her trunk in the air back at her affectionately.

Alister smiled. "What in the world is in this vial? She's doing great. She healed so fast, I can't even believe it," he said, grabbing the monkey figurine hanging around his neck.

"It came from the river…" Tillie said, but Elinora came back to the portal. "Alister, you need to know, Tillie and Lina read Coddlefin's diaries. Tell him," she said.

"I read more, much more than what I let on," Tillie answered.

"I suspected as much," he laughed.

"We know when he's coming to Waterbridge. I read he will be there June twenty-second—just under a month from now. That will put the circus close to us here at Kellandale, as close as he will get," Lina added.

"That is very helpful information," Alister replied.

"So, we have until then to come up with a better plan than the last one," she said. "But we're worried. Will everyone be safe for that long?"

"I made a deal to keep Ghant and the others away from the animals now. We have Nigel, Stinky, and Lark helping us. And Coddlefin seems to like me for some reason. We should be all right for the time being."

"There's more," Tillie added. "Lina has read his travel itinerary—that's how we know the date. But I read his personal journal—he's absolutely wretched. Awful. More than we ever guessed. You really must be careful."

"I know, Nigel told me everything," Alister said looking down. "I didn't want to tell you and worry you any further, but I know."

"I read about a strange chariot he's building, one that appears to fly in the air. He's stolen from an inventor to make it—not that it comes close to the other things I read about."

"He didn't tell me about that part, but yes, it sounds quite tame compared to other things he's got going on."

"Alister, there's something else."

But he suddenly turned away when a tiny pebble was thrown his way. He looked back to the portal. "We don't have much time, but I'm glad we have a way to meet. I'll come back tomorrow, and the day after that, and every day until we get out of here. We have people on our end that we can trust now, and we'll find more, as many as we can."

"Alister," Tillie said quickly. "I must tell you. Coddlefin knows about Kellandale Wood. He's obsessed with it. And from what I read, it seems like he's had it in his sights for a very long time. He knows the history somehow, and about the animals living here.

He has been trying to get at them for years. He doesn't know why he can't, but they are protected by the forest. It's the only thing stopping him. Do you know about the Lady of the Forest?"

"I do, Henry told me everything."

"Coddlefin saw her when he came to Kellandale when he was young; he's been searching for her ever since. Now he just sends his men to look." She paused. "And you know about the other horrible things?" she asked.

"Nigel told me all about the Red Barn, if that's what you mean," he said, wrinkling his nose. Just then two more stones came flying and plinked on the edge of the carousel. Alister could see Stinky and Lark waving a little more urgently at him. "I'd better get Henry and Wildflower out of here quick. You can tell me anything else you know later, and I'll do the same. We'll stay on guard. You be safe, too, all of you. See you soon."

Elinora returned to the portal. "When?" she asked quickly.

"In two days. Same time. That will give me time to talk to others around here to see what else I can find out. We're stealing an entire circus; we've got some serious planning to do."

"All right then, we'll be here. Alister…be careful."

"I will," he promised.

Graham poked his head in. "Righto, we'll put our minds to it."

Tillie, Jamie, and Lina peered through the portal one last time, and everyone said their goodbyes quickly. Henry wagged his tail vigorously.

"We love you, Henry!" Tillie yelled as the portal door closed.

29

The Delivery

Tillie put the key in the lock, turned it, then jiggled the door handle, but it was stuck. She tried again using both hands with more force.

"What did you do, break it? Here, let me try," Jamie grinned as he nudged her out of the way.

"Very funny. We were in a hurry to get back downstairs last time if you recall, Mister *Witling*. I locked it like any normal person would."

"Ha!" Jamie barked.

"It's probably jammed with rust and just needs to be cleaned," Graham offered.

"Well, you're no fun, I'm *trying* to give Tillie a hard time for being such a foozle." He pulled the key out, stooped down, and blew into the keyhole.

"Ha, ha!" Tillie replied.

"I'm just stating the obvious," Graham added.

Jamie stood back up. "Right, of course, nothing out of the ordinary there, Gray."

Elinora and Lina both snickered.

"What!" Graham said to them.

"Look at you, Jamie!" Tillie cackled. "You've got rust particles on your face. Serves you right!"

Jamie furrowed his brow, wiped the grime off, then reinserted the key, wiggling it to clean out the locking mechanism. Then he tried turning the key again. This time there was a click. He bowed in victory.

"As I said." Graham replied smartly.

"At least I can unlock a door."

"Touché," Tillie praised.

Elinora shook her head. "You're all *impossible!* Come on then, I want to get in there sometime this century."

"Oh, who's the impatient one now?" Tillie teased.

Elinora wrinkled her nose.

Lina laughed at all of them.

Jamie turned the knob and opened the door. "All right everyone, get thee to Sir Edward's treasure room," he said, pointing the way.

It had been several weeks since their failed rescue attempt at the circus and they were still traumatized by the encounter. Alister was on their side now and they had continued to meet him at the carousel over the ensuing weeks to plan their next attempt. But they recognized the dangers they faced and were aware that it was imperative they develop a much more solid strategy, considering the situation had grown in both scope and complexity. They knew Coddlefin would eventually visit Waterbridge, and it was likely their only opportunity to act; but still, it was a long distance by foot from town to Kellandale Wood—too far, and much too risky to have an entire circus trying to escape in that manner. They had all grown increasingly frustrated by this logistical stumbling block.

But through her recent reading of Sir William's journal, Elinora realized how deeply connected he had been to Kellandale Wood. It was her idea to go looking for his other journals, hoping they might contain more passages about the magic of the forest that could potentially help them free Henry and the others. Everyone agreed returning to the storeroom to search for them was a good use of their time. "Look everywhere," she directed when they finally entered.

They stood at the entrance, candles raised, revealing the heaping mass of treasures. They walked forward into the room as a group, but quickly dispersed as they began to explore.

Graham was drawn to a carved wooden shield and the tarnished sword that lay near it. He lifted the shield off the wooden table; it was surprisingly heavy, so he set it back down gently and surveyed the area for other treasures. "James, come have a look at this one, it's something you might've read about in one of your history books," he called out.

Jamie hurried over. "That's old, *really* old. A suit of armor from Toku, or perhaps Kolin—a perfect specimen from the sixteenth century. Razan empire if I had to wager a guess." He reached out and put his hand on it, marveling at the rich rust-red color of the fabric and the golden chain mail breast adornment.

"I had a feeling you'd know," Graham said, smiling. He wandered off and came upon a small dagger with a handle made of jade on another table; the jade matched the eyes of the monkey figurine that Tillie had found. He picked it up and pulled it out of its scabbard then turned it over in his hand. The face and body of a dragon was intricately carved into the blade, and the letter "V" was carved into the handle.

Tillie was on the other side of the room, also exploring, and had been lured by a rack of hanging, colorful blue, black, and green silk tapestries, some of which were adorned with golden threadwork.

Elinora and Lina, meanwhile, had made their way to the far corner of the room together, forgoing exploring the other treasures to look in the area where Elinora had found the first journal. There they picked through a stack of old maps.

Lina opened one and studied it. "Trade routes," she reported.

They continued searching and Elinora quickly unearthed a large, old chest. She felt around for a latch. A loud click caught everyone's attention.

"You found them!" Lina exclaimed.

Graham carefully slipped the dagger back into the scabbard and into his pocket, then made his way over to Elinora and Lina, carrying it with him. Tillie and Jamie also made their way through the maze of treasures, passing by an old globe, a cabinet full of bayonets, and a stash of jewelry boxes. Elinora was stooped over, already reading a journal when they got there. Inside the chest next to her were many other journals lashed together in small stacks bound with silk cording. An old, feathered quill pen was tied to one of them.

"Here, there are more," Lina said, carefully pulling them from the chest and handing them to Tillie, who began lining them up on a nearby table.

"They're definitely Sir William's journals," Elinora said, picking up a random stack and pulling on the cording to untie it. She grabbed the top journal and removed the feather pen, then opened it to the first page. "Property of Sir William." She handed it to Jamie.

He leafed through and found a drawing of the tower. "It looks like a child drew this," he said showing the others.

Elinora continued to sift through the other journals, handing another stack to Graham, then she sat down and began reading passages from another. "This one is dated much later. Listen," Elinora said. She read out loud.

288

It is hard to believe our beautiful forest has suffered such a terrible reputation through the centuries. If only the rest of the world knew the way it really was. But then again, perhaps it's best they do not. There are so many animals living here, and while the tales have warded most people off, today I was surprised to discover trespassers within Kellandale Wood. I told Mother and Father, and we chased them off at once.

There was a quiet knock on the open door, startling them back to the present.

"Hello!" Abigail called from outside the storage room. "It's nearly supper; your mothers have returned early and are unpacking."

Elinora looked up. "Thank you, we will be right there," she called back.

They quickly gathered the journals and made their way to the door.

Graham eyed the jade dagger again. "I've never seen anything so beautiful," he said.

"Abigail didn't seem to think there was any harm in taking the journals," Tillie reminded him.

He nodded and smiled, then placed it in his trouser pocket for safekeeping.

"We have a lot of reading to do," Elinora said as Jamie locked the door.

"Let's split them between us," Lina suggested.

"If anyone comes across anything of importance, we can meet in the music room tomorrow before everyone else wakes," Elinora added.

Later that night, they each fell asleep reading passages from Sir William's journals, and glimpses of life at Kellandale more than two hundred years ago seeped into their dreams...

As planned, they met in the music room in the wee hours of the morning. Tillie and Graham were taking a break and resting their eyes as Jamie practiced his viola. Meanwhile, Elinora and Lina had gone back to the storeroom to look for any other journals they might have missed.

"Don't be daft, Gray," Jamie said between staccato strokes on his viola.

Graham was lounging with his head upside down and hanging off the settee, open journals strewn around him. Velvet was sleeping beside him. "You don't think Mister could take Coddlefin in a fight?" he mumbled, half delirious from hours of eyestrain from the night before.

Tillie snorted. "Mister can do anything."

The sound of shuffling feet and then someone dropping, then picking up, something outside the music room echoed in the hallway.

"Elinora's back," Jamie snickered.

A second later she entered the room with Lina, who walked over to the grand piano and set down another large stack of journals. Elinora followed and placed hers next to the others, wiping away some of the dust. "He was relentless with his pen. There are at least fifteen more to read through," she announced. "He must have written daily, pages and pages each day. We found these on the other side of the room. They were written much later in his life."

Lina passed some to Tillie, Jamie, and Graham.

"I think I might go cross-eyed," Graham replied, as he took four more.

They got settled and began reading again. After twenty minutes had passed, Elinora sat up abruptly. "Listen to this. This was written just after Lady Vivienne died." She sat down on the floor on her knees and carefully set the book in front of her, placing the old feather pen she had found on top of it as she read.

It has only been a few days since Mother passed. It was sudden, and my heart aches. And while my grief is unbearable, Father's is even more so. I cannot bear to see him suffer. He has grown weak from a broken heart, and I am afraid for his own health.

Just the other day I found him, returning from the woods, where he had gone the day she passed. He has since asked me to promise, when it is his time, that I will lay him to rest in the river just as he had done for her.

Elinora looked up. The others were staring at her, waiting to hear more. She gingerly leafed ahead a few pages, careful not to damage the old, fragile pages. "This is dated a few days later."

Father has told me of the wish he made at the river and says it has come true. When pressed further, he claims the river transformed mother into an immortal being, and that she is now there, watching over Kellandale Wood, living deep within the forest in the form of a...

She looked up at the others.

"In the form of a what!" Tillie exclaimed.

"...in the form of a great river serpent," Elinora mumbled. She read the next passage very quickly, growing louder with each word.

He has gone looking for her every day, but he is beginning to grow weak. All he wishes now is to be with her. I fear he may be losing his faculties.

She put the journal down and the room fell silent.

Does that mean . . . oh, Elinora, read more," Tillie managed to choke out the words.

Elinora turned the page. "There is a bit of a delay, a few weeks from that entry to this one." She continued.

> *Everything I have written, everything I thought I knew, I must now confess that I was wrong. Father is not mad. I have seen with my own eyes and I can feel it, too. Mother is still with us—she lives within the river, deep within the forest, just as Father said.*

She leafed through the pages, her hands shaking.

> *Father lost the will to carry on in this life without Mother. My heart is broken. As promised, at his passing, I placed him into the flowing current of the Iveria. But I know in time I will see him again, though in what form I cannot even guess. And while I know that they both will always be near, it is difficult to bear that both of my parents, as they once were, are now gone.*

> *I now resolve that it is my life's duty to protect the forest with every means. Though I once thought it was but a child's tale, I can sense the energy of the forest, and I feel it deeply. It is much more powerful than anyone could ever imagine.*

"That's all there is," Elinora said looking up incredulously. "It can't stop there!"

The others began rifling through their journals, but nothing continued from that point. As they searched for the next passage, a stirring came from outside the room. It woke Velvet. Jamie looked up. Mister was at the window and he assumed he had come to listen to him play his viola.

But instead of asking to come in, Mister remained at the

windowsill and began to chatter frantically. Without Henry, and without being in the forest, they couldn't quite understand him as they had grown accustomed to, but they knew it was something very important.

Just then, two loud knocks sounded at the door of the music room. Then the door was pushed open, but no one was there to announce the arrival.

Graham got up quickly, but before he reached the door a striking gentleman stepped silently into the room.

Velvet stood up suddenly, her eyes widened and her gaze fixed on the man.

He said nothing and kept his hands in the pockets of his navy velvet waistcoat.

"Hello," Graham said to the stranger. "How may I help you?" When there was no reply, he continued. "I am Graham O'Conor, pleased to meet you. My mother is Camille O'Connor, James Wolton's sister."

The man bowed politely but still said nothing in return.

"This is my brother, Jamie; and this is Elinora and Tillie Wolton, and Lina Meade," Graham said, introducing everyone. "Who might you be then?" He put his hand out for him to shake.

Instead of reaching for it, the stranger pulled a book from his coat pocket. He turned to look at Elinora, then bowed to her.

She paused and her mouth dropped open.

Tillie caught a better glimpse of him as well and she sucked in her breath. She looked over at Lina, who also looked stunned.

The man motioned for Graham to take the book.

"Thank you, er, I didn't catch your name," he said, taking it, but the man bowed politely at him again, then turned and quickly exited. Graham followed him into the hall, but he had already vanished. He returned to the others. "That was awfully strange…" he muttered.

"Gray," Elinora said.

"He didn't even..."

"Gray!" Tillie interrupted.

"What?"

"Did you get a good look at him? Did you see his face?"

"Of course I did."

"Have you ever looked at the paintings in the portrait hall?"

"What do you mean?" He looked down at the book in his hands. "Erm, he brought us a...this is a journal. One of Sir William's journals." He looked back up and locked eyes with Tillie. She nodded.

Just then Mister chattered again. They looked out the window, and Mister was gazing at the sky. They looked up.

Off in the distance a familiar shadow fell onto the ground and was heading toward Kellandale Wood.

"And there goes the Messenger..." Jamie muttered.

Graham stared at the gift in his hands. "It's bookmarked," he said.

"Open it!" Lina exclaimed.

It, too, was in Sir William's handwriting, and it continued where the other journal had left off. Graham began reading the passage.

> *The magic of Kellandale Wood runs deep indeed, deeper than I can even comprehend—a protective magic for all its inhabitants.*
>
> *After I lay Father to rest, Mother appeared to me. The forest, it seems, has given her magic of her own. Of course, there had to be something fitting that speaks so much of who my parents were, or I should say are—loving and tragically comedic all at once. Mother, still a novice with her powers, has transformed Father. But his beloved monkey, Chi,*

would not leave his side and they seem to have become immortally entangled as not one, but two monkeys—one great, one small. Both emerged together from the river after I laid Father to rest. I am not yet certain which one is Father, and which one is Chi.

If one were ever to find this journal of mine, it would sound nothing short of a fairy tale, and perhaps it is. Perhaps I shall share with the world about the river dragon and the great ape that guards the forest. That should be enough to keep the hunters away...

Jamie fell onto the sofa, covering his face with his hands, kicking his feet in the air.

Tillie and Elinora locked eyes.

"Is there more?" Lina asked, reaching for the journal. Graham handed it to her. She picked another passage and read it out loud.

Today a hidden path that leads deep into the woods revealed itself. This is not a place Mother or Father had ever seen. I followed it, and upon reaching its terminus, I found a place to lie down, which, feeling tired, I did so contentedly. As I lay there, I felt something inexplicable—as though the Earth itself was speaking to me. It shared with me great secrets and told me of the three waterfalls. It is a special place, and one that needs to be protected for eternity. I have decided when it is my time to join Mother and Father, I shall ask to watch over Kellandale from the skies.

"The Messenger delivered his journal to us," Lina said, stunned.

"This isn't for real is it?" Tillie exclaimed.

Elinora had been tinkering on the keys of the piano absently as she listened to them read, but when she heard this, she abruptly stood up, her eyes wide. "How can we do this...how will we get

Henry, Alister, and the rest of the circus here, safely? Our plan has seemed impossible to me all along, and yet with all that has happened in Kellandale Wood, nothing feels impossible to me now."

Tillie looked up in surprise. "Elinora Wolton, is that you talking?"

"I think you're right, Nor. And it seems to me Sir William, er, the Messenger is trying to tell us something," Jamie replied.

There was a knock at the door, halting the conversation. "Breakfast is almost ready," Abigail said brightly as she entered. But she was astute and knew something was afoot.

"Abigail, can I have a moment?" Elinora asked, then turned to the others. "We can tell Alister what we've discovered when we meet later. For now, I'd like to tell Abigail everything that's happened." She walked over and picked up the journal Lina had been reading. "Tillie?" she asked. Tillie nodded.

"Right. We will see you both in the breakfast room shortly, and we can talk this out later," Graham replied, exiting the room with Lina and Jamie.

Tillie followed Elinora.

"Well?" Abigail asked. "You both look like you've seen a ghost!"

"It's…something like that," Tillie replied.

Elinora shared with Abigail the plan to free the circus they had been struggling to work out.

"All of them? A whole circus, coming here to Kellandale? Sir William himself would never have believed it. You've got his blood in you, that's for certain."

Elinora glanced at Tillie. "You can tell her the rest."

Tillie recounted what had just happened with the man in the blue velvet tailcoat and the journal he had brought them. Elinora handed it to her.

Abigail gasped as she flipped through the pages. "Oh, what a clever man. Is it really true? All that power, all that magic in the forest, and I didn't even know the half of it. Well, if this is what it takes to bring Henry and everyone else home, then it's what's meant to be. We'll just have a busy forest out there!"

Elinora took Abigail's hand. "Abigail, there's another problem. There are people in the circus that need help. We saw how they live, and how they are treated by Coddlefin. We have to help them, too, we just can't figure out how to get everyone here, safely."

"Théodore Coddlefin is an evil, frightening man," Tillie scoffed. "And yet his followers think he's wonderful. How is it possible for people to be fooled so easily? And how can someone just be so awful and cruel?" Tillie asked.

Abigail smiled wanly. "The world can be a harsh and terrible place, indeed. But it can also be a beautiful, wonderful place, too. You're doing your part to make it the most wonderful it can be, and that's what counts. I know in my heart you will find a way to help everyone."

"I hope so."

"I've been such a coward and now I'm *really* scared," Elinora said in a whisper.

"Then I am a coward, too, Elinora," Tillie replied. "I'm very afraid."

"Come now, you're *all* very brave! And you have each other." Abigail exclaimed. "Have faith in yourselves. Don't you know? Courage isn't the lack of fear—courage is when you're scared out of your mind, but you find it within yourself to move forward and pull off exactly what you've set out to do anyway."

30

The Impossible Plan

For better or worse, the big day was approaching fast, and the escape weighed heavily on everyone's minds. Throughout the summer a dozen or so other circuses would be passing through Waterbridge—Stan Dillon's and Harold Piston's among them. Each of them was anticipated with excitement, but it was, of course, Théodore Coddlefin's Amazing Feats and Extraordinary Traveling Menagerie everyone was clamoring to see, and the crowd would be surprised when he arrived.

But they would not be surprised. Just as Coddlefin's private travel journal had revealed, they knew his caravan would be appearing in Waterbridge within the month. Elinora and Tillie, Graham, Jamie, and Lina would be waiting, ready to take down his circus, freeing Henry and the others, and bringing them all to the safety of Kellandale.

It was early into the night, and at the manor house everyone was tucked away. Elinora, however, was restless and had been tossing in bed for some time. Their plan played out in her mind over and over, making it impossible to sleep. "Oh, this is ridiculous!" she exclaimed throwing off her sheets and sitting up.

She couldn't help but feel on edge and decided to think their plan through once more to settle her mind. It was bold and risky, Coddlefin a terror to contend with; he also had Rikona and Kano and a loyal army on his side. She knew it wasn't out of the question he would resort to violence to prevent his circus from getting away.

"We can do this," she reassured herself for the twentieth time. She missed Henry so badly and wanted nothing more than for him to be with her, safe at home. They had not just the animals of the forest, but the brute strength of the animals at the circus on their side. Alister, Henry, and Wildflower, with the help of Nigel, Stinky, and Lark—all smart, brave, and just as determined—were leading the charge to freedom on that end.

With help, it seemed even more believable that their plan could work. But how could they lead an entire circus to safety from Waterbridge to Kellandale Wood without being stopped, and without harm coming to anyone?

She looked up at the ceiling and sighed, then lay back down, only somewhat appeased. She was about to give in to sleep, her eyes just starting to close, when something caught her attention. She rubbed them and focused closely, only to find a little brown and orange spider—a young marbled orb weaver—dangling from a thin wisp of a web just above her head.

"Silly girl, I think you'd be happier outside, wouldn't you?" she asked.

The spider dropped closer.

She sat up and stretched. The spider swayed in front of her. "Here, let me help you." She stood up, grabbed a book, and gently let her fall onto the cover. It cautiously stepped onto it and scrambled about as Elinora walked over to the window. But at the last moment she set the book back down on her bed, careful not to lose her in the blankets. She slipped on her robe and slippers, deciding that since she couldn't sleep, perhaps she could at the very least take her new friend outside.

"I have a better idea. You can make a nice little home in one of the delphinium in the garden," she offered. "And I think you need a name while we're at it."

She tiptoed down the staircase and through the manor house, careful to keep the spider upright on the book, then silently made her way to the sitting room, out the door, and into the garden. The moonlight illuminated the summer flowers, helping her find her way in the dark. She knelt and placed her on a purple flower spike. "There you go, enjoy your new home, my tiny friend...June," she said, naming the spider as she watched her crawl down the flower stalk to perch on a leaf. Elinora knew inside somehow the spider understood her. She smiled.

Instead of returning to bed, she decided in the moment to slip out into the night forest. She picked a small stalk of flowers from another delphinium plant, and then walked the darkened trail alone for the first time. It was quiet except for the rushing of the river, bubbling and churning alongside the trail and catching the reflection of the moon. It was her only companion as she walked upon the path that had grown so familiar. The soft moss kept her footsteps light. She thought about the day Henry had entered their lives. "Hello, Ole Warty," she said when she passed him by.

Finally, she reached the amphitheater. It was quiet. The carousel was there, spinning so softly it made no sound. No animals were to be found.

"Mister?" she whispered, placing the delphinium blossoms in the grass next to her. There was no response, so she tried again a little louder, then lay down in the middle of the amphitheater to wait for him. As she did, she fell into a gentle slumber.

When she awoke, Tillie was sitting beside her. She sat up. "When did you get here?"

"Just a moment ago. I couldn't sleep either." She studied Elinora's face.

"It's so peaceful out here. I'm glad you're here—I just wish Henry was with us, I miss him so much, Tillie."

She looked down and nodded quietly.

"I wish Alister was here, too."

Tillie gave Elinora a nudge.

"What?" she asked.

"Oh, nothing. I know you do."

Elinora looked down, trying to hide her grin. "I don't know how to explain it, Tillie. I just feel like I've somehow known him forever. Like we've always been best friends and we're there to look out for each other."

"I think I understand. I feel exactly the same way about Lina."

Elinora grabbed her sister's hand.

"And Alister feels the same about you," Tillie added.

"How do you know?"

"Do you even have to ask? Because I can tell, silly." She nudged her again.

Elinora's smile grew bigger. "I knew you and Lina cared about each other way too much to give up. I'm really glad you found your way back." She leaned her head on Tillie's shoulder.

"Me, too." She sighed.

A sudden stillness followed, enveloping them in a deep drowsiness. Elinora and Tillie both leaned back and rested their heads upon the earth.

"Elinora, what is happening…" Tillie asked, but her own voice seemed to echo and fade.

"Tillie?" Elinora called out to her, but the same happened to her. It was as though words lost all meaning. Feelings washed over, then came another voice. Neither of them knew it if was the other that was speaking.

But it was the forest.

You know what you need to do.
The answer is inside you.
It is inside all of you. Listen, and trust in yourselves.

They both bolted upright. Elinora gasped.

Tillie cried out in frustration. "Yes, of course I know what it is we need to do—we need to bring Henry home, and all of them here. But how? How!?"

More thoughts flowed, even as they were awake. The heart of the forest began to share tales from the present, acknowledging what Jamie had supposed—that the vortex was where the great river serpent, the Lady of the Forest—made her home. It was a special place, immensely powerful and a pure source of protective magic and healing energy that shielded the inhabitants of the forest.

Then, it revealed to them more about the day they had found Henry. The Lady of the Forest had rescued Henry from certain death when he was thrown into the river. She had pulled him into the vortex to recover, which had given him the empathic ability to speak the universal language of the forest. She had then guarded him until Elinora and Tillie could help him. She had been watching them curiously since they were young children, and had recognized their love for Kellandale Wood, and for all living creatures. For this, she had entrusted Henry into their care, knowing they would most certainly love and protect him. Then they could hear the heart of the forest in clear, undeniable words.

Just as the forest is the heart, the earth is
strength, and the sky is knowledge...the river is
the way. Do not push the river. Follow it. They

will help you, the Forest, Earth, River, and Sky.
Together, what you wish to do is possible.

Then came a vision. It took place there in the forest, centuries before their time. They fell back upon the ground, watching it play out like a dream.

"Do you see what I'm seeing, Elinora?" Tillie whispered.

"I see a man. I know who that is."

"Yes, it's Sir Edward."

They watched as he carried someone—it was his beloved wife, Lady Vivienne—deep into the wood. He plodded through the muck and puddles as rain battered the earth around him.

He moved over to the low spot along the edge of the riverbank and gently laid Lady Vivienne on the ground. He paused, struggling to catch his breath, then sat by her side and wept. After a moment, he lifted her into his arms once again to make his way down to the little rocky beach where it met the water, a place they knew well.

He stood with his bare feet sinking into the silt, stopping to listen to the hypnotic sounds of raindrops falling onto the crystal-clear river. He watched the river swirling around the rocks in its path.

Finally, he waded out deeper into the river, first knee-deep, then headlong into the tumbling current. The sleeves of his shirt were soaked as he held her close in his arms. The water rushed around his waist, grabbing at him, almost sweeping him away, forcing him to brace his legs against its pull.

The crimson and pink proteas from her garden had been lying in a bouquet across her chest. He lowered her into the water and placed them in her hands, then cast her off into the bounty of the river.

As she drifted, her delicate, green gown fanned out like large, billowing fins. Her hair, pulled back in a tight chignon, now cascaded freely in the water. Elinora and Tillie watched as she was enveloped and swallowed up by earth, river, and sky—by the rolling current tumbling over her, by the misty haze rising high in the air from the surface of the water, and by a cloak of willow branches that skirted along the river's edge. Then she vanished from sight, leaving behind a trail of petals.

He wiped his eyes, then returned to the shore, kneeling quietly with his head bowed down at the water's edge for another moment. He placed his hands to the ground ceremoniously. "The earth, the earth, it is the heart," he said.

He then turned back, climbing the embankment. He reached for a branch on the young, sturdy sycamore growing along the edge to pull himself back onto the trail.

Faster came the rain, driving down upon him. He turned his head skyward, letting the drops pelt his face. The breeze shifted violently as a cold wind quickly descended upon the river valley in the approaching summer storm. The treacherous sky was illuminated by a flash of lightning, striking the ground at the same moment the rumbling thunder shook the earth underfoot.

Elinora and Tillie watched as he reluctantly returned to the trail.

Mister darted into the amphitheater with such force it startled them both and the images vanished.

Monkey has just spoken to you!
He has told you their story.

He was frantic, excited. Pipe was at his side, as were the wolves and the fish crow. The sound of heavy wings came from behind as the Messenger landed in a nearby tree. They had all heard.

It was a moment before Tillie and Elinora could muster any words. Elinora looked beside her. Her flowers had disappeared.

Finally, Tillie caught her breath. She looked around. "Monkey?" she called out. But she did not see him. Mister replied instead.

He has returned to the deep forest.

Elinora took a long look at the Messenger. "Sir William—that really is you, isn't it? And Lady Vivienne…"

The bird bowed his head.

"You're all here—you're a part of the forest," Tillie said.

He flapped his wings.

"Oh, Sir William! You're our family! Can you please help us? Elinora pleaded. "I think I know how we can do this."

Tillie turned to look at her sister. "How?"

"It will be difficult, but we can do it, I know we can. Will you help us—you, and Lady Vivienne, and Sir Edward? I have a plan; I *do* know what the answer is. We just need help. A lot of it."

He bowed again.

"Elinora, tell me!" Tillie exclaimed.

"It's the river, Tillie," she replied calmly. "The river can bring them here."

"Oh?"

Mister chattered, understanding what she meant. He promised he would help, as did Pipe and the fish crow.

The wolves stepped forward. Their leader made a promise, too.

> We know the ways outside this forest,
> and we will also be there to protect you when
> the time comes.

"Thank you, all of you," Tillie replied.

Mister chattered loudly to the Messenger, who then set off to share the news with the rest of the forest council.

"We will let the others know. When we return tomorrow, we will speak to Alister and tell him our plan and we will work out exactly how to go about it," Elinora said to Mister, then she and Tillie exited the forest and returned to the manor house.

There they woke Lina, and the three of them tip-toed to Graham and Jamie's room.

305

Tillie knocked on the door, and Graham opened it. "Come in, hurry," he ushered them in. "I heard you leaving your rooms earlier. What is it?"

Tillie let loose in a single breath. "We went to the forest to ask for help, and it did. It helped us...it told us we know in our hearts what the answer is...and Elinora was the one who figured it out, the impossible plan. She's solved it. Tell them, Elinora!"

"The way is through the river. We can lead everyone from the circus site at Waterbridge into the Iveria, and then make our way back home, flowing back into Kellandale very quickly, protected by Lady Vivienne. We can move an entire circus with the help of the river."

Jamie jumped up.

"The Messenger is already delivering word to the others in the forest. He and Monkey will be there to help, too," she added.

"Elinora, I really think your idea will work," Graham replied.

Lina tipped her head sideways. "An entire circus floating down the river."

"It will be quite a sight," Tillie replied. "The biggest challenge will be getting everyone into the river safely in the first place."

"Where will the people from the circus go?" Lina asked. "Can they live in the forest? And what will your parents say, how would we explain all of them living here?"

"I'm not sure. The forest would certainly provide a place to live," Elinora replied after a moment. "The question is, would they want to live there? Maybe, but maybe not. But if they leave the circus, right now they won't have anywhere else to go. I've been thinking about this a lot, too. And then I remembered there is another place they could go if they wanted to. And it's far enough away, Coddlefin would never think to look for them there."

"Of course," Graham replied.

Tillie looked over at her sister. "The community school!"

Elinora nodded. "For once I don't care if our parents are shocked when they first learn what is going on," Elinora said. "We will have to tell them everything eventually. But they will see it for themselves. We can't keep this from them any longer, and I know they will want to help once they understand."

Jamie began to piece the last bit of the plan together in his mind. "So, they will need to make a break for the river in Waterbridge. It makes most sense for this to happen just after the parade when they first reach the camp at the river. We'll need a signal to set everything in motion. Then, everyone should run together, all at once. It will be such chaos that Coddlefin won't be able to stop us."

"We need to think of every possible thing that could go wrong," Tillie added.

"Well, who are *you* starting to sound like?" Elinora teased.

"Very funny."

"Tillie is right though. We need to be prepared when Coddlefin comes for us, because we know he will," Graham said.

"I am prepared to fight back," Lina replied. She looked at Tillie.

"Me, too. We will stick together and fight our way to the river together."

"The river it is, then. We can tell Alister tomorrow evening." Elinora said. She drew in a deep breath.

"It will be the wildest escape ever!" Tillie proclaimed. She threw her arms around Elinora. "We can do this. We can bring Henry home, all of them home. If we can get to the river, Lady Vivienne will help us make it the rest of the way, I'm sure of it."

"You mean *when* we get to the river," Elinora corrected her.

Summer

31

Wildman

The weeks passed quickly, and it was not long before it was time for the circus to load up the private trains at Cavendish depot, preparing for the first scheduled stop one hundred miles away in the little town of Derby. Alister had been able to communicate with Elinora through the carousel just prior to the move, and she had shared with him the rest of the plans for the escape. But once the circus left the training grounds and set off on its summer journey, the opportunity for communication between them had been lost.

Coddlefin, meanwhile, had chosen from the many hundreds in his care who would be traveling for the season—the best of the best, the most outlandish of the outlandish, and the most stunning and exotic animals—those guaranteed to draw a big crowd. Paranoia had caused him to leave the other half of his collection behind in Cavenwell for safekeeping.

Evening was creeping in on the sunny, breezy day as the hungry crowd began to gather. A feverish excitement hung in the air. Posters had been plastered in shop windows and on lamp posts all over town with their bold declarations promising a show beyond one's wildest dreams. *Opening Night of the Season! See the World's Ugliest Man!* and *Fear the Vicious Lost Men of Ancient Gilla!* read one poster. Another announced the newest act, *Boy and His Gargantuan Dog Ride Untamed Wild Stallion!* Beneath that, in very bold letters it elaborated, *For the First Time Ever: See Snapdragon, the Warrior Wolfhound as He Rides Alexander!*

The crowd came in droves. They waited in long lines at the ticket windows and flooded the four entry areas when the gates finally opened. Then they spilled into the menagerie to view the exotic animals on display, and onto the boardwalk to gawk in voyeuristic delight at the man with the ten-foot-tall hairdo, a woman who could turn her head three hundred and ten degrees, and the man who could remove his eyeball from his own head.

"Step right up!" the ringmaster shouted, beckoning everyone to the big top just as the sun began to set. Everyone rushed to their seats and the tent went dark. A spotlight fell onto Coddlefin, and as always, the voracious audience roared when he appeared.

"My dear audience!" he shouted. "Théodore Coddlefin's Amazing Feats and Extraordinary Traveling Menagerie takes great pride and pleasure to present to you the best acts in all the land. This first one is our newest act and is guaranteed to take your breath away. Behold the magnificent treasure of rulers and kings! Please, stand and applaud as I present to you, the one and only, Ancient Warrior Wolfhound, Snapdragon!"

Three spotlights searched the crowd, flashing around the arena wildly, a drum roll pounding to accentuate the suspense.

"This is it; we might as well give it our all," Alister whispered to Henry, Wildflower, and Alexander. Henry moved forward into the arena and the spotlights joined and fell upon him. The crowd gasped. He walked forward, then paraded around the ring as rehearsed, showing off his size; then he began a slow trot. The circus band started a slow waltz, and as the tempo of the music increased, so did his momentum. By the finish of the first lap Henry had broken into a full canter.

Alexander and Alister appeared from the shadows and joined him in the ring. Alexander reared up, bucking, and thrashing about, then galloped across the arena, catching up to Henry, snorting like an out-of-control wild horse.

Alister stepped forward and raised his hands over his head. Henry waited patiently at his side as Alexander raced solo around the track. Then he flicked his wrist and Henry crouched down, ready to spring. Alexander made his return and was now twenty feet away, approaching fast. Alister pointed in the air.

Henry waited for the right moment then leapt onto his back. Alexander reared up, and Henry held on, climbing higher on the stallion's back. Then he, too, raised up his front legs, balancing on Alexander's shoulders with his back legs. The crowd hollered in delight. Before they could recover, Wildflower appeared, charging in from the wings, painted from head to toe and adorned with bells and a velvet saddle. The crowed cooed in delight over the tiny elephant. Then, when she caught up with Alexander, Henry gracefully leapt from his back onto hers, and together the three of them continued around the ring, heading back to Alister.

Alister crouched, waiting for their approach. As they galloped past, he jumped onto Alexander's saddle-less back with grace. The stunt was flawless and the crowd cheered. Alister raised his arms above his head and the crowd cheered harder. They took their bows and the lights went out.

Alister, Henry, Alexander, and Wildflower exited into the wings quickly. Alister stooped over to catch his breath. The sound of a whip echoed from the arena and Henry snarled. Alister reached over and patted him. "Not much longer we have to endure this, Henry. Hang in there, boy," he said gently. "Wildflower, let's get that hideous paint off you." As they made their way backstage, Coddlefin walked past, returning to the ring to announce the next act. His step was light, his mood elevated.

But Mudd entered and pulled him to the side. "We have a problem, Boss."

Coddlefin was smiling, but he turned his head abruptly, the smile fading fast.

"Quackenbush won't be able to perform tonight," he said quickly, shrinking back after delivering the news.

"Why wasn't I informed of this?" he snapped. His face turned a beautiful shade of red.

"Eh, not sure, but Quackenbush broke his leg during a cannon malfunction at rehearsals late last night. It looked painful, bone protrusion and all."

Coddlefin's eyes bulged. He made a grab at Mudd. "What a weak fool that man is!" he yelled, then gave him a shove forward. "Well then, Ira. Looks like you're up next, then."

Mudd laughed, sure that he had misunderstood.

"Get in costume and get out there. *You're* the Great Quackenbush now!"

Mudd put his head down and ran off into the wings to change. He returned minutes later, his outfit haphazardly thrown on, but there was no time to fix it as Coddlefin was already in the ring introducing him.

"My dear gentlefolk, it is with pleasure I present to you another new addition to the show." He looked over at Mudd's attire and grinned devilishly. "Please welcome the outrageous, the untamable, the daring, Wildman!"

Mudd emerged to the exuberant music of the band, wearing nothing but a skimpy yellow and red leotard. He looked over at the large golden cannon, strategically aimed at a massive net on the other side of the arena; his stomach turned. He slumped in resignation, then awkwardly climbed up a ladder into the barrel.

The fuse was lit with dramatic flair and the crowd watched intently as the sparkling fuse grew shorter.

"Come on, Wildman, show us what you got!" an audience member heckled.

As they waited, Coddlefin narrated the fictitious story of Wildman, trained as a young boy by wrestling with wild wolves, and surviving off raw snakes for breakfast. A loud explosion silenced the crowd fifteen seconds later.

A woman screamed as Mudd launched into a high arc, half of his already scant costume falling away, the backside torn in the blast. Parents of young children covered their tender eyes when the bare cheeks of Wildman's buttocks flew past. He sailed by, his arms flailing like a giant bird, but the rest of his body was limp with fear.

He yelped insanely, but the crowd only cheered harder.

The stunt looked amazing, but Mudd knew he was in trouble from the start. The cannon had shot hard, and he had no idea how to position his body to get where he needed to land safely. His approach to the net was much too high and fast, and he watched the landing pad with a sinking feeling as he jettisoned past it. Twenty-odd feet in the air, he collided with the center pole of the big top at an angle, then continued to plunge downward toward the sidewall of the tent, where he bounced off it. The tent fabric swayed from the impact as Mudd continued to drop.

Nigel had been thinking fast and was on his feet when he had seen Mudd launched in the air. With the help of Hector, he was waiting on the sidelines with a thick bale of straw, hurriedly calculating where Mudd would land—a desperate attempt to help soften the blow when he did. With a dull plop Mudd just barely, but safely, landed in the deep pile.

Mudd was conscious when he touched down, but he couldn't move his arms or his legs. By his own diagnosis, he was sure he had broken all of them. The wind had definitely been knocked from his lungs. He looked up at Nigel and Hector and eked out a nod of thanks for saving him, then he shut his eyes.

Coddlefin sauntered over and grabbed him by the arm, lifting it up in victory. Mudd groaned in agony as he was plucked off the ground and pulled to his feet by Coddlefin, who forced him to bow. "Let's get a round of applause for the spectacular Wildman! Able to withstand tragic falls and get up unscathed!" he gushed.

Mudd winced in pain and the strange guttural sounds coming from him only enhanced his new persona.

The crowd yelled for more.

Wildman fainted on the spot.

Many days and many performances later, Mudd sat despondently with his back against the rails of his cage. His feet were already calloused and roughened after his shoes had been taken away, his pants were cut off at the knees, and his hair was tangled and dirty. His left leg throbbed from a nasty bruise inflicted during the performance two nights before, making it difficult for him to walk the rare times he was let out of the cage to get a hose down while standing in line with the animals.

The cage was another of Coddlefin's innovations. The reception to Wildman had been so overwhelming that he wanted to make sure Mudd looked authentic. As such, he had ordered him to be treated like the wildest animals in his collection, and the results were, unfortunately, effective.

Mudd had pleaded with him. He was Coddlefin's trusty

sidekick, his childhood friend. He couldn't figure out what he had done to have lost favor so severely.

But Coddlefin only slapped him on the back and congratulated him on a wonderful performance. He also gently suggested there were other uses for him if he didn't like being Wildman. Ghant was thrilled by this turn of events.

As Mudd sat dejectedly in a pile of hay in his cage, his head swimming with misery, and his body broken, the door swung open at the far end of the stable. "No, no, no!" he pleaded, shrinking back when he saw two figures approaching. But he breathed a sigh of relief when he saw it was only Alister and Henry. He knew despite his tough act, Alister was very kind. He also knew Henry would not hurt him, even though he could if he wanted to.

"I've got something for you from the mess hall," Alister offered.

Mudd hobbled to his feet and limped to the other side of the cage, grabbing the bars for support. He looked down at the basket full of food. As hungry as he was, he turned away. "I'm not eating that slop," he said, his voice hoarse and weak.

"No, no," he stuttered. "I watched the Legatos prepare this, it's safe."

Mudd grunted. "One can never be too sure."

Alister slid a plate and utensils through the bars to him, then placed the basket on the ground.

Mudd sat down in the dirt, reached through the bars, and picked through the food. He voraciously devoured the stale bread, beans that were not quite fermented, and limp zucchini, leaving the utensils untouched. As he ate, a single tear flowed from his eye. "Thank you for looking out for me, boy."

"You're welcome." He had hated Mudd for what he'd done to Henry, and for playing a part of Coddlefin's operation, but still, he didn't want to see anyone suffer. He also sensed Mudd was beginning to rebel against Coddlefin, something he was eager to encourage.

Mudd grunted again.

"Come, let's go get some clean dressings for your leg. Coddlefin would love to see it go infected. I'm sure he'd find a way to work that into the act, but who knows what would become of you." He unlocked his cage for him and helped him up.

Mudd leaned on Alister as he was quietly led to a stall in the barn across the way. Henry followed closely.

Alister pulled out the monkey figurine. "This will help. First I need to clean you off."

"Is this what you use on the animals? I heard something about that."

"Yes. It might sting a bit. There, how does that feel?" Alister asked as he soaked the wound with warm water.

"It stings a bit, yep," he said, cringing.

Alister dried his leg, then applied the tincture.

"Aw, that's better already, thank you, Alice." He looked up at Henry. He was so large he had to crane his neck to see, but for the first time, he looked at him—really looked at him, into his soft eyes. And then, visions began to swell in his head. He swooned, like he had lost his balance.

"Are you all right?" Alister asked.

"I think that medicine is making me funny in the head."

Alister stopped wrapping Mudd's leg and looked at him.

Then, in a flash, visions flooded into Mudd's mind. He felt everything Henry had felt—the confusion, the fear of being pulled from his family, the sense of abandonment. He suddenly realized who Henry was and remembered what he had done to him after the show in Waterbridge the year before. He was tiny then, a runt, not fit for performing with his mother and her other pups. He had his orders, though he'd thought that perhaps finding somewhere

318

to dump him along the side of the road would be easier to bear than what Coddlefin had in mind. But Ghant had grown short with him, and in the end was the one who had thrown Henry over the bridge.

Mudd now saw from Henry's viewpoint—the enveloping darkness, the terror he felt when he was thrown into the river. He could feel the dull, numbing sensation as he sank, unable to breathe. "I had a hand in that, didn't I?" he asked, putting his head down.

Then the feeling was suddenly replaced by a warmth, and a sense of calm. Then he saw the creature pulling Henry to the bank of the river.

"The river serpent…" he gasped.

Alister turned to him.

"Coddlefin…he's been after her since we were young. You came from Wyches Wood, didn't you?" he asked Henry.

"Kellandale Wood, yes," Alister corrected.

"Théodore and I first entered Wyches Wood when we were young, on a dare. It was innocent fun. But he stumbled upon the serpent one day, just by accident, and he only just got a glance. She disappeared so quickly I was unsure what we had even seen. But he became obsessed with finding her again. He wanted to show everyone what he had found—a legendary creature, a water dragon. We returned again and again, but never found her. I began to question whether we had ever seen her at all."

"But you did see her," Alister said.

"We saw her, yes. And that was the beginning of his undoing. The last time we entered the forest looking for her together, we became disoriented when Coddlefin's compass got mixed up. We ended up in an area where the forest had been devastated. Something happened to him there, I don't know what, but I saw his eyes. I scrambled to find our way out, and lucky I did, and it seemed like whatever had happened to him had subsided.

"But now and again that look would reappear in his eyes. He was never able to prove what we had seen. They teased him and said he was fibbing, making it all up—all in good fun, of course, nothing any kid wouldn't do or say. They didn't mean anything by it, but it made him angry, aggressive even—something he had not been before. He wanted to make people believe him, and he wanted to impress them, and then he began to do terrible things. He was not the friend that I had grown up with, and in time I grew afraid of him. But I continued to follow him, I followed his orders...I don't know why. Fear—perhaps. Greed—probably that, too. And perhaps because I believed, or hoped, that his heart had only been damaged, not destroyed, not gone rotten..." He drifted off. He had memories of his own to share. They played out in visions, too.

In a flash Henry and Alister could see in their minds the acts against other living beings that Mudd and Coddlefin's army had carried out in his name.

Mudd began to weep openly.

Henry lay down next to him. He could sense his emotions, his remorse. Then, in an instant, Henry shared his own feelings. He conveyed his desire to free his family, Wildflower, and the rest of the circus.

"How can I understand you?!" Mudd screamed at Henry suddenly. But he caught himself. He understood everything now. He looked into Henry's eyes again and asked him for forgiveness.

Henry gave it to him.

Alister began to tell Mudd everything. He told him about Kellandale, and the escape plan. "Come with us. Coddlefin cares about no one, and none of you are happy. You can help us when we get to Waterbridge. We are going to make a run for it when we get there. There will be others waiting to help, and we have somewhere safe to go. There are already some here who will be coming with us and we have a plan in place. You of all people can help make it happen."

He grunted and signaled for Alister to help him up.

Alister reached his hand out to pull him up and they returned to the stall.

"I will help you," he said.

"Come on then, let's get you back. I'll return later to tell you the rest of the plan."

Outside the stall, Byron had scurried away hurriedly when he heard their footsteps approaching. He had been passing by when he'd heard voices speaking in hushed tones about Waterbridge and an escape plan. He wasn't sure who the voices belonged to, but he rushed off to alert Coddlefin about the trouble brewing within his ranks.

32

The Escape

Under the shroud of twilight, the carriage meandered down the winding woodland road. Patches of purple and red sky backlit the trees, and two modest lamps illuminated the rising fog as Emil gently coaxed the horses forward. Abigail was at their side for the journey, as was Albert. Inside the coach, Elinora, Tillie, Graham, Jamie, and Lina sat pensively.

Abigail had eventually confided in Albert and Emil about the truth of the forest, where Henry was, as well as the plan to rescue him, in the event the children should find themselves in trouble and in need of more help. Elinora, Tillie, and the others agreed that this was a good idea. Abigail had then asked Emil to provide the ride to Waterbridge.

Emil eagerly agreed. Though they were stunned to learn about Kellandale Wood, they were relieved to learn Henry would be coming home finally, and that they were playing a part in making that happen.

Elinora gazed absently out the window as the carriage bumped and swayed. Tillie sat beside her, and Graham, Jamie, and Lina were in the seat across from them. The Messenger perched quietly on Jamie's shoulder. A meditative silence consumed everyone. It did not feel like any of the other times they had traveled into town—there were no light-hearted games of Worst Dessert, no teasing of one another. "I see you're wearing your battle trousers," were the only words uttered, spoken with unnatural seriousness by Jamie to Tillie.

Elinora craned her neck and looked out the window when she heard the rushing of the Iveria flowing fast and hard beneath the bridge as they crossed it. She thought of Henry and that fateful morning in the tower.

They followed along the river and traversed untamed forest, with random, darkened homes appearing sporadically. Just as the sun rose, they turned away from the river to where the houses were clustered closer together, signaling the approach into town. Emil halted the horses near Main Street on one of the cobblestone side streets. Only a few early morning delivery carriages were about. The gas lamps were still lit and there was no sign of the circus yet.

Jamie opened the carriage door and the Messenger flew into a nearby tree. Emil stepped out of the driver's seat and assisted Abigail and Albert out of their seats, then walked around to help the others. They looked up at the bird and back at Jamie, grinning incredulously. "I won't even ask," they laughed.

"Thank you, Emil," Elinora smiled. "For everything."

They clasped their hands together and bowed. "You're very welcome. Good luck to you—I look forward to seeing Henry again. And if you aren't all back home in a reasonable amount of time, you can be sure I'll be coming after you!" they said before returning to the front of the carriage.

"Thank you, Emil!" Tillie and the others called out in unison.

Abigail approached with Albert.

Elinora gave her a kiss on the cheek. "I hope we will all be home soon. Kellandale Wood will be very busy for a while after that, I should think."

"We will see you back at the manor house in time for supper," she replied, smiling warmly. "Now go find Henry and bring him back."

Tillie reached over and squeezed her hand. "See you for supper. Make sure Cora and Jeppe set some food aside—he'll be hungry when he arrives home."

"Thank you both for helping us," Graham said to Abigail and Albert.

"I'm happy to help, but please *do* be careful," Albert replied.

"Listen to Albert, my loves," Abigail said. "I know you have the forest on your side, but my goodness, please look after one another." She looked up at the Messenger. "And you, please keep them out of harm's way, will you?"

The Messenger fluffed his wings back at her.

She blew a kiss as she and Albert returned to the front of the carriage. Emil helped them back into their seats.

"See you soon!" Jamie called as they drove off, then he, Elinora, Tillie, Graham, and Lina turned and walked silently down the road.

"Well, here we go," Elinora said, a shiver running down her spine. She breathed in and out deeply. "Just like we planned."

"Let's walk through it again one more time, just to be sure," Jamie said.

"Right. Graham, you will head into town to find spot to wait for the parade." She paused and furrowed her brows.

"Don't worry, I told you I'll be all right," he reassured her. "He never saw me; he doesn't know who I am. I'll just be another face in the crowd. I can handle finding Alister and signaling to him on my own. You just concentrate on positioning yourselves at the river. Find Lady Vivienne and be ready for us when we arrive. Although, I'm not too sure what everyone will do when they see a water dragon swimming in the river they're supposed to get into…"

"Let's hope Alister has prepared everyone for that. Oh, Gray, you know I just really don't like the thought of you going alone."

"Alister will be there with Henry and Wildflower. I won't be alone."

"All right then," she sighed. "The rest of us will head to the river and wait." Her demeanor shifted as she focused and confidently directed the others, detailing the plan. "Last orders, and most importantly—don't do anything stupid, and keep a look out for one another. Everyone, confirm you understand the plan."

"Confirmed," Graham, Jamie, and Lina replied in unison.

"Confirmed," Tillie echoed. She turned to Graham. "Be *careful*," she stressed.

"I will—promise. You, too. See you in a while, Tills."

He started off toward town but then came running back. "Here, take this. Just in case," he said, pushing the little jade dagger he had kept from Sir Edward's treasure room into her hands. It was still in its scabbard.

Tillie took it and regarded it closely. "Thank you. I sure hope I won't need it," she said, tucking it into the belt on her trousers.

Graham took a good look at her. "No one will get away with anything with you there," he said. She balled her hands into fists and raised them in the air. He did the same, then turned and made his way into the center of town.

Tillie turned and followed Elinora, Jamie, Lina, and the Messenger, and they quietly slipped into the outskirts of the camp in the woods. It took them the better part of twenty minutes to reach their destination. Once at camp, they climbed down the embankment of the river to find the Lady of the Forest. A flash in the water let them know she was there, waiting.

Jamie waved his arms at the Messenger, signaling him to find Graham and let him know they had arrived.

He bounded out of the trees and soared through the air heading back to town.

As Elinora, Tillie, Jamie, and Lina hunkered down at the river's edge, a rustling sound came from within the trees. Jamie stood up, poked at Tillie, and pointed. She turned and they stood speechless as a man in a tailcoat stood at the edge of the woods. A monkey was sitting on his shoulder and they were both looking right at them. The man waved, then vanished. A moment later, a very large creature, primitive and apelike, reappeared in his place. A tiny monkey of a different sort sat on his shoulder.

"Monkey..." Jamie gasped. He waved to them, and the little one waved back. "That one is Sir Edward, I'll bet, and that means the bigger one is Chi."

Chi gave a familiar, low rumble in reply. Jamie grinned.

Just then, voices drifted over from the camp on the ridge above them. Chi turned abruptly toward the sound. The little monkey made a motion for everyone to hide, then the duo disappeared back into the shadows.

"Come on, hide," Tillie said to the others. They ducked down, but it was too late.

"Oliver! There's some kids over there," a voice yelled.

"How daft can we be? We forgot to make sure no one was up there," Jamie whispered. He looked up and two men were staring at them from above.

"Well, look at that. You're the ones who were snooping around in the boss's tent a while back," one of them said. He turned to the other man. "Go find Ghant and let him know Dillon's rats are back!"

"You're not my boss, Byron," the other man replied.

"Will you shut up, Oliver and just do what I say? I'll keep them here until he arrives. Oh, he's going to be mad." He trained a gun at them carelessly.

Lina locked eyes with Oliver who didn't reply to Byron, but instead dropped behind him, put his finger to his lips, and winked at her. Then he sprinted down the path toward the parade. Byron continued to brandish his weapon at them.

Lina shot a sideways glance at everyone and they all nodded discreetly, all thinking the same thing.

"All right, get up here, or that one gets it," Byron said pointing his gun randomly at Jamie. But he suddenly fell to the ground, and the gun was knocked out of his hand.

Monkey appeared from behind, grabbing him by the ankles. Then he reached out and covered Byron's eyes with his giant hands.

Byron instantly blacked out from fear.

Monkey conveyed to Jamie he needed his help, so Jamie followed him. Byron was slung over Monkey's humongous shoulder as he carried him to one of the camp tents. Little monkey sat on top of him for the ride.

Jamie studied Monkey as they walked, awed by his size and strength. Once inside the tent he rooted around for some ropes. Together the trio tied Byron's arms behind his back, then placed him out of sight behind a stack of hay bales. Monkey pulled a handkerchief out of little Monkey's jacket pocket and Jamie secured it over Byron's mouth. When they left the tent Monkey slipped back into the woods.

Jamie returned to his position at the water's edge. Elinora turned to him with raised eyebrows. "Don't worry," Jamie said. "He'll be fine, though Monkey made sure that man won't be interfering with our plans anymore."

33

The Way of the River

A bass drum boomed in the distance at the edge of town, summoning the residents of Waterbridge. A substantial crowd quickly gathered as everyone rushed onto Main Street, eager to greet the oncoming the parade and to catch a glimpse of Théodore Coddlefin. Graham was amongst them, silently observing and watching for the Messenger's return.

Shortly after, a familiar bird call came from high in the trees above, letting him know everyone was in position at the river. He breathed a sigh of relief, nodded back, then moved to the edge of the crowd.

As the drumbeats drew closer, the rest of the band joined in with a bright circus march. But when the parade finally came into view, the reception was not the usual expected cheers from the crowd. Instead, there were gasps of disbelief. Confused by this, Graham turned to see what was causing the commotion. At the front of the parade, gliding high in the air and leading the way, was a large contraption making a peculiar and very powerful humming sound. Coddlefin's head was visible, poking out the top of it as he waved ceremoniously. The onlookers gawked and waved back. Rikona and Kano were at his side gripping their swords, standing at attention.

Then came the rest of the circus—a long procession of animals and performers, all dressed in their finest. Graham scanned the line and spotted Alister, Henry, and Wildflower walking in front of a large parade float. His heart pounded, gravely aware that the signal he was about to give would set off an undo-able chain of events. He stepped forward to get their attention with a simple nod. Alister nodded back, then Graham disappeared into the crowd and followed along, keeping them in his line of sight.

"Here we go. Stay on your toes," Alister conveyed to Henry and Wildflower. At this, Henry threw his head back and howled, and Wildflower trumpeted, setting the plan in motion.

Mudd, who was behind them locked in a cage, responded with a fierce growl, beating his chest with his fists. The crowd reacted just as they had hoped, cheering loudly, making lots of noise. The animals and people who were in on the plan responded with yells, growls, and roars, further adding to the chaos, providing cover for what was about to happen next.

Very quickly and quietly, Nigel, Hector, Stinky, and Lark jumped into action, moving from animal to animal and cage to cage, stealthily picking and unlatching locks, removing shackles, and unbuckling halters. Nigel, who was on the float with Mudd, was able to discretely unlock his cage.

Lark was still wearing the blue woolen cape that Elinora had given to her back at the training ground and used it to hide her actions as she and Stinky darted about together, unlatching as many enclosures as they could, leaving the doors ajar. Many of the sideshow performers, and even circus folk such as the Tall Man and the Elder Man were on display in cages on the floats for dramatic effect. Their locks were systematically picked as well. When finished, they slipped back in line.

Meanwhile, Hector unclipped Alexander's harness, then dropped back to where his terriers were, trying to keep them quiet as he removed their leads. His hands shook nervously as he worked. He looked around, making sure the coast was clear before moving on, unlatching the cages of the alligators, snakes, and the rhinoceros.

But while he worked, he had failed to notice that his every move was being tracked.

Ghant, as well as Coddlefin's army, had been on high alert after Leopold had reported mutiny. He had been spying from a position behind the backdrop of one of the floats, hoping to be the one to catch the traitors. "Gotcha," he muttered when he saw Hector in action. Then he crept out from his hiding spot and followed him from behind, quietly redoing the cage locks he had undone.

At the front of the parade, Coddlefin continued to soar above the crowd on what everyone was now referring to as the mystical chariot. His admirers cheered and followed him to the circus grounds as he waved to them from above.

"He's flying, mother! How can he do that?" a child asked.

"Why, he's magic!" was the answer.

It was not magic, of course. It had just required a little thievery of a recent scientific discovery—one that involved harnessing the properties of magnetism. After getting his hands on the invention, Coddlefin had pressed his men to work tirelessly until they were able to create the behemoth, levitating craft for him. *He* called it The Mosquito. The results were spectacular.

Oliver emerged from the edge of the woods. When he heard the whirring of the chariot in the distance he looked up in surprise.

Ghant spotted him immediately and made his way over to him. "Idiot! Why aren't you back at camp keeping watch?"

"We saw some kids poking around the site, but they ran into

the woods when they saw us. We think they might be up to something. Byron is there making sure they don't come back. I came to warn you." He shifted anxiously, scanning the area for Alister.

"What did they look like?" Ghant looked around suspiciously.

"Three boys, all about age ten. Probably Stan Dillon's bunch, like you said."

"Dillon's gotten to Hector, too. I'm not sure who else is in on it, but I'm watching. All right, I'll find Leopold and let him know, this is a full-scale alert," he said, then moved on.

Oliver exhaled deeply, then rushed to find Alister. He discretely joined in the parade line and walked alongside him to report what had happened.

Alister looked around, his eyes wide with worry.

Graham saw this reaction and made his way through the crowd and over to them.

Alister met him at the edge of the parade under the guise of shaking hands with the children in the crowd. Then he quietly shared the report.

Graham furrowed his brows when he heard the bad news. "Monkey is there, and he will protect them, but I'll head back right now to make sure. We'll be waiting for you. Watch your back, this could go very badly, Alister. If they suspect you're in on this...."

"Don't worry, I'll be all right. Ghant won't dare interrupt Coddlefin right now. When we reach camp we'll make our move, and by then it will be too late for them to stop us. Hurry now, and I'll see you at the river."

Graham nodded, then dashed off.

Back at the river, Graham cautiously climbed down to the waterfront and found Elinora, Tillie, Lina, and Jamie unharmed and hiding in an alcove they had dug into the side of the embankment just beneath the camp. They were covered in mud, but otherwise safe. The Lady of the Forest was nearby, hiding at the bottom of the river, waiting.

"We saw Monkey, Gray!" Jamie whispered. "He grabbed one of Coddlefin's men and I helped him! We tied him up in the tent. Monkey's huge!"

"You saw him? I wish I could have seen that. And I'm glad you're all still safe. Oliver found us and told us what happened. Alister and Henry are still with the parade...they'll be here soon, but Ghant saw some cages being unlocked. There could be trouble. And I had time before the parade started so I left a note under Lovii and Lucerne's shop door telling them about the plan. I don't know if they'll get it in time or what they could possibly do, but at least they know what's going on." A trombone slide cut the air, not too far in the distance. Graham looked up. "This is it, is everyone ready?" he whispered.

"Ready as we'll ever be," Tillie whispered back as they hunkered down.

A few moments later, the noisy parade rounded the bend and entered the circus grounds. Coddlefin teased the crowd with glimpses of the carousel, the big top, and some of the attractions they would soon be treated to. Then a whistle blew, and he stood up. Rikona and Kano held on as the chariot lurched to a stop. He produced his megaphone, put it to his lips, and shouted into it. "Children and gentlefolk, I welcome you! The best show in all the land will open at high noon tomorrow, when our amazing feats will be waiting for you. Until then, have a good day, and thank you for coming!"

This was met with grumbles of confusion and disappointment.

"No, no, don't do that!" he said, swatting his hands at them. "We will see you again tomorrow. Be sure to arrive early!" He looked to Rikona and Kano, and they quickly began shooing everyone away. But two members of the crowd hovered nearby, then hid in the woods on the outskirts of the camp.

After he was certain the parade-goers had been cleared out, Coddlefin motioned for his chariot to be lowered. He stepped down and grinned. "I had them hanging on my every..." A loud screech came from the sky above, startling him into silence. He looked up, and for a moment, no one moved.

Then, without warning, an explosion of sound filled the air as all at once cage doors were bashed open and animals and people rushed by in a violent, thundering stampede. Wildflower threw her trunk into the air and trumpeted loudly, declaring freedom as Jazz and Tango roared and led the charge to the river. Lovii and Lucerne re-emerged from the woods and joined in freeing the animals. When they had done all they could, they slipped away, returning to Waterbridge.

Those who were able escape fled quickly—Thunder, Lightning, Earthquake, Caelus, Henry's family, Mudd, and scores of animals, circus laborers, and performers—all rushing to the safety of the river. But those whose enclosures and leads Ghant had re-secured were trapped and left behind. The animals rattled their cages, and the circus folk screamed for help. Stinky, Lark, Hector, Nigel, and Oliver desperately tried to free as many as they could while keeping out of sight from Ghant and Coddlefin's hovering army.

"Stop! I command you!" Coddlefin screamed as he surveyed the chaos. He clutched his head in his hands, pulling at his hair, sweat beading on his forehead.

The stampede continued down the embankment toward the river. The sounds of thundering hooves, whinnies, screams, and roars muddled his brain. He stood frozen as the mob rushed past.

"Where are you going? Why are you leaving me?" he demanded. His voice was strained and childlike.

But they continued to flee, running for their lives to get away from him, charging toward freedom. He instinctively reached for his pistol and fired blindly. A stray bullet struck a young woman in the leg. She fell to the ground and tumbled down the embankment out of sight. Amidst the pandemonium, he didn't notice who had rushed to her aid.

Mudd picked her up and carried her to the river, setting her into the current. The river swelled and enveloped her, healing her, then carried her to safety within the center of the swirling mass of water. Flashes of the river serpent's fins were visible, but they weren't afraid of her. Scores of people and animals continued to scramble into the river with her.

Coddlefin gritted his teeth and squeezed his eyes closed, trying to regain focus. He reopened them. "Rikona! Kano! Call in my guards and stop this mess at once!" he bellowed. He grabbed another pistol from one of his captains then staggered toward the river after the deserters in a rage.

"Guards!" Kano shouted.

Coddlefin's sentries materialized, armed with tranquilizer guns and quickly they surrounded many of the animals and the circus performers within their proximity. More than half the circus, including Alexander, the giraffe, the rhinoceros, half of Hector's dogs, the Tall Man, and hundreds more of the circus folk and animals, were darted and hauled away, and held captive.

Down the embankment, Graham, Elinora, Tillie, Jamie, and Lina remained concealed in the alcove, helping escapees into the river as they approached. Alister remained up the hill at the camp with Henry and Wildflower, trying to free anyone else they could get to without being discovered.

Alister could see Leopold off in the distance and hurried to unjam the lock on the cage of a beautiful parrot. Sweat dripped from his forehead as he worked. Finally, the lock popped open and the bird flew off toward the river. Alister turned to Henry and Wildflower. "You have to go now, while you have the chance."

Henry's ears drooped.

"Don't look at me like that, boy, your family is here for you. This is what we've been waiting for. Go find them, quickly. You, too, Wildflower. I'll be right behind you; I just want to help anyone else while I can."

Henry nuzzled Alister, then put his head down. Wildflower stroked the top of his head with her trunk.

"I'll be all right, I promise. Quick, I hear footsteps. Go!" he said, nudging them on.

Henry and Wildflower headed down the embankment to the river, reluctantly leaving him behind.

Alister heard someone shouting nearby, and quickly took cover behind Coddlefin's chariot, which was lying immobile on the ground.

It was Ghant. "Leopold! Find Hector and bring him to me!" he demanded.

Leopold rushed down the embankment, scoping out the area near the woods—an unfortunate location to go searching, as without warning, an oversized, furry arm reached out and knocked him unconscious. He was hauled away and took his place next to Byron in the darkened tent.

Once Ghant was out of sight, Alister scrambled out from behind the chariot and found Stinky, Lark, Nigel, and Hector. "Hurry, head down there and get in the river," he directed them. Ellis, who had not been part of the escape plan, was with them and followed eagerly, making the split-second decision to defect.

The river continued to swell and churn, and it began to form a protective wall. Alister could see Mudd at the river's edge, helping others into the water. "Hurry, get in!" he called out.

Mudd shook his head. "I've got to help them, as many as I can, first." He led a water buffalo calf into the river to safety, but when he heard Coddlefin yelling in the distance, he ducked into the brush, out of sight.

"Mudd, where are you?" Coddlefin mumbled almost deliriously. One of his pistols had run out of bullets and he chucked it to the ground.

The wolves, who had been watching over the river and lying in wait, saw him and crept out from the brush. The pack circled, hackles up, drawing in on him. The leader growled.

Coddlefin froze. Seeing his hesitation, the Messenger swooped down, flying at his face. The fish crow joined him, flapping his wings frantically and grabbing at him with his talons. "Mudd! Ghant!" he roared. He thrashed about, attempting to swat them away, but lost his balance and twisted his ankle on the uneven ground. He tumbled over.

The wolf leader was on him instantly, grabbing his leg in his mouth, biting down and holding him in place.

He screamed in pain. "Ghant!" he shrieked again when he saw him in the distance, coming his way.

Ghant came rushing toward him, firing warnings with his pistol when he saw the wolves, accidentally emptying his weapon.

The pack leader released his hold but stood his ground.

"Help me Ghant! Draw these filthy animals away, then get back to camp! Help Alister, Rikona, and Kano hold down the fort and retain order—you're in charge until I return!"

"Yes, Sir!" Ghant grinned, then dashed off, leaving Coddlefin to his own fate.

"Wait! Help me first, you buffoon!" Coddlefin cursed at him. But Ghant was already gone.

As Coddlefin struggled, Graham, Elinora, Jamie, and Lina

were making their way into the river, waiting for Tillie. She was standing at the river's edge, scanning the shore for any more escapees before getting into the vortex. The water began to swell in preparation for the move down the river. Elinora kept her eyes on the shoreline, frantically searching for Alister.

Tillie was only somewhat obscured by the embankment and hadn't noticed Coddlefin in the distance, but she did see Alister downriver in the opposite direction, helping a very old man into the water. "There he is!" she yelled.

"Hurry! We've been waiting for you!" Elinora called out to him.

"Tillie! It's time to go, come on!" Graham yelled much louder.

Coddlefin heard Graham's shout and recognized the name. *Tillie.* He looked up, scanning the riverbank from his position on the ground, and he saw her. He remembered the girl. Then he glanced to the river and saw Jamie, Lina, and Elinora—with his prized wolfhound. He bared his teeth. Suddenly, his reflexes returned, and with it, his rage. He stealthily pulled out the second pistol from his pocket and fired from a distance. "Tillie!" he roared.

The wolf snapped at his leg again and he shrieked.

Tillie turned with a start and Alister ducked down when he saw what was happening.

"Tillie, come on! Get out of there!" Jamie screamed.

But Coddlefin cocked his pistol again and pointed it at her. The wolf froze, afraid to provoke him. He stood up. "*You* did this!" he shouted.

Henry came bounding out of the water to Tillie's side, flashing his teeth in warning. Wildflower followed and rushed past Tillie, charging at Coddlefin.

"Revolting creature, get out of the way!" He fired at her and she stopped her attack. He advanced slowly, limping in pain, but he was now close enough to easily hit any one of them with a bullet. "Call these ugly beasts off or I'll kill all of you," he barked at

337

Tillie. He paused in thought. "Or—you can give yourself up and come with me, and the rest of them can run free like cowards. I don't need them anyway."

"Tillie!" Elinora cried out. "Don't listen to him, just hurry and get in the water! *Please!*" she pleaded.

Coddlefin turned and trained his pistol on her.

"Elinora, it's all right," Tillie yelled calmly.

"I warned you last time, young lady, to never come near my circus again. And yet, you are here, helping to destroy all that I have created." His eyes were bloodshot, he was sweating and lightheaded, and his leg was throbbing. But he was so consumed with rage that, despite his circus disintegrating before his very eyes, all he wanted now was revenge, to punish her, and her alone. He pointed the pistol again. "Call these filthy animals off me. Now!"

Tillie nodded at the wolves and they retreated, but stood protectively around Elinora, Lina, Graham, and Jamie.

Tillie's eyes remained steely.

"You will pay for what you have done with the rest of your days on this earth, and your friends can't help you," Coddlefin said to her. "But if you come with me willingly, I'll give you a consolation gift and I'll leave them alone." He turned to the others. "If you try to help her, I will shoot her right now!" he shouted at Elinora. "I will call my men over, and it will be the end of all of you. Stay back, and she will live."

"Please, Tillie, don't listen to him!" Lina begged.

She kept her eyes trained on Coddlefin, his cold gaze eating into her. "It's all right, Lina. I'll be fine. Stay with Henry and get his family and Wildflower into the vortex where it's safe," she said calmly. Silently, she conveyed to Henry and Wildflower. *I will be right behind you. Make sure everyone gets to Kellandale and I will catch up down the river. Trust me, I can do this!*

Wildflower ran her trunk along Tillie's arm. Henry brushed against her, and she stroked his back. But they understood what she was planning and could feel her resolve. Then they reluctantly left her side and returned to the river.

With a start, Coddlefin's gaze shifted behind Tillie to where Alister was creeping out from the undergrowth.

"Ah, perfect, grab her, Jeffries!" Coddlefin ordered.

But Alister didn't obey.

"What are you going to do, chop off another one of my fingertips?" Tillie taunted as Alister moved closer to her.

Coddlefin lifted his pistol and pointed it at him. "You're dead if you try to help her, son."

He halted. He looked at Tillie, and then into the distance to Elinora.

"Alister, go. Get in the river with the others and help them," Tillie whispered. "I'll draw him off while you finish what we planned. I can jump in downriver and catch up. He's too weak— I'm not even sure he can aim properly. I'll be all right."

Alister took a deep breath and put his head down.

She regarded him closely.

Then he peeked sideways at her and winked, quickly slipping something around her neck before raising his hands in the air. "All right, Boss, you win. She's all yours. Be safe and hurry back," he whispered to her before backing away.

Tillie reached down and clutched the monkey figurine. "It's me he wants, Elinora. Go on home. Alister will stay with you," she called out to her sister.

"Tillie, are you crazy!" She doubled over, crying hysterically. "You monster! Take me instead!" she screamed at Coddlefin.

Alister turned to her, a look of horror in his eyes. He shook his head.

"Elinora, no!" Tillie said, choking on her words. "All of you, hurry, get in the vortex, go on!"

At this, Elinora, Graham, Jamie, and Lina joined Henry, his family, and Wildflower in the rushing spiral of water; everyone was crying.

"Aw, don't worry, she'll be just fine. I have good things planned for her," Coddlefin tutted them as he shuffled closer to Tillie. He grabbed his throbbing leg.

Alister stepped into the river and plowed through the waves, rushing to Elinora's side. He took her hand in his and she grabbed it. "It'll be all right, she's going to draw him off. She's planning to jump in down river. He can't catch her; he can barely move," he whispered. Elinora closed her eyes and gritted her teeth.

Tillie quickly surveyed the area, searching for the best exit. Then she eyed Coddlefin's pistol; it shook under his unsteady hand. She smiled. "All right then, but you're going to have to catch me first!" she said, then sprinted into the woods along the edge of the river.

He fired erratically, then hobbled after her as fast as he could. He, too, disappeared into the forest.

Just then the river began to swell. "I hope she knows what she's doing," Jamie said. His eyes were red rimmed and filled with tears.

Elinora suddenly let go of Alister's hand. "Oh, no you don't, not without me, you bloody Queen of Mischief!" she shouted at Tillie, fighting the current and sprinting back to shore.

"Elinora, wait! I'll come with you!" Alister shouted above the roaring water. Henry howled sorrowfully. "Stay here boy, stay with your family." He turned to Graham, Lina, and Jamie. "Don't worry, I'll protect her," he said to them, then he chased after her, catching her hand again.

She stopped at the water's edge and turned to him. "Alister, I can't let Tillie do this alone, I just can't. You understand, don't you? Stay here with the others. Please, I know you can protect them. Go with them, help them however you can. I won't be gone long, and I will see you in Kellandale." She threw her arms around him.

He hugged her back. "Promise me," he said. She nodded and he pressed his forehead to hers. "Be careful, Elinora," he said, his chest pounding. He fought back tears. "Promise me again you and Tillie won't get hurt."

She squeezed tighter. She, too, was crying. "I promise." She turned to the water. "Henry, help Alister watch over everyone!" Then she pushed away and ran.

"Elinora!" Alister yelled once more as she raced into the woods.

Monkey came bursting out of the river, following her, then vanished into the distance.

The river began to swirl with frenetic energy. Jamie, Graham, Lina, and Henry were pulled into the center of the vortex with the others, and they, along with half the circus, were engulfed in a wall of water. They grabbed on to each other as waves came crashing down around them. Jamie yelped as water battered his face and body.

"Alister!" Nigel yelled. "Don't you dare get left behind!"

"Alister, hurry!" Lina called out.

He glanced back at the woods one last time, but Elinora was long gone. He turned toward the others, fighting the current, but it was too powerful. Just then a piercing whinny came from the direction of the camp. He stopped and turned.

Wildflower burst out of the river, racing back up the embankment toward the horse's call of distress.

Nigel, Stinky, and Lark came out of the water, too. Together they chased after Wildflower.

Alister turned back to the river. "Wildflower is trying to help Alexander. I can't leave them behind!" he shouted. "Nigel, Stinky, Lark, and I will stay back with the others who are stuck here until we can bring them to Kellandale. Tell Elinora I will find a way there as fast as I can. Go now!"

"Alister!" Jamie's muffled voice rose above the rushing water; within seconds the spiraling vortex washed downriver with a rush.

Alister turned and hurried away.

When he reached the camp, Wildflower had already been surrounded and was bound in shackles. Thankfully, his hand in the escape had not been exposed. "Well then, looks like everything is under control here," he said to Rikona and Kano, discretely wiping the tears from his eyes. "I'll just look after this one," he said moving over to Wildflower.

Oliver appeared from the tent when he heard Alister's voice. He had been cut off from the river and had missed his chance to escape, so he had stayed hidden. Alister winked at him and he heaved a sigh of relief. Nigel, Stinky, and Lark were there, too, and he took his place next to all of them.

A moment later Ghant reappeared and sauntered over. "Make sure no one else gets away," he ordered no one in particular. He turned to Alister when he noticed him. "In case you didn't hear, Alice, the boss put me in charge until he gets back, and who knows when that will be—if ever. So, for the time being, Coddlefin's show is *my* show, and you will do as I say." He grinned in a way that looked more like he was baring teeth, then spit on the ground and fiddled with his pistol, glancing at the river. While he had been searching for Hector he had caught a glimpse of a large, shadowy figure in the water. And with the water swirling around it unnaturally like that…he thought about what Coddlefin had sent them into the forest to find, time and time again, and his wheels began to turn.

Off in the woods, Elinora had skirted out of sight from Coddlefin and eventually overtook Tillie from the side.

She was taken by surprise, but she grabbed Elinora's hand and kept moving. Together they dashed through the forest, ducking through the underbrush, leading Coddlefin astray as the river serpent and half the circus advanced downriver.

He trailed from behind. His pupils were dilated, his hair dampened and plastered to his head. Now and then he let out a guttural sound. He could see Tillie was running with someone else now, just ahead—too far for his pistol to be of use, yet close enough to continue giving them chase, and so he relentlessly continued to follow.

"Hurry! He's coming!" Elinora yelled, and they raced on.

Finally, an all too familiar bridge came into view. Beyond it they could see Sir William's tower rising in the sky. Tillie was breathing hard and stooped over to catch her breath.

"Quick! We can jump in over there!" Elinora gasped.

A rush of sound came from the river, roaring like the engine of an oncoming train. They turned to see as the vortex of water washed past them, the Iveria and the Lady of the Forest carrying everyone back to safety.

Coddlefin jumped out from behind and fired his gun in the air, startling them both. At once he was on them, grabbing Tillie by the arm and pulling her toward him.

Elinora ran toward the edge of the bridge, stopping when she heard her sister scream.

Tillie struggled, trying to free herself from his steely clutches, but he was much stronger than she expected him to be, his rage transformed into sheer brute force. She jerked her arm back, fighting against his tight grasp. "What are you going to do, kill me?" she shouted. "Your adoring crowd would love to find out you're a cruel, murderous man, wouldn't they?"

343

"No, no, you misunderstand, I'm not going to kill you," he replied evenly, jabbing the pistol into her side to keep Elinora back. "I have much better plans than that. I think it would be far more useful, and rather poetic, if you joined my little family. You will be coming back with me to make up for my losses. Your little accomplice can come, too. It will be splendid. The first order of business will be to pay a visit to my medical staff; they will do a little cleanup on you—some, shall we call them, *alterations.*" He laughed. "Maybe I will have them take your nose off, or maybe your earlobes this time...and obviously your annoying tongue. You'll become hideous and mute, unable to yell. The perfect new specimen. What shall I call you? The Earless...no, the Tongue-less Wonder. Perhaps. I'll have to work on the name first." He smiled broadly. "We certainly have room for new acquisitions."

Tillie struggled again. "Amazing Feats," she snorted. "You try to impress everyone with your bizarre, grotesque ideas. But how many have had to suffer for this? You think everyone adores you?"

He waited to hear more.

Elinora glanced down at the hilt slung around Tillie's hip.

"Your circus might be extraordinary. But *you're* not. It's all lies, and you're a liar! Your crowds are silly and stupid for believing in you, and they are ridiculous to not look beyond the lies and realize you're a crooked, cruel man. Your journal? I read every word. Now that you've lost half your circus everyone will see how rotten and wicked you really are," she said without breaking her stare. "Your own circus fled from you, that's how much you're hated. You're a joke, did you know that? Except you're not even funny at all."

Coddlefin would never willingly give Tillie the satisfaction of knowing her words affected him deeply, that he was exploding with rage because of them. But the veins in his neck bulged and sweat dripped from his forehead involuntarily, betraying his innermost thoughts. He trembled and his blackened saucer-eyes returned.

Tillie looked at him and spit, and he flinched, just as Mudd burst forth from the woods, distracting them all.

Coddlefin had been unaware of Mudd's role in the escape, but considering all he had done to him, he wasn't sure where he stood. But he saw he had a gun. "Ah, splendid. Shoot the other one first, Ira," he ordered.

"Oh, it's Ira again, is it? I thought I was Wildman," Mudd said, dropping the hand that was holding the pistol.

Coddlefin turned a cold eye to him. "You were part of this, weren't you?" His face turned purple. "I'll kill you all!" he screamed, lunging at Mudd and releasing his hold on Tillie. She pulled away and tried to run, but he quickly snagged her by the hand and took aim at her again. She stopped squirming when she heard him cock the pistol.

Mudd, anticipating such a move, jumped in between the two of them, intending to knock the pistol out of Coddlefin's hand. But he was a split second too late.

Coddlefin fired three times, and in the commotion, Mudd took a bullet. He shrieked in pain and stumbled back; Coddlefin shoved him into the river, and he was immediately washed away in the rough current.

In that same instant, Monkey jumped out of the brush, distracting Coddlefin and allowing Elinora to grab Tillie's dagger. Coddlefin turned to confront the hulking figure, but Monkey sprang at him, pressing his face into Coddlefin's. He growled and the vibration shook the ground.

Coddlefin lurched back, reeling from the sound, though he managed to keep his pistol trained on Tillie, desperate and single minded on exacting revenge upon her. He fired again. Tillie screamed, and with all her might, Elinora heaved the tiny jade dagger toward him.

It connected.

He dropped his pistol and grabbed his shoulder, the searing pain taking him to his knees. Monkey charged again, and this time his massive head collided into Coddlefin's belly with great force. They toppled backwards, and both went over side of the bridge. As Coddlefin fell his head knocked against the edge of the bridge. Then with a splash he hit the water and was pulled into the surging wake of the vortex.

"We need to get out of here!" Elinora screamed in a panic, looking over the edge, searching for him. When there was no answer, she glanced back at Tillie.

She stumbled into Elinora, collapsing into her arms. They, too, tumbled over the edge of the bridge and plunged into the mighty Iveria, drifting back to Kellandale together.

34

Emergence

Jamie scouted the river from above. "Still no signs of them," he said anxiously to Graham and Lina. Henry was with them, pacing, watching for Elinora and Tillie.

Graham leaned his back against Ole Warty and sighed deeply.

Behind them there was a flurry of activity as the animals of the forest welcomed the people and animals of the circus—Caelus, Thunder, Lightning, and Earthquake, the Legatos, Hector, Guinness, Snicker, and half of the canine troop, Ellis, Jazz, and Tango, and the others who had made it into the river. Everyone was out of breath and dazed, but they had made it. They were free. And they had only seen but a glimpse of the magic of their new home.

Henry's family was there, too. He raced over to Azalea, Aster, Basil, Sage, and Yarrow, kicking up the dirt up as his paws thundered against the ground. Tails wagged frantically as they nudged each other with their noses and jumped up on their hind legs in excitement. Henry could hardly believe he was with his family again…but this time within the safety of Kellandale Wood.

After the first wave of evacuees from the circus arrived, another group suddenly emerged from the river, more animals and people, and a familiar face.

"It's Emil!" Jamie shouted when he saw them.

Graham stood up quickly, then he, Lina, and Jamie dashed to the water's edge.

"Emil, how did you get here?" Graham asked, reaching for their hand to help them out. "I thought you were taking Abigail and Albert back to Kellandale after you left us in Waterbridge."

"I did. But I returned. I told you, if you were gone too long, I was going to come looking for you. I couldn't sit there and worry and wonder what was happening to everyone. I had Abigail's blessings."

"What?" Lina said. "Are you hurt?" she said, looking them over. Though they were lightly scratched up and bruised just like everyone else, they did not appear to be injured.

"No, I'm all right, Lina, thank you," they replied. "I wanted to keep an eye on all of you, and I suspected others might need help, too, when this was all over. I was there when the breakout happened, and then started helping everyone I could to get into the water just as you were. I couldn't get to you in the commotion."

"I'm just so glad you're all right," Jamie said.

There was a loud splash, interrupting their conversation and suddenly Mudd appeared at the shore of the river. Slowly, he pulled himself out of the water; he was breathing hard, but his gunshot wound had begun to heal rapidly when he was pulled into the heart of the forest by the Iveria.

"I know who you are," Graham said, rushing over to him, his jaw tightened and his teeth baring. "Get out of here!" he seethed, picking up a downed tree branch and charging at him.

But Henry dashed over and quickly conveyed Mudd's story, assuring everyone that he had aided in the escape. Graham dropped the branch. He looked directly at Mudd, who just nodded.

Mister scurried over to Emil and Mudd, running circles around them. Then he stood up and chattered loudly, inviting the escapees into the amphitheater so they could rest and heal. Everyone, including Emil, Mudd, and the people and animals of the circus, followed as Mister led them. Henry's family stayed behind to be with Henry.

"Emil!" Graham called out as the entourage began to make its way to the trail into the amphitheater.

"I'll be fine! I'll return in a bit," Emil shouted back. "I'll check to see if anyone needs tended to while I'm there."

Graham nodded and smiled.

Monkey and Chi emerged from the water next. "Fernph!" the little Capuchin called out to them. A low rumble came in response, then Monkey and Chi swiftly disappeared into the forest.

"I see Elinora!" Jamie shouted suddenly. He ran to the riverbank as she was carried in by the current. Henry, Graham, and Lina followed on his heels, scrambling down to the rocky beach to meet her. "Oh, Elinora," he said, pulling her out of the water.

She coughed and stood up. "Tillie! Where is Tillie?" she asked at once. She was trembling. "She collapsed and we fell into the river together—I think something was wrong. And I think I may have killed him," she mumbled. "I *killed* someone! He's dead, I'm sure of it! But he was going to kill her. Where could she be? We got away; she's coming, I know she'll be here soon, she has to..." she continued to ramble. She turned to the water, shivering uncontrollably.

Lina rushed across the rocky beach and waded into the river, searching for Tillie.

Graham placed his damp coat over Elinora's shoulders and led her to the bank to sit down. "Elinora, I think you might be in shock. I will help Lina find her. You need to rest. Jamie and Henry can stay here with you," he said gently, then he joined Lina at the river.

Henry brushed up against her and sat down beside her.

Elinora stroked Henry's fur, and it calmed her a little. "Henry," she said, leaning into him. "You're *home*," she sobbed.

"She should be here by now, Gray," Lina said after several minutes had passed. Her eyes were fixed on the river. She was shaking now, too. Graham's face was slack and pensive.

"Tillie will be all right. She's got to be," he replied firmly.

Elinora looked down river again, panic blazing in her eyes.

"Elinora, what happened?" Jamie asked.

"I don't know, she just fell into me," she said. "We went into the water and I was holding onto her, but we were separated by the current, and I lost her somewhere in the river. And where are Alister and Wildflower?" She looked around, searching for them.

Jamie put his head down. "Alister couldn't get back into the vortex after you left. Then Wildflower tried to help Alexander, and he went back to help her. Stinky, Nigel, and Lark stayed behind with them and they are all going to help free the others that got left behind. Alister said to tell you he promised he would find his way here with everyone else as soon as he could. He will be all right. I'm sure of it."

"What? What have I done!" Elinora slumped forward and covered her face.

As she wept, Tillie was on the other side of the forest, her body drifting quietly within the vortex.

In the skirmish on the bridge between Coddlefin and Mudd, she, too, had been shot. The bullet Coddlefin had intended for her had connected, piercing her skin, and had ripped through her collar bone; not even Monkey knew it had happened. Elinora had been pulled away from her by the current and carried away quickly. Tillie had drifted limply back to Kellandale and her wound was deep enough that even the soothing waters of the Iveria struggled to heal her.

But she had been clutching the little monkey figurine.

As she had drifted into the forest, it slipped from her fingers, falling to the bottom of the river. It called to The Lady of the Forest, who was at the base of the waterfall where she had been recovering from the escape.

When she sensed the monkey figurine in the water, she swiftly came to Tillie's side, and wrapping her fins around her, she pulled her through the underground cavern beneath the rocky beach, into her home at the center of the vortex. There she let her rest until she regained consciousness.

With a jolt, Tillie thrashed about, drawing in a deep breath and struggling to fill her lungs with air. Instead, she felt them fill with water and she thought that she might drown; but the water was pure, and it felt good. It coursed through her body, healing her with each breath. Once she had regained strength, she attempted to swim to the surface.

The river serpent swam to her and pulled her back down into the water again. At first she struggled, but she instinctively trusted her and ceased resisting, allowing herself to be taken by the flow. The monkey figurine was back in her hands, and she clutched it tightly as she clung to the river serpent's massive fins. Together they sped back through the underground tunnel, emerging in the center of the Iveria, and breaking through the surface of the water with a sudden splash.

Elinora was the first to notice the flash of light in the corner of her eye. Startled, she turned to look. The Lady of the Forest breached the water. There in the middle of the river was her sister, her wild and crazy sister, Queen of Mischief, riding on the back of a great river serpent.

Tillie let out a primal scream, fierce and loud, filling her lungs with air. She raised her fists high above her head as together they rose into the sky.

"Tillie!" Elinora screamed.

"Elinora!" she yelled back. "We did it!" They plunged downward, into the river with another splash.

Everyone rushed to the riverbank as The Lady of the Forest carried Tillie to the shore.

She stepped out of the water and grabbed Elinora. She felt different somehow, but she wasn't sure how.

"Oh Tillie, I think I might strangle you," Elinora cried, clinging to her.

Mister scrambled down the bank and ran circles around her. He chattered, relieved to see her. But he sensed something different about her, too.

She has given you a gift!

He said this as though even he was surprised.

"A gift?" Tillie asked.

Mister was still scampering in excitement.

Your wounds were very great, but she healed you.
In order to be able to do that,
she needed to give her powers...to you!

"To me?" Tillie exclaimed, looking down and pulling the collar of her shirt back, revealing the scar the bullet had left in her chest. It had healed already. Elinora gasped when she saw it.

Tillie walked back to the river's edge. "Why me? I don't want to take your powers from you," Tillie said to Lady Vivienne, her voice still weak.

The river serpent came close and for the first time she spoke directly to Tillie. Only she could hear her.

There are those who work against nature,
and there are those who understand that humans
can work together with nature.
But you and your family are brave and strong,
and you understand more than this.
You know that humans are a part of nature.
Use these powers not just to help others, but to help
them understand this, too. You are worthy of this.

Tillie looked around. Everything looked unusually vivid. She felt things even deeper than before. She looked at her hands. She didn't seem any different on the outside, but something had changed within her. Lady Vivienne spoke again.

When the river took me, it gave me these powers.
It transformed me with its energy. It saved me, too,
but it also bound me to the water. When my family
came to the river, I was there with them.
I helped guide the river to give them powers so they
could return to their mortal form if they chose to.
That is something I have been unable to do,
and I have not been able to walk upon the earth by
their side since that time.
Now I will be free to do that one last time.

Tillie looked up. "You miss them. You want to be able to see them, and walk with them through the forest, don't you?"

The great river serpent lowered her head down.

Tillie stepped back into the water and approached her, placing her hands upon her head. "I am forever in your debt—but we still need you here, you know. Tell me. If I have your powers, then I can choose to use them as I see fit, can't I?" she asked. But she knew the answer. She closed her eyes. Then, in a flash, before the river serpent could stop her, Tillie wished Lady Vivienne could walk beside Sir Edward and Sir William in her human form whenever she wanted, just as Monkey and the Messenger could do; then she wished for the powers she had just been given to be returned to her.

The great river serpent looked into Tillie's eyes and knew what she had just done. She bowed to her in gratitude, then she swam off into the depths of the river, her beautiful tail fanning out gracefully as she did.

Henry bounded over to Tillie and knocked her down. She buried her head in his fur. "Oh…Henry, you're home!" she squealed. She looked behind her. His family was there, too. "Come here, all of you!" she called to them. They rushed over and sat beside her, their tails wagging furiously. She hugged them all.

Pipe came down to the river's edge next, along with the squirrels, Mitch, Vita, Popo, Ronda, Fernph, and Boing. The big animals were there, too, watching from above, as were the wolves and the fish crow.

Tillie sighed and threw her head back. "You're here!" she said to them. "I know we all have a lot of work to do to get everyone settled. But right now, I think it's time for us to rest—but only for a moment, right?" she smiled.

"Oh, Tillie," Jamie said, tears in his eyes as he, Graham, and Lina came to her side.

Lina knelt beside her and kissed her cheek. "Don't you scare me like that ever again, Ottilie Wolton." She was crying very hard.

Tillie's face brightened. "Lina! Oh Lina!" she blurted out. She grabbed her and hugged her.

"You're one crazy kid, you know that?" Graham teased. He extended his hand and pulled her to her feet. Together they walked up the bank and he helped her sit down in her favorite spot next to Ole Warty.

Elinora and Lina sat down beside her and each took one of her hands into theirs.

"We did it," Tillie said, leaning her head on Lina's shoulder.

"All of us—together." She smiled at Elinora, then looked around. "Speaking of, where is Alister?"

Elinora closed her eyes and leaned into her, tears welling up. "He didn't make it into the river, Tillie. I begged him to stay behind when I went after you, but he couldn't get back in. I can't even bear the thought of it."

"What?" Tillie gasped.

"He's back at the circus," Jamie said to her quietly, then told her what had happened after Alister had gone after Wildflower when she heard Alexander call out in distress.

Tillie looked down and put her arms around Elinora. "Don't you dare be afraid. We'll get him back. We will get the rest of them. I know for a fact you won't rest until we do." Elinora nodded and wiped her eyes.

"None of us will," Lina added.

"Coddlefin?" Tillie asked.

Elinora shook her head. "He fell into the river after I threw the knife. I don't know what happened to him after that."

"You *what?*"

Elinora locked eyes with Tillie and nodded. "It hit him in the shoulder, then Monkey charged at him. They both went into the river. And Coddlefin hit his head."

"I'm not even sure what to say," she said with a gasp. She cocked her head. "So, that means Alister is at the circus with... who? Who's in charge now?"

Elinora looked down. "I don't know." She growled in frustration. "But I can't believe we are all here, and he's still there." She looked up. "Mudd was there, too—in the forest on the bridge, he was the one who tried to help us..."

"Mudd is here," Graham replied quickly.

Tillie looked at him with surprise. "Coddlefin shot him," she said, remembering. "He tried to stop Coddlefin from shooting me!"

355

"He's going to be all right. Mister took him and some of the others to the amphitheater," Jamie said to her. "Emil is here, too!"

"What!" Tillie exclaimed. Lina explained to Elinora and Tillie what Emil had done, and how they were helping the recovering animals and people who had followed Mister into the amphitheater.

"Oh, Emil!" Elinora exclaimed.

"I suspect they're all going to be hearing all about this place from the heart of the forest!" Graham added.

"Emil is about to be amazed!" Jamie said, smiling.

Tillie leaned her back against Ole Warty and stroked Henry.

Elinora sighed deeply.

"Don't worry, Nora," Graham said. "I know what you're thinking. But Alister is smart and he's tough. I know he will be all right. He will protect the others until we can get them here. And when it's time, he'll have all of us to help."

"He's right. I *know* Alister will be here soon," Lina said.

Henry put his head down and sighed at the thought of Alister, Wildflower, and all his friends that had been left behind.

Tillie ruffled his fur. "We are going to help them, Henry, don't be sad," she said. Then, she sat up with a familiar, mischievous glimmer in her eye.

"Tillie?" Elinora asked nervously.

She cracked a grin. "Today wasn't very dull at all, was it? I wonder then, whatever shall we do now?" But the reply was not at all what she expected. Before anyone could answer, she felt a surge of energy that seemed to be coming from directly behind her. She looked up, then over at Elinora with wild eyes.

"Tillie, what?" Elinora demanded.

"Did you hear that?"

"Hear what?"

"I think I just heard Ole Warty answer my question!" she exclaimed. "What the heck in the world!"

35

The Light and the Dark

The vortex ceaselessly churned—it worked its magic, unseen and mysterious. It was not just Tillie, but Coddlefin, too, who had been taken there after the escape.

The Lady of the Forest, remembering him from long ago, and still sensing a ray of goodness still buried deep within him, had not left him behind. In her wake, as she pulled Tillie into the heart of the forest, she had pulled him to safety, too; then she had given him to the whim of the forest. He had passed through the vortex, pitiful and meek, and there he had remained—evolving, changing, even learning while he healed.

The vortex swirled around Coddlefin as he recovered at the base of the waterfall. The forest had revived him—rewinding time for him, giving him new life, and a new chance.

He, too, had healed within the pool, and now awoke. He drifted within the crystal-clear water, understanding the forest in ways he never imagined possible. He had listened. Now, stretching his legs, he tested the water and swam with the current. Around and around he went, swirling in all directions until he was able to resist enough to make his way back through the passageway to the river.

There he emerged, into the Iveria as a protected inhabitant of Kellandale Wood, ready to discover the powers he now possessed.

Coddlefin could see two girls and a dog resting at the water's edge by a large tree as he swam past. There were three others off in the distance, and there were other dogs with them. He ducked down and drifted silently, undetected. His eyes remained steadily fixed on them and he felt a seething anger bubbling up inside, though he didn't understand why. Then, all at once, the memories returned as he swam closer. Scattershot images and thoughts rushed in, enraging him. The circus. The Water Dragon—he had seen it again! And the girl, now he remembered her. *Tillie,* the one who had taken everything from him. He recognized Henry, and Lina, too.

He recalled the moment on the bridge. He felt the flat of the blade, the pain of the fall, the closeness and panic of suffocation as death circled him. Then came the memory of warmth from another being, feelings of compassion and goodness that he hadn't experienced in so long he had forgotten them; the feelings had washed over him and infused him as he entered the vortex.

Now free, he fought off those useless, pesky feelings. He wanted back everything that had been taken from him—fame, fortune, adoration, control over everyone. The more he acknowledged these thoughts, the more they festered and grew. His old friend rage returned and he became hungry for revenge at once.

Another memory buried deep in his mind returned as he floated much farther downstream. He recognized the barren landscape now surrounding him, remembering his days of youth he had spent here with Mudd at his side. He knew this particular spot from long, long ago, and he remembered Kellandale Wood. He drifted over, moving deeper into the outer edge of its boundaries, finding a place along the riverbank to exit the river.

Once at the edge of the Iveria, waist-deep in the water, he stood up and looked down at his hands. No longer were they rough and worn, they were much smaller, smooth, and youthful now—just as they were when he was a child. He felt his cheeks and his shoulders. Then he glanced down. As he did, he caught his reflection in the water, cursing when he saw his twelve-year-old face staring back at him. Then he emerged from the water and disappeared deep into the malevolent forest.

Author's Note

Themes in this story and principles that inform my writing include animal rights advocacy & activism, kindness & compassion for all living beings, family, friendship & friendship issues, creativity, respect, communication, collaboration, problem solving, mental health advocacy, disability rights, human rights & humanitarian issues, trans rights, lgbtq$^+$ equality & equity, racial equality & equity, social justice principles—equity, access, participation & rights, environmental activism, nature, mother earth & peace.

In a world suffering from greed, threats of animal extinction, social injustice, and threats to the environment, this tale is a reflection on the importance of cherishing our own interconnectedness to nature, to one another, and to all living beings. It's been my purpose to write a story for a young audience that is hopeful to read, one that encourages kindness, compassion, open communication, the recognition and celebration of diversity, and working with others to enact positive change—told within the context of a fantasy adventure. The story takes place in an imaginary world with fictitious countries, and is set within Eldmoor—a country I envision to have overcome most human-related barriers to equality. In the story, the only social barrier that exists is the unequal access to and control of education.

As a first time novel-writer, my idea of a perfect book is one that celebrates diversity, is inclusive in nature, and is respectful of all readers. I hope I get it right, though I know I may stumble in my early attempts. I am still learning how best to achieve these goals and to express myself in this way, and will never stop trying learn, as I believe that is the only way forward.

There is a world of diversity in children's literature out there, with diverse voices, stories that reflect the lives of all youth, and authors who get it right writing for representation and diversity. So many of these authors and stories have inspired my own writing. There are many excellent places to help you find them, if you haven't already, and I urge you to go seeking—both online and in your own library!

At its core, this story is also about the human-animal connection, and the caring and respect for all creatures. The following list includes a few of the many organizations you can explore that are doing amazing things to promote animal welfare and well-being. Each provides support and care for animals in need of help in their own, unique way. ACOC Angel Fund provides services for domestic animals, while Sheldrick Wildlife Trust dedicates their time and resources to aiding wildlife and elephants in Africa, and PAWS provides sanctuary for performing animals. Sheldrick Wildlife Trust and PAWS were also wonderful resources that helped elevate my writing through the knowledge I gained regarding elephant care, and of their body movements, and behavior, and for that I thank them deeply. You can visit the websites of each organization for more information.

ACOC Angel Fund
Chardon, OH
www.facebook.com/acocangelfund

Animal Clinic of Chardon's Angel Fund was created to help pets in need with treatable conditions that have no owner or have owners that cannot provide the needed treatment for the pet. Through this fund, we will grow our goodwill, provide educational opportunities to our staff, and help to find loving homes for pets that would have otherwise faced a life of needless hardship.

Sheldrick Wildlife Trust
Nairobi, Kenya
www.sheldrickwildlifetrust.org
Instagram: @sheldricktrust

Born from one family's passion for Kenya and its wilderness, the Sheldrick Wildlife Trust was established more than 40 years ago and is best known for its Orphans' Project, the first and most successful elephant orphan rescue and rehabilitation program in the world. The Sheldrick Trust is a pioneering conservation organisation, dedicated to the protection of wildlife and the preservation of habitats in East Africa.

Performing Animal Welfare Society (PAWS)
Galt, CA
www.pawsweb.org

PAWS captive wildlife sanctuaries care for retired, abandoned or abused performing animals and victims of the exotic animal trade. These captive wild animals live in peace and dignity with absolutely no aversive methods used to maintain them. For more than 30 years, PAWS has been at the forefront of efforts to rescue and provide humane sanctuary for surplus animals providing the space, natural habitat and quality of care which they deserve.

Acknowledgments

This book would have never happened without the input, assistance, and encouragement of so many people. Everyone in my orbit in some way, has touched this project and helped make it become what it is. In short, that is what family is to me. You know who you are! Thank you for this love and support, and I hope you feel it back.

I would like to express my infinite gratitude, love, and thank you's to my children for their massive amounts of energy, and creative contributions to this story (and beyond), starting when they were very young, when they asked me quite earnestly why *The Tales of Henry* wasn't a book yet. I had no good answer, and that's what got this ball rolling. Thank you for always challenging me, for creating this book with me, and for believing in me. Love you both, this book is for you!

Extra special thank you's go to my small but mighty family—I love you all. First, to my dad for the original *Tales of Henry* that began as a series of collaborative bedtime stories, first told when I was a child, that never disappeared, and ultimately sparked this project. I think we knew one day it would become a book! To my mom and step-dad for their never-ending encouragement and their advice and help with the mechanics of writing a novel; to my artist husband who understands how much time and effort is required when a creative endeavor is afoot, for his quiet and steady support, and for graciously providing me an environment that allowed me to work years on end on this epic project; to my sister, who is integral to this story's creation and existence and for her unwavering support, and to her husband and his sister, all three of them joining in with their infectious positive energy and advice; to my aunt and uncles, my nephews and nieces, and all my cousins and their families for their input and excitement throughout the writing of this story; to my dear grandmother, my in-laws, step-sisters and their families. Also to my dear friends who supported me and acted as a reliable, creative sounding boards over the years as this was being written; to my editor for her discerning eye, pushing my writing and helping to make this book the best it can be; to my trusty beta readers; to my Graphic Design Forum family for all the collaborations and wacky, creative adventures we have shared through the past decade, my Clash blog network of friends, and my Mag6 global sisters; and to all of the generous Kickstarter donors who believed in this project enough to support it and help make it a reality. Thank you—this book is for all of you, too!

In memory of my grandma Maxine, and my grandpas Dave & CD, who were all loved and are so insanely missed.

As an independent author, your support means more than you can ever know! If you enjoy *The Way of the River: Kellandale Wood (Book One)*, every time you tell a friend about it, share a post about it on social media, or leave an honest review on websites such as Amazon, Goodreads, Barnes & Noble, Bookshop.org, IndieBound, or any other major online bookstore, you help bring the story to a wider audience. You can also request books to be shelved in your local library. All of the above are ways to spread the word, and turn enables me to continue writing and creating. Onward to Kellandale Wood (Book Two)!

THANK YOU!

This book was designed in Adobe Caslon Pro 12pt
Chapter titles set in Brioso Pro
Section headings in Olicana Smooth

What the heck in the world?

Shan L. Spyker loves to make things with words and ink! Her passion for writing was first ignited when she discovered the world of publishing through her love of music, when at age 14, she created her first zine about her favorite band (it was Duran Duran!). Her drive to write, design and publish has never diminished and she's been 'zine making ever since that time, originally creating in the traditional cut and paste method using Letraset press on letters, up to current times producing several online publications for creative writing, music, art, and photography. She grew up along the shores of Lake Erie in Northeast Ohio, earning a BA in studio art while working for a screen printer where she learned the process. She later earned a secondary degree in IT focusing on web design and development. Today, her graphic design business Tulip Tree Creative Studios blends all these experiences, offering design and writing services to small businesses, academic publishers, and non-profit organizations, in addition to interior book design services to independent authors, and creating screen printed goods, her true passions.

She lives with her family, all artists and creatives in their own right: her husband and two amazing...kids isn't the right word anymore, their two very unique felines, and an aquatic frog named Gerard. She wishes she could also be a companion animal owner to an elephant, a water buffalo, and a humpback whale, but since this is impractical, and she recognizes it is best they remain in the wild, she instead supports them through organizations who help take care of those in need. She has deep interest in nature, the environment, the pursuit of animal rights, human rights, and social justice, and these issues strongly influence and inform her art and writing.

Cilantro, rivers and waterfalls, outer space, sandstone hoodoos, and her Faber-Castell India Ink pens are among her biggest little joys in life. Some of her creative influences—artists, authors, musicians, some more recent and some life-long—include Hayao Miyazaki, Jamie Hewlett, Vashti Harrison, Mary Stewart, Grace Lin, Kurt Vonnegut, Joseph Campbell, Jason Reynolds, Holly Black, Damon Albarn, Joe Strummer, Jeff Tweedy, and Fatoumata Diawara. The Way of the River is her first full length novel.

For more information and to purchase copies of this book visit

shanspykerauthor.com

This first edition of The Way of the River was made possible by the generous support from all of our Kickstarter backers.
Thank you!

Special thanks to
Wendy & Tom Frankmann

Debbie DeLuca Lambros & Carl Ecelbarger
Judy Spyker & Matthew Spyker
Adrienne LL Blatcher & Jeffrey M. Blatcher
David Wilkinson

Nicole, Brandon, Owen & River Hall
Melissa Perkins & Justin Neidermeyer

Cathy & Bruce Neidermeyer, Noona, Charles,
Andi White, Mel Ladner, Dawn Rossbach,
Scott & Jennifer Spyker, Arioch Morningstar,
John H. Bookwalter, Jr., Thomas Bull

Early Backers
Wendy & Tom Frankmann for Helen Frankmann
Wendy, Tom, Arden & Ryder Frankmann for
The Animal Clinic of Chardon
Cathy & Bruce Neidermeyer for Owen & River
Julie M. Covert
Nicole, Brandon, Owen & River Hall for Katy Godar
Noona for the Mag6 global sisters—
Joanne, Mercedes, Noona, Shan, Silvia & Marianne

This adventure was brought to you by

...once upon a time, the end. - PL